Secrets of the Chocolate Girls

Annie Murray was born in Berkshire and read English at St John's College, Oxford. Her first Birmingham novel, *Birmingham Rose*, hit the *Sunday Times* bestseller list when it was published in 1995. She has subsequently written many other successful novels, including *War Babies* and *Girls in Tin Hats* and the bestselling novels *Chocolate Girls*, *Sisters of Gold* and *Black Country Orphan*. Annie has four children, all Birmingham born; she lives near Oxford.

Birmingham Rose
Birmingham Friends
Birmingham Blitz
Orphan of Angel Street
Poppy Day
The Narrowboat Girl
Chocolate Girls
Water Gypsies
Miss Purdy's Class
Family of Women
Where Earth Meets Sky
The Bells of Bournville Green
A Hopscotch Summer
Soldier Girl
All the Days of Our Lives
My Daughter, My Mother
The Women of Lilac Street
Meet Me Under the Clock
War Babies
Now the War Is Over
The Doorstep Child
Sisters of Gold
The Silversmith's Daughter
Mother and Child
Girls in Tin Hats
Black Country Orphan

ANNIE MURRAY
Secrets of the Chocolate Girls

PAN BOOKS

First published 2022 by Pan Books

This paperback edition first published 2022 by Macmillan
an imprint of Pan Macmillan
The Smithson, 6 Briset Street, London EC1M 5NR
EU representative: Macmillan Publishers Ireland Ltd, 1st Floor,
The Liffey Trust Centre, 117–126 Sheriff Street Upper,
Dublin 1, D01 YC43
Associated companies throughout the world
www.panmacmillan.com

ISBN 978-1-5290-6496-4

1 3 5 7 9 8 6 4 2

A CIP catalogue record for this book is available from the British Library.

Typeset in Stempel Garamond by Jouve (UK), Milton Keynes
Printed and bound by CPI Group (UK) Ltd, Croydon, CR0 4YY

MIX
Paper from
responsible sources
FSC® C116313
FSC
www.fsc.org

Visit **www.panmacmillan.com** to read more about all our books
and to buy them. You will also find features, author interviews and
news of any author events, and you can sign up for e-newsletters
so that you're always first to hear about our new releases.

I would like to dedicate this story to all readers everywhere who have enjoyed my stories over the years: those who kindly keep in touch through social media, the book buyers and library goers, the passers of books among friends and all of you who like to catch a glimpse of the past by reading about the lives of others in this way. I realize books have been part of helping everyone through the COVID-19 year – which as I write is turning into two years – so if I have contributed to taking people's minds elsewhere for a while, I'm very glad of it.

Although this novel is part of a series that follows *Chocolate Girls* and *The Bells of Bournville Green*, this is a new story about a different family – so please come to it without expectations of it following on from the others. I hope you will enjoy meeting the Gilby family: Ann and Len, Sheila, Joy and Martin, and starting to share in all the ups and downs of their lives.

I have recently started a newsletter which will appear from time to time. If you would like to sign up, go to the home page of my website www.anniemurray.co.uk and you will find the sign-up form if you scroll down. Or do keep in touch on Facebook @Annie.Murray.Author or Twitter @AMurrayWriter.

With warm wishes,
Annie xx

Summer 2021

I

September – October 1940

One

'Ouch – blast it!'

Ann Gilby straightened up, sucking her bleeding finger, in the middle of pinning the remains of an old sheet on as a fresh cover for the ironing board. To her annoyance, a couple of pinpricks of blood spotted the white. Wrapping her finger in a frayed ribbon of the leftover cloth, she folded down the wooden board.

'This is just one of those flaming days!'

She leaned the board against the wall instead of putting it away. The wash, hanging outside on the line in the late-summer breeze, would soon be dry and she could get most of the ironing done today if she got on with it. At least it wasn't raining – that was the one thing that hadn't gone wrong today.

That morning she had hurried along to the shops with their ration books only to find, after queueing for nearly an hour, that there was only a scrap of bacon ration left – that would have to be Len's; the rest of them would make do with bread dipped in the fat – and all the butter had gone. At least margarine was off the ration.

While she waited, two women behind her were rattling on in low voices about the raids. It had started last month, raids every few days and no one knew where or when they would be. They had already caused so much damage – the Market Hall in town was burned out. And they were bombing the hell out of London now. Everyone was living on their nerves. All summer people had been saying, 'There'll be Germans marching along the streets soon . . .'

Ann closed her eyes for a moment, queasy. She was tempted to turn round and give them a piece of her mind. Oh Lord, if only they'd stop *keeping on*. Careless talk, that was what those posters said – and even if it didn't cost lives, it certainly frayed her nerves.

'Mrs Terry at number eight said she was sure there was someone in her garden last night . . . She heard this funny noise but when they went out . . .'

Ann opened her eyes and counted how many people were in front of her in the queue. Do this bit of shopping, get home, do the washing, keep busy . . .

When she had eventually got the water heated for the wash, she found less than a handful of Sylvan Flakes at the bottom of the packet. After dashing out to get some more and reaching home in Beaumont Road for the second time, she realized they were almost out of Izal and Len wouldn't half create if they started having to cut up newspaper for the lavatory . . . The whole morning had gone with her hurtling up and down the road to Bournville Village to the shops and then racing to get the washing out.

And even with all this going on, she still could not distract her thoughts. It was the war, stirring everything up again. Today, she would not be able to hold back from going upstairs to the bedroom, going to her drawer and reaching inside to look; to look back, to *feel* – however much she wanted to stop herself . . .

She hadn't made the bed yet, her mind reasoned. That was an excuse to go up, and . . . At this rate she wouldn't get the ironing done before tea . . . With her eldest, Sheila, living back at home now her husband, Kenneth, was in the RAF, Ann had taken on all her washing again – and the baby's.

'Why don't you get her doing her own washing?' her friend Hilda asked, after Sheila arrived home again with only a suitcase and Elaine in her arms. ''Stead of waiting on her like that. Hardly knows she's born, that one.'

'Oh, I don't know,' Ann said. She knew Hilda thought she had not prepared Sheila for life properly – though God knew, she'd had some hard knocks lately. 'I s'pose it's easier than having her fluffing about in my kitchen. You know Sheila – makes such heavy weather of everything.'

'Only yourself to blame then, Annie.'

Good old Hilda – you always knew you'd get a straight opinion from her and no flannel. Ann smiled as her feet took her upstairs, pretending to herself that all she was doing was bed-making . . .

Ann and Hilda had been friends for years, ever since they started together at Cadbury's when they were fourteen. They had worked side by side in their white overalls and caps in the filling room, over trays of chocolate shells. And since they had left work, many cups of tea had been drunk together while looking after small children and as they all grew up. There was nothing she couldn't say to Hilda. Well – almost nothing. And now, with the war on and men going off to the forces, Hilda was back working at Cadbury's so she saw less of her these days anyway.

On the landing, she looked in through the open bedroom doors. Even if it was hard work, it was nice having the whole family here under one roof again. There was Len's and her room and Joy's next door, with all her fripperies on her dressing table – hairpins and make-up and ribbons – a pretty, peach-coloured skirt flung on the bed. She loved getting dressed up, Joy did.

Martin's room was quite different – books, chess board, his train set in a box, bits of Meccano. She smiled though

5

at the sight of the little animal figures on his desk – Brother Rabbit, Percy Parrot, Freddy Frog – happy that he still kept them there. Martin had been a keen member of the Cadbury's club for children, the Cococub Club, when he was young. He used to save to go on their trips and holidays while the girls had not shown much interest. But the Cococub animals were given away with Bournville Cocoa through much of the thirties and they had bought a lot of cocoa in those days, to collect Martin's animals for him! It had been quite hard to get hold of at times with everyone so keen on the little toys.

And now Sheila and Elaine were home and sleeping in the attic. Smiling at the thought of Elaine – the dear little poppet! – Ann went to her own room. The walls were papered in a fawn colour, pattered with little nosegays of white flowers, and it was nice and bright in there now, with the blackout screens taken down and curtains pulled right back. She opened the window to let out the faint smell of sweat.

Ann set about making up the bed with clean sheets, shaking out the blankets and turning back the dusty-gold eiderdown – Len felt the heat in bed and was forever throwing the thing off on to the floor. She folded his pale green pyjamas under his pillow; her peach-coloured nightie under her own.

Once she had tidied everything she sank down on her side of the bed, rubbing her hands which were red and sore from all the soap. Only then did she notice how shallow her breathing was – she was almost panting. She couldn't keep the thoughts out of her mind for ever.

War. Again. All these terrible things happening – in Poland, in Belgium and France. Now it looked as if they were going to be next to be invaded. Things had been quiet for a while – the Phoney War they called it, after all the hoo-ha when they thought, last autumn, that they were going to be bombed any minute. Then nothing happened – not in this country – for months. Until now. And now Sheila was back home when she should really be with her husband – and . . . These memories which came flooding in, now they had entered this, the second war of her life.

Beside her was her chest of drawers. On the edge, within reach of the bed, were a bottle of aspirin, a screwed-up handkerchief and a glass of water. And resting on a long, crocheted mat, her Mason Pearson hairbrush, a few hairpins beside a cherry-red lipstick and the box of face powder with its pale pink puff, in front of the folding, triple mirror, which gave back the window's light to the room . . .

Her face looked back at her, the soft wave of her brown hair round her forehead, her dark eyes that so many people had called pretty, her smooth complexion. There were a few threads of grey in her hair now though. She was a middle-aged woman of forty-six, she reminded herself. A matron.

Kicking off the worn old slippers she wore around the house, she stretched her toes on one of the rectangular flowered mats which covered the floorboards each side of the bed. It was suddenly so quiet. She let out a long breath. A faint ticking came from the living-room clock. Len and Joy were at Cadbury's, Martin at school, and Sheila had at last taken Elaine out in the pram for a bit. It felt a long time since she had been alone or that the house had been this peaceful.

Almost as if it belonged to someone else, her hand reached out towards the top drawer. No. She tried to stop herself. You mustn't. It will only make you feel bad, for days . . . The stirred feelings, the ache of memories – it was better not, better without. Her emotions already felt like a bucket full to the brim. She must not be shaken, must not let them spill . . .

But still, her hand reached out. It was a long time since she had allowed herself this. Pulling the drawer open, stealthily, even though there was no one else in the house, she looked down into it: a tangle of stockings; panties and an old roll-on; a spare brassiere atop a couple of warm vests . . .

Her fingers felt their way to the back of the drawer, under the bundle of knitting patterns – and there it was, the velvet-soft feel of the old brown envelope. She stroked it gently with her fingertips, was just pulling it out—

'Cooee! You there, Annie?'

Ann jumped, jarred. Margaret, her mother-in-law, only lived a few houses away along the street.

'I've brought a bit of cake . . .' Her voice floated up the stairs.

'I'm up here – coming!' Ann pushed her feet into her slippers. 'Just making the bed!'

Margaret Gilby was someone she had loved and respected right from the beginning, as much as anyone in this world. But all the same, her heart was pounding and she felt irritable, guilty, forced back to reality . . .

'You all right, bab?' Margaret was in the hall, swathed in a green-and-yellow flowered frock, a plate in her hand. She was a big-boned woman with ham-joint hands, almost a head taller than Ann. Her blonde hair had faded to grey and had, for as long as Ann had known her, been worn swept back from her face and pinned into a bun. The brown eyes which looked so striking against the pale hair were still as warm and kindly as they had ever been. 'You look a bit flustered.'

'Oh, I'm all right – it's just been a bit of a morning.' For a moment Ann felt bathed in shame. What she had been doing upstairs! Then, as usual, she pushed it away again where it belonged – into the past and forgotten. 'Ooh – thanks for that. Martin'll be pleased.'

'It's only plain – and a bit dry. You could put a bit of custard on it. Cyril and I don't need all of it . . .'

Ann took the plate and they went into the kitchen. 'Want a cuppa?'

'If you've got time, bab.'

Margaret sank down at the table. They always went through this rigmarole. Ann always had time. She set the kettle on the gas.

'I keep seeing that broom handle in our cupboard,' Margaret said, wiping perspiration from her forehead. 'Gives me a turn every time.'

'Len did one just like it . . .' Ann went to the cupboard under the stairs and brought out the old broom handle with a carving knife tied tightly to the top. Cyril, her father-in-law, had showed Len how.

'Like them bayonets we had in the last lot,' Cyril had said grimly. 'You go in and up!' He gave a horrifying demonstration in the air. 'That'll see 'em off.'

'He says we should keep the bath full of water,' Margaret said. 'Buckets. Just in case.'

'What for?' Ann said.

'Well, fires, I s'pose.'

'We've got a stirrup pump – and a sand bucket . . . S'posed to be for bombs or summat . . . I don't know how you stop a bomb with a bucket of sand, though.'

They'd both been stocking up on food ever since it all started – squirrelling things away in the larder – a tin of ham or salmon here, a few raisins there.

'You all right?' Ann said, sitting across the table from her. Margaret did look tired today. She was nearly seventy-two years of age and active with it – as was Cyril, a small

9

man and chirpy as a budgie most of the time. Ann sometimes looked at Margaret and saw how her daughter
would look – Sheila, not Joy, who was entirely different –
when she was an older lady. The long, big-boned face that
Len also had, seemed to carry distinctively down through
the generations.

'Oh, I'm all right. I've had that WVS woman round
again . . .' Margaret was saying, when a kerfuffle broke
out at the front door. 'Oh my word – is that Sheila . . .?'

They heard Sheila pull the pram inside, shut the door
with a bang and burst into dramatic sobbing.

'Mom?' she wailed.

Little Elaine was starting to cry as well, no doubt at
the sight of her blarting mother.

'Oh Lor'.' Ann and Margaret rolled their eyes at each
other.

'Sheila?' Ann went into the hall, arms folded, as Sheila
flung her box with its gas mask down on the lino as if it
was to blame for everything. 'You're soon back!'

Sheila, her eldest, was now twenty, a solidly built girl –
even more solid since giving birth to a child – with wavy,
abundant brown hair, rolled back from her forehead and
pinned attractively at the sides. It was hair that seemed
made for the current fashionable style. At this moment,
Sheila's already high colouring was heightened by her
upset so that her cheeks almost matched the colour of her
pink-and-white spotted frock. Little Elaine, seven months
old, was also pink-faced and squirming in her arms.

'Here – give her me.' Ann held out her arms.

'No – she wants feeding.'

'All right – come in the back and for heaven's sake
calm down.' She beckoned Sheila towards the kitchen,
making herself be patient. 'Whatever's the matter?'

'What's ailing you, bab?' Margaret said.

'All right, Nanna?' Sheila sat, heavy with emotion, and unbuttoned her frock so that Elaine could feed. Ann made tea.

'I thought you'd gone to Betty's – I mean, *she*'s the one to be upset.'

'I *was* at Betty's.' Sheila starting sobbing again. 'Of *course* she's upset – she's no idea when she'll see Fred again. It's so *awful*. I mean, at least I know where Kenneth is . . .'

Sheila's old friend Betty had a child of nearly two. Her husband had been – they thought – captured at Dunkirk but they could not be sure of anything.

'But then her mom came round. I mean, you'd think she'd try to find something cheerful to say, the way things are, but you know what she's like. *On and on* she went about how they're going to bomb us until there's nothing left. I just wanted to stuff a cushion in her mouth! She said they'll soon be marching along the Bristol Road . . .'

'Yes – well, you can always rely on Vera to be cheerful,' Ann remarked, bringing the teapot to the table. Her granddaughter's round cheek could just be seen, sucking away at her mother's milk, and it melted Ann's heart.

This had been going on all summer, since the Germans had marched into Paris. The government leaflet which had dropped on to the mat a few weeks ago was sitting on the sideboard in the front room. *If the Invader Comes! What to Do and How to Do It!* When it arrived, Ann had been tempted to hide it from the rest of the family – it was enough to frighten anyone to death. They were all to stay where they were, report anything suspicious. The thought of Germans suddenly parachuting in at any time of the day or night was truly terrifying.

There had been so many changes already: the sandbags and shelters, their Cadbury factory – it felt like theirs since everyone in the family except Martin had worked there – swathed in camouflage. The carillon bells were, like all the church bells, to be silent unless there was an invasion, so that now the thought of hearing a church bell was too horrible to imagine. And there was a barrage balloon tethered at Rowheath, the Cadbury recreation ground where they had all swum and danced and played. It hung there like a great big fish and everything beneath it had changed too – what had been playing fields were now part of the Dig for Victory campaign and had been carved up into allotments for food.

'I should never've come back here.' Sheila had dried her eyes but her long face was still as mournful as a hound's.

Ann looked over the rim of her teacup, trying to forget how much nicer tea had been with more sugar in it. Another thing to get used to.

'Well – that was then. None of us were to know how things were going to go.'

Kenneth Carson, Sheila's husband, who was in Air-Sea Rescue, had been posted to the east coast in the New Year. Sheila went with him, heavily pregnant with Elaine, and had had a frightening time, going into labour with no one there until a neighbour took pity on her. She had then spent most of her time alone, in their two squalid, rented rooms. After two months of that, with a new baby, she had had enough of coldness and loneliness and feeling like a foreigner and fled back home. According to Sheila, Kenneth had also been relieved, much as he had wanted his wife and daughter with him. Ann could believe it, knowing just how miserable Sheila could be, but she could see that the girl had had a hard time.

'If Birmingham's where most of the industry is, they're going to bomb the living daylights out of us!'

'That what Vera said?'

Sheila nodded tragically, then looked down at Elaine, more tears falling.

'Oh Lord – I should've stayed in Grimsby with Kenneth . . . But I don't want to go back there. I know it's not his fault that he has to be on duty so much and never knows when he's coming back – but I can't stand it.'

Ann sighed. 'No. You're better off here. Look – instead of getting all wound up and expecting the worst, why don't you just wait and see?' She felt irritable, even though she knew it was serious. Everyone was frightened and edgy with all this talk of German spies and more bombs about to fall any moment.

'No – I think I ought to take her out of Birmingham.'

'Oh, d'you think so, bab?' Margaret sounded very doubtful.

'But you've just said . . .' Ann put her cup down, exasperated.

'No – to . . . I don't know . . .' Sheila wailed, looking tragically at them. 'I don't want to leave you all – but I'm a mother now and, you know, being a mother comes with responsibilities.'

'Yes – I do have some idea,' Ann said.

'I'm going to go and find out where else I can go – for evacuation!' she announced dramatically.

'But Sheila,' Margaret pointed out, 'we're not even *in* the evacuation area here.'

'Oh, for goodness' sake!' Sheila erupted so suddenly that Elaine's head popped up, startled. 'D'you think they're going to mind where they drop their bombs just because the corporation have drawn some lines round Birmingham? They could wipe out the whole city and we'll all be killed in our beds!'

Two

'Mom!'

Just a few hours later and it was Joy, crashing into the house and arriving in the back kitchen, tears streaming down her cheeks.

'Oh, good Lord – what *now*?' Ann, bent over by the oven to check on the shepherd's pie, stood up, mopping her face.

Joy more usually lived up to her name. In looks she resembled her mother, but somehow with the volume turned up, Ann often thought. Joy was slight, nippy on her feet, with glossy black hair nestling in waves into her neck and round her forehead; big, liquid brown eyes and a dimple in each cheek. She was only two years younger than Sheila, but the gap seemed much wider. Sheila had become more matronly than her age, both in outlook and in the thickening of her waistline. Whereas Joy looked as youthful as her eighteen years, bursting into the kitchen in a dress of white-spotted navy with a white collar and a full, swinging skirt. But her cheeks and eyes were teary pink.

'It's Al – he says he's gone and joined up!' Joy wailed, as if the world had actually ended. 'And he never even told me he was *thinking* about doing it!'

Alan and Joy were the same age and had both started work at Cadbury's on leaving school. They had been good pals ever since they got to know each other – friends, but never anything more, so far as Ann knew. He

14

was also Joy's main partner for the thing that was her life's obsession – dancing.

'Well,' Sheila said, sitting at the table, feeding Elaine a spoonful of mashed carrot and gravy. 'There's a war on. In case you hadn't noticed.'

'But why didn't he *say* anything?' Joy wailed. 'He's going in the Army – starts training in a week or so! Who am I going to dance with now?'

'For goodness' sake – you think you've got problems!' Sheila twisted round in her chair, exasperated. 'It wasn't as if you were walking out with him, was it? Not so far as I could see.'

'No – but . . .' Joy looked confused and really upset. 'I thought . . . I don't know. But we always went dancing!'

'If he wanted to go out with you properly, I'd say he's been a bit slow on the uptake,' Sheila commented, adding smugly, '*Kenneth* wasn't backwards in coming forwards – he asked me out the second time we met.'

'Yes – we know,' Joy said, wiping her eyes miserably. 'Don't we just. There's no need to be nasty. Alan's just a bit shy. And it's none of your business anyway.'

Joy bent over Elaine, running a finger down her round cheek.

'Hello, squeaky! Aren't you beautiful? Aah – she's enough to make anyone feel better. You coming to Auntie for a love?'

'Yes – she's about finished.' Quarrel at an end, Sheila wiped Elaine's smeary cheeks and handed her over, smiling. Elaine gave Joy a grin, showing her four little teeth, and Joy's natural optimism began to reassert itself. 'Who's a gorgeous girl then?'

'Sheila's saying she's thinking of taking her out of Birmingham,' Ann said.

As she spoke, she felt a desperate pang, the full implications of this only just sinking in. If she was honest, it was a mixed blessing having one of your married children move back into the house, but the thought of them *not* being there, and not seeing her little granddaughter every day, was awful. But even if it felt safer having them here, it didn't mean it *was* safe.

'Oh no – you can't!' Joy wailed all over again. 'What – you mean go back up there where Kenneth is?'

'No . . .' Sheila began.

'What's going on?' Martin came crashing in, dumping his school bag on the chair by the door. 'Ooh – something smells nice!'

Ann softened, as she so often did at the sight of her boy, pale-faced, with his freckles, straight brown hair and wide, pebble-grey eyes. Martin, at thirteen, had a fresh innocence about him still and he seemed so even-tempered and uncomplicated compared with the girls.

'Shepherd's pie,' she said. 'More spud and turnip than mince, but there we go. Oh – did you put your bike in the shed?'

'What – in case the German spies steal it?' Martin made a face, raising his arms in a monster pose. 'Raaaargh!'

'It's not funny, you idiot,' said Sheila.

'*Yes* – I put my bike in the shed.' He went over and eyed the stove, lifting the lid of the boiling carrots to sniff them. 'Glad to see you haven't given away *all* the saucepans.'

'Well – they said we had to.' A WVS lady had come round collecting scrap metal. Making aeroplanes with your old pans seemed far-fetched but that's what she said. Ann had parted with a saucepan, a battered old colander and a bowl that had been kicking around in the garden (though she was not really sure what that was made of and just hoped it would be useful for something). Len had kept the shell of an old motorbike sidecar in the shed for years, so they had thrown that in too.

'Your dad'll be in in a tick so lay the table, Joy, will you?'

'But you can't just take her away,' Joy was saying, in between kissing Elaine's downy head. 'What're we going to do for cuddles without little Lainy?'

Still in her apron, Ann slipped out into the back garden, a long, narrow space scuffed by Martin's football and cricket games. Not that there was much room for that any more. The path ran along one side down to the shed and the washing line had had to be shortened to about half the length now they had a much bigger veggie patch and a hen coop that Len had knocked up, like the one his father had built at the back of their house along the street, each with four hens pecking about in it. They were good layers as well. And, right at the end, the Anderson shelter which had arrived last year.

All that kerfuffle! she thought, looking at the curved shape of it, now shrouded in late-afternoon gloom at the bottom of the garden. When they had come round delivering them, Len had quietly – as he did everything these days – got on with digging down to the right depth to put the curve of corrugated iron in and shovelled earth over the top. Now, more than a year on, it was covered with grass and weeds. He had tried to make it as comfortable as possible inside with wooden benches along the edges. But in all this peculiar time of nothing much actually happening, they had never used the shelter at all except for keeping a sack of harvested potatoes in there.

Looking at the humped shelter, Ann felt that chill, dreadful feeling again. What a pathetically small, defenceless thing it looked . . . The thought of Sheila taking

Elaine away made her throat ache and she knew if she went on like this there'd be tears. It was no good – she needed to pull herself together.

She unpegged the washing, folding the stiff cotton, enjoying its clean scent of soap and sunshine and dropping the pegs back into the cloth bag, glad to be away from the emotional hubbub going on in the kitchen.

Len would be back any minute – and then no doubt go straight out again. What with helping out at a nearby ARP post and the Local Defence Volunteers at Cadbury's, he was hardly even in these days. He seemed so quiet – tired, nervy. That must be the war – and all this training they were doing.

That's what she told herself. It was easiest to blame the war. But was that the truth? Sometimes it felt as if Len was deliberately avoiding her. He was so remote lately, hardly seeming to meet her eye. Ann had started to feel that she was living with a stranger and whatever she did, she could not seem to bring back the man she'd married who had laughed and joked and seemed so much lighter and more carefree. Even with the troubles they had had they had pulled together. All that seemed so long ago now. Life took its toll, she told herself – and bringing up a family. He was just tired and worn down.

But carrying the basket of dry washing along the garden, she felt suddenly sad and weary to her bones. They were always busy, it was true. But, beneath the hard work and busyness of every day, she knew her husband was unhappy – and deep down, that it was all her fault.

Three

'Where's Dad?' Martin said, just as Ann was about to call them all in for tea.

'Out there.' She jerked her head towards the garden.

'I s'pose he's going out again?'

' 'Fraid so.'

She knew Martin wanted to listen to the wireless with his dad after tea – laughing along at Tommy Handley and the ITMA gang. Martin could also do an impression of Lord Haw-Haw, the propagandist for the Germans, that was so unnervingly good that Ann sometimes whipped round to check that it was really just her son in the room!

'OK. How long 'til tea?' He stood holding the doorknob. Of course, Martin was almost a man now and the same height as herself. But for a second she saw the small boy in short trousers, freckle-faced, as now, fresh home from school – 'What's for tea, Mom?'

'Couple of minutes.' She smiled fondly. 'Go and wash your hands.'

As Martin went out she saw Len pass the window, pushing his bike along the path to the shed, the hems of his trousers still tucked into his socks. Instead of coming straight in, he brought out a hoe and started attacking the weeds between the now-empty bean sticks and last few marrows, still to be harvested.

She watched, a tea towel in her hand. Len, her husband of twenty-one years, looking much as he had always looked – at least, since he came back from the first war and they were finally able to marry. Then he seemed so much older and more gaunt than when he had left. His flesh had filled out since, of course, but the joking lightness of his youth before the war had never quite come back.

Len was of medium height and sturdy build, and had the strong, sandy-brown hair which Sheila, unlike either of the other two, had inherited. His had a wiry curl to it, sitting neat and close-cropped, with little soft bits round the back of his neck that always wanted to curl as soon as they were allowed to grow. For some reason she had never understood, he called these his 'bum-fluff' – though wasn't that supposed to be elsewhere on the body? (Was there even a proper answer to that or had he just made up the name for it?) He had always had a pink, healthy complexion, eyes blue and wholesome-looking; a quiet, humorous nature. Except that these days there was a lot more of the quiet and less of the humour.

She watched as he jabbed at something by their patch of radishes. *Who are you?* Twenty-one years sleeping, breathing through the nights side by side and three children later. But who was this man, out there, bent over, burdened-looking, in a world of his own?

She realized her hands were clenched, wringing the tea towel tighter and tighter until it was a tangled knot. She shook herself and hurried to the pan of boiling cabbage, just as Martin came back.

'Call Dad in, will you, love?'

The rest of them were already round the table when he came in. Len went straight to the sink to wash his hands, without a word. Even though he had been in the garden, she caught the sweet, caramelly smell that he carried home from work and which was hardly ever absent from him for long. He was in the chocolate-making department at Cadbury's. He spent all day feeding chocolate crumb into the great vats, or *melangeurs,* where they were swirled with condensed milk and sugar to make smooth, liquid chocolate. This was carted in tanks to the other departments for tempering and moulding into bars or Easter eggs or individual chocolates – the full range of Cadbury delights.

Len sat down with a sigh, sleeves still rolled. Ann liked him to unroll them at mealtimes – it looked better, less like having a labourer at the table. But she didn't say anything.

'What's up, Dad?' Joy said, as Ann handed her a plate of shepherd's pie. 'Ooh – nice. Pass us the cabbage, Mart. There any mustard?'

'Not much point in mustard if there's no actual meat,' Martin said.

'Yes, there is,' Joy argued. 'Makes it taste of *something.*'

'And there *is* meat,' Ann pointed out, passing it over. 'A bit, anyway.'

'Nothing's up,' Len said. ''Cept I'll have to get this down me and get out again. It'd be nice to stay in for once.'

Would it? Ann thought, watching him shaking white pepper over his cabbage. He was only in for a couple of evenings a week and even when he was, it did not feel as if he really wanted to be with her at all.

Len dolloped mustard on to the side of his plate, then looked round the table and for the first time almost smiled.

'Where's the little 'un? Asleep?'

'Yes – she's just gone down,' Sheila said wearily. 'I hope she'll give me a few hours' peace now!'

'Shall I put the wireless on?' Martin said, through cabbage.

Before the war the wireless had been in the front room,

21

only turned on sometimes, for some entertainment. Now though, Len had moved it into the back room, on the sideboard with its accumulator. All summer they had been listening to it during meals, bulletins about the air battle raging over the southern counties, scores of how many planes had been shot down on each side. It felt indecent to her – too much like a sport.

'No,' Ann said. 'Let's have a rest from it.'

Martin nodded, then looked at Len. 'How's the old "Look, Duck and Vanish" going?'

'They're calling it the "Home Guard" now,' Len said, rolling his eyes. 'Even though they've sent out all our LDV armbands!'

He had volunteered – 'better do my bit' – for this home defence force since it was set up in May and was in the 27th Warwicks, in a unit established to guard the Cadbury works. It had all been quite sociable at times with the families invited out for a picnic now and then with their 'fighting men' when they had to go off for a weekend training camp.

Martin had been teasing him ever since. 'Tonight could be the night! All those "aliens, fascists, communists, pacifists" – oh no, not those terrible pacifists! – "religious dissenters under Nazi control . . ." You might capture some prisoners!'

Martin had been mugging up on the Training Manual. 'They're going to be terrified of those broom handles of yours – at least you've got a tin hat! Are they handing out walking sticks as well?'

Apart from armbands and helmets, the uniforms or any kind of weapon were proving a long time coming.

'Glad you find it so funny.' Len was on his dignity. In fact, he was getting annoyed. 'Those of us who went through the last lot might not be the youngest but we can pass on a lot of our experience.'

'I know, Dad,' Martin said good-naturedly. 'I was just kidding around.'

'Have you got much homework?' Ann asked quickly. Martin's school was still managing to function, even though they were short-handed.

'Nah – won't take long.'

Ann sat eating the stodgy shepherd's pie – though the mustard helped. She had been on edge in case Martin pushed it too far with Len. He was such a sunny boy, always the amiable tease, but it was hard to predict whether her husband would take it all in good part or suddenly get the hump.

'Have you told Dad my news?' Sheila said, looking woefully round the table.

'He's only just got here,' Joy pointed out.

'What?' Len looked wary.

'I'm going to have to evacuate.'

'Evacuate what?'

'Oh, don't be dense, Dad! I mean take Elaine out of Birmingham before it all starts!'

He nodded, mid-mouthful.

'Well, don't you mind?' Sheila saw herself as her father's favourite.

'Not if you want to keep safe,' he said. 'It's not for me to say – you're a married woman now . . .'

'I might just as well not be,' Sheila said woefully.

'At least you know where he is,' Joy said, attempting a cheerfulness which would only irritate Sheila further.

'Not for much longer – he says he reckons some of them will have to get posted overseas if things keep going like this – while we're all dying here in our beds!'

For the first time Ann's eyes met those of her husband and in each was a knowing glint of amusement.

'That's it, Sheila – look on the bright side,' Len said. 'But you'll have to do what you think best.'

'And Alan's gone and joined up!' Joy erupted, not to be left out. 'I never even knew he'd gone for the medical!'

'Who's Alan?' Len said.

'Dad! You *know* who Alan is – I've been dancing with him for *years*!'

'Oh yeah – him.' Len got up, his plate cleared. 'Well, good for him – he's a good lad. I'd best be off . . .'

'D'you want some pears?' Ann said. 'With evap?'

'No – gotta go. See yer later.'

Oh well, Ann thought. At least he got paid an extra one and six for a night shift – that was something at least.

It still felt strange, going to bed on her own. A relief, in a way, Ann realized guiltily. But that night, as soon as she lay down, she wished Len's warm, solid body was beside her. He had never been away before – hardly ever in the day during their marriage except to his mom's up the road, let alone at night.

Lying in the strange silence, without his breathing – or snoring – going on beside her, she found dark thoughts crowding her mind. The war – closer now and closer. The slightest sound from outside felt terrifying. Was this it – were they coming at dead of night, across the fields, heading into the cities? Boots marching along New Street, out along Linden Road . . .?

She tried to get hold of herself. Ridiculous. She was being silly. But the idea of a German in a helmet creeping along the garden towards her back door was so compelling she actually got up and pulled one of the blackout boards out of the way to look, though she could hardly see a thing. She tugged the window open a few inches.

Tossing and turning, neither her body or mind would lie still. By the time the first glimmers of light began to appear at the edges of the curtains, she was not sure whether she had slept at all.

She heard the back door opening, very carefully. Len must be home. She heard him moving about downstairs. Finally, he came up, quiet, in stockinged feet. As the door opened she closed her eyes, pretending to be fast asleep as he peeled off his clothes and sank, with a heavy out-breath of exhaustion, into the bed beside her.

Sleep still would not come. Her mind was flashing memories, images of the secret past she had tried to forget, both precious and painful, which just kept arriving in her mind whether she wanted them or not.

Four

1915

She was working on fillings, alongside Hilda. The two of them had been taken on at Cadbury's in the batch of school leavers in 1908, once they had passed the stringent tests of good character and clean habits expected by their Quaker employers.

Mrs Elizabeth Cadbury, Mr George Cadbury's wife, had herself inspected their hands, to make sure they were clean and free of any kinds of blemish. They all knew what a fine lady she was, doing all sorts of good things for people in the city. The Cadburys seemed a very grand family, living in their big house, Manor Farm, off the Bristol Road, but they seemed to spend all their lives working for good causes in the city and they were always giving away their money. Even though she knew how kind she was, Ann found Mrs Elizabeth Cadbury faintly terrifying when she came along the line, with her long, serious face and tightly curled hair. Ann's hands were trembling as she held them out to be inspected.

'It's all right, my dear,' Mrs Elizabeth said, with a slight smile. 'I won't bite.'

Afterwards, Hilda, who was standing next to her, nudged Ann and said, 'She looks a bit like the old Queen Mary, doesn't she?'

Ann turned to see a girl with very dark brown hair

smoothed back from a pale, heart-shaped face with rounded cheekbones, full pink lips and laughing brown eyes. They started giggling together then – and never really stopped, over the years.

They'd worked side by side on fillings for a long time, for the boxes of chocolates – marzipan and caramel, or strawberry and orange crème – to be pressed or squirted carefully into each chocolate shell.

There wasn't to be much chat in the factory, of course, as they sat in front of the piles of trays of chocolate shells waiting to be filled. Cadbury workers were expected to be calm, sober and obedient – and in return, the young ones carried on their education in classes at the Continuation School on Bournville Green one day a week. They worked forty-eight hours a week – shorter hours than other factories in the city. And they had access to opportunities undreamt of in any other workplace: art clubs and acting and singing and sports. Anything you wanted to do, you could find a club and join in. Getting work at Cadbury's was a dream job.

As soon as there was a break, Ann and Hilda would be together in the girls' dining room each dinner time, and in summer, out in the garden specially set aside for the girls of the factory, where they could sit in the shade of the trees or at the edge of the pond, the breeze rippling its surface. They had always been a proper couple of chatterboxes.

1908 was the year Cadbury's launched the new dark bar, called Bournville, which Hilda was mad about and they used to have teasing arguments.

'Dairy Milk's much better!'

'You ought to be in the advertisement for that one!' Hilda teased her. 'I think it's too sweet.' 'No, it's not!' And so on. Was it better when they added fruit and nuts?

Ann, yes, but *still* not as nice as Dairy Milk on its own – Hilda, no!

But over the years they had talked about almost everything. Ann had found, all her life, that there was no one she could confide in, or while away hours chatting to, the way she could with Hilda as they grew up together; Hilda with her happy nature and blunt, straightforward manner. Their lives, over time, ran in parallel, living through the Great War, getting married, having children.

The factory had been expanding then, before the war broke out, with building works all round, new blocks going up with the cryptic names 'M', 'Q' and 'T'. Milk condensing factories, they heard, were being set up away from Bournville, at Knighton in Staffordshire and Crampton, Gloucestershire, places close to canals so that the milk could be brought gliding along by water to the wharf at Bournville while other ingredients came into the Cadbury's railway siding.

Chocolate was mixed and moulded, the bars moving along conveyors to be wrapped and packed and sent out all over the country and to other countries round the world. Everything felt safe and prosperous and promising.

And in the months before war started, Ann met Len. Every time they went out together, she told Hilda all about it, because Hilda was also walking out with Roy by then – or Carrotty Roy as he was called, after his very noticeable hair. It was still a long time before she found that she had secrets she could not even share with Hilda.

Once taken on at Cadbury's, in one department or another, that was where you generally worked and stayed. So, although Len had been working there even longer than she had, Ann had never come across him before. That day, because someone was off sick, Len was doing something different. It was a warm summer day, 1915. Ann and Hilda were outside, aprons off, in their light summer frocks, walking back from the girls' grounds to work after the dinner break. One of the tanks of liquid chocolate was being pulled, trundling along towards them, on its way from the chocolate-making department. Not that this was anything unusual. Once the chocolate was mixed it was poured into a tank on a three-wheeled bogie with a towing arm to haul it along to the other rooms for moulding into bars or individual chocolates. And this time, it was Len pulling the thing. Afterwards it felt like fate.

Ann wasn't taking any notice to begin with, but gradually she took in his energetically curling hair, his jaunty walk and – as he came up close – the very blue eyes and cheerful smile. And Len's gaze was fixed, she realized, blushing, very definitely on her. Not on Hilda, with her sultry looks, who Ann always thought was the more striking of the two of them. Ann was pretty enough with her dark, wide eyes and hair with its pretty waves – but Hilda was a bit of a stunner.

Len nodded at the two of them as they walked by, a grin spreading across his face. Once he was well past, they broke into giggles.

'He looked nice,' Hilda said, nudging Ann again. 'He was staring straight at you.'

'He wasn't!'

'Yes, he *was*! And he went all red – don't tell me you didn't notice!'

She had noticed. And she was flattered and a little bit shaken. She was very soon to turn twenty-one then, but she had been very sheltered. Her mother, Mrs Jessie Williams, was a strict pillar of the Methodist Church and

29

Ann, like her two younger sisters Ruth and Elizabeth, had almost no experience of men except her father.

'I wonder who he is – he's quite a looker,' Hilda was saying.

Ann shrugged.

Hilda leaned round and peered mischievously into her face.

'Look at you, all blushes as well!'

'Oh, for goodness' sake,' Ann said. 'I don't even know who he is.' It seemed unlikely that she would see him again anyway.

But she did – and soon. Then it really did feel like fate. She passed him in Bournville Lane after work one day not long after – and from then on, Len seemed to keep appearing in Bournville Lane, miraculously, at that time. By the third or fourth time, he stopped right in front of her. She looked up, startled, to find him smiling down at her from his few extra inches of height. He looked shy and bashful, but the smile crinkled up his face in a way that she liked immediately.

Len, *that* Len, before he went away to war, was light-hearted about everything. They only had three months before he joined up – he agonized about it, but he felt he must – but they were lovely times. Len was fun and being with a lad was all new to her. They went about for walks, to the Cadbury's leisure area at Rowheath where they ate picnics beside the little lake and, now and again, she watched him play football. He was crazy about football – and Birmingham City in particular. And Len taught her to ride a bicycle, holding her at the waist and running along beside her until she was laughing so hard she could hardly cling on to the handlebars.

Best of all, she met his family. Len had one brother,

Ron, who had already joined up in the 14th Royal Warwicks. Ann only ever met him through his photograph – a new one, on the dresser in the back room, in his Army uniform. He had a longer face even than Len, his hair darker and eyes more serious – or perhaps it was just the new thought of being sent to France.

Right from the start, Ann loved Len's parents. Margaret and Cyril Gilby were both in their forties then. Ann was not especially close to her own mother who she found severe and not especially sympathetic. She realized, when she met Len's mom, how joyful a person she was compared with her own mother. It was only much later she began to ask herself what the relationship – on the face of it, calm and dutiful – had really been between her own parents. Had they ever loved each other? It was not something she would ever really know.

But in Margaret Gilby, tall, with her long, pink-cheeked face, affectionate eyes and easy laugh, she found a person who was warm, welcoming and able to keep her head up and see the funny side of things even when at her most sad. They took to each other straight away. And she could see that Margaret and Cyril, Len's dad, were what she thought of as properly married. They loved – and liked – each other. They seemed like a team, sharing things, little and large, in a living friendship. They created something – an atmosphere, bigger and more enveloping than just themselves – and she was gladly embraced within it.

In those days they had a dog called Trigger. He was some sort of mutt with enough boxer in him to give him an iron-hard body, all muscle, which wiggled with endless happiness at the sight of any visitor, his thin tail whipping at their legs. His face – not like a boxer, just wide-eyed, and somehow smiling – seemed to beam even more broadly at the sight of her.

'Look at him – he likes you!' Margaret exclaimed the first time Ann went to the house. She was wearing a cream dress sprigged with tiny pink flowers and a baggy fawn cardigan over the top. Ann sensed that she was careless of her appearance, was comfortable and unconcerned with such things. 'Look at Trigger, Cyril – he's really taken to Ann!'

And Cyril, a short, stocky man from whom Len inherited his build, if not his features, came obediently into the back room, rocking on his heels as he laughed at the way Trigger was making up to Ann, his head resting hopefully on her lap and his tail swinging.

'You've made a hit there, bab,' Cyril laughed. He was an ordinary-looking man, with receding mousey hair and regular features. But his personality radiated kindness and good nature. When he smiled, his lips shaped upwards with an almost cartoonish glee.

'Right – I'll get the kettle on,' Margaret said. 'You'll have a cup of tea, won't you, Annie?' She had called Ann 'Annie' right from the start.

The back room, with its iron range, its table and store cupboard, and its muddle of jugs and ornaments and bits and pieces on the mantelpiece, all indicated a homely contentment. Trigger came and sniffed at Ann's hands as she sat down by the table and Len laughed.

'I think he's decided Ann's all right! She's passed the test.'

'What test?' Ann asked.

'The sniff test.'

'Does everybody have to smell of chocolate?' she asked, laughing. This was a Cadbury family – everyone had worked there at some point.

'I wouldn't be surprised!' Margaret said, filling the pot. 'He doesn't know anything else.'

'Go on with yer,' Cyril said, giving the dog a shove as he sat down beside Ann. 'Leave her alone, you hairy hound!' He twinkled at Ann. 'I hear you're on fillings, bab? Our Len's in the mixing department – but then he'll've told you that, I s'pose?'

Ann agreed that he had. It was nice being in a household where everyone worked – or had worked – at Cadbury's because at home she was the only one. It was another family they all belonged to.

They drank tea and ate cake dotted with sultanas and sprinkled with brown sugar. As they sat there round the table, with the pot and milk jug and the cake on little flowery plates, the Gilbys chatted in a relaxed, friendly way. Margaret told her about Ron, how much they missed him and how odd it was not having him at home. Ann could see she was worried but trying not to show it. Cyril talked about cricket and he and Len had a friendly ding-dong over it and Ann and Margaret rolled their eyes. It was quite unlike home where having any visitor was an ordeal of stiff tension.

Len looked round and his eyes met hers. Aren't my mom and dad nice?

He was always proud of them. So kind, so *right* in his eyes. And they were. They were the nicest people she had ever met. And sometimes she wondered, looking back on the way she and Len had grown together, how, before he went away, they had promised to marry just as soon as he could get back again – whether she had in fact fallen in love more with Len, or with his family.

Five

Saturday 21 September 1940

Elaine's eyelids fluttered in her sleep. Sheila leaned against the train window, feeling the reassuring weight of the little girl in her lap and watching the country scenery pass outside.

Birmingham was a long way behind them now. Sheila felt lost and afraid and terribly unsure if she was doing the right thing. She had no real idea who these people were who said she could come and live in their house and she had to resist the urge to jump out at any station where they stopped and catch a train going back the other way. But at least having to look after Elaine made her feel stronger.

The weather was still pleasantly warm and the train rumbled along coughing smoke and occasional smuts in through the window above her head. By now there were not many people left in the carriage. There had been servicemen and a whole crowd of others when they started out, but they had all got down at the bigger stations. Oxford was the last, where she had changed on to a local train, and now she sat with just an elderly man snoozing in the opposite corner.

Soon they slowed again, pulling into another small station. It was no help looking out to see where they were – all the signs had been taken down when the danger of invasion became imminent. No good helping the enemy by signposting where they were. But this only increased her nerves as she was frightened of missing the right stop.

'Cholsey!' a voice shouted outside. 'This is Cholsey!'

Panic rose in her. Weren't they supposed to be getting off at the next stop? She did not know how far that was, but they seemed to be stopping rather often. Holding Elaine carefully, she stood up and laid her on the seat in order to lift the suitcase down in readiness, sitting with it on the floor by her feet.

'Oh, Kenneth,' she whispered, as the whistle blew outside and the train got up steam again. 'Why can't you be here with me?'

The ache of missing him rose in her like sickness. Missing him and worrying about him. His latest letter had arrived just before she left and she had it in her handbag. It was short, as ever – Kenneth wasn't the letter-writing sort. A few details about what he and his pals had been up to in their spare time. But he always ended with loving words. *'That's my girls – you give Lainy a big kiss and a cuddle from her dad – and all my love to you, She-she.'*

Her eyes filled with tears at the thought of Kenneth's (never Ken, he hated that) face – the face she loved. He had light brown hair, hazel eyes and a cheery personality. He was a steady, kindly lad – they were both secure in each other's love.

And all I ever wanted was a normal life, Sheila thought miserably, as the train trundled along again. There was a glimpse of the river from a bridge, water sparkling as it passed beneath them. Not like Joy, out dancing and gallivanting, needing all the attention. She just wanted a home, husband, kids, a little house near Mom and Dad.

And now with the war, even that was being snatched away.

She had felt guilty when she first ran away from Grimsby with Elaine, only two months old, in her arms. Kenneth had meant well, had rented two cold-water rooms so that they could be together as a family. But he hadn't got much clue what was needed and the rooms were dark, damp and cheerless. Even though the neighbours were kindly enough, Kenneth had hardly been there, leaving her alone for hours – days even – on end. It wasn't his fault – they had to go out to sea in the boats looking for survivors whose planes had come down. It was impossible to predict how long any of it would take and she lived in fear that he might not come back at all. But there was nothing they could do – the war and its demands had to come first.

When she went into labour with Elaine, alone one evening, she had been so frightened and embarrassed. And with the strain both of them were under and with a new baby, things had changed even when they were together.

'Can't you leave her – even for a moment?' Kenneth snapped one evening, when Sheila was back and forth, looking in on the little girl in their bedroom. 'It feels as if she's taken over everything! It's not as if we get much time together!'

Sheila tried to make it up to him, sitting over their evening meal with her fists clenched in her lap, her breasts aching and tingling with the peculiar feel of milk arriving in them. She tried to keep her mind on what her husband was telling her about one of his pals – because she really did want to pay him attention. But by the end of their meal of chops and potatoes the front of her dress was wet with milk.

Try as she might she could only find Grimsby foreign

and bleak, rough grey waves crashing in all the time, filling the air with spray. And you couldn't even go on any beach because they were all edged with rolls of spiky barbed wire. Sheila felt a complete fish out of water. She got very low in herself and Kenneth was worried. She did not want to be parted from him really, but in the end she could stand no more and ran home to her mother's.

Kenneth had been very loving before she left, saying how much he would miss them both. But she was peeved to realize that he was also relieved, as if he felt she had become a ball and chain, not just someone who was always there putting his needs first.

Afterwards, though, he had written loving letters saying how much he missed them both but that they had been terribly busy – even if he could not say with what exactly because it was all hush-hush. But that made her feel better. What was the use of her sitting up there in Grimsby on her own if he was not even there?

'*Dear Kenneth,*' she had written to him a few days ago:

I'm very worried about being here in Birmingham now, with our daughter.' (Our daughter sounded rather grand, she thought, like something you might read in a story.) 'It does not feel safe. There are bound to be more raids soon. At night the sky is full of searchlights – it's eerie. It's very bad in London, they say, and Portsmouth has been bombed as well. They are coming for the big cities and I know we'll soon be next as it's already begun. I'm frightened to death here. I've applied to the council to be able to take Elaine away and they've told me there's a family will take us in somewhere down south. They've got small children so Elaine will have some company. It's

*not a nice thought having to go and live among
strangers but all in all, I hope it's for the best . . .*

Her hosts, whose name was Vellacott, had sent a telegram
instructing her to wait at the station that Saturday afternoon where she would be collected. Telegrams being the
way they were, the instructions seemed terse and forbidding, and had only increased her nervousness about who
she might be going to live with.

After a few minutes the train slowed again, and she
saw another anonymous station similar to the last. Unsure,
she threw her coat on, scooped Elaine up with one arm
and picked up the heavy case with the other.

'Goring and Streatley!' she heard.

Managing to get the compartment door open – the
sleeping old man still being oblivious – she scrambled to
the outer door of the train and stepped out into a whorl
of smoke and steam.

Only one other person, a middle-aged woman, got down
from the train – and she walked briskly away. Looking
across the station, Sheila was not sure which side to go as
there seemed to be two ways out. Someone in a railway
uniform disappeared up the steps from the platform
before she had a chance to ask him anything. Her arms
were shaking with the effort of holding the case and
Elaine, who was now waking up. The thought of lugging
them up and down all those stairs just felt too much
for her.

'Don't wriggle, Lainy, I'll drop you, else.' She stag-
gered over to a nearby bench.

She dumped the case and sat down holding Elaine. She
felt hot and sticky in her coat which was too warm for
the day, and close to tears. It just felt like Grimsby all

over again. If only there was a kind, welcoming face waiting for her. And Elaine was starting to grizzle.

'No – don't *you* cry – please. Here – have a drink of
water.'

She found Elaine's little beaker and pacified her. It
wasn't a bad day – comfortable enough, sitting here. And
what else was she supposed to do with no one to help, she
thought, feeling very sorry for herself. Whoever was
meant to be meeting her would have to come and find her.

Six

A few minutes passed. Footsteps hurried back and forth somewhere but she could not see anyone until they started to come down the steps on to the platform. She saw feet in brown shoes, blue trousers, a sleeveless V-neck woolly with a hectic Fair Isle pattern over a white shirt, and finally a panama hat at a jaunty angle over a frowning face.

He hesitated halfway down the steps, catching sight of the mother and child perched tensely on the bench.

'Mrs Carson?'

Sheila struggled to her feet, nodding, clutching on to Elaine. 'Yes . . . Are you . . .?'

He completed the steps two at once and landed in front of her. A man in his mid-thirties, his face long and rather rectangular, a sharp, chiselled nose, thin lips and black hair just visible from under the hat. It was almost a handsome face, but stern and forbidding, until he managed to give her a second's hint of a smile which softened things briefly. He had an equally clipped way of speaking.

'Right, er, well . . . How d'you do? Maurice Vellacott. Delighted to meet you.'

He spoke with a certain charm, but this expressed delight did not translate to his features, apart from that glimmer of a smile. After a second, he held out his hand before realizing that she could hardly spare one of hers to shake his.

'Ah, yes – let me take your case. Motor car's out at the back . . .' He seemed in a hurry, with other things on his mind. They were halfway up the steps before he thought to say, 'Good journey?'

'Er, yes – thank you.' Sheila did not feel at all at ease with this man with his piercing grey eyes. He was polite enough, but her spirits sank. Grimsby had been bleak and cold, but at least most of the people around her had been warm and down to earth. What on earth was his wife going to be like?

A maroon Austin Six saloon was parked at the back of the station. Mr Vellacott handed her case in and, with a thinly veiled air of impatience, held the door open for her to get in the front with Elaine.

'Thank you,' Sheila said. Her voice sounded thin and uncertain. This chilly reception was draining away the last drops of her confidence.

'It's not far.'

Maurice Vellacott leapt in behind the wheel and they set off at high speed. Soon she saw the main street of a pretty village with wonky little houses, shops and pubs. Even here, she saw, there were tapes against blast on the windows and she could see glimpses of blackout curtains inside. Surely a place like this would not be bombed – that was why she had come here!

Sheila glanced nervously at Maurice Vellacott. Sitting beside him on the luxurious leather seat, she felt like a lumpish, rough incomer from the city – almost as if she had arrived from another world altogether – and she started bitterly to regret having left Birmingham. Mr Vellacott's eyes were focused on the road and she found his silence unnerving.

'It's nice of you – to let me come,' she offered.

'Audrey's idea. Her way of doing her bit. Fancies some company.'

Sheila waited, wondering why Mr Vellacott spoke as if

words were on the ration as well as foodstuffs and petrol. It was very strange. Although he was perfectly polite, she already felt that he did not like her.

'I'm hardly ever around in the week. Work in London. Here on her own with the boys – and Mrs Blisset, of course, in the mornings.'

'Your boys – how old are they?'

'Eddie's seven – not that Audrey likes him being called Eddie. Edward, it's got to be, according to her. And Charlie's five. Good little lads.'

'I'm sure,' Sheila said. She stroked Elaine's plump leg. The little girl was sitting quiet and wide-eyed. Two boys – a lot older, but they might be nice company for her.

There was a silence before he said, 'Bad, up there?'

'Pardon?' she said foolishly.

'You're from . . . *Birmingham*, I gather?' The way he said Birmingham sounded distasteful, as if he was talking about something foreign and rather squalid. 'So how are things up there?'

'Well – all right. But my husband's away, you see – RAF, Air-Sea Rescue. Before – I mean his real job – was at the Cycle Company, in Greet. But he's too young to be reserved. I was living back with my mom and dad, but . . .'

'I see.'

Do you? she thought. Then felt surprised by how prickly she felt with him.

'There have been raids – the sirens keep going off even if there isn't a raid in the end. We've already spent a few nights out in the shelter, down the garden . . . I thought I ought to bring her somewhere safer.'

Maurice Vellacott glanced at her for a second, just before swerving off left from the main road on which they were now driving.

'I've a flat in London. Work at the Old Bailey, you see. Not sure how that's going to be – things have been frightful this month. Just have to wait and see.'

He sensed that she did not know what he meant.

'It's the main criminal court – in London,' he said. 'The Old Bailey. I'm a barrister.' After a moment he added, 'I send people to prison.'

The satisfaction with which he said this was not lost on her. It felt almost like a threat, as if to say, you'd better behave yourself. But then he laughed, a sudden belt of sound which made her jump.

'Don't worry – not going to clap you in irons!'

Well, why would you? she thought crossly. I've done nothing wrong. She was surprised at how cross she felt, as if he looked down on anyone like her, as though they must all be criminals. But before the war she would have been cowed by him, not annoyed.

He steered abruptly left again and suddenly they were at an angle, shooting up a drive so steep that Sheila gasped and clung to the edge of the window. On reaching the top, he braked the car with a jerk outside a long, beautiful, brick house. It had gabled windows, little pink roses growing in a sprawl up the front of it, a glass conservatory at the far end and a flowery front garden surrounded by hedges. Sheila almost gasped. It looked like a holiday hotel. She couldn't wait to tell Mom and Joy about this!

'Oh!' she exclaimed. 'It's lovely!'

'Yes,' he said drily, getting out of the car. 'I think one might say that you've fallen on your feet. Right – come along then.'

'Ah – here you are!'

At the door stood a neat, petite young woman, two little lads peering out from behind her. Sheila realized they had been waiting to see the car come back and get a look at these strangers who were to live among them.

Audrey Vellacott hurried out to meet them. Sheila, scrambling to get out of the car with Elaine in her arms, found herself looking into friendly, deep-blue eyes set in a pink-cheeked, heart-shaped face which had a natural sweetness. Audrey must have been in her early thirties, an English rose, her sleek, jaw-length hair the colour of conkers, parted at the side and held back from her face with a mother-of-pearl slide. She wore a floral shirt-waister dress in patterns of pale blue and pink and belted at the waist.

'Well done, darling,' she said to her husband, rather heartily. 'Good timing!'

Maurice Vellacott marched into the house as if he had now done everything expected of him. As he passed his wife, Sheila thought she heard him mutter to her, 'Stupid woman – no initiative at all – just sat there on the platform.' Was that what he said? she wondered, feeling her heart pound faster with embarrassment. Surely she must have been mistaken?

'I'm Audrey. And these two little reprobates are Edward and Charles.'

'I'm Eddie,' the older boy contradicted her. He was dark-haired like his father and looked sulky. The little one, Charles, sweet-faced, almost blond, stood with his mother's skirt clutched in his hand, looking at Sheila and Elaine with sad-seeming eyes.

'Say hello,' Audrey Vellacott said.

'Hullo,' Edward said. There was no smile.

'Charlie? He's very shy,' Audrey laughed as the boy coyly hid his face.

'Hello, boys.' Sheila, who was still stinging from what Maurice Vellacott had said, forced her face into a smile.

'I'm Mrs Carson – but you can call me Sheila if you want. It's very nice of you to have us to stay.'

'Oh, and look at your little one – who have we here?' Audrey gave a warm smile. 'Isn't she *lovely*?'

'Elaine,' Sheila said, encouraged by her genuine appreciation of her daughter. 'She's seven months – and a bit.'

'Isn't she a *poppet*!' Audrey took Elaine's pudgy hand for a second, chattering – Sheila realized – nervously. 'Oh, they are *so* lovely at that age. Anyway, do come in. I'm sure you've had a dreadful journey but at least you got it over early in the day. Let's get you settled and I'll make some tea. Then we can all get to know each other. It's going to be fun having you here!'

She led the way into the house. Sheila was hurried through a wide, dark hall and up a broad staircase with a sage-green runner of carpet. It all felt very grand. All the way, Audrey talked, like a runaway train.

'We've only lived here for a few years – Maurice so *loves* to come home to the country after a week in London. I can't *bear* living in a city. Can't imagine living in Birmingham – even Reading would be too big for me! I'm a proper country mouse, so I hide away here with the boys and Maurice gets his fill of city life ... Although I do worry so now all this frightful bombing has started ... I keep saying he should come home ... Anyway, here we are!'

They had passed along a carpeted landing and she flung open the door into a room facing over the back garden. It was carpeted in cream, the walls painted a soft blue, with two elaborately framed mirrors giving back light to the room reflected from the huge window. Sheila saw a double bed with a thick, pale-blue eiderdown on it, a dressing table with another tilting mirror, a table, armchair and, near the bed, a little cot. She almost burst into tears.

'Oh!' she breathed. For a moment the memory of her cramped, damp room in Grimsby came to mind. 'It's beautiful!'

'For you,' Audrey said, seeming touched by Sheila's delight. 'I made sure you got the main guest room. No good being cramped when you have a child to look after, is it?'

Sheila realized Audrey had gone to a lot of trouble to make it as nice as possible for her. Tears filled her eyes suddenly.

'Oh, my dear – are you all right?' Audrey said. 'Leaving home and all this change must be rather overwhelming for you.'

'Yes – thanks.' Sheila wiped her eyes quickly. 'I'm just tired and it's all so . . . So nice.'

She couldn't say what she was feeling: that though she and Audrey did not know what to make of each other yet, she could see, to her enormous relief after meeting Maurice Vellacott, that his wife was a kind, warm-hearted person.

'Thank you – so much.' She was about to plonk Elaine down on the bed, but realized in time that her nappy was well overdue for a change.

'I'd better see to her . . .'

'Look,' Audrey said. 'I'll show you where the bathroom is, then you can settle in for a few minutes. Sort little . . . I'm so sorry, I've forgotten? I'm a proper numbskull – Maurice is forever telling me!'

'Elaine.' *And you're not*, Sheila wanted to add.

'I'll make us a drink – some coffee, tea?'

'Tea, please.'

'Of course. And then I can show you everything.'

Audrey hovered in the doorway for a moment, her hands clasped as if she was about to say something, but she seemed to think better of it. She turned to go, then paused again.

'By the way, this room has not been used for a while, so I haven't done the blackout and it's quite a job. I wondered if you might give me a hand putting it up?'

Sheila smiled. 'Yes. Course I will.'

Audrey was looking out for her as she came down the stairs carrying Elaine.

'I need to give her something to eat,' Sheila said. 'Look, I can pay you, every week – for our keep . . .'

'Yes, yes, dear – don't worry. We can discuss all that. Come and have your tea.'

The way she spoke was comfortingly motherly. Sheila realized that Audrey must be ten years or so older than her, though in her own way she seemed young and uncertain.

Audrey led her to a room overlooking the back garden, where there was a round table close to the window on which she had laid little bone china cups, white and painted with delicate blue flowers.

'I made a bit of toast – I thought you might both need a little something – and look, she can use our old high-chair at the table.'

They sorted Elaine out and Audrey handed her a finger of toast. Elaine looked uncertainly at Sheila for a moment before taking it and chewing happily.

'Thank you,' Sheila said. She felt as if she was going to spend her life saying thank you to Audrey from now on.

Sitting at the table she could see Maurice Vellacott through the wide window, whacking at the undergrowth with a hoe. The oldest boy, Edward, stood watching, very still, as if he had been told to watch and learn. A couple of hens pecked about the garden as well.

The younger boy, Charlie, had stayed inside and was standing by the table watching them all with solemn interest. Audrey fluttered about, finally settling on a chair and pouring tea, which Sheila sipped gratefully.

'With Maurice working in London during the week, he gets very tired, poor lamb – it's all rather a strain. But then travelling in from here every day is *exhausting* as well . . . So, he's keeping on the flat for the time being. But it did seem very silly, me here in this big house with just the boys when there are people needing somewhere to go. We really don't know what's going to happen next, do we? They've even put little watchtower things – I'm sure that's not the right name for them – sort of bunkers, along the river. Little concrete cabins with slits to look out of. It really is horrible to see them – makes me all of a quiver – as if the Germans are going to come paddling up here from London any minute.'

She paused for breath and topped up Sheila's cup.

'Do tell me about yourself. Your family?'

Sheila was about to answer when Maurice Vellacott erupted into the room.

'For heaven's sake, Audrey – where are the hedge clippers? It's not safe to put anything down around here!'

And though Sheila had a shrewd idea that Audrey had no clue where they were and had not touched them, she leapt to her feet.

'Oh, darling – I'm *sorry*! Let me come and help you look.'

'I'm here in a great big house,' Sheila wrote to her mother that night. *'You should see it – I'm living in the lap of luxury!'*

She was sitting up in bed, in her old pale-yellow nightie which, against this luxurious blue room with its

48

gilt-framed mirrors, looked suddenly scruffy. There were long, powder-blue curtains with gold brocade – now with the blackout curtains behind them as well, which she and Audrey had put up late that afternoon.

She looked at Elaine, asleep beside her. The little girl had taken a while to settle. It had been such a strange day. But she was tired out and eventually grizzled and fed herself to sleep at the breast. It was cosy, this room, the cot right beside her bed. If only Kenneth could be here to get in with her and they could cuddle up side by side! She tried not to think about Kenneth or she knew she would start to cry.

Even so, she felt a surge of homesickness, thinking of her attic room in Bournville. What would they all have been doing this evening? Martin poring over his homework, making jokes, teasing everyone; Joy doing her limbering-up exercises at odd moments in the kitchen or living room. Joy seemed to hear dance music in her head all the time. Making an exhibition of herself, Sheila often thought to herself rather snottily when she was at home. But she missed it now. Mom knitting or mending, Dad out, as usual.

'*The lady here is called Audrey. She's very nice. Very kind. I don't think . . .*'

She crossed that bit out. '*I'm not sure about her husband yet . . .*' It felt wrong to write anything more about the Vellacotts. It felt as if he would know, somehow. And it felt rude and ungrateful. She told her family the bare minimum, just to let them know she and Elaine were well settled, and promised to write again soon.

Seven

For those first two days, Maurice Vellacott was at home. Sheila felt very awkward at first, trying to look after Elaine, make sure she got fed at the right time while she hardly knew where anything was in the house and had to keep asking.

Audrey was very kind and bustled about showing her everything. Beside her petite form, Sheila felt like a carthorse.

'Now look, just help yourself, Sheila. If you prefer to cook things for Elaine yourself, here are the pans – and the larder . . . Don't be shy. I'm sure we'll all get used to each other very soon.'

Audrey always seemed eager to please and Sheila liked her. But she found the idea of only having your husband at home for the weekend rather strange. When the Vellacotts had come back from church on Sunday – Sheila stayed behind – and she and Audrey were in the kitchen, filled with the delicious smells of roasting chicken, she could see Audrey was looking tense. Or looking something – sad? She could not be sure.

'We'll all have lunch together,' she said cheerfully. 'Sunday lunch is rather sacred in the house.' Yesterday, Maurice Vellacott had been out over lunchtime, apparently playing golf. 'Of course, in the evening, I have to get Maurice on to the London train . . .'

'It's a shame,' Sheila ventured. She was drying up the morning teacups by the sink.

'What?' Audrey turned to her brightly, forehead wrinkling. 'Oh – you mean Maurice being in London? But you're worse off, aren't you? You're having to live apart from your husband?'

'Well – yes.' She found unexpected tears in her eyes and saw Audrey notice this. She quickly pressed them away with her fingers. 'But – is it just because of the war?'

'Oh – no, the war's made no difference to that! Maurice has always spent the week at the flat. He's *so busy*, poor dear – all those briefs to read. And being in easy reach of chambers and the courts – he'd be quite worn out and grumpy if he had to go in every day.'

Sheila thought Maurice Vellacott was quite grumpy enough as it was, but obviously this was not something to say to Audrey.

They all sat round the table at dinnertime – or 'lunch-time' as Audrey called it, in the dining room – not the sunny room where they had drunk tea. It was a darker room, mostly taken up by a long, mahogany table with stiff, high-backed chairs placed all around. Maurice was seated at the head of the table and stood to carve the chicken.

'These are our own potatoes,' Audrey said, passing round a dish of mash. There was a large vegetable patch at the bottom of the garden.

'Sweat of my brow,' Maurice Vellacott said and Audrey laughed though Sheila was not quite sure why. Things were very formal and she felt tense and on her best behaviour. She was praying that Elaine, strapped into the high-chair next to her, wouldn't play up. It was a mercy to have her little one to pay attention to, though. Elaine kept looking at her, wide-eyed, not at all sure where she was, but she enjoyed the mashed potato with chicken gravy.

Maurice Vellacott ate hungrily and mostly in silence, except to tell Edward off for reaching to get the salt instead

51

of asking politely. Sheila felt he gave off an atmosphere of impatience at all times. The boys sat stiffly, also quiet. Audrey, on the other hand, hardly ever stopped talking, as if she needed to fill every chink of silence with cheerful chatter – which in turn seemed to annoy her husband.

'You really do have the most beautiful hair,' she said to Sheila, as she handed out slices of home-made apple pie. Sheila was startled and was trying to think of something to say but Audrey rattled on. 'We have our own apple trees as well. So much fruit at the moment I can scarcely keep up! Here, do have some custard, I thought Elaine might like some as well? – Yes, it's so lovely and thick and is that a natural wave? I'm so envious!' Sheila, still trying to keep up with whether she meant her hair or the custard, could think of no reply and Audrey sat down after serving the pie. 'You've no idea how hard I have to work to get any sort of curl in my hair.'

'That's Audrey's idea of hard work,' Maurice Vellacott said suddenly. He looked at Sheila as if wanting her to join in the joke – to side against his wife. Sheila smiled faintly, out of politeness.

'But it *is*!' Audrey laughed. 'Curlers and pins every night – it's such a business and any sort of wave I manage drops out by midday!'

Maurice Vellacott let out a loud sigh at this point, as if this conversation really was too silly for him even to have to listen to.

'My mom says the same,' Sheila said, thinking, Damn you – you say something then if you're so bored with us. She had had the same thoughts about her own father sometimes, the way he was so silent. And here was another one. 'I got my hair from my father – and I think hers will be like mine.'

She took refuge in feeding Elaine a mouthful of the

stewed apple filling. It was all such a strain and she felt homesick for Mom's stews and all the family round the table, even if she and Joy were bickering. This place may have been grand but it certainly didn't feel homely. Audrey was very nice and was trying hard, but she felt a great longing to retreat into the kitchen, finish feeding Elaine and have done with it.

Later she wondered if it was what she had said that caused it – mentioning that Maurice Vellacott would soon be gone again. Trying to get any sort of conversation going, she turned to him and said, 'So you've got to get back to London this evening, have you?'

'Can we get down?' Edward interrupted.

'Can we get down, *please*,' Audrey said quickly. She looked at her husband.

'Go on then – off you go,' he said.

Edward and Charlie slid down off their chairs, even though the adults were still eating their pie.

Sheila was still wondering if she would get any reply from Maurice Vellacott as Edward passed behind the back of her chair. Instinctively, she leaned forward and pulled her chair in even though there was plenty of room. As she straightened up she saw that Edward had stopped next to the high-chair and was staring at Elaine. There was no expression that she could read on his face. He was a pale, cold-eyed child. She had scarcely seen him smile yet.

She was about to say something to encourage him – about Elaine, or just something friendly. After all, they were strangers who had suddenly arrived in his home.

With no warning, Edward shot out his arm and slapped Elaine hard round the face. Sheila leapt to her feet.

'What the hell're you doing!' she cried. 'You little . . .'

She managed not to finish the sentence with the words that came to mind. Elaine was howling and she lifted her into her arms. Audrey had also jumped up, completely mortified.

'Edward, how *could* you! How awful, Sheila – I'm sure he didn't mean it.' She came round, fussing over Elaine, who was yelling and in tears.

Sheila knew perfectly well that he had meant it and she was seething, but she did not want to say anything to poor Audrey. She clenched her teeth and cuddled Elaine.

'Come here, boy,' Maurice Vellacott said, in a tone so icy that Sheila almost felt sorry for him. Audrey went to protest, but he held his hand up. 'No. Leave it. I'll deal with this.'

He left the room, with Edward pinned tightly by one arm. Audrey watched, her eyes wide, upset. Little Charlie started to cry and for a while the two of them were left to pacify their sobbing children. Sheila heard a yell from Edward, followed by more crying from somewhere outside.

'Oh dear,' she said, almost in tears herself. 'Is it us coming here that's caused this?'

'No,' Audrey said, kneeling with her arms round Charlie. She sounded tearful too. 'I don't think so, Sheila. The boys are always unsettled on Sunday afternoons – with their father going again. It's not easy for them.'

The whole thing was horrible and Sheila realized she did not want to mention it to everyone at home – or even think about it if she could help it.

Later on, when Maurice was shut in his study and the children were calmed down, the boys playing with a little model railway on the sitting-room floor, Audrey said in a light voice, 'Maurice finds it a bit difficult to adjust back to domestic life after the days he spends in court. It'll be a bit more relaxed in the week.' There would just be the two of them. 'We can get ourselves sorted out then.' And she smiled, her eyes full of anxious appeal.

Eight

'What's up with you, Joy? – Joy?'

'Eh? Oh – sorry.'

Joy looked up from the tray of chocolates she had been staring into without moving for the last she didn't know how long. Her friend Norma, with her freckly face, curly strands of her bright ginger hair escaping from under her cap, was staring at her indignantly.

'You'd better get on with it – you're lost in your own little world and those chocs aren't going to pack themselves.'

Joy and Norma were working together in the boxing department at Cadbury's, at one of the many tables in the long room, packing up the selection boxes of Milk Tray. They had both worked there for several years now, so the desire to keep eating chocolate had long worn off. All the workers were allowed to sample chocolate while they were in the factory but not to take any of it home. New to the job, Joy had been nibbling on and off all day at first, coming home queasy from too much sugar. She soon stopped and now she was so used to the smell and taste of it that she hardly gave it a thought.

She could do the job in her sleep – strawberry, lime barrel, caramel, fudge, marzipan . . . *Cadbury's Milk Tray Assortment – covered with blended chocolate*: words printed in cursive across the half-pound boxes which arrived flat, in piles, and had to be assembled and packed. Her mind often drifted off. It was a good job for daydreaming. Except today she wasn't so much daydreaming as trying not to cry.

She quickly got on with her work again – strawberry, lime barrel, caramel . . .

'What's up with you – is it 'cause of *him*?' Norma went on, filling her boxes from the trays of chocolates like lightning, as she did everything. Norma was Hilda's daughter and as their mothers had done before them, the girls often worked side by side.

'Just shurrup, OK?' Joy snapped. 'I'll tell you in the break – just not now.'

Norma rolled her eyes, but she could see she was not going to get anywhere.

'You know they want more people to go over to the munitions work? Girls can do it – you gunna go?'

Cadbury's was converting to doing more for the war effort: a new company had been set up called Bournville Utilities Ltd. Since the fall of France to German occupation in June, everything had become much more urgent, more frightening. Parts of the factory were already being used by the Lucas and Austin companies, who were making vital items for the military, and there was talk of this expanding.

Joy shrugged.

'They're gunna need us,' Norma said. 'Now so many of the men are joining up.'

Which was the wrong thing to say, because Joy then burst into tears.

Joy and Norma – just as Ann and Hilda, their mothers, had done when they worked there together – snatched a few minutes outside in the dinner break. They sat on the grass in the girls' gardens, which were tucked away at the side of the factory, in the last of the autumn sunshine.

Other female workers were scattered across the grass in groups, laughing and chatting, getting a bit of sun on their faces before the afternoon's work began.

'You've got to admit – he's pretty hopeless,' Norma said.

'I know,' Joy said resentfully. She had been in tears again and her chest hurt from trying not to let go and really sob.

Norma looked at her, shocked that Joy was not disagreeing with her. Normally she leapt to Alan's defence if she ever said anything. Joy was picking at the grass, not meeting Norma's eye. It wasn't just that he hadn't told her he was going to join up. Only now, she realized, there were so many things about Alan that puzzled her. He was so strange sometimes and he hardly ever told her anything.

She did look up in the end, her huge brown eyes and dark hair showing off how pale her face was today.

'I just can't make him out, Norm. We've been dancing together for a year and we're such good pals – well, I thought we were anyway. I mean – more than pals, or that's what I was hoping . . . I know he's shy – in that way, anyway. But you know, when you dance with someone . . . I've tried to show him how much I like him and I thought he *did* like me, really . . . And then out of the blue he goes and says his papers have come and I never even knew he'd been to sign up!'

Tears rolled down her face despite her trying to control them. Joy was hurt – and affronted. She was so pretty and lively that a lot of boys liked her and wanted to walk out with her. But the one she had really set her heart on was a mystery to her.

'I think he does,' Norma said. 'The way I've seen him look at you sometimes.'

'Have you?' Joy was grasping at this shred of hope. She knew Norma was not the sort to say something like that if she didn't mean it. But Alan was strange. There was that night when they kissed – and what happened afterwards . . .

'Well, I think so. But I'm never sure with lads either.'

'You're sure with Danny.'

'Yes – but he's . . . Well, he's just Danny.'

'And you've known him since you were in your pram!'

'Well, practically, yes!' They both laughed. 'The boy next door. Or next door but one, anyway.'

'You're lucky,' Joy sighed. 'I don't want to spend all my time guessing. Why doesn't he *say* something? It's humiliating. I feel as if I'm going to end up throwing myself at him because he's being so peculiar!'

Norma put her head on one side.

'What're his family like? You've never said much about them – is there summat wrong there?'

'His family?' Joy frowned. Then she looked confused. 'I've never met his family, Norm.'

'*Never met them?* In all this time? Why not?'

Joy found herself questioning everything suddenly. She and Alan had got along well at work, each finding out that the other liked dancing, and soon they were going as often as they could. There were dances in the ballroom at Cadbury's Rowheath Pavilion, a few streets away from the factory, with its lovely grounds round it and the lake. And they went to the dance halls in town when they could. Joy adored all of it. She was very good at it and so was Alan: they made a fine pair. And somehow she had just thought that because they liked each other one thing would eventually lead to another – and maybe then she would meet Alan's family.

'They live quite a way away, in Edgbaston,' she said.

Norma giggled. 'You make it sound like the ends of the earth – you've only got to get on the bus! Anyway, you went to the Tower with him.' The Tower Ballroom was right next to Edgbaston Reservoir.

'I know, but . . . We just never went there, somehow. I s'pose he never invited me. Is that strange?'

'It is to me,' Norma announced. 'I'd say, never get too far with a bloke without meeting his mom – then you'll know everything there is to know about him.'

'Oh, come on, Norm – that's a bit much,' Joy laughed. 'Not everyone grows up knowing everything about their other half like you!'

'But it's just common sense.'

'Well, what about his dad?'

'Him too – but the mom. Especially the mom.'

Joy stared ahead of her tragically. 'He might get killed. And then I'll never know . . .'

'He's only training at the moment.' Norma picked up a buttercup head and peered at its metallic yellow petals. 'I don't think that'll finish him off.'

'No, but . . . You'd think he might have *said* something!' Joy's outrage surged again. 'Why didn't he even *tell* me? He's just . . . Oh!' She let out a groan of frustration.

'Come on.' Norma nudged her. She screwed up her eyes, peering at the sky. 'Time to go in. It's getting chilly.'

The other girls were starting to get up and make their way towards the various blocks where they were working at Cadbury's. Laughter echoed across the grass. The two girls got reluctantly to their feet.

'Ugh – that fish was a bit ropey,' Norma said. 'It's repeating on me already.'

'They're doing their best, I s'pose,' Joy said.

The fish they had for lunch in the works dining room was a greyish white and a bit like eating cardboard. The only saving grace was the tinned peas which added a splash of colour to the otherwise dishcloth grey mass of fish and a bit of boiled spud. And one of the male staff had played the piano which livened things up. Some of them sang along once they had finished eating. A bit of 'We're Gunna Hang Out the Washing on the Siegfried Line' and 'Roll Out the Barrel'; the sound of all their young voices surging round the dining room set them up for the beginning of the afternoon.

'Alan'll be home on leave before they send him anywhere, won't he?' Norma said. 'You can see him then – set things straight.'

Joy gave her a wan smile. 'Thanks, Norm.'

Norma's mom and dad, Hilda and Roy, lived in Sycamore Road and Joy had known them all her life. She had always enjoyed going round to their house. Norma's mother and her own were such old friends and they were like aunties to each other's children. Nowadays, though, when she saw Hilda and Roy Baines together, laughing and joking, she realized how quiet her own mother and father were, in comparison.

'You'll just have to shake some sense into him,' Norma said as they went back inside. 'That's what I'd do, anyway!'

At work again, her hands fitting the chocolates into their slots in the trays at top speed, Joy tried to shake off her annoyance with Norma. Norma's advice rankled. Just because she and Danny and their families lived in each other's pockets – that was easy when you lived spitting distance from each other! There was plenty of time for meeting families and all that. And wouldn't it have seemed a bit forward, or formal, for Al to have invited her over to meet his family? After all, they were only sixteen when they met.

Alan worked in the box-making and printing department at Cadbury's and for a time he had been one of the lads bringing round a trolley stacked with flat Dairy Milk selection boxes to the packing department. Any lad who came in was fair game to be eyed up and ran the gamut of the women's whistles and ribald comments. Joy had seen many of them blushing until their ears went pink as they passed through.

The first time she saw Alan, a neat lad with healthy-looking skin, slender but broad-shouldered, with a friendly blue-eyed face and ready smile, she had liked him straight away. He dealt light-heartedly with the girls' banter and when he kept coming in day after day, she and he started to exchange a few words. They had found out that each of them liked dancing and – well, that was how it started.

Joy had loved dancing almost as soon as she could stand. If the wireless was on at home, even as a tiny girl she would be jigging and jumping about. When she got to the age of five, Mom took her to a Mrs Lyndsey in Selly Oak, who played the piano and gave lessons to a few children in the big front room of her house on the Bristol Road. Mrs Lyndsey taught them the usual things, the basic ballet positions and some country dances. As Joy grew older and left school, she used almost every bit of the wages she didn't give Mom for dance lessons and shoes and full-skirted frocks.

She went to the Bocker & Bettridge school in Bristol Street where she learned ballroom dances, then jazz. The best, most fun and invigorating and joyous thing in the world was to be dressed up for a dance, spinning and whirling with the music, your feet so in tune with it that you didn't have to think about it. And in time, it was she and Alan, warm from the exercise, lit up by the music – in harmony. There was nothing like it.

Alan had not had so many lessons as she had but he seemed able to pick up dances very quickly and he had a natural flair for it. They got into the habit of a regular weekly date for dancing: at the West End Ballroom, the Tower in Edgbaston, the Palais de Danse for jazz dancing – and any hop or dance going locally. They were thinking about starting to enter serious dance contests.

And then the war came. At first Alan had said he was going to stay at Cadbury's. As the gas masks were handed out and piles of sandbags appeared around buildings, he volunteered to be a fire watcher and aircraft spotter at the factory. But thinking back, she realized Alan had changed recently. He seemed quieter, as if worried by something.

Her hands filling boxes as they did day after day, her mind was on a track all of its own, going back over things that had happened with Alan.

The first time they kissed was one night last winter; they were on their way back through the blackout, from a dance at Kent Street Baths. Ballrooms had been closed since the war started. The Palais de Danse in Monument Road was being used as a warehouse for rationed foods. But the bigger swimming pools like Kent Street Baths could have sprung floors laid over the pool so that the place could be used as a dance hall.

They had had a lovely evening but now Alan was quiet as they walked, hand in hand, through the freezing darkness to the tram stop. It was difficult – and unnerving – trying to get along in the blacked-out streets with only a pencil line of torchlight between them and you could easily lose each other if you didn't hold hands. But Joy thought it meant more. You held hands with a lad if you were walking *out* with him, instead of just walking *along* with him – didn't you?

'You all right?' she asked into the gloom.

'Yeah. Course,' he said. Joy shone her little torch at him for a moment and Alan smiled his broad, infectious smile. 'Why wouldn't I be? That was a good night!'

But then, as they stood waiting on the Bristol Road, he pulled her aside from the other people waiting. He's going to kiss me – at last! she thought, her heart juddering.

She had never known a lad as slow to try and steal a kiss as Alan. Though he was full of vim when dancing, he seemed very unsure of himself in other ways. For a long time, they had definitely just been pals, even though the wartime blanket of darkness cast over the Birmingham streets meant no one could see what you were doing. It gave a new kind of freedom. Now, at last, it felt very exciting, feeling Alan reaching for her and she putting her arms round him, even tighter than when they were dancing, feeling his lips exploring hers, the very slight bristle on his upper lip.

'That's nice,' she said, hugging him, full of happiness. It was so dark that they could only sense other people close by somewhere and it felt as if they were in a world of their own.

'Yeah. It was, wasn't it?' She heard him give a little laugh. They were both young, very inexperienced – especially him, it seemed. Alan put his arms round her and kissed her again.

Even though there were more kisses, now and again after dances, it was as if something was holding Alan back. Joy was puzzled and confused by it. She didn't want to do anything untoward but at the same time it would have been nice if he had seemed a bit more keen!

And there was another time, after a dance, when something odd happened that she still could not understand and it left a bad taste. More than that – it had frightened her.

By then, because of the pressures and obligations of the war, they did not have the freedom to see each other so often, though she was very keen for those kisses to happen again. But Alan never said anything. Never came out with any of the romantic, loving words Joy was hoping for – *you're beautiful, I love you, you're the girl of my dreams . . .* It was more as if he was daring himself, to see if he could kiss her, but did not have any idea what to do apart from that.

That balmy night – during the summer – they were making their way through town to get home. They were walking in the smoky, uncertain light of dusk and Alan put his arm round her shoulder. She was wearing a sleeveless summer frock in buttery yellow-and-white stripes, a cardigan flung over her shoulders. Soon, Joy thought, excited, he'll pull me aside and we'll have another kiss. But he didn't. In her disappointment she started needling him, mucking about.

'Come on, let's run – I dare you,' she goaded him. If he wasn't going to kiss her, she was at least going to make something happen!

'Don't be daft – you'll fall over or summat,' Alan said crossly, as she pulled on his arm.

'You gunna stop me?' She yanked her arm out of his grip, tugged off her heels and with a shoe in each hand, set off, tearing barefoot along down past the post office, towards Navigation Street.

She heard Alan running after her and she got the giggles at being chased in the uncertain light, guided by the pavement's white-painted edges but hoping there were no holes or uneven bits of paving. She hardly felt the bits of gravel jabbing into her feet. Soon she was laughing so much she could hardly run.

It was not long before Alan caught up, at the bottom, grabbing her arm.

Still laughing, she turned and went to put her arms round him, thinking he was laughing too, that this must surely have broken the ice . . .

'Get off me! Don't do that!' He pushed her away, so roughly that she was flung up hard against a wall. There was a sharp pain at the back of her head and she was so shocked, she felt as if she had been doused in iced water.

'Just leave me alone!' he yelled back over his shoulder as he strode off along the street.

Joy was stunned, rubbing her head as tears of pain and shock started to come. She had no idea what to do. What the hell had come over him? Was that Alan? Whoever that was did not seem at all like the Alan she had known all this time. Surely he would come back and ask her to forgive him, say it was all a terrible mistake?

After she had stood there for what felt like an age, there was no sign of him. Shivering now, she put her shoes back on, slipped into her cardigan and, still tearful, made her way to the tram stop.

The increasing darkness made it impossible to see far, but she still hoped he might come back – that he would wait at the stop with her until her tram arrived as he usually did, that they could make things up. But the tram slid into view and all she could do was to get on. Utterly miserable, not having any idea what had happened, she caught her tram. Alan must have gone straight home.

She saw him at Cadbury's the next day, during the morning break, in Birdcage Walk, the passage that ran along the long, imposing brick frontage of the factory.

She realized he was looking out for her and he came straight up, looking awful, upset, with dark rings under his eyes.

'Sorry about that – last night.' He could hardly look at her and she was glad because her tears immediately began to flow. She felt so hurt and confused. 'Don't know what came over me – I was just in a bad mood. I dain't mean anything.'

'It's all right,' she said tearfully. Even though it wasn't yet. She still felt very raw. But she could see he really was sorry and was shaken up by what had happened. Gradually, over the next days and weeks, they got back to normal, went dancing, and things seemed all right.

Until the evening when he suddenly made his announcement. They were in town, near the library, about to go for her tram, when Alan pulled her aside. She could tell at once that this was not because he was going to kiss her or anything of that nature. He seemed tense, stood facing her with his hands at his sides.

'Look . . .' He kept his gaze on the pavement. 'I need to tell you something . . .'

'What?' She didn't take in quite how serious he sounded. She was still caught up in the music and dancing they had just enjoyed, her voice light and joking.

'I've joined up.'

'Joined up what?' she joked. 'The wires in your brain?' But she realized, just then. '*Joined up!* What – you mean . . . ?'

'The Army. I start training next week. Catterick.'

Even now she was in shock. They were friends, weren't they? At least *friends* even if she was not sure about anything else with Alan. And friends tell each other things – don't they?

Within days he was gone, promising to write – which

was big of him. She felt so hurt and angry. Why had he not told her what he was thinking? How could he just go off like that and not say anything? She had known, over the last year for sure, that she was in love with Alan, but they were both young and having such a lot of fun there didn't seem to be much hurry about anything. That night when he pushed her – well, that had put a brake on her feelings, it was true. But he had never done anything like that before, ever, and she told herself it was just something that happened once, that he was upset for some reason. But then suddenly this announcement out of the blue . . .

Standing at her worktable that day, seeing Alan's lovely face in her mind, thinking of the two of them jiving and waltzing, so good it was like flying, the pain twisted in her. She was hurt – and so was her pride.

Well, Alan Bishop, she thought, angry and defiant, if you're just going to play Mr Mystery Man all the time and go off and leave with barely a word, I'm going to have to find someone else to dance with!

Nine

'D'you think I should?'

Ann looked round the tea table. It seemed so quiet without Sheila and Elaine and she ached with missing them, especially her little granddaughter. Len was quiet, Joy seemed woeful about something. The only bright spark was Martin, whose sunny face and jokes could always cheer her up.

'Well Norma's mom's back at work,' Joy said. 'On the munitions side – that's where they want people.'

'What d'you think, Len?' If only he'd say something, she thought.

Ann felt very mixed up about it. Perhaps she ought to go back to work for the war effort like her best friend – but there was quite enough to do at home and Martin was still quite young. Hilda's two, Norma and John, were both out at work. She hardly saw anything of Hilda these days, now she was back at Cadbury's.

'Well – the way things are . . .' Len trailed off, vaguely. Ann felt frustration boil up in her. There he was, forking up the hash of corned beef with potatoes – just half an onion for flavour as they were in short supply – his hand going mechanically up and down to his mouth but he might just as well not have been there.

She was filled with sudden rage. For a moment, another face, so tender and loving, came to the forefront of her mind. A face close to hers, gazing, gazing at her. When was the last time Len had actually *looked* at her?

'Len, are you listening?' she said, more sharply than she'd intended.

'She wants you to tell her what to do, Dad,' Martin teased, winking at her. 'Little woman – can't make a decision by herself.'

Len looked up as if surfacing from a dream. 'Well – yes. Good idea. They need the workers . . .'

'Well, they do . . . but it's a lot to manage,' she said, immediately backtracking. How could she possibly manage to work as well as everything else? 'And if we're going to spend a lot of nights in that damp blasted shelter – and how's the shopping going to get done, not to mention the washing and ironing?'

Len looked at her as if such things had never entered his head.

'Best not, then,' he said. 'It'll all get too much. I'll lay a better floor down in the shelter when I get a minute.'

Relief warmed through her – she knew this was true. How could she possibly manage everything if she was at the factory all day every day? She didn't have to go – she had a family to look after. But for those moments she had suddenly thought how nice it would be to get out and do something other than the endless domestic round – feel actually *useful*. Nobody ever thought of housework as useful. It was always there, always just *done*, somehow. No one pays you for that, she thought.

'I mean, you're hardly here these days,' she reminded him sharply. 'What with the Home Guard – did you really have to volunteer with the ARP as well?'

Once, there was a time when he wanted to be with her, always, every possible minute. And even as she almost snapped at him, she realized that the last thing she wanted was him here every minute, his moody presence taking up the room. Not the way things were now.

And whose fault is that? the scolding voice said in her head. She felt as if she was going to explode.

'It's only a couple of nights a week,' Len said. 'They're a bit short.'

This was the trouble these days – you couldn't complain about anything. It was *all for the war effort.*

'Your mom's been on about me doing things with the WVS,' she said. 'P'raps I'll do that instead.'

'Yeah. Why don't you do that then?' Len glanced up at her. He was hardly listening. It was as if he had a tune playing in his head.

'There's a bit of tapioca,' she said, getting up, trying to quell the restless anger inside her. 'We'd better get it down us in case the siren goes off again.'

'Mom?' Joy stood in the kitchen doorway as Ann was filling the teapot. Her tone was enough. Ann turned. She felt calmer now after her anger at tea time. Of course she couldn't go back to work – that was a stupid idea. That she didn't mind. She just wished that once in a while her husband would pay attention to a word she said.

'D'you think it's peculiar that I've never met Alan's mom and dad – or been to his house?'

'Not especially.' In her turn, Ann forced herself to listen. 'Don't they live quite a way out?'

'That's what I said. Only Norma said she thought it was odd.'

'It's not as if you're engaged.' But immediately, wreathed in steam as she filled the pot, she thought of Len's mother, how much she had loved going to his house from early on. Sometimes, she thought, apart from the kids, Margaret and Cyril felt like the only glue left holding her and Len together.

'You seen Nanna?' she asked, thinking to cheer Joy up. 'Pop in and see how they're getting on, will you?'

'Yes – in a minute.'

Joy hovered still. In the shadow of the doorway, she looked so pretty: her lovely, trim figure in her navy dress, a belt tied at the waist, her dark hair curling into her neck. But her eyes were troubled.

'What's up?' Ann said, softer now.

'It's just – Alan. I thought I knew him – like the back of my hand. And now I feel as if I hardly know him at all.' She was close to tears. 'How could he just go off like that? I know he's not the forward sort – sometimes I wished he was, a bit more. But he seemed like a gent . . .' Her voice went husky. 'Only now I feel as if he's been hiding from me – and he doesn't really like me at all!'

'Oh, I'm sure he does.'

Since their house was not too far from the Cadbury works, Alan had been round quite a few times. He seemed a nice lad, with his sunny smile – and he was fun for Joy. They got a lot of pleasure out of their dancing.

'He was probably just frightened to tell you – didn't want to hurt your feelings . . .'

Joy leaned her back mutinously against the door frame. 'Well, he flaming well did hurt my feelings anyway! And who am I s'posed to dance with now?'

'Oh, you'll find someone – pretty girl like you! There must be one or two left from all those classes you've been to?'

'Hmm.' Joy frowned. 'Maybe.' Ann could see that she was really bothered. 'Mom?'

'D'you want to come and sit down?' Ann indicated the table. 'We seem to be OK tonight so far.' There had been no air-raid warning yet, no dashing round trying to get a hot drink and their things down to the shelter.

Joy pushed herself off from the door and came to the table. She seemed tired, listless. She took her teacup and stirred in a half-spoon of sugar.

'I don't understand men.' She gave a heavy sigh. 'Tell me about you and Dad. How you met and everything?'

'I've told you – lots of times!' Ann laughed. 'About how I met Dad in the factory and we went to see Nanna and Grandad – not that they were grandparents then. They were always so good to me.'

'Yes, but you weren't marrying *them*, were you?'

'Well, in a way I was . . .' She tried to keep the conversation light as Joy's eyes burned into her – wanting to know, really wanting it, not just in a 'tell me a story about when you were young' way. 'If you marry someone, their family is very important as well.'

'Tell me again. Was he the first man you were ever in love with? I mean, he was *the one* – and you knew straight away, for always?'

'I . . .' Ann flushed. It took her by surprise. It was so easy to skate over the past. The details. The feelings. Children never needed to know any of that. They just thought of you being there, Mom and Dad, forever the same.

She stared back at Joy. She was an honest person – tried to be. The problem with answering was that the answers to Joy's two questions were so impossible that she could not think how to begin. *Yes. No.*

She smiled, as her heart pounded hard with all her own secret truths.

'I'm not sure everyone is so certain from the word

go,' she said. 'We all have to carry on and hope for the best.'

'Huh.' Joy sat back, obviously not happy with this unromantic answer. 'Well, I want something better than that!'

Ten

February 1916

'Nurse?'

Ann Williams looked round to see which of the patients was calling her. The afternoon was a quieter time of day, if they were lucky; once the ward rounds were over, the busy morning routine of bed baths, observations and dressings complete, and dinners finished. There was often a lull then, when it was possible to stop and spend time with someone who wanted company.

'Over here, please!'

The patient calling her was in the bed tucked into a shadowy corner, at right angles to two others which were arranged with their heads abutting the wide window. From the middle of the room, she could only make out his outline as he lay there in the bed, and the white dressing over his left eye. She had seldom seen him awake before and it was not she who had changed his bed and washed him that morning.

Ann squeezed past the neighbouring beds, nodding to one patient whose eyes were open. He tried to move his mouth into a smile, but his face was very sad.

She was getting more used to this now. During her swift training as part of the Bournville Nursing Division, with other girls who had volunteered from the factory, she had wondered if she was really up to this sort of work.

Part of it, she had learned, was just a matter of habit. You simply got used to handling people's bodies – men's bodies – in a way you never would except in the most intimate of family life. And they just expected you to do it. They handed themselves over to you with childlike trust, most of them seeming to welcome a chance just to put themselves in someone else's charge.

She approached the man who had called out to her. There was not much space beside the bed and it felt wrong standing over him so she perched for a moment on the edge of the chair squeezed in by the bed-head.

'Hello?' she said softly. 'Is there something you want?'

Amputation of left arm at the shoulder, she remembered, from the handover report on the ward. And his left eye had had to be removed. She could recall his injuries but to her shame could not think of his name.

'My arm back?' he said huskily. After a moment, very quietly, he began to sob. 'I was left-handed, you see,' he said.

Tears overtook him then – but almost silently. This gentle anguish, this one person among so many, with his soft voice and manner which said, *I don't want to make any fuss, but . . .* tore at her. It pulled off the protective skin which she had to keep growing over the feelings about what she saw and heard and smelt, what she learned, in horrifying snatches, about their experiences. Her chest ached. There was something about this lad which reached right into her, from the start.

Oh goodness, she thought, I mustn't start crying as well.

She reached out for his one remaining hand and laid her own over it. He turned his hand over and held hers, so tightly that she felt a lump rise in her throat.

'I'm sorry,' he said, trying to recover. 'It's only today

75

I've really come to, sort of thing. My arm. My eye.' He was silent, frowning for a moment. 'Actually – where am I again, exactly? Birmingham, someone said?'

He looked at her and they managed to exchange watery smiles.

'Yes, you're in Birmingham,' she said. 'This is Fircroft – an auxiliary hospital. It was a college before. It belongs to Cadbury's.'

'Cadbury's? Ah.' He seemed so glad to talk – a welcome distraction, she thought. 'Good people, I gather.'

'Yes. I was working at Cadbury's before the war – most of us working here were.'

'Were you?' He sounded interested. 'What did you do?'

'I was filling chocolates. We all sat at a big stone table – granite – to keep the chocolate cool . . .'

Even though she had only moved up the road a mile or so to work at Oak Tree Lane, before the war now felt like another life.

'But you decided to do this instead? Treat yourself?'

Surprised, she realized he was teasing.

'Yes.' She smiled. 'Well, I suppose I wanted to do something to help with the war.'

It had been more than that. As soon as she started training – only basic nursing, bed baths and first aid and hygiene – she realized she had wanted something else. To know more about life, do something other than work in the factory year in year out.

She saw him eyeing her uniform, the white veil tied back to cover her hair, her long, starched apron swathing the blue-grey uniform.

'You're lucky you're doing that here and not out there,' he said. 'They see some sights, those girls . . . I don't know how they do it.' He was silent for a moment. 'Did you volunteer?'

Ann nodded. 'They gave us a choice at the factory. The Cadburys are meant to be conchies – and they are, most of them. Well, Mr Lawrence – Cadbury, I mean – started the Friends Ambulance Units so that they could go out and help. Without having to fight and kill anyone, I suppose. But they said everyone in the factory should make up their mind according to their own conscience.'

He nodded gently and seemed interested, so she kept talking.

'Some of the lads joined up. And then Mr Cadbury – Mr George, that is – asked some of us whether we wanted to volunteer.'

He had turned his head a fraction and she felt him watching her, one grey, serious, interested eye.

'What's your name?' he said. 'If I'm allowed to ask.'

'Nurse Williams. Ann. Williams.'

'I'm Tom Somers,' he told her, to her relief as she would have felt embarrassed having to ask. He seemed to need these introductions, as if this was a normal social occasion. She could see it was tiring him out to talk, his voice had become slower, but he did not seem to want to let her go. 'So will you go back to the factory – when it's all over?'

'I . . . I suppose so, yes. They said so. Only – it feels . . .'

'Impossible to imagine?'

Ann nodded. *And I'm engaged*, she could have said, *to a man called Len Gilby. So I'll be getting married, not going back.* But Len was somewhere in France, a place she could barely imagine. He was part of that other life and it felt as if to mention the future they had planned would be to jinx everything. All the same, she saw Mrs Gilby every week.

'It's so quiet with Ron and Len both away,' Margaret

said to her. 'I'll be ever so pleased to see you, Annie – don't stay away.'

She asked Tom where he had been and he said he was in the Second Hampshires, and was at Gallipoli.

'Let's not talk about it,' he said wretchedly. 'There's a lot I can't even remember about it – or about getting from there to here. Probably for the best. Please, tell me about you. Your family. Just anything.'

So, still holding his hand, she chatted away to distract him, saying she lived with her parents and two younger sisters, and a little bit about Cadbury's and Hilda her friend who was still working there.

'Hilda's far too squeamish to be a nurse,' she laughed. 'But they do other things for the war effort. The factory makes up parcels for the front – chocolate and books and postcards of here, Bournville. Familiar things from home – for the ones who joined up.'

'How . . . nice . . .' Tom Somers said. His voice was drowsy now.

'Hilda does that – she helps make up packages, but she says she's not up to bandaging anything else . . .'

Ann realized that Tom Somers's hand had slackened on hers and he was now drifting into sleep.

Oh well, she thought, with a faint smile. I suppose that's what he needs the most. She slipped her hand out of his and stood up, feeling that for once she really had delivered some comfort, or at least soothed him off to sleep.

She lingered for a moment looking down at him, taking in his thin face, one dark, arched eyebrow, his lips slightly parted as if he was now completely relaxed. The left side of his face was mostly covered by the gauze and bandages over his eye. There were some small, healing gashes on the visible part of his face, raw against his pale skin. His slender body lay, defenceless in sleep, under the counterpane.

Something about him moved her. All the men were wounded, of course. Many of them were very young, some of them having to come to terms with terrible internal injuries, with loss of limbs or of sight, like Tom, with disfigurement. Perhaps it was because she had only been here for two months; she was still not inured to it all, hard as she tried to be. Things shocked her. Sometimes, as she tried to fall asleep at night, images of the day would crowd in and she would find herself weeping, letting out the sorrow and tension that built up during a shift in a way she knew she must never do in front of the men. This young lad was just another who had gone off, innocent, into the fire and come home maimed. And yet . . .

For a moment she had a tender impulse to lean down and plant a kiss on his sleeping cheek.

'Nurse Williams?' one of the other nurses called her softly. 'Could you come and give me a hand?'

She shook herself out of these strange feelings and went back to work.

Looking back, she realized that if Tom Somers had been discharged soon after that, she might well have remembered him, or at least the feelings she'd had during that conversation, the tenderness that had crept in more than usual. He would have been gone, to be replaced by countless more boys mourning for the young, whole-bodied creatures they had been before the war.

But Tom was not gone. Not yet.

Two days later, when she came back on duty, he was still lying there. He did not call out to her but his gaze met hers as she walked past and she felt drawn to him.

'How are you today?' she asked, in her nurse's voice. It was a role you had to step into.

'Well . . .' He considered. 'I still only have one eye and

one arm – although the arm is still with me somehow, even if I know it really ended up somewhere in Turkey. It *hurts*. Which is strange, isn't it? They've given me something for the pain. But apart from that . . .' He twinkled at her. 'I suppose mainly I just feel lucky to be alive.'

His tone had changed. He was more alert, brighter. They smiled at each other.

'I'm glad to hear it,' she said. 'Working here makes me feel lucky to be alive as well.'

She was moving away as he said, 'Nurse, when you get a moment will you come and talk to me again? That was the best medicine of all.'

The patients often said that. It was hard to find time to get round to everyone, to share herself out between men who were often far from home – some very far, from Australia and Canada, a few who did not speak English. Tom told her he was from Southampton.

'You could have joined the Navy?' Ann said, perched on his chair again that afternoon, glancing to see if the ward sister was about and trying to look as if she was ready to get up again at any moment.

'Not very keen on water – bit rich really, living by the coast.' Tom grimaced. 'I left my arm somewhere in the sea when we were trying to wade our way on to "V" beach – near Sedd el Bahr.' He swallowed. 'I'm one of the lucky ones that didn't drown.'

He seemed to regret even mentioning this. 'Would you mind helping me sit up, please?'

Ann helped him into a comfortable reclining position, conscious of the intimacy of linking her arm to his remaining one, leaning close, their breath mingling, so that she could have rested her cheek on the top of his head.

'Tell me about your family,' she said. 'You had some letters, didn't you?'

She knew a little about him from his notes, looking at them with what she had tried to persuade herself was only for practical, nursing reasons. Tom Somers, aged twenty-four.

'Well, the best member of my family is my dog, Raggles.'

She looked at him uncertainly and Tom started laughing.

'I'm joking. Raggles is a crazed mongrel bundle of legs and fur and ears who follows me everywhere. I would have taken her to work if I could – I was apprenticed in marine engineering before the war. But the rest of my family aren't bad either!'

Tom was the only boy, with three sisters – no wonder he had had so many letters, Ann thought, with all those doting females!

'They can't wait to get me home to convalesce – in the sea air, ho, ho,' he said.

'You can't really hate the sea? I've never even seen it, living here. But everyone wants to go to the seaside!'

'No, of course I don't hate it exactly,' he said. 'But I respect it. You never mess about with the sea – it can reach out an arm and you're gone in a blink. When I'm finished with all this, I think I might move inland!'

'That won't be very good for marine engineering, will it?' she said, before wishing she could cut her tongue out. How was he ever to do *any* engineering now, with only one arm, and not even his best one?

'I'll cross that bridge when I come to it,' he said, with a wry expression.

They kept the conversation light, joking. As they did whenever she came to sit beside him – which, over the next three weeks, was every possible time she could.

Eleven

The corner of the ward where Tom Somers lay for those weeks became a magnet to her. Ann could not walk into the room without her eyes darting to see if he was still there. She was not certain when he might be discharged so she came back from her days off desperately hoping he would still be there – for her sake, at least. And she could not stop her feet from moving close, from seeking out the searching gaze of his one remaining eye that always seemed to be fixed on her as if willing her to come over to him.

And come close she did, as often as the work routine would allow. They fell in love swiftly, within a few conversations, with brief glances, the touch of a hand. Fell deeply, in a way she had never known before. So that very soon Tom Somers was all she could think of. He filled her mind, her heart. She knew he thought of her constantly because he told her so.

One spring Sunday, while Tom was still on the ward, Ann was off duty and she visited Margaret and Cyril Gilby – her future in-laws. As ever, they were kind and made her welcome, and Trigger's greeting was uproarious. How lucky she was, she thought, sitting at the tea table in Beaumont Road, the dog's tail beating her leg, to be thinking of marrying into such a nice family, to have such a mother-in-law.

As usual Margaret had baked a sponge and Cyril had

brought misshapes from the factory – all Milk Tray chocolate, the new selection introduced last year.

'Go on – you have the orange ones,' Cyril urged. 'I know it's your favourite.'

With a grin he laid four wonky chocolates in front of her.

'That's enough!' she laughed, loving the way he liked to spoil her in a way her own father had never done.

'Have you seen the new box they've brought out? A half-pounder – looks very nice.'

'No, not yet.' Now she was working at the hospital she felt a bit out of it.

'Go on, bab –' Cyril held the plate on to which he had tipped the chocolates out towards Margaret – 'tuck in.'

'No, I'm all right,' Margaret said.

Ann and Cyril exchanged a worried glance. *She's fretting*, Cyril's expression said.

Over these last months, Margaret's kindly face had shrunk thinner, emphasizing her cheekbones. She worried constantly about her boys, both in France. The lists of dead in the newspaper were a torment to everyone, day after day.

'I shan't be able to rest until they're both back here, sleeping in their own beds,' she said, moving a teaspoon restlessly round in the cup in front of her, as if in some way she had to be moving at all times. 'Ron's such a home boy, bless him – I can't imagine how he's managing out there . . .'

She stopped, close to tears. Ann felt a terrible pang. This was not the Margaret she had first got to know. She had not met Ron. He had started his working life as an apprentice carpenter at the Bournville Village Trust, the Cadbury housing project, and later moved to work in the factory. He sounded like a gentle sort of lad.

'He'll be all right, love,' Cyril said. 'It's got to be done. You can't spend your life fretting over them all the time.' But despite Cyril trying to remain cheerful, Ann could see that he was almost as emotional as his wife.

'I had a letter from Tom,' Ann said, wanting to cheer them up.

Margaret Gilby looked blankly at her. 'Tom who?

'I mean Len – your son!' Her mistake pierced through her and her cheeks burned. How *could* she have got that wrong? 'What did I say?' She tried to cover her dismay with a laugh. 'Sorry – all these patients I've been with, I can't keep up with the names! I'm just a bit tired, that's all.'

'You must be,' Cyril said. 'Hard work what you're doing, bab. We're proud of you.'

Which made her feel even worse. But she had had a little letter from Len – not saying a lot, just that he was getting along all right, and she was able to tell them that. She burned with guilt, sitting there. It was as if she was going through the motions of her feelings for Len, playing the faithful fiancée, when all the time . . . She told herself it was a period they would all wake from one day and things would go back to normal. And Margaret and Cyril were their usual kind selves, so pleased to see her. Of course, Len was to be her husband and they would live close by, be a loving, happy family . . .

Walking home, along Linden Road, she tried to take herself in hand. It was not far from here, the park in Bournville where she had promised to marry Len. That now seemed a hundred years ago but was in fact about six months.

'Come on,' Len had said. They had just stepped out of his parents' house into another kind of day altogether, blustery winds sending the falling leaves whirling through the air and skittering across the ground. 'Let's go somewhere nice, like – I want to talk to you.'

'Talk to me?' she teased. 'Do we have to wait to get to the park before we can say anything?'

He had never been the world's greatest talker even in those days, but he was a happy, cheerful soul.

Len grinned and linked his arm, in his brown tweedy jacket, through hers. His cheeks were bacon-pink in the cold, his hair still lying in thick waves under his cap – he had not yet had his soldier's haircut – and he had a brown-and-white scarf Margaret had knitted coiled round his neck. He had a way of walking, when he was with her, bouncing from foot to foot as if he was excited and pleased with everything about himself and his life – and his girl, here on his arm. She knew that she made him happy – pleased as punch, in fact – and that was a gratifying feeling.

He was a straightforward lad, Len was, happy and without any side to him. There were certain things that made him happy: a win by his team at football, his bike – they had been out for some rides together – his food, her. It was as simple as that. He was decent, enthusiastically keen on her, could make her laugh and she him. And she already loved his parents. Everything felt happy, in a calm, mild way. It was nice. What more could she possibly want?

They turned in to the little park in Bournville. It felt as if something momentous was about to happen. She looked down at their feet walking side by side: Len's big black boots, her neat, brown boots buttoned at the sides. A moment later Len, as if he could not hold back any longer, stopped her at the edge of the grass and put his hands on her shoulders.

'Ann . . .' His earnest, somehow innocent eyes searched hers, pleading for her to make the reply he wanted. 'I've got to say it. You know what I'm gunna ask, don't you?'

She looked back at him solemnly from under the green brim of her hat.

'Try me,' she said.

'I'm gunna be gone soon. I don't know for how long. And I know it's gunna be hard. What I want most is knowing you're here – waiting. 'Cause I love you, Annie – I do.'

She smiled sweetly. What a lovely lad he was! And how pleased her mother was going to be – first daughter off her hands to a good, steady lad.

'Will you be promised to me? Say you'll be my wife – when I come home?'

She reached for one of his hands and cradled it in both of hers. This moment, so exciting for a woman, everyone said. And it was exciting, in a quiet sort of way. A proposal of marriage – of course it was! Dear, familiar old Len. He was going away to war and she was to be his sweetheart! What better thing could she ever want?

'Course I will,' she said, her heart fluttering. 'Yes, Len, dear – I will!'

Len let out a cry of joy, yanked his cap off and flung it in the air. She had seen him do the same thing when his beloved Birmingham City Football Club scored a goal. He was unerringly faithful to them, even though they had been relegated to the second division . . . Faithful, that was Len, she knew, through thick and thin. And here he was, so delighted!

'Oh, Ann!' He flung his arms round her and kissed her cheeks again and again. He reminded her of a very enthusiastic dog.

'Stop!' She giggled helplessly. 'You're tickling me!'

'You've just made me the happiest man there ever was!' he'd said. 'Come on – let's go back and tell my mom and dad!'

Guilt gnawed at her as she walked along now, thinking of this – it happened just over there, she thought as she stepped into the park, trying to calm herself. There was a feeling of new life in the air now, the grass beginning to grow again in the weak spring sunshine.

She *did* love Len – course she did. How could she be feeling the way she was? How ungrateful and disloyal could you get? She clenched a handful of the stuff of her skirt – a grey serge – in one hand, looking down at her boots again as she walked, just as she had that day when she had promised to marry Len, standing almost on this very spot. On that distant day when she had no idea that she was capable of feeling the intense, extraordinary way she felt now . . .

She tore her gaze away from the place where they had stood and turned back. She must get home, give Mom a hand with the evening meal. Both her sisters were working now and they were all stretched. She tried to think about practical things – about anything but *him* . . .

But within seconds it was all she could think about, the burning longing which would not leave her, the feeling of being moved, lifted and changed by another person who affected her so strongly, so obsessively. It was the way she felt whenever – which was most of the time – she thought about Tom Somers.

Nothing was said between them, not for a long time. Each occasion when she was on duty they talked. It was all she could think about and she could read in his scarred face – his eye now wore a lighter dressing – how deeply it mattered to him that she came to be with him.

When the ward sister announced that Tom was soon to be discharged, everything changed.

'My father is coming up to fetch me,' he told Ann one afternoon as she sat beside him. 'On Saturday we'll go back on the train together.'

Two days away. Ann actually felt a pain, a kind of buckling of her heart. No. He could not be going! This man who had changed her, opened up a world of feelings she had not known existed, even if the two of them had never put this passionate love into words.

She nodded at him, trying to force her lips into a smile. He was out of it at least. Unfit for duty – so his life would be saved. That was a great blessing.

But then she could not stand it. She looked down, fiddling with the tassels which fringed the bedspread. She had to pull herself in tightly before she could look up again.

'What will you do, do you think?' She knew it was a hopeless question. His training from before the war could not count for anything, surely, now he only had one arm.

Tom shrugged, with a bleak look. 'I don't know. I'm going to have to find something though. I can't just sit around for the rest of my life, can I?'

A silence stretched between them then. Ann felt herself grow more and more tense. Any moment now she would be called away to tend to some other patient and there was an ocean of things they might say, might begin on – but somehow could not. And should not.

She fiddled with the cotton tassels, trying to find something to say – words which were kind and fond but would not give her away. *I shall miss our little talks . . . I do hope you enjoy convalescing for a time . . .* She felt like weeping at the hopelessness of talking when every time she was in the ward she knew his eyes were following her; she was always aware of him there, in his quiet corner, to which so much of her tenderness was directed, that so much flowed between his gaze and hers.

'Ann?' He spoke first, very quietly, because there was precious little privacy.

Their eyes met again. Something in his tone made her tremble.

'I . . .' He stumbled over it, put his remaining hand to his head, rubbing at his hair, as if despairing of how to begin. 'I – look . . . I don't know how to . . . I just *love* you, my dear. So much. That's the only way I can put it. And I don't want to leave here without you knowing.'

Paralysed, she stared at him. Now was the moment, she knew, when she had to thank him, to say *how kind* or one of those things you could say to fob off the boys who got too fond of you which of course they did, every so often. But she just could not. Not with every fibre of her loving him back, longing for him. And now was the moment to say that she was already engaged to a boy called Len Gilby who was in France. Len – her fiancé, from that distant other world before the war . . .

Her mouth went dry. She tried to lick her lips. She had to say it. Say what every atom of her body and the passion of her nature demanded her to say. Boys like him were dying every day. Time was short, life so frail – all of them like moths with only days to live . . .

'I love you too,' she heard herself say. Tears ran down her face, suddenly, though she hardly noticed until Tom reached out and with the back of his hand, tenderly wiped her cheek.

'Why are you crying?'

'I don't know,' she whispered. Then she shook her head. 'No – I do know. I must be truthful with you, Tom. I'm promised – to someone else. He's in the Warwicks.'

The pain registered in the twitch of a nerve in his cheek.

'You never said.'

'I know. I'm sorry.' She pulled out a handkerchief and blew her nose. 'I should have. Only . . . What's happened here . . . I mean – *you*. I never expected . . . I've never felt like this before.'

Tom nodded. 'Nor me.'

They sat quietly.

'Look,' he said, with an effort. 'I'm leaving, very soon. I'll give you my address. And maybe I could have yours? And then . . .' He looked ahead of him sadly for a moment and she could see he could not bear to give up hope, not completely, and it would have been cruel to force him. 'We can just see, can't we?'

She was able to be the one who escorted him down, when he left. She made sure she was, even though she had to put up with teasing from one of the other nurses.

'You're very eager – why would that be now, Nurse Williams?'

Tom was dressed in his blue convalescent uniform, the empty left arm neatly pinned and a black patch worn over his missing eye. Seeing him dressed for the first time, she thought he looked older, taller, wincing as the shoulder of the jacket touched his still-healing wound, his jaw clenching.

They walked slowly down, she carrying his bundle of belongings. He said his father would be bringing a bag to put his things in. When they had left the ward, the swift goodbyes of the other nurses behind them, he took her arm gently. She realized this was not just his fondness for her: he had not done a great deal of walking and was unsteady. But making her way on Tom's arm along the corridor to the stairs, they glanced at each other and she wondered if he was thinking the same as her – that it was how they might have processed along the aisle of a church, to the wedding march. But they did not speak.

She saw him flinch as they came out into the sunlight, screwing up his good eye. There were people coming and going and he pulled her aside for a moment.

'It's a long time since I've been out. Feels very strange,' he said. 'Officially a cripple now, I suppose.' She took a sharp intake of breath. 'Mustn't feel sorry for myself. I've got my legs, after all.'

Time pressed on them.

'Dad'll be here any minute,' Tom said.

'I must go back inside.' They looked at each other, wanting every second to go on and on.

'Ann . . .' Tom stepped towards her and reached out his remaining arm. For a moment she wrapped her arms round his slight form, wanting just to stay there, stay and hold him. They released each other gently.

'I'll be . . . You know where I am. If . . .' He stopped and looked down. A well of tears was rising inside her. This could not be – this man disappearing out of her life . . .

'Goodbye, Tom.'

She reached up to kiss his cheek, then forced herself to walk inside, fists clenched, her throat aching and holding back all her unshed tears as she climbed the stairs up to the ward, to continue her work.

Twelve

27 September 1940

'D'you think we really need to keep doing this?' Joy grumbled.

Arms full of blankets and cushions, the Gilbys felt their way down the darkening garden and into the Anderson shelter, the blood-chilling howl of the air-raid siren turning their legs to water.

'Your country needs you!' Martin growled, tripping over the end of a rug and just managing not to fall flat on his face.

'See – less of the blather and more looking where you're going,' Joy retorted.

'Anyway, aren't you used to it by now?' Martin said.

They had been up and down the garden like this for several weeks.

'No,' Joy grumbled. 'I'll never flaming well get used to this. Have we shut up the chickens?'

'Yes,' Ann said, panting as she caught them up. 'Poor things – this isn't going to help them lay. There's nothing else I can do though.'

She had dashed about the house to pick up bits and pieces – a torch, a scarf, the Ludo board, her knitting. She left all their papers in the shelter now – insurance papers and their wills, all in an old chocolate wafers tin, just in case. Len had put a concrete floor down which was a big improvement on finding a muddy puddle inside. Len was hardly ever in there himself and tonight he was on Home Guard duty at Cadbury's.

'I've got the kettle on,' Ann said. 'I'll go in and make us a cuppa in a while. I can't get through this without. Let's hope it won't last long.'

'It smells bad in here tonight.' Joy wrinkled her nose as they all ducked inside. There was a musty smell of soil and of the damp concrete.

'Well, just thank your stars there are only three of us,' Martin said, dumping his rugs and cushions on the narrow bench. 'Eric's got nine people squeezed in. Even if Nanna and Grandad are in here it's not that bad!'

'Norma's mom makes her put on clean knickers,' Joy giggled.

'Well, that's Hilda all over,' Ann said, putting the torch down and sorting out the stuff she had brought in.

'What – in case they all get killed?' Martin asked cheerfully.

'That's enough,' Ann snapped. 'Come on, move up, Martin – let's all get settled in. I hope Margaret and Cyril are all right . . .'

Now and again her in-laws had come and sheltered with them, but they assured Ann that they were quite all right in their own shelter. As it was only a few doors down, they could run along during a lull and check on them.

They settled on the benches each side with the door ajar for the moment, as it was not too cold yet. If they leaned to look, they could glimpse the jittering search-lights across the sky. Martin was reading a book by the light of the torch. Ann fished out her knitting – a fawn, sleeveless jumper half made for Martin. Joy sat tapping her feet, as if she was listening to music in her head. And the siren stopped.

'Oh Lor', what does that mean?' Joy said, breathless. 'It's almost worse when it stops – ooh, I'm all goose pimples.'

They waited, in the sudden ominous quiet. Though her ears were pricked, Ann laid her knitting in her lap and forced her mind on to other things than the terrifying threat outside. Having this rare moment to sit still, she looked across at Joy and took in her daughter's dark hair and lustrous eyes. Joy was turning into a real beauty. With a pang she thought of herself at the same age, eighteen, so innocent and under her mother's thumb: so many things in front of her . . .

The ack-ack guns started pounding. Martin looked up from *The Grapes of Wrath*, more frightened than he wanted them to know. Distantly came the drone of engines, then the thumping, crumping sounds of explosions; a lull, then more of them – and soon as they all sat, too tense now to do anything but listen, the bells of ambulances and fire engines.

'Roy'll be out there somewhere,' Ann breathed. 'And your dad, of course – but Roy could be right in the middle of town . . . God, I hope Hilda's all right – shame she can't come in here with us.'

Roy, Hilda's husband, a big, amiable redhead, was an engineer at Cadbury's but also in their fire brigade. This meant that they had one of the firemen's houses in Sycamore Road, with a bell to summon them if there was any fire at the factory, day or night.

'It's enough to wake the flipping dead, that bell!' Hilda said, years ago when it had gone off the first time. 'Nearly frightened the life out of me. Nice house though – can't complain.'

But now Roy was out with the Auxiliary Fire Service, under the bombs.

'I've got to go and make that tea in a minute, Hitler or no blasted Hitler,' Ann announced.

'Mom, no!' Joy said. 'It's not safe!'

'Well, I can't just let the kettle boil dry,' Ann said, getting up. 'Look – it's gone quiet. I'm going to make a dash for it.'

'I'll go if you want,' Martin said. 'Although . . .' He grinned. 'This is a very good book . . .'

'I'll make the tea,' Ann said firmly.

'Ha – don't trust mine?'

'To be perfectly honest – no, Martin, I don't. You'll probably put cloves or flour or something in the teapot . . .'

Ann peeped out of the shelter. There was a lull in the gunfire, though the searchlights were still etching their restless patterns against the black lid of the sky. She could smell the night, soil and grass and the hint of the last autumn roses after a warm day. As she dashed along the garden, she thought, Thank heavens it's been dry – imagine all this in the pouring rain. And then, I wonder where Len is . . .

Standing in the blacked-out kitchen which was now full of steam, she spooned tea, poured water, then stood a moment, stirring, staring. Where is *he*, now? Tom Somers's face, his intent, loving eyes, filled her mind for a second as if he was standing right beside her. Would there ever, ever, be a moment when she saw him again, in this life? For a second her body sagged, as if infected with grief.

Stop it, she raged at herself. *It's no good – just stop it.*

She put the cosy on the pot and hastily grabbed some cups to make up a tray.

✻

Joy sat thinking about Alan. Next month he would be home on leave after basic training and she was getting more and more nervous about it. It's now or never, she thought, full of bullish determination. He's got to say whether or not he feels anything for me or whether I'm just wasting my time. She knew they made a good-looking pair on the dance floor – she with her flashing dark eyes and lively looks and Alan with his limber body and sunny, handsome face. People would turn to look at them – they were excellent dance partners.

Alan was always fun. He kept things light, held her carefully within the positions of the dances, smiled, made jokes. He had definitely become a heart-throb for her. But after the things that had happened – that night in town, the way he had pushed her with real force, and then him just taking off into the Army, she realized Alan was a closed book to her. It hurt – both her pride and her deeper feelings. Getting to know him was like trying to hold water in your hands. Maybe she had been kidding herself all this time that she and Alan were made for each other.

'I can't stand just sitting here like this,' she said, fed up with her thoughts going round and round. 'Come on – d'you want to sing some songs with me or something?'

'Not particularly,' Martin said, nose in his book.

'You'll go blind, reading like that.' She started tickling him until he was laughing and fighting her off, lying back along the bench.

'OK – I surrender!' He sat up. 'Hey – know what? Once I'm fourteen—'

'Two days to go!'

'I'm going to volunteer to be a messenger – Scouts are doing all that sort of thing.'

'I thought your job was paper collecting?'

'It was, but now I can do volunteering for the ARP – deliver messages.'

'Where to?'

'*I* dunno!' Martin shrugged. 'Where they tell us. I can go on my bike.'

'What, when there are raids?' Joy said. 'Mom'll never let you do that, Mommy's boy!' She started tickling him again so that he lay back laughing helplessly. 'Mom's favourite!'

'I know,' Martin gurgled. '*Of course* I'm the favourite child – the boy and prince of the family!'

'Oh, shut up!' She thumped him. 'You are though – Mom's little prince!'

Ann appeared, struggling through the door with the tray, just as the guns started banging away again.

'You do love me best, don't you, Mumsie?' Martin teased.

'Depends what day of the week you ask me on,' Ann said. 'Keep still! You'll kick the pot over and if you do I swear I'll . . .' She sat down wearily. 'God, even making a cuppa tea's an ordeal in all this. Pour it, will you, Joy?'

Joy handed round cups.

'That's too much sugar, Mart!'

'Sorry. Forgot.'

'Martin wants to work for the ARP,' Joy said, as they sat with their hands cupped round the warm tea mugs. 'After his birthday.'

'Really?' Ann was not taking this in fully. 'I ought to get round to doing something, I really ought . . .'

'Well, Dad's always out,' Joy remarked. 'He might just as well have joined the army for all he comes home.'

She was shocked, after a moment, when, in the dim lamplight, she thought she saw the glitter of tears in her mother's eyes. Oh dear, she'd said the wrong thing again.

'You all right, Mom?'

'Yes.' Ann tugged the backs of her wrists across her eyes and forced a smile. 'Course I am.' After a moment she said, 'I'll do something about the WVS this week.'

The All Clear went some time in the small hours. At last they could all stumble back to the house, stiff and cold, for a few hours' sleep in their own beds.

Ann crawled in between the cold sheets, dead tired, but it was a long time before she could sleep. She felt churned up, a tolling bell of sadness inside her. Memories kept coming to her of Len as he had been when they first got to know each other – the cheerful, puppyish, loving boy who had disappeared into the war and come back quieter, still loving, but more serious and remote. But he did come back – not like his brother. And now, the way he was these days, her husband of all these years seemed to be moving further and further away, shrinking smaller, until he was like a tiny dot on the horizon. She felt like calling to him, *Come back! I'm sorry . . . I'm sorry. Don't go!*

Ann had barely managed to fall into a doze when Len came home. She heard the click of the bedroom door opening. It was hard to know what time it was with all the blackout on the windows. She felt as though she had barely slept and was still full of doom-like feelings. Suddenly, she wanted urgently, *this moment*, to make things better, as if there was some key word she could utter, some spell, to bring them close again.

Len sat down on the side of the bed with a low grunt. Ann sat up and switched the light on next to her bed.

'Hello, love,' she said quietly. 'How was it?'

Len finished a yawn. 'All right. No damage at the factory.'

She was ready – ridiculously ready – to talk, to heal things. A smile was waiting on her face. But Len twisted round without even looking at her, threw back the covers and fell into an exhausted sleep.

Thirteen

'Two letters for you.'

Sheila sprang to her feet almost knocking the cup of tea across the breakfast table in her eagerness as Audrey handed them to her, smiling. A letter from Kenneth – her heart rate picked up – and the other from Mom by the look of it. Tears filled her eyes. She hadn't realized until that moment how much she longed to see them.

She wiped her eyes carefully so that Audrey did not see her tears – not wanting to seem ungrateful – and read her mother's brief letter in her careful, childish handwriting. Everyone was all right, including Nanna and Grandad. Mom was still trying to make up her mind whether or not to volunteer with the WVS. Dad and Joy were both busy at Cadbury's . . . And Martin had taken it into his head to help the ARP as a messenger as soon as he turned fourteen and she really didn't want him doing it but the Scouts were encouraging it.

We had a nice little tea for Martin's birthday at Nanna and Grandad's. I think Nanna must have dug into all her emergency supplies for the cake! We all missed you of course, and Elaine. She must be growing by the day. Apart from that not much news. We've been up and down to the shelter, of course and there have been quite a few raids on and off – not much damage round here though. I did hear they bombed Fort Dunlop and quite a few other places have been hit . . . But we're all all right and you're not to worry, Sheila . . .

'How are things?' Audrey asked carefully as she carried a plate of toast to the breakfast table. 'I hope your family are going along all right?'

'Yes. Thanks.' Sheila glanced up at her. Was Mom really telling her everything? she wondered. Mom had always tried to protect her from things. 'I think so,' she added distractedly. 'They're getting a lot of air raids up there.'

'Bournville, isn't it?' She was always polite, but Sheila got the feeling that Audrey, who had grown up in villages and towns in the south, thought of Birmingham almost as some foreign land, like Ireland. 'You never hear much about it in the news.'

'It's been going on since – early in August,' Sheila said, her eyes still on the letter.

'August? Goodness, I had no idea.'

'They're not bombing Bournville – not yet anyway – but there's an awful mess in some parts of Birmingham.' Again she felt like crying and had to swallow hard. 'Before I left they hit the Market Hall – it was one of those places everyone goes to shop. Mom took us there as kids and we loved it – full of fruit and veg and all the smells and everyone bustling about. We bought pet rabbits there once . . . But they say it's just a wreck now, all burned out,' she finished bleakly.

'How absolutely awful.' Audrey's face was filled with genuine sympathy.

Sheila had been going to save Kenneth's letter to read upstairs, but since Audrey was busy clearing the boys' breakfast things and Elaine was happy in her high-chair, she could not resist tearing it open.

'*Dearest Sheila,*' she read. '*Only time for a quick note*

101

to say I hope you and Lainy are all right and settled down south and so that you don't worry. We've been out on a rescue for two days and I'm not long back – need to get my head down for a bit but first to send you all my love . . .'

A smile spread across her face.

'Your husband?' Audrey asked.

'Yes – just a note. Says he's been out at sea for two days . . .' Her face clouded. 'He's all right at the moment, but it's ever so dangerous and difficult.'

'I'm sure. But he's written to you when he must be so tired out – what a very nice husband!' At that moment Sheila hardly noticed the wistful edge to Audrey's voice, but she would remember that moment later.

'Yes,' Sheila smiled. 'He is – he's a good 'un.'

It was a Tuesday, which meant that Maurice Vellacott was in London. Audrey had been up early and dressed, her hair done and make-up on, to wait with the boys for the pony and trap that was now taking them to school.

'Petrol rationing,' she told Sheila. 'It's rather nice for them – it's only a couple of miles away. In fact, I believe some of the children are being paddled along the river to get there!'

Sheila liked Audrey. Though they came from different backgrounds, they both wanted to get along together and had quickly grown comfortable with each other. Audrey was a kind-hearted person, forever eager to please.

And during the weekdays, when it was just the two of them, both she and the boys were so much more relaxed – though Sheila had to admit she found it hard to take to Edward, with his pale, angry-looking face. Even knowing that it must be difficult for them suddenly to have strangers invading their house, she still could not forgive his viciousness towards Elaine when they first arrived. At least there had been no repeat of that. Charlie, on the other hand, was timid but sweet with Elaine and would sit playing with her.

This was now their second week together. The best part by far, Sheila had quickly realized, was all the time that Maurice Vellacott was not at home. When he was here, Sheila felt all she wanted to do was keep out of the way. Audrey suddenly became more formal, always dressed in a smart frock or twinset, the ends of her hair tightly curled, lipstick at all times. And she was constantly nervy and anxious to please.

When it was just the two of them, Audrey softened into someone different. In the evening, once they had eaten and the children were all in bed, she sometimes came down in her slippers and cream, silky dressing gown, curl-pins in her hair, and they would drink cocoa by the fire and chat.

The thing Sheila soon noticed about Audrey was that she was genuinely interested in other people. She told Sheila a little bit about herself – her people were in Sussex and she had a married sister who lived near Cheltenham. Evidently she did not see any of them very often – even less now the war was on. But Audrey seemed far more interested in hearing about Sheila – her family and their work and, most of all, Kenneth.

'So how did you meet?' she had asked a couple of evenings ago, curled up on a chair next to the fire, her feet tucked under her, hands nursing her cup of cocoa. She had only put a few pins in her hair and she looked warm and relaxed. 'Tell me a romantic story – do!'

'Well,' Sheila smiled, suddenly feeling shy. She was still in her skirt and jumper. It didn't feel quite right yet, wandering about in someone else's house in her nightclothes. 'It was a little bit. We met at the Cadbury Lido – Kenneth never worked at Cadbury's but his best friend does . . . Well, did. He's joined up as well.'

'Lido?' Audrey said.

'Oh yes – at the swimming pool. If you work at Cadbury's there's a lot laid on for you. The Cadbury family are very good to their workers and there are all sorts of clubs and entertainment and sport. We all learned to swim there and as well as the indoor swimming pool there's a sports area called Rowheath – it's got a pavilion with rooms inside, even a ballroom! And there's a big outdoor swimming pool. It's *packed* in the summer, and it's lovely – everyone goes.'

'People from the factory?'

'Mostly – and family, friends. You can swim and there's all sorts going on – galas and dances and socials. There's a club at Cadbury's for everything you can think of – acting and stamp-collecting and painting . . . Anyway, Kenneth's pal, Eric, was sweet on a friend of mine and that's how we met – actually in the water! Kenneth came along to all sorts of things after – well, 'til we got married and I had to leave. He works at one of the cycle maker's, but he was called up . . .'

Audrey was staring at her. 'I do rather wish I had gone out to work,' she said wistfully.

'Have you never?' Sheila was amazed.

'Daddy didn't like women working. We were just bred up for marriage.' There was a bitter edge to her voice. 'And of course, I met Maurice and married before I was twenty. It seemed the only thing to do.' She rolled her eyes, then sat up straighter and drained her cocoa cup.

'All of us went to Cadbury's at fourteen when we left school,' Sheila said. 'My grandparents, Mom and Dad, my sister, Joy. Martin – our brother – he's the only one who most likely won't. He's the one with the brains – wants to stay on at school and be an engineer or an architect or something.' As she spoke she felt a surge of pride in Martin. At times when they were growing up her little brother had seemed alien – not only a boy but so bookish and obsessed with all sorts of things that meant nothing to her and Joy. But now she said, 'He's a good kid. He'll go far.'

Audrey was watching her, as if trying to work something out.

'My sister, Evelyn, was quite sure she wanted to be an actress. Daddy soon scotched that. Shocking idea! Poor Evelyn – she was so furious and disappointed. I mean, I was never sure about being anything, so I had less to be disappointed about . . . Bit of a mouse, I always was.'

'Yes, me too,' Sheila said.

'Really?' Audrey said. 'I wouldn't have guessed that. Anyway, I don't think Evelyn's ever forgiven him for shuffling her off into marriage with Clive. He's pretty stuffy. That's what I liked about Maurice. He seemed . . .' She hesitated. Sheila did not like to interrupt. 'Fearfully clever, of course – but lively as well.'

She leaned down and put her cup on the floor. Sitting up, she said brightly, 'I must show you more of the village. It's very pleasant here.' She smiled. 'I'm glad you came. I was nervous – how was I to know whether we would get on? But it's very nice to have your company, Sheila, instead of sitting here on my own night after night.'

Sheila was touched by the way Audrey almost made her feel that she was the one doing her a favour instead of the other way round.

'Thanks. It's ever so kind of you. And I'm glad I'm not up and down the garden to the blasted shelter of a night, I can tell you!'

*

Audrey did show Sheila around the village, sometimes just with Elaine in the boys' old pram, and sometimes with the boys when they were home. It was a very pretty place with a lot of old houses, a beautiful, peaceful grave-yard around the church and two bridges spanning the two branches of the river that flowed through the village.

Audrey was a friendly, chatty person and stopped to talk to all sorts of people, introducing some of them. Audrey always tried to be positive about everyone. A number were frostily polite, quite snobbish, Sheila thought, looking down their noses at her as if wondering what on earth Audrey was doing offering a home to some riff-raff from the industrial north. That type always spoke just to Audrey, as if they thought Sheila might not know how to speak English. One elderly gentleman told her he had been posted in India as if this and Birmingham were somehow equiva-lent. Others were warm and welcoming and said they must both come round for a cup of tea. A couple of them even meant it.

And Sheila drifted off for walks by herself sometimes, to get Elaine to sleep – all the more when Maurice Vella-cott was at home. The second weekend with him there had not been a comfortable experience, despite all Audrey's bright efforts to keep everyone happy.

Maurice Vellacott arrived back on the London train on the Friday evening and Audrey, who could drive but was terrified every time she took to the road, put the boys in the car – 'they like to see him before they go to bed' – and went down to the station to pick him up. Sheila, who was upstairs still settling Elaine, heard them come in.

'Now, darling – dinner's ready. Boys – up you go. I'll come up in a moment!'

Sheila stood over Elaine's cot, stroking the soft down of hair to help her settle. She tensed as the boys came thundering up the stairs and along to their bedroom in case they woke her again. But Elaine seemed worn out, her breathing soft and even.

'Audrey?' Maurice's voice rose tetchily from downstairs. 'What have you done with the post? I *told you* to leave it on my desk!'

'It *is* on your desk, darling . . .' The rest of the sentence, spoken in terms of someone pacifying a convalescent, must have been muffled by Audrey going into his study, as it was called.

Sheila felt nervous now the 'master of the house' was back. It made her want to keep out of the way as much as possible. It all seemed so strange, this way of living. She thought of her dad coming in night after night from the factory, always there with his kids. This was another way of living altogether.

She heard Maurice Vellacott come wearily upstairs and a little later, once all the children were settled in bed, the three of them ate an awkward dinner of lamb chops and vegetables. Sheila could not work out what it was exactly that made her feel so uncomfortable with Audrey's husband.

At home, Mom and Dad had seemed distant with each other lately. Having gone back to live with them after her failed attempt to live with Kenneth in Grimsby, she had seen it more plainly. Dad just seemed . . . well, just not there – even when he was. There was no fighting between them, just a sort of . . . freeze, was the word that came to mind.

No one shouted. They did what they had to do every day. But they seemed like strangers to each other. It scared her. Was this what happened? Years of habit just wearing you down so you had nothing left to say to each other?

How she and Kenneth would be, somewhere along the line? Surely not? The thought made her miserable.

But here, with Maurice Vellacott, it was something different. Audrey had dressed for that Friday evening in a soft apple-green frock with a cream cardigan and her best make-up. She was not a dazzlingly pretty woman but she could look very nice, Sheila thought. And Maurice was halfway to being very handsome though Sheila found his long face, the beaky nose and pink cheeks off-putting – his grumpy frown even more so.

He responded wearily to Audrey's questions – 'So have you had a *terrible* week, darling?' – as if speaking was all too much trouble. No, it wasn't all that terrible, but *of course*, the air raids had been bad, and utterly exhausting. And yes, he was tired.

Sheila felt sad on Audrey's behalf. It wasn't as if he had had to talk to her all week – could he not make a little bit more effort? But then, Sheila thought, her own father wasn't much better when Mom tried to keep the conversation going.

'I do wish you'd stay here,' Audrey persevered as they waded through the meal. 'Sheila says –' she glanced over at her half-apologetically, trying to bring her into the conversation – 'that Birmingham is having some very bad raids as well.'

'Oh, not as bad as London,' Maurice said.

How the hell does he think *he* knows? Sheila thought. But she looked down at her potatoes and beans and kept quiet. She mustn't say anything or be rude. These people had been kind enough to take her in, after all – but what an arrogant sod he was! She was quite taken aback by the way her mousey little self seemed to be toughening up!

There was a silence, then Maurice Vellacott suddenly sat back, wiped his lips on his napkin and smiled.

'So how have you ladies been getting along all week?'

The change was so sudden Sheila felt almost dizzy. Like a charm switch being pressed. And he *was* charming, and suddenly, with that smile, he became handsome and she could see how Audrey had come to fall for such a person.

'We've been getting along famously!' Audrey said. 'Haven't we, Sheila?'

'Good. Good. And the boys? Behaving themselves?'

And so it went on. He hardly spoke to Sheila at all but then she did not expect him to. There was nothing he did that was truly terrible, other than being tired and short-tempered, but she found his presence off-putting, oppressive even.

As the weekend passed, Maurice Vellacott spent snatches of time when he was not away on the nearby golf course with his friends (that was most of Saturday) or in his study, and now and then, playing with his sons out on the lawn. Some sort of cricket game. Sheila kept Elaine away from them because the ball was flying far and wide. She played with her inside, but she could hear the voices through the open window.

'Come on, Eddie – no, not like that! Oh, for heaven's *sake*, can't you throw in a straight line? Charlie, *don't* stand there, you're right in the way . . . For goodness' sake, boy, show some initiative!'

Poor lads, Sheila thought, hearing the hectoring voice. He hardly gives them a chance.

Sheila had taken to Charlie, a frail-looking, sweet-faced little boy. Now and then she had heard him erupt into streams of giggles if Audrey tickled him, romping about with him on his bed or out on the lawn. But he was a timid child. Edward, on the other hand, had a hostile air about him almost all the time. He reminded Sheila of a self-important businessman who had far better things to do than listen to anything a woman said. But with a father like that it was not really surprising.

'I thought we might go to the river – for a picnic,' Audrey suggested on the Sunday. 'Maurice likes to do a bit of fishing. Do say you'll come with us?'

'I think,' Sheila said, 'it would be nice for you all just to be family. I'll be happy here, honestly – Elaine'll need her nap and I can write to Kenneth.'

'Of course,' Audrey agreed. Sheila could see she was relieved. 'You can have a nice bit of peace and quiet.'

As they were preparing to go, with a picnic basket, Sheila heard Maurice Vellacott's voice, hushed, but still reaching her up the stairs.

'Is it a good idea, leaving her here on her own?' Audrey must have given him some sort of challenging look, because he added heatedly, 'No, there's no call to flash your eyes at me like that. We've invited this stranger into our home who we barely know – and frankly, she's hardly our sort of person. You don't know what she might get up to while we're out.'

'Like what?' Audrey's light, appeasing laughter floated upstairs. 'You may not know her, but I do, Maurice. She's a very *nice* person. Now do stop being so ridiculous, darling – you spend far too much of your time with criminals!'

Sheila's heart was pounding – both with anger, but also in humiliation at someone talking – *thinking* – about her in that way. As if she and her family were all somehow dirty and inferior, when he hardly knew the first thing about any of them!

Furious, she sat in her room listening as the Vellacotts piled into the car with picnic and fishing rods, the engine started up and the sound faded down the steep drive.

Elaine was asleep and Sheila drew in a huge sigh of relief and took out her Basildon Bond to write letters at the little table.

But she found herself just staring out at the garden, wondering why the man made her feel so uneasy. It was impossible to relax when they were in the same room. It was as if there was something coiled up in him, in his gunfire speech and his impatient ways, waiting, like a cobra, to jump up and sting you.

Fourteen

October 1940

'Oh, go on, Norma,' Joy pleaded. 'There's a dance at the Y tonight and I've got no one else to go with! You know you like a good hop!'

Norma, ever steady and sensible, looked doubtfully at her.

'You could bring Danny, if he doesn't like you going out on your own?' Joy had not been dancing for several weeks and she was longing to be back in the swing of things, just for a night at least – raids or no raids.

'Danny?' Norma giggled. 'Oh, he doesn't mind. And he's got two left feet, bless him. But I thought you said Alan was going to get leave some time soon?'

'I dunno.' Joy shrugged, looking down to hide the tears welling in her eyes. 'I haven't heard from him in nearly two weeks. He's *hopeless*,' she added, her hurt and anger bursting out.

'All right, I'll come with you then, I s'pose. Our mom's not going to like it though – or yours. What if there's a raid?'

'There won't be!' Joy said, with no other justification than hoping and praying. 'Thanks, Norm – you're a pal!'

She spent the rest of the shift at Cadbury's packing chocolate boxes even faster than usual in her excitement. Looking across the huge room full of stacked purple boxes and her lines of fellow workers packing them into cartons, all she could see was her dance dress with the full, shimmery, silver-grey skirt and her dance shoes. The thought of going out was the most exciting thing that had happened in ages and she couldn't wait to climb into her dress and go sailing round the floor. She had learned every style of dance she could – ballet, a bit of tap and even jazz – but her favourite and, she thought, the most romantic by far, was ballroom.

As she worked away, her mind was full of the sound of music, her feet wanting to take off straight away into a waltz or foxtrot. She was quite startled later, as she looked up, to realize that other music was going on around her as her end of the room had broken into a sing-song. She had been so much in a world of her own she had not heard 'When You Wish Upon a Star' going on all around her! But as soon as she did, she joined in, her voice sailing up into the final moving words that always brought tears to her eyes.

'See you later!' she called to Norma when the bull had echoed across the factory announcing the end of the shift and they had grabbed their coats and hurried outside. 'I'll meet you at the tram stop!'

'You're in a great hurry,' Mom remarked, as Joy got her tea down her as fast as she could, hardly tasting the stew. Watery as it was, that might have been just as well.

'Me and Norma're going for a dance . . .' She didn't really want to go into it, have Mom trying to stop her. Dad hardly said a word, as always these days, and to her surprise, her mother's only reaction was to look a bit put out, but she didn't say anything. Mom and Dad both seemed to have their heads in the clouds all the time! She knew Mom was worrying about Martin – he had just had

113

his fourteenth birthday and was on about doing messenger work for the ARP. Mom was frightened to death about it. Joy wasn't sure whether to be pleased or offended that she had got away with saying she was going dancing so easily!

'How'll you get back?' her father asked her. So he had been listening! 'There's hardly any buses or trams after it gets dark.'

'You can take my bike if you want,' Martin offered.

'Very funny – in my dress!' Joy had to admit she had not really thought this through. 'We'll manage. There are trams – unless there's a raid. We'll just have a long wait. We'll *walk* if we have to – but I've *got* to go!'

'Well, take a coat,' Mom said, finally taking notice of her. 'If you're going to be standing around. It's cold at nights now. And if there's any trouble get yourselves to one of the shelters.'

Joy left the house half an hour later with a coat flung over her dress, dance shoes in her bag and bubbling with anticipation. A bit of life at last amid all the rationing and dark, boring nights! But if only Alan was here to dance with. Hurt pierced her excitement for a moment, as it did every time she thought of him. But she pushed the feeling away. At least they were going dancing – that was really something!

She hurried all the way up to the Bristol Road and when she made out Norma waiting at the stop in the gloom, she waved and started to run.

The YWCA at 64 Wheeleys Road had also once belonged to a Quaker family, the Sturges, living close to their neighbour just along the street, Richard Cadbury, one of the original founders of the Cadbury chocolate business. The families had a tradition of donating their homes to public use when they moved elsewhere and the Sturge home had been given over as a women's hostel.

By the time Joy and Norma arrived, they could hear waltz music, faintly, from behind the blacked-out windows of the mansion.

'Ooh!' Joy said. 'Come on – let's get in there, quick!'

They were admitted swiftly into the darkened hall so that no light should spill out on to the street. Excitement bubbled inside Joy. All these things she loved – the thrill of dance music coming from the main room, the air in the hall warm and stuffy and tinged with the smells of sweat and cheap perfume, face powder and lipstick. They paid their entrance fee and went along to the ladies' cloakroom to peel off their coats and change their shoes.

'What if there's no one to dance with?' Norma said.

'Don't be daft – course there will be,' Joy said, hurriedly slipping her shoes on. 'We'll just have to dance with each other if not. I've not come here to be a wallflower!'

They stood side by side for a moment in front of the mirror. Norma looked magnificent in a night-blue dress with a swirling skirt, her wavy auburn hair now freed from the cap they wore at work and pinned back stylishly from her face. Joy stood beside her, her dark hair curling at her neck, with big, shining eyes, her curvaceous figure sheathed in shimmery silver-grey. They grinned at each other.

'Not bad, eh?' Norma said.

'Thanks for coming – you're a pal.' Joy squeezed her arm. 'I can't wait for this!'

They had missed the very beginning of the dance, girls and lads standing in huddles – bold or bashful – each side of the room, waiting for the music to start up. As soon as it did, they would surge forward and pick partners, everyone praying not to be the wallflower left behind.

The music was being played on a gramophone, its volume turned right up, at one end of the room. There were more girls than boys at the dance and so there were always a few who either danced together or stood aside waiting and hoping to be picked next time around. The lads were a mixture of those in civvies and others in uniform. Joy looked wistfully at the uniforms. Was Alan going to other dances near where he was training? The thought gave her a nasty, insecure, jealous feeling.

Trying to forget these thoughts, she waited with Norma at the side. Norma was not such an expert dancer as she was but she liked a good night out. They stood tapping their feet, watching as a waltz finished. Everyone clapped and made a little bow to their partners and the girls looked about, trying to catch the eye of someone who might want to dance. It did not take long.

A lad in civvies came up shyly to Joy and they launched into the cha-cha-cha. He was thin, with slick, black hair and a long, pale face.

'You're a good dancer!' he said as they twirled back and forth, with more flair and adventurousness than most of the other dancers.

'So are you!' She was surprised at how skilled he was.

She saw Norma as they went flying past, who gave her a small grimace as her partner towed her about and felt lucky in the lad who had picked her to dance.

The room was heating up, the smells of sweat and perfume, smoke and Brylcreem all mingling. Her partner's hands were clammy and she felt the familiar prickling of heat under her arms. At last, she thought! Life again! A smile of pure pleasure spread over her face and seeing it, the lad, who was not much older than her, smiled back.

As the dance came to an end they bowed, laughing.

'What's your name?' he asked, leaning towards her.

'Joy.'

She was about to ask his name when over his shoulder, she saw something which made her freeze to the spot, his question wiped from her mind.

'Joy?' was the next thing she heard him say. 'Are you all right?'

'Yes . . . Yes, thanks.' She was far too horrified and upset to worry that she was being rude. 'I've got to go – thanks. Bye.'

Leaving him standing bewildered, she slid away and round the side of the room until she found Norma, who was having a laugh with the lad she had been dancing with.

'Norm, we've got to go home – now!' She took her arm and started dragging her.

'Joy, what are you doing? We only just got here – gerroff!' Norma snatched her arm away, only for Joy to grab it again and start dragging her. 'That lad was nice and he'll think I'm really rude – I never even said goodbye!'

A foxtrot was starting up and everyone was pairing off again as Joy hauled Norma out of the crowded room, weaving around everyone. Norma finally ground to a halt like a donkey, outside the ladies.

'Just stop, Joy! What's got into you? I don't *want* to go home – I'm enjoying myself!'

'I'll tell you – soon as we get out of here,' Joy said. 'Just get your coat. Please, Norm. Just take my word for it, all right?'

They stepped out into the city's darkness, the only lights being a tiny shred of the waning moon and the dance of searchlights across the sky.

'O–oh,' Norma said, looking up. 'I hope that doesn't

mean . . .' But she was drowned out as the air-raid siren raised its unearthly howl over the city. 'Oh my Lord, I knew it! That didn't half make me jump! Should we go back inside?'

'No!' Joy yelled, grabbing her arm. 'Come on!'

Clinging together, they started groping their way back through the blanket of darkness, made more difficult by the searchlights, to the Bristol Road.

'We ought to find a shelter!' Joy yelled. 'We'll never get home!'

'No, look!' Just along the road, like a miracle they made out the solid, trundling shape of a tram moving towards them in the distance, its front lights shielded.

'Quick!' It was Norma's turn to grab Joy's arm this time, so tight that she yelped. 'It's going our way – he'll want to get out of town. Run – quick!'

The road was quiet and they belted across, breaking into giggles at the frantic nature of the whole business and made it to the stop just as the tram slid to a halt.

'Thank God for that!' Norma panted as they sank into a seat. The tram lumbered off again. 'Let's hope to God we get out of here before anything comes down.' Norma turned to her then, remembering she was cross. 'What the hell was that all about?'

Joy swallowed, the excitement of the moment fading and the desolate memory coming back to her so that she knew, as soon as she opened her mouth, she would be unable to hold back the tears.

As the waltz finished and she and the lad were thanking each other, she had seen, just behind him, a young man in army uniform, his hair cropped like all the rest of them. He was laughing with a girl with long fair hair, his arm round her shoulder as they shared a joke. It seemed obvious that they were two people who knew each other very well and fondly. It had taken her a moment, seeing the unfamiliar shape of the hair, then the cheek, the shape of the nose, that smile, to realize that the young man was Alan Bishop. 'Her' Alan.

Fifteen

Across town, in Bournville, Ann and Martin were in the shelter, one each side, facing each other.

'Well, Ma – this is how you like it, isn't it?' Ann saw the teasing gleam in Martin's eyes in the light of the oil lamp. 'Alone with your favourite child? Not for much longer – I'm going to be out risking my life in the streets!'

'Don't say that,' Ann fretted, too worried to joke about it, even though Martin was trying to keep her spirits up. 'I do wish you wouldn't do it. And God knows where Joy is now – or your father.'

The siren had gone off before eight and they had grabbed all the necessaries – blankets, flask of tea, biscuits, pack of cards – and run down the garden in the night chill. They had been sitting there for the best part of an hour with no sign of any German planes coming over.

The two of them had chatted, Martin about his hopes for the future – to train as an architect. Or at least that was this week's plan. At one point she had sent him dashing down the road to check if his grandparents were in good spirits – which they were.

'Nanna's still knitting me that enormous jersey,' Martin said. 'It'll be down to my knees, I think.'

'Never mind,' Ann laughed. 'You'll need it if we're going to be sat here half the winter!'

Guiltily she thought, it was true – she did enjoy just being with Martin on his own from time to time. Much as she loved her daughters, it had to be said there was always *something* with them. When Martin was around it was easy, she felt in tune with him. He was calm, funny – good company.

'It's so damp in here,' she complained after a while. 'I can feel it getting in my bones. Oh, hark at that!' The All Clear howled into action. 'Right, they're not after us tonight then! Thank heaven for that – we can go and sleep in our own beds. Let's just undo the door so they can get into the run in the morning.' She stooped over by the hen coop. 'There you are, ladies – should be a peaceful night now.' Straightening up, she added, 'Poor things.'

As she and Martin came into the house from the back, Ann heard the front door open and close. She hurried through to find Joy in the hall.

'Oh, thank goodness – am I glad to see you back!' Still wrapped in a blanket over her coat, she pulled Joy into her arms. After a moment she took in the expression on Joy's face. 'Everything all right, love – did the siren break up the dance?'

'Yes . . . No, not really . . .' Joy was avoiding her eyes and Ann could see she was on the verge of tears.

'Joy?'

'I'm going to bed. Night.' She ran off up the staircase.

'Oh dear, oh dear,' Martin said, doomily shaking his head.

Joy was curled up on her bed in the dark. Ann could see her outline from the light on the landing, her slender form in her silvery dance dress, shaking with sobs.

Slipping into the room, she sat down on the bed, leaving the door open to let in the landing light. She laid her hand on Joy's thigh and stroked gently.

'What is it, love?'

Joy shook her head, sobbing, and wouldn't answer at

first. Eventually she sat up. Ann reached over and opened a drawer to get a hanky for her.

'Come on – have a good blow and tell me. It can't be that bad, surely?'

'It's Alan,' Joy burst out. 'Norma and me were dancing. It was nice – to be out doing things again. And then I turned round and saw him. I didn't recognize him for a minute with his hair all short and in uniform. But he was there. And he'd never even said he was back, or been to see me! *And* – he was with some girl and—'

Sobs broke out of her again and she pulled her knees up, shoulders hunched, looking just how she did when she was a little girl and one of her pals had let her down. Joy had always felt all her friendships very strongly. Ann put her arm round her and hugged her close. She knew she had to be careful what she said.

'You sure it was him? And he didn't see you?'

Joy nodded miserably.

'That does seem peculiar . . . But you and Alan were never . . . I mean, he was your dance partner but you were never actually courting, were you?'

'Courting!' Joy managed a snort of amusement. 'You do know Queen Victoria's dead, don't you, Mom?' She straightened up and blew her nose. 'This is the thing – I don't *know*.'

'It never seemed that way to me. He was friendly enough when he came round here – nice lad. But he didn't seem . . .' She shrugged.

'What?'

'Well – sort of *fixed* on you, like boys are sometimes.' Joy's dark eyes were staring at her in the gloom. 'I mean, even your dad wasn't backwards in coming forwards when it came to . . .'

'Courting?'

122

They both managed a laugh, though Joy then started crying again.

'No. I know.' She seemed really confused and hurt. 'I just can't work Alan out. I thought we were – that there was *something* between us. We spent so much time together dancing and with dancing you're very – you know – *close*. And we had a lot of laughs together. I really like him. I've written to him, but he hardly ever writes back and when he does he's got next to nothing to say . . . But if he's had another girlfriend all this time why did I not know about her?'

'That is a queer thing,' Margaret said when she popped in the next day and she and Ann were sitting over the tea-cups. 'How could any lad resist our Joy? She's a real beauty, she is – and a live wire.'

'I know. Poor lamb – she was ever so miserable last night,' Ann said. 'To be fair on the lad though, if he's never given her any real sign, he's not deceiving her, is he? Unless there are things she's not saying.'

Margaret sipped her weak tea philosophically. 'Ah well – plenty more fish in the sea.' This was followed by a yawn.

'You all right, Mom?' Ann had long felt closer to Len's mother than her own. But she had only taken to calling her 'Mom' since her mother, Jessie Williams, had died in 1924.

'I must admit, I feel tired out,' Margaret said. 'I don't know if I'm coming or going with all these sirens going off. Puts the fear of God into you.'

'I know. Even the sound. You can always come and sit with us, you know . . .'

'I know, bab – we will. We're not very quick off the mark with getting organized.'

Ann found her mother's in-law's presence very comforting, as she always had. Margaret's solid body was dressed in a soft blue frock, her hair once sandy-blonde like Sheila's, now vivid white and pinned back over her ears in a bun as it always was. Many were the hours they had spent in each other's houses, drinking tea between household chores.

Over the years Margaret had reminisced about her own childhood, growing up in Kings Norton when it was more or less countryside, playing in the fields with her brother Stanley. Whatever the ups and downs of her marriage, Ann knew she had been very lucky having in-laws like Margaret and Cyril, who she loved deeply.

'It might be better if you and Martin was to come in our shelter, if you like?' Margaret offered. 'And Joy if she wants. There's only Cyril and me and the cat. He's in there before us most nights now. I expect he'll make room for you if you ask him nicely!'

After a series of dogs, Margaret and Cyril had decided a cat might be easier and along had come Sinbad – named because though mostly white he had a black patch over one eye – who was well known for perfecting his personal comforts at all times.

'Ta. That's nice of you,' Ann said, nibbling another Lincoln biscuit. 'Especially if Martin's going to be doing this ARP work – it's with the Scouts.'

Margaret grimaced. 'He's doing it, is he?'

'I wish he wouldn't but I don't feel I can tell him not to either. If everyone's out except me, I'll run down and join you!'

'Well, the side gate's open for you, bab.' Margaret drained her cup. 'You're all faster on your pins than we are.'

There was a moment's quiet, only the sound of the clock.

'Wicked, all this,' Margaret remarked, sitting back and crossing one leg over the other. 'I can hardly stand having the wireless on. Never thought we'd have all this again after the first time.'

Neither Margaret nor any of the rest of them ever usually referred to the first war, to Len's brother Ron, who had never returned from the Somme. The pain of it was buried too deeply. Ann watched her face, the shadow of grief that passed across it.

'It's a wicked world.' With a twist of pain at her heart, she thought of Tom and was overcome by a sense that things in her life never seemed to have lain straight, her feelings like a log pile dropped from on high, lying all in a tangle. Here she was with her mother-in-law, who she had loved for as long as she had known her – and yet she sat suffering these pangs of feeling for a man who was not Len . . .

Ann sat up, shaking herself out of it.

'I think I'd best get out and do something,' she said. 'I can't just keep talking about it. Hilda's in the WVS already and Roy's a fireman, of course. Who do I go to, to volunteer?'

That night was one of the few in the week when Len was at home all evening and sleeping in his own bed – air raids permitting. Ann knew he was dog tired, what with work and all the extra Home Guard duty. But as they got ready for bed in exhausted silence, all her old guilt rose up. I wonder what he feels he's coming home to? she thought. Was it her fault that he was so silent and closed off?

Len climbed into bed beside her, lay down and gave a jaw-splitting yawn.

'Seems quiet tonight, thank goodness?' she offered. 'Let's hope we get a whole night in our own bed.'

'Yeah,' he said in a flat voice. 'Should be all right.'

She was about to ask him more, but he had closed his eyes and seemed to be asleep before she had even switched the light off. Ann looked at him, this man resting beside her, at that face she knew so well, the hair, still thick and tending to stick out, boyishly out of control, the full lips, like his mother's, his strong cheekbones. Every inch of him was so familiar to her. And everything felt suddenly so painful and unbearable.

'Len?' Clicking the light off she lay down and snuggled up to him as he had always loved her to do, her arm across his warm, solid body. There was a time when they would have been immediately in each other's arms, his lips seeking out hers, hungry to make love.

'Love?' she tried again. 'I just . . .'

Just what? She ran out of words. Want you to look at me. Want you to hold me, love me. I want us to love each other.

'Let me sleep, will you?' he managed to say – not aggressive, just desperately tired.

Ann withdrew her arm and turned away. He must be worn out. She had chosen the wrong time, and it was selfish of her. But she lay, lonely in the darkness. However much she tried to stop it, her mind wandered down the path of the past to other times, to that other loving face.

Sixteen

1916

After Tom left, Ann worked her shifts at the hospital. She smiled at the lads in their beds, slowly trying to mend. Each of them seemed to long for a woman's cheer; a smile, a chat, someone to be their sister, mother, lover, nurse, all rolled into one. It moved her the way they handed themselves over to the nurses, these men, many of whom were older than she was, humbly putting themselves in her care.

She loved the work, she discovered; tending them, listening to their jokes and stories and the way, on a night shift, all the bluster of the day would disappear. Some woke sweating or crying out, while others wept like children.

But now, the ward was not the same. That corner, Tom's corner, was the first place to which her gaze had leapt each time she entered the room. She could not seem to help it. Even now sometimes, when she glanced across the ward, it seemed to her that he was still there. Her mind transposed his face on to that of whichever patient occupied the bed, and for a second Tom lay there again and her pulse galloped . . .

It was as if a light had gone out. She had a pain, all the time, in the left side of her chest. It took her days to realize what the feeling was. She was heartbroken. He was gone, this man. She would never see him again.

The news that summer was overwhelming. The name of Ronald Gilby, Len's elder brother, appeared in the lists of dead and Ann went to see Mr and Mrs Gilby, full of dread at facing their grief. As ever, Margaret and Cyril welcomed her. They shared with her their sense of stunned horror, the fact that they could not yet believe he had gone.

Ann sat with Margaret, their hands clasped in each other's as she wept. Margaret was a lively woman then of forty-eight, but she had aged overnight, the lustre gone from her sandy hair which, over the next weeks, faded quickly to grey.

'How can all these lads be gone?' she kept saying. 'They should have sent us – not let them kill all our children.'

The first days of the Battle of the Somme claimed an unthinkable number of lives and it was as if nobody's soul could catch up with the reality. A pall of death hung over the country, grieving families the length and breadth, all trying to take in the enormity of the slaughter.

And even then, Ann could not stop feeling the way she was feeling, ashamed and guilty as it made her. She was promised to Len: Len whose brother had just been killed, Len who was risking his life every day for his country. Len who now felt like part of another life that she could scarcely remember.

What's the matter with me? she raged at herself. While at work, she was kept busy. It was when she got home she really felt the weight of her heart.

'Poor Margaret,' her mother, Jessie Williams, said. 'Having only sons. I'm sure Len'll be all right though,' she added. 'Try not to fret so much, Annie.'

Ann nodded, feeling even more guilty because of course she *was* worried about Len, in the way she would have been terribly worried about her brothers, had she had any, and if they were in France. She tried and tried to force herself to make Len the one her heart was aching for. Because that was not how it was – but it was how things had to be.

One afternoon in August, she came downstairs after working an early shift, out into the sunshine of Oak Tree Lane. The old oak which the place was named after had been cut down a few years ago and she could still not get used to the bareness of the road without it, like an old friend who had gone missing.

She went along, past the People's Hall, a big place sometimes used as a 'Picturedrome' that she and Len had been to once or twice. Drifting along, weary after the hours of work, she found someone blocking her path. Startled, she looked up. A man, the left sleeve of his jacket pinned up, a patch over his left eye – the remaining features were suddenly familiar. Ann gasped, her blood starting to churn.

'Hello, Nurse Williams.'

'Oh! My goodness – hello!'

They stood face to face in the street, both clueless about what to do next. Tom Somers's face wore a healthier colour than when she had parted with him, though she could see the nervous tension in it, mirroring how she felt, immediately, on seeing him.

'What're you doing here?' she said. 'I thought you lived in . . .'

'Southampton. I do.'

An awkward pause followed. They both moved aside, by the wall of the People's Hall, topped by neat railings.

'I'm on my way to . . . to, let's see . . .' He was talking in a light, joking way. 'To London.'

'But . . .' She could feel herself frowning.

'Birmingham isn't on the way to London?'

'No.'

'No, it's not. To get to London from Southampton, you very definitely do not need to go via Birmingham.'

She stared at him, baffled.

Tom shrugged. 'I came to see you. See if I could find you.'

She felt as if she was living in a dream suddenly – or rather the reverse, that she had been in a dream from which she was now being startled awake. She had made so much effort to stay in the dream, to wrench her feelings back to Len, where they belonged. Little by little she had been schooling herself to forget the feelings she had had for Tom and remember where she belonged – with Len and his family who had already welcomed her so warmly. And now here he was again.

'Why?' she asked brusquely.

'Because . . .' He dropped his joking manner. She saw confusion, wretchedness even. 'I just can't stop thinking about you, Ann Williams. I've been so restless – it's not easy to settle back, after . . . But it's not just that. Meeting you, talking to you. It was just the best thing – and I had to come back and see you, just to see if—' He cut himself off abruptly.

She could feel her face drowning in blushes as all those feelings surged through her again; all the emotion she had tried to suppress and force away.

'I thought your shift might end about now from what I remembered.'

She nodded, unable to speak. It felt as if all her efforts to forget him had melted in the face of one hot breath of his presence.

'Do you have to be anywhere urgently now?' he asked.

'N-no. Not really.' Her voice was hoarse. She had been going home to Heeley Road and Mom would be expecting her but not needing her especially for anything.

'Walk with me for a bit, will you? So we can at least have a little chat.'

Nothing in this world would give her more pleasure. 'All right.'

'Might as well walk past for old times' sake,' he said, nodding along Oak Tree Lane towards Fircroft, the hospital.

They started walking in a silence suddenly so awkward and full of unspoken feeling that Ann began to think she might explode. She tried to force herself back into 'on duty' and ask him questions as a patient.

'So how have you been?'

'All right. As far as one can be all right with one eye – actually, that's less of a bother. One arm is far worse. You've no idea what you do with an arm until it's not there. But look, never mind all that. Tell me about everyone. How's Nurse Jenkins?'

Ann did her best to chat away about the other nurses, the few patients who Tom would remember and life on the ward in general until they reached Fircroft.

'It seems a long time ago,' was all Tom said as they paused outside. He gazed at the building. 'I can hardly believe I was in there now.'

It felt easier to talk once they had turned off into the quiet back roads leading down to Bournville, wandering slowly side by side. Ann kept glancing down at his legs, moving beside her, his black boots. *He's here, now – really here!* And it all felt like a dream.

'I know I'm grateful to be alive,' Tom said. 'To be out of it. I'm one of the lucky ones – to be injured before July when it all kicked off on the Somme.'

Ann nodded. She could see what he meant, if this was what being lucky meant – and these days, it seemed it was. He sounded so wistful and sad though.

'My father's got me a little job in one of the chandleries – that's where they sell marine equipment. I can just about manage to be a shopkeeper with one arm.'

'That's – well, that's good,' she said carefully, thinking of men she had seen begging at the side of the road, men with missing arms and legs, missing work, missing lives.

'It feels ungrateful to say it, but . . .' He trailed off, looking ahead. So sad, his face. All she longed to do was to stop him and put her arms around him. She was flooded with tenderness, with love for him. He turned and looked deeply into her face.

'It's just bloody, in all honesty. Trying to settle down. Fit back in. People say the most—' He stopped himself, shaking his head. 'You must think me a self-pitying fool. It's just very difficult to explain to anyone.'

'I think everyone finds it like that,' she said gently, feeling hopeless. What could she say?

They were walking along the green lanes, passing clusters of the neat Bournville Village Trust houses with their little plots of land – the garden estate, another Cadbury undertaking – each side of the road. Tom looked wretchedly at her.

'I'm sorry, Ann. I know you told me you're engaged. That I'm not . . . That you can't . . .' He turned away, stumbling over his words. 'Only, the thought of you is the one thing keeping me going. I feel a fool – coming up here like this . . .'

She thought for a moment he was going to weep and her own feelings buckled inside her.

'I think about you all the time – day in, day out,' he rushed on. 'I kept thinking when I left that it would

132

fade – that I could put you in a place in my mind that was sort of neutral.' He looked back at her again. 'So far, no luck. I love you, Ann. I can't think what else to say. I've been in love with you since the first time we talked and every time afterwards and . . . And I just can't seem to help it.'

She had a second, just a second to decide what to say. She was so moved and overwhelmed that he had come all the way to tell her this – so full of trembling love for him that words failed her. Instead, holding his gaze, she stepped towards him. Tom looked uncertain for a second, then held out his one arm which he wrapped tenderly round her as she embraced him. He was slender, thinner than Len, but muscular. She could feel him trembling.

'Oh, Ann,' he said. 'Ann, Ann.'

She could not speak. All the pent-up feelings for him started to pour out and she was sobbing against his chest, her hands on his back, hardly able to believe he was here, this body, this man who she never thought she would see again.

After the first storm of emotion had passed, she looked up at him, starting to try and draw back.

'No!' He held her. 'Don't go, please. Stay with me – be mine, Ann. I *ache* for you. Just say you'll be mine and be with me for ever!'

She was all confusion – desire, tenderness, loving him . . . If she were to get on a train with him now, start a new life . . . She could if she really wanted to – she was free. She and Tom. But there were so many unknowns. Tom, his family? Southampton? She had never been out of Birmingham let alone all the way down there. To her it felt like the ends of the earth. What would life hold for them? How could she desire this man, love him so much, when she hardly knew him?

'I can't,' she said. 'I love you, Tom. I do – so much. I think about you too – you're in my mind all the time. But I can't be with you. I promised Len. And his mother and father – they're so good to me and they lost Ron, Len's brother, on the Somme. I can't just . . .'

She released him and turned away, wiping her cheeks.

'Call me a coward.' She looked up at him again. The sight of him, the tender desire on his face made her feel weak with longing. 'I'm sorry, Tom. But I just can't do it. There's too much I have to stay here for – I promised Len and I've got to keep my promise.'

Seventeen

Sheila woke, hearing a whimper from Elaine in the darkness. She slipped out of bed and lifted her from her cot.

'Shh – it's all right, babby,' she murmured, her own voice thick with sleep as she lay the child beside her.

Wrapping her arms around the warm little body was comforting for both of them when there was no Kenneth in bed. If only she could reach out and find his long, muscular back beside her, so warm to cuddle up to. If only he was here breathing beside her, that comforting sound. The dreaded images came to her then, the ones she tried never to think of: the North Sea, waves crashing against the stones and the black, terrifying depths of it. Where was Kenneth? Was he out somewhere now in the freezing darkness, trying to rescue some fallen pilot? Her husband, so kindly and solid, out there on the great dark of the water? When these thoughts forced themselves into her mind they filled her with such desperation she hardly knew what to do with herself.

Elaine had slid back into sleep, but now Sheila was wide awake. Bother it, now she needed to go to the lavatory as well! Getting carefully out of bed, leaving the light off, she felt for her dressing gown and slid it on. She didn't like wandering about in a house where there was a man not her husband, and it was the weekend. Maurice Vellacott had come home tonight on a late train, looking white and strained.

Sheila crept to the door, feeling for the pretty china

doorknob and turning it, managing to get the door open almost silently. For a moment all the things she hated about the situation she was in rose up in her. It was true she was living in a safer place, a prettier, quite luxurious place compared to what she was used to. And Audrey had been kindness itself. But in the end it was not home; she had to play gooseberry to another couple while her own husband was doing heaven knew what. And here she was, a stranger in someone's house having to creep back and forth to the lav, feeling out of place and at that moment, really homesick.

She hurried along the landing, the carpet soft and silent under her slippers, the air still laced with the smell of their supper, a beef stew. It was all so embarrassing. It didn't seem right to flush the lavatory in the night in case of disturbing any of the family, yet it felt wrong not to do so either. In the end, with the door still shut, she gave the flush a quick tug, hoping it might do the trick without too much disturbance. The clunk and whoosh of it sounded deafening and she stood in there cringing for some minutes until the cistern had quietened again, before venturing on to the landing.

Blinded, once she had turned the light off, she stood still waiting for her eyes to adjust and became aware of a sound coming along the landing from beyond the bathroom. For a second she misread it and thought it was Elaine. She was about to go tearing back to her bedroom when she heard it again and realized it was coming from the room the other side – the Vellacotts' room which faced over the garden at the back.

It was a desolate noise. For a moment she wondered if it was a cat outside. But no. Stepping closer to the Vellacotts' bedroom door, she listened, so tense that she could hear her own blood beating in her ears. Someone was weeping, heartbrokenly, and it could only be Audrey. She was obviously trying not to make too much noise, but the way the anguished sobs broke out of her, it was beyond her control. Sheila felt her own emotions tangle into knots of sadness and pity for her. Whatever was wrong? Surely Maurice Vellacott could not be sleeping through that?

There was nothing Sheila could do except wonder what on earth had brought on such upset. She was just turning to creep back along the landing towards her room when she heard a door open behind her. She froze. Not knowing why, she felt terrified, as if she might be caught out doing something wrong. It was the feeling of being a stranger in the house again, who should not be caught out of place.

Pressing herself against the wall, she stood very still, heart pounding. On the opposite side of the landing to the bathroom, and at right angles to the Vellacotts' bedroom door, was another door. Sheila had never been into any of the rooms at that end of the house.

This door had opened, letting a wedge of light on to the landing, and she saw Maurice Vellacott come and stand in the doorway. He was dressed in blue-and-white striped pyjamas, barefoot, with no dressing gown, as if he had just got out of bed and come to listen.

Sheila held her breath. She did not know why – after all, what was wrong with going to the lavatory in the night? But there was something so odd and intense about the way he was standing there. What was he doing in another room and why was he up at what must be the small hours of the morning? She knew, by instinct, that he would not be at all pleased to know she was standing there watching him, but she just could not move.

Maurice Vellacott went to the main bedroom door and

stood listening. Sheila could just hear the faint sound of Audrey weeping, more quietly now. Maurice Vellacott leaned his head against the door for a moment, his hands hanging by his sides. Then he opened the door. He stood with one arm leaning on the frame, staring for what seemed an age into the room. There was no light inside so he must not be able to see Audrey – but she would be able to make him out, standing there. There was no sound from the room now.

Sheila stood frozen in the shadows. She felt so frightened she was sure Maurice Vellacott must be able to hear her heart beating. It seemed an eternity, him just standing there. When he finally spoke, loudly and abruptly, Sheila jumped, the noise jarring through her body.

'Do stop that ridiculous racket.' His voice was full of contempt. He stood for moments longer. Sheila could not hear anything from Audrey, not a sound. He closed the door and turned, so suddenly that Sheila had no chance to shrink back into the deep shadow. To her horror she realized he could see her. There was nothing she could do but stand there, feeling foolish and scared and embarrassed.

Maurice Vellacott stepped across the landing and she shrank back. His voice was low, full of contempt.

'And what in God's name are *you* doing?'

'Nothing. I've just been to the . . .' She was filled with horrible confusion about which word to use. 'The bathroom.'

'*Have* you?' He spoke rudely, as if he didn't believe her, not even troubling to keep his voice down now. Sheila waited for him to accuse her of something, of stealing, or some other suspicion he might have. Being a German spy even – there was no knowing what he might come out with.

'I don't like having some . . . someone creeping about in my house,' he hissed through his teeth.

'I wasn't, honestly. I just—'

'Oh, just get back to your bed. Now.'

He turned and strode back to his own room as if sick of the whole situation and shut the door, leaving Sheila trembling in the darkness.

Sheila was full of dread at the thought of going downstairs the next morning. She already felt as if she was in the way – at the weekends, anyway – disrupting this household. The harrowing noise of Audrey's weeping still sounded in her head, and how was she ever going to face Maurice Vellacott? However much she tried to tell herself she had done nothing wrong, she had a sick, uncomfortable feeling about what had gone on last night.

Elaine seemed to take in her mood and was fractious and tearful.

'Come on, babby,' Sheila said, getting her dressed and trying to hold on to her patience. 'Don't be like this – please. Maybe Lainy and Mommy should go home next weekend and see Nanny Ann and Nanna Margaret. D'you think we should?'

It was a long way, and so expensive. She knew she probably wouldn't do it but it was nice to think of being able to get out of here.

Carrying Elaine downstairs, aflutter with nerves, she went into the morning room where they ate breakfast. But she found only Audrey and the boys at the table.

'Ah, good morning!' Audrey said, with a broad smile. An apron was tied over a neat, milky-coffee colour dress. She was in the process of putting a plate of scrambled eggs in front of each of the boys. 'Would you like some, Sheila? The hens have done us proud this week – we've so many eggs I can hardly keep up!' She gave a merry laugh, stroking little Charlie's head as she gave him his breakfast. 'There you are, *darling*. Now eat up, do!'

'That'd be nice – yes, please,' Sheila said. Audrey was behaving so normally that she felt confused. Had she dreamt what happened last night? 'I can make it—'

'Don't be silly!' Audrey said merrily. 'I've got the pan on – it won't take a moment. More toast coming as well.'

Sheila settled Elaine in the high-chair and sat down beside her, feeling very uncomfortable. The boys were gobbling down their breakfast, ignoring her.

'You all right, both of you?' she tried. She was always friendly to them, really did her best not to seem like a wicked witch who had been foisted on their household.

Edward nodded without looking at her and little Charlie gave her a long stare, swallowed a mouthful of egg and whispered, 'Yes, thank you.'

'Where's your daddy this morning?' Sheila asked.

'Maurice?' Audrey came in with two more plates of golden scrambled eggs and laid one in front of Sheila. 'Oh, he got up very early. Said he wanted to make the most of the day. He sleeps so much better here than in London – they're having the most dreadful time of it. So he was up with the lark and off to the golf club.'

As if reading Sheila's mind – but he's only just got home! – Audrey added, 'He needs to unwind, poor darling. They've had some absolutely ghastly raids down there. He says the sky's criss-crossed with those trails from the planes almost all the time. Quite awful. It's just exhausting.' She sat down, shook pepper on to her egg, her face a mask of cheerfulness.

Are you all right? Sheila wanted to ask, as she fed Elaine a little spoonful of egg. But she knew she could not. She felt sad, seeing the smile pinned on Audrey's

140

face, but at the same time she admired her bravery, after the heartbroken sounds of last night. She knew Audrey was never going to say anything. It made her feel tender and protective towards her, and suddenly stronger in herself. Whatever had happened, she was quite sure it was not Audrey's fault.

Audrey looked up and smiled round the table.

'Now – what shall we all do today?'

II

October – November 1940

Eighteen

'Oh, go on – *please*, Norm! It's at the Queen's Hotel – it'll be lovely!'

Joy clung to Norma's arm. The bull had sounded for the end of the shift at Cadbury's and she and Norma, overalls off, coats on, were walking out through the factory gate to Linden Road. The sky was low, and there was a grey autumnal tinge to everything which seemed to heighten the golden glow of yellowing leaves in the gloomy light.

'We haven't had a raid for a while – maybe they're over now?'

'I wouldn't be so sure,' Norma said. 'It'll be our turn again soon. All the same, it's time we had some fun.'

Joy turned round for a moment and skipped along backwards, facing Norma, a beguiling grin on her face. She could see her friend was coming round to the idea.

'It flippin' well is! I'm trying to do my bit – I've volunteered for everything I can think of for the war effort.' She counted off on her fingers. 'I've given blood, I'm knitting scarves and socks for the Naval Comforts Committee – you wouldn't really want to wear the socks though, I've never knitted heels before . . .'

'Could anyone even get their feet into them?' Norma laughed. 'Look, just walk properly!' She grabbed Joy's arm, pulling her round. 'You'll knock someone over, else!'

'And *now* we're making bits of aeroplanes all day – even if we've not the first idea what they do . . .'

'And all this, just to mend your broken heart?' Norma teased her.

'No, to take my mind off it,' Joy said, with an air of melodrama. Wondering why Alan hardly ever answers my letters, she thought, but she didn't want to go into all that with Norma. 'As well as helping with the war effort, naturally,' she added virtuously. 'And because Mrs Elizabeth is hard to say no to.'

Norma's blue eyes flicked a glance at her, then away.

'It'll just be like last time. We'll get all dressed up and then spend half the night freezing in some shelter!'

Joy squeezed her arm. 'It'll be worth it though. We'll have forgotten how to dance soon. And anyway – I reckon we're going to have to work nights somewhere along the line!'

'The Queen's Hotel?' Norma said. 'That's right in the middle of town!'

'Your mom'd be all right about you going out for once, wouldn't she?'

Norma's mother, Hilda Baines, was busy working back at the factory now and Roy, her dad, already a fireman at Cadbury's, was helping out with the AFS when needed. John, Norma's brother, was in the RAF. So Norma, while doing bits and pieces where she could, was helping to hold the fort at home as well.

'It depends. So long as we all get our tea. By the way, she said to tell your mom she'll pop round, soon as she can. She hardly seems to have a moment these days. But yes, she'll probably be all right about it.'

Opening the front door, Joy immediately breathed in the delicious milky-nutmeg smell of a rice pudding baking. Her mouth began to water.

'Mom?'

'We're in here, love,' her mother's voice came from the back room.

'Pudding smells nice . . . Oh, hello Nanna – Miss Prince.'

The three of them were bent over the table, which was covered in a muddled heap of old garments – immediately the sweet scent of the pudding was superseded by a musty, off-putting mix of old clothes tinged with mothballs and sweat. Scattered about the room on chairs or heaped on the floor were various untidy piles: folded trousers, shirts, children's clothes and various muddles of socks, underpants, even a corset or two. A couple of pale blue teacups and saucers teetered dangerously close to the edge of the table. The blackout was over the windows and the gas fire was blasting away, so the air in there was fair pickled.

Miss Prince lived further down Beaumont Road, a gentle, bespectacled lady with a flowery overall tied over her drab grey skirt, hair that was somewhere between brown and grey and a set of dangerously loose false teeth. Nanna's broad hips were wrapped in a pleated fawn skirt and she wore a white blouse, spotted with navy, with a floppy bow at the neck. Beside her was Mom in her old green housework dress, her sleeves rolled up.

'All right, bab?' Nanna Margaret beamed at Joy as she straightened up, wiping her face. 'Look at your lovely rosy cheeks!'

'Well, it's chilly out, now,' Joy said, removing the teacups before any harm could come to them. The room seemed stifling in comparison with the cold air outside.

'We're almost finished and then I'll lay the tea,' Ann said, shaking out a man's shirt with a frayed collar and torn under the arms. She looked doubtfully at it.

'Can't afford to be fussy,' Margaret said. 'Some of 'em

147

are only left with what they're standing up in if their houses are gone.'

Miss Prince tutted, her teeth clacking. She gave Joy a rather jaw-clenched smile.

'We're getting these ready for the woman to come and collect with the van – any minute now . . .' Ann said. 'Once she's been, I can put the tea on the table.'

'Hilda says she'll be over to see you, soon as she gets a moment,' Joy said, slipping all this in while her grandmother was here. 'And Norma and I thought we'd pop out for a bit later.' She made it sound as if she was only going out for five minutes, and Nanny Margaret tended to take her side over things like this. But Mom was not taken in. She immediately stopped what she was doing and Joy could see her face objecting to the idea.

'It's at the Queen's Hotel – and we won't stop there for long,' she pleaded.

'Well,' her mother said reluctantly, 'I suppose it has been quiet . . .'

'She loves her dancing,' Nanna said to Miss Prince. 'She's a marvellous little dancer, our Joy – and it keeps everyone's spirits up, doesn't it?'

'Oh yes, they need to have some life, these young people,' Miss Prince said sweetly, this kind statement accompanied by the faint clack of her teeth slipping loose again.

Her mother's words, *Make sure you know where the nearest shelter is*, were still ringing in Joy's ears when she and Norma climbed into the tram again.

They got off at Navigation Street and walked round to the hotel behind the railway station, fronted by the London and North Western Railway enquiry office.

'Bit grander than Kent Street Baths, isn't it?' Norma

said. As well as the swimming baths, more of the hotels were holding dances now that the dance halls were being commandeered for storing rations. 'It'd look a lot better with the lights on though.'

In the blacked-out city, instead of the hotel looking like a great, lit-up ship at sea, all they could make out was its dark, imposing, but slightly sinister bulk.

'It'll be nice inside,' Joy said, excited.

She was not going to let Alan Bishop and his behaviour to her spoil things. She pushed her chin up. They were going to have some fun and she'd dance with whoever she liked and that was that. That was how she felt at the moment. At other times, all the hurt and sadness of Alan's odd behaviour – *nasty* behaviour, she would think then – washed over her and she sometimes had a little cry.

They took off their coats, laid them over their arms and in their flimsy, swinging dance dresses, rushed in through the grand portal of the hotel, out of the cold. After hurrying to change into their dance shoes and touch up their lipstick, they followed the sound of 'Tuxedo Junction', already singing and dancing and laughing before they arrived at the room set aside for the dance.

A band was playing at the far end of the long space, the windows swathed in crimson velvet curtains, packed with swaying couples circulating around it like the currents in a river, the air thick with smoke and scent and Brylcreem.

'Aah, smell that!' Joy said, pulling Norma in, the two of them squeezing round the edge of the floor. She felt instantly as if life had begun again. 'Come on – there must be a free bloke or two around somewhere!'

Joy stood on tiptoe, her eyes automatically searching out Alan, even though he surely could not possibly be here. For a moment all the pain she felt came flooding

back and a lump rose in her throat – the hurt she had felt
seeing him with his arm casually wrapped round that
girl's shoulders in a way he had never done with her,
she thought, enraged. Why was he so flaming *peculiar*?
She forced these thoughts away. If that was how he
was, she was not going to go chasing after him. And she
certainly wasn't having him spoil her rare night out!

She and Norma were both lookers and as soon as the
dance ended there was no shortage of offers for the next.
Norma went off with a friendly looking bloke with
closely cropped hair even redder than her own, and Joy
found herself in the arms of a fair-haired man called Frank,
who worked at a machine tools firm in Highgate. Soon
they were swinging their way round the floor to Cab
Calloway's 'Jumpin' Jive'.

'It's reserved, my job,' Frank shouted down her ear
over the music. He smelt clean, of Lifebuoy. He was
obviously keen to let her know that he was not some kind
of shirker. Even though he was a good few years older
than her, he seemed dazzled by her and painfully shy. He
held her just a bit too tightly and every so often leaned
forward and shouted, 'Enjoying yourself, Joy?'

She could see he was trying his best so she kept nodding and smiling back, thinking it would be nice when
she could get away – but even though he wasn't the best
of dancers, he wasn't bad. The fact that she was so good
at it lifted him and soon they were both laughing with the
fun of it and a few heads turned to look at them. Joy felt
as if she was fizzing, full of energy and life.

'Cor!' Frank said, when the music ended, still gripping
her hand. 'You're like a professional dancer! Shall us
dance again – only if you want, that is?'

'All right,' she said, smiling at him. He wasn't Alan, but
she could have been lumbered with a far worse dance

partner. The band launched into a foxtrot and off they went, reaching the end of the dance warm and breathing heavily and Joy loving every moment. But she didn't want to give Frank any ideas when he asked for a third dance.

'That's nice of you but I need to go and find my friend,' she said, looking round for Norma. She added the female catch-all escape excuse. 'I need to powder my nose. But thanks – I enjoyed that!'

Turning away from Frank's wistful expression, she was moving across the floor between the knots of people trying to sort themselves into couples for the next number, when from outside came the rising wail of the air-raid siren.

A great roar of dismay went through the room and Norma's face surfaced among the crowd, mouthing her name.

'I don't want to go,' Joy said desperately. 'Can't we stay?'

There was confusion around them. The band held their instruments down as there was a hubbub of everyone deciding whether to stay or go down to the cellars. Knots of people were waiting to get out through the door.

Norma looked torn.

'If we were in here when a bomb hit . . . Even in the cellar . . .'

Their eyes met. Joy felt an instant sense of claustrophobia. They linked hands and, as soon as they could escape, hurried to the cloakroom to get their coats.

Nineteen

Outside, the siren was still wailing. Joy had linked arms with Norma so as not to get separated and in the dark street she could sense, rather than hear or see, the presence of people all around her, hurrying this way and that below the searchlights and silver of an almost full moon.

Her first thought was to find a shelter – her mother's advice to make sure she knew where they were beforehand had slipped right out of her mind. Her eyes were searching for the dim, S-shaped light that would indicate the entrance to a public shelter.

But suddenly, along with some of the other people who floated dimly in and out of view in the deep murk, both of them were gripped by some kind of madness.

'Come on!' Norma was dragging her now. 'Let's have a look around!'

'What d'you mean, look around?' Joy was giggling, almost hysterical already. 'I can't see a flaming thing!'

'Let's go to the Market Hall – I haven't seen what they've done to it.' Norma said.

The Market Hall, gutted by a bomb back in August, was mourned by the whole city.

'I'm not sure this is quite the moment . . .' Joy was laughing so much now she could hardly stand up straight and Norma was catching the giggles as well.

'There won't be any bombs yet,' she yelled against the siren. 'We can get to a shelter when they start.'

Somewhere along the street, its darkness only broken by the little pencil-thin torches people carried to get about, they heard a warden shouting.

'Get under cover now! This is an air raid not a flaming party! Go on – shelter's over there!'

But the girls, almost helpless with giggles, hugged close to the sandbagged fronts of buildings along New Street and made their way down to the Bull Ring. They began to make out the faint, jagged outlines of smashed masonry against the sky. Light from the haze-covered moon silvered the high arch of the market entrance that was still standing.

'Oh, my word,' Joy said. They stood, sombre for a moment. Even now it was hard to take in that something so solid, so familiar, could be burned and smashed. But they just could not seem to remain serious. Joy felt Norma tugging at her sleeve.

'Come on – let's dance!'

They had seized each other, Norma playing the man's part, to dance a jig outside the entrance to the Market Hall like two crazy people, when the siren groaned to a stop. For a moment the silence itself seemed to reverberate. A moment later it was filled by the steady buzz of engines.

'Get under cover!' they heard again, in the far distance. It broke the spell.

'Quick!' Joy said. 'We'll have to find a shelter!'

They tried to run, tripping in the darkness. The sound of the planes was building like a swarm of bees and Joy felt her legs turn to jelly. What the hell had they been playing at? If Mom could see them!

'There!' Norma dragged her arm towards the faint S sign she had been looking for. They ran to the entrance and a man standing just inside hauled them in.

'That's it, ladies – get yerselves in! 'Bout time!'

And they heard the first of the bombs falling somewhere in the distance.

Inside was a fuggy gloom. In the middle of the shelter an oil lamp was burning, but there were so many people crammed in that they were blocking the light and the place seemed full of stirring shadows.

'Move along a bit, everyone – got some newcomers,' the man who had let them in ordered jovially. The lower part of his face was half-hidden by enormous walrus moustaches, the top half by a black steel helmet. 'Just a couple of tiddlers!'

Joy made out that there were benches round the sides of the shelter and the other people standing, who had also only just arrived, were all trying to squeeze into the dank space.

'There's a bit o' room over 'ere,' someone said to Joy's left.

'Shift up a bit – there's a place for a little 'un 'ere!' a voice called from the other side.

She and Norma found themselves separated and on opposite sides, but, crushed as it was, it was a relief to sit down. Joy looked around her, able dimly to see the gathering of tense faces, already tired from working flat out all day and now facing another broken night. She realized that the rank smell in the place came from behind a curtain at the end where there must be some sort of bucket lavatory.

The person who had called to Joy was a middle-aged man, thin and exhausted-looking, and soon he let his head loll back against the wall. Despite the terrifying sounds from outside and the place shaking at times, he remained fast asleep.

The man on her other side was leaning forward, resting his elbows on his knees, and wore a trilby hat so that she could see nothing of his face. She looked across at Norma and they rolled their eyes at each other.

Well, she thought, this is going to be a jolly night. Only then she was gripped by guilt. Mom was going to be beside herself wondering where they were. If only she could let her know! But then Mom had told her to get to a shelter and that was what they had done.

There was not much noise in the shelter. Up the far end a woman kept coughing, a real phlegmy old hack, and a few people had murmured conversations. But most people were focused on what was going on outside, sitting in grim silence as the noise grew, the explosions coming closer. Sometimes, when a bomb fell horribly close, there was almost a collective moan. The plane noise receded again, and then they were waiting for the next wave to come over . . .

The smell grew worse. Even the cigarette smoke could not disguise it. Now and then someone would get up to relieve themselves behind the curtain – the fear did not help. Joy vowed that she was not going in there, whatever. She wished she'd thought to bring her WVS knitting with her – that would at least have kept her hands busy.

Squashed in between the two men, she found her mind wandering to Alan again. She still felt sad and rejected – and foolish. How vain she had been in thinking that Alan must fall for her just because she was pretty and a good dancer. How had she got it all so wrong? And now, with a little distance from what had happened, she sensed that under Alan's strange behaviour there was something troubling him, something she did not understand at all. But he had not seen her as enough of a friend to talk to her about it and that hurt almost more than anything else.

155

Defeated by these sad thoughts, she forced herself to think about the dance. At least they had had a couple of dances before the blasted air raid! She let the music flow through her mind. Her feet started tapping automatically, her knees jiggling gently up and down as she traced the steps to the music in her head.

The attention of the man next to her, who was sitting forward, was drawn by her movements. She realized he was watching her feet and after a few moments he suddenly sat up, flexing his back, accidentally elbowing her in the ribs.

'Sorry!' he said, speaking quietly. It felt necessary to speak in barely more than a whisper so as not to have to share any conversation with the whole shelter. 'I was sitting forward to make a bit more space, but I can't keep it up for ever.'

'It's all right.' She shifted along a fraction. 'Here – there's enough room. Your back must be aching. Sorry if I disturbed you.'

He turned fully towards her and she just made out a lean, interesting-looking face with dark eyebrows, a long nose and a slender moustache. He smiled and the face became even more interesting.

'So – foxtrot? Am I right?'

'Oh!' Joy laughed. 'Very good! Yes, my friend and I were at a dance at the Queen's Hotel. D'you like dancing?'

'I do,' he said. 'Very much – though I've not been doing a lot of it lately.' He started humming 'Boogie-Woogie Foxtrot' and they both moved their feet for a few steps, side by side, laughing.

'Oh, it was the first time we'd been out in ages,' Joy said. 'Course, there had to be a raid tonight!'

'Full moon tomorrow. I gather it's been a bit quieter

here the last week?' he said. 'But we've been copping it down in Southampton.'

'*Southampton?*' Joy said. 'What're you doing here then?'

'Ah, well . . .' He smiled, then held out his hand to shake hers. 'Lawrence Dayton.'

'Joy Gilby.'

'Joy? How nice!' She wondered how old he was. Years older than she was, she thought. She found him fascinating. Something about the way he moved, his voice, low and smooth, like dark treacle.

'I had a few days' leave – had to arrange various things. I should have arrived back up here hours ago, but my train was damnably late. And of course it's hard to tell where you are . . . Anyway, I came out to find a bite to eat and then . . .' He made a gesture that encompassed the raid, the shelter and all. 'I'm at the shadow factory at Castle Bromwich for the time being. I was at the Supermarine Woolston until . . .' He shook his head and his face fell into sober, miserable lines. 'Course, it was a prime target. Everyone was jittery all the time. Terrible. Terrible thing.'

'Were a lot of people killed?' she ventured.

'Yes,' he said tersely. 'It was . . .' He shrugged. 'Anyway, most of the Spitfires will have to be made at Castle Brom for now. So I reckon I'm going to be here for a while.'

'Don't pay any mind to what people say – Brum's all right really,' she said, trying to cheer him up.

He flashed a grin at her. 'Oh, I'm sure it is. But what I've mostly seen of it is the factory and pitch-dark streets and this shelter!'

They laughed together. Joy saw Norma glance across at her, as if wondering who she was talking to. And she found now that she was glad they had been separated because it

157

meant she could sit talking to this man, Lawrence Dayton, as they helped one another pass the time and tried to keep each other's minds off the raid.

'Oh, here we go,' she said, a moment later.

The guns were hammering like mad and they instinctively curled their bodies in, ducking their heads as the planes roared overhead. Bombs whined down and there were several explosions near enough to shake the ground. Someone screamed and there was another, lighter sound, almost a collective whimper.

Gradually, Joy realized her hand was clasped in someone else's and Lawrence only let go as they heard the sounds die away. She felt herself blush. His strong, warm fingers holding hers felt very intimate, almost as if they had shared more than a brief pressure of the hand.

'Phew,' she said as the moment of terror passed. Someone cracked a joke and there was some tremulous laughter.

'So you're a keen dancer?' Lawrence said.

'I love it! I've been dancing since I was a little girl. One day I'd like to run my own school.'

'Ah, you want to be another Josephine Bradley! Are you a dance teacher now?'

'Oh no!' she giggled, flattered at the idea of her being likened to the First Lady of Ballroom. 'I work at Cadbury's!'

'The chocolate factory?'

'I'm not making chocolate now – I went over to munitions. Bournville Utilities – it's a new company for the war effort.'

He asked her all about Bournville and the factory and told her something of how he had come to be apprenticed at Woolton. She realized he must be very clever. She liked the lively way he talked, the expressive way he moved his hands.

'I used to dance a lot,' he said. 'What's your favourite?'

'Oh, I don't know – all of them!' she laughed.

'Not good enough. You must have a favourite!'

'All right – the jive, then.'

'My favourite as well, with a spot of Glenn Miller!'

Softly, he started humming, moving his feet and hands, and she joined in, tapping along until they were both dancing side by side in the confined space.

'Look at them two!' someone laughed. 'Should've brought my tin whistle! Go on, give us a number!'

Joy saw Norma watching them and felt proud that she was the one with this man, with this Lawrence Dayton.

'I wish we could,' Lawrence laughed, looking round at what had now become an audience. 'If there was the room to do it. You going to be the band?'

The All Clear sounded at last. A few people left the shelter, letting in blasts of cold, fresh air as the door opened and closed. Others stayed, asleep, leaning on each other or with their heads cricked back against the wall. There were coughs and snores.

Joy looked across and saw that Norma was dozing. For herself though, she had never felt more awake in her life. During the last wave of bombs, she and Lawrence had gripped each other's hands again and somehow never got round to letting go.

'There won't be any trams or buses yet,' Joy whispered, pulling her coat closer round her as another man, looking weighed down with exhaustion, left the shelter and smoke-laden air poured in.

'Tell you what –' Lawrence leaned close and whispered

so that she could feel his breath on her neck. 'Fancy a dance?'

Their eyes met. She grinned. 'What – out there?'

'Why not?'

Suppressing giggles of glee and with a glance at Norma to make sure she was asleep, Joy got up and followed Lawrence out of the shelter. Outside it was still dark, the moon sinking in the sky, visible behind a haze of cloud and the smoke and cordite which hung rank over the city, stinging the nostrils. Looking round, she saw the glow of fires somewhere not far away and the sky was tinged bronze. The other shelterers had gone and for the moment, here, in front of the shelter, they had the place to themselves.

'Madam . . .' Lawrence took her hand. 'May I have this dance?'

'You may!'

Joy was still wearing her dance dress under her coat, which she unbuttoned. She found herself with this tall, slender dance partner who bowed, clicked his fingers and started to sing 'Doo, doo be-do-do' jive music. And they were off on the flat space outside, under the hazy moon, stepping and turning, each of them in tune, practised, gifted dancers.

She could faintly see the pallor of his face, hear his voice marking the music, sense her own body moving and warming and feeling, in these moments, her life enchanted, that this was heaven – it was how things were supposed to be.

Lawrence was out of breath by the end of the dance as they stopped, laughing softly together.

'It's hard lines having to make all the music at the same time!' he panted.

'If we'd known we should've brought a gramophone!'

160

He was still holding her hand. There was a moment's pause as he drew her close and they moved into each other's arms. It seemed the most natural thing in the world to be in town at some hour before dawn in the now quiet, injured city, kissing a man she had only just met, their bodies pressed close and urgently together like hungry animals.

Twenty

Ann heard the back door quietly opening and closing. She leapt out of bed and rushed to the top of the stairs.

'Joy?'

Footsteps came through to the hall.

'It's me.' Len's face turned up to her, ghostly in torchlight. 'Sorry if I woke yer.'

'I've not slept. We're only just in from the shelter and Joy's not home!'

Ann could feel tears coming, she was in such a state. She had sat out there with Martin all through the raid, and Margaret and Cyril had come to join them which was a comfort. But she had spent the night fretting about Joy.

'I should never've let her go out,' she kept saying as they all huddled together. She had felt so frantic with nerves that she wanted to pace up and down, but you couldn't pace in an Anderson shelter. Martin, bless his heart, did his best to distract her and cheer her up.

'You know our Joy,' he said. 'She's like a cat – she's like three cats rolled into one, with twenty-seven lives!'

Ann had to laugh at this, because it was true. Joy got herself into little scrapes and somehow or another got herself out of them with her tail in the air.

'She'll have found a shelter somewhere like you told her to,' Martin insisted, leaning up close to her.

Ann reached round him, thankful that at least no one had asked him to risk his neck out there for the war effort yet. She cuddled him and stroked his head and he let her.

Her boy, her dear, beloved lad. He was so sweet – always had been.

'I expect you're right,' she said.

'Course he is,' Cyril said.

'She knows which side her bread's buttered, that one,' Margaret added.

But she knew they were worried too – about Joy and Len.

They had spent all those hours hearing the Luftwaffe's engines droning over towards the middle of Birmingham. Every time the roar of the planes drew nearer her stomach felt as if it had turned to ice.

She knew in her logical mind that if Joy had gone into a shelter, she might not have been able to get home. That now the raid was over and no trams were running, she might even be walking back, through the night. But she was still filled with a terrible feeling of foreboding, wanting all the family gathered safely together.

Len followed her into the bedroom. She checked that the curtains and blackout were properly in place and turned the light on. For a moment they stood each side of the bed, Len undoing the top buttons of his Home Guard uniform.

'You're soon home.'

'They didn't need me,' he said. 'Not once the raid was over.'

'Oh? It sounded bad.'

Len nodded. He seemed in an odd mood, keyed up and strange. The strain of it all, she thought. Still unbuttoning his tunic, he looked up at her, seeming on the point of saying something. Ann felt as if it was the first time his eyes had met hers in months. All she had on was a pale pink nightie. It came well down her shins, but the soft

163

material gathered into the yoke accentuated her breasts and she saw his gaze fasten there for a moment.

'Well, you can get some sleep for a bit anyway.'

'What about the lad?'

'He's asleep.'

She expected him to throw his clothes off and tumble into bed with hardly a word, as he usually did. As she climbed back in herself, shivering, Len got undressed with jerky movements. He seemed on edge, she thought. Angry even. Watching him as he stood turned away from her, she felt her stomach tighten again. When he was down to his underpants and vest, his back to her, he said quietly, 'Ann?'

'Umm?' She was arranging the bed, pulling the eiderdown on straight, getting ready to lie down.

He turned round and hurriedly climbed on to the bed, giving just enough time for her to see how aroused he was. Lying down, he leaned on one elbow and clumsily fastened his lips on hers, reaching to grab at her breasts. For a moment she was gratified, wanting to lie back and open herself to him, to be loved for the first time in a long time. But things felt wrong. The mood Len was in made him a stranger – rough and mean and frantic with need.

'Len?' Her voice came out small and frightened.

'Just lie back!' he ordered.

He straddled her, pinning her down, and leaned over her.

'I'm gunna have yer! Me – *your husband.*'

She sank back, bewildered, scared even. This was not Len. Was he drunk? But Len had never been much of a drinker and she could not smell it on his breath.

'Len, don't. I don't—'

'What? Want me? You never did, did yer?'

His hands were pressing down hard on her shoulders

so that she could barely move. Her chest tightened and she was suddenly panicking, afraid she would not be able to breathe. She started trying to push him off, slap at him, but she could not move her upper arms. A second later, he released her shoulders and his hands fastened round her throat. It lasted a few seconds. She felt her eyes stretch wide in terror but he was not looking at her – he turned his face aside as if at a distance from all that was going on. He let go at last, leaving her to gulp in air.

'Get your legs apart . . .'

She lay back, and he pushed into her hard, moving feverishly, not as if he was enjoying it, but simply trying to relieve his own tensions. It made her feel like a lifeless shop dummy or a lavatory that he was just using for his own ends. He finished quickly, frozen for a moment, face contorted and his head back so that she could see all the tendons in his neck. He shuddered, his body losing its tension, then fell forward on to her, burying his face in the pillow beside her. A few seconds later he broke into loud, helpless sobs.

Ann lay trapped under his weight, paralysed with shock as her husband wept, loud and distraught. How could she comfort him after what had just happened? But soon all the old guilt crept in. This was Len. Gentle Len who had never, ever done anything like this before. Len who she had hurt, so badly, whose love she had betrayed and made him feel terrible things he never wanted to feel. And she longed to make things right, for them to find the sweet innocence they had once had, as kids when they first met, before life and experience took their toll.

'Len . . .' She managed to ease her arms out and wrap them round him, holding him as his body shook. Was the war bringing everything to the surface for him as it was for her? Of course – it must be. All those things he saw in France during the last lot. He never wanted to go into it once he came home. All he wanted was to forget, to get married and make a life with her. But she knew it had not been that easy. How could she be so selfish and blind to what it must mean now, being out in the night as the planes flew over and the bombs came falling at them from the sky?

Brimming with guilt, with shame and sorrow, she found herself sobbing as well. Len pushed himself up on his hands, distraught.

'I . . . I'm sorry . . . I never meant . . .'

Ann could not seem to stop crying, sobbing from the very heart of her for all that they had been, for what had been lost.

'Ann?' He seemed really dazed. He did not know how to face her emotion. 'I dunno what came over me . . . Eh now . . . No need for that, is there?'

He tried to put his arms round her, but she shoved him away.

'You nearly throttled me! You frightened the life out of me, Len!' She sat up. He was sitting beside her now, in his place in the bed. They sat for a moment, both stunned. Then, less harshly, she said, 'What brought that on?'

He looked into her eyes, as if searching for something. He seemed frightened, she thought. She could not understand what was happening to him.

'Is it the bombing?' she asked. She forced herself to touch his leg for a moment, doing her best to be kind. 'I know, after the first war – I mean, it messes up your nerves.'

He looked down into his lap.

'I s'pose,' he said. 'Yeah. I think that must be what it is. I'm sorry, Annie – I never meant to hurt you.' He paused. 'Don't tell our mom, will you?'

'*No*. Course not!' Did he really think she talked about their private life with her mother-in-law?

Len patted her on the shoulder, a wordless attempt at sorrow and comfort, and lay back, closing his eyes as if everything had become too much.

It felt only moments later when Ann heard the front door open, so that she was not sure if she had slept at all. She jolted upright. What time was it? Seizing a cardigan and her slippers she hurried downstairs, to find Joy in the hall, taking off her coat.

'Oh!' Ann's hand went to her heart. 'Where in heaven's name have you *been*?' It came out more shrill than she intended. 'I've not slept a wink worrying! I'm putting the kettle on – come on in here.' She led Joy into the kitchen.

She opened the curtains and put the kettle on the gas. It was almost light now and glancing at the clock she saw it was gone six. She stood in front of her daughter.

'Well, you look all right. For God's *sake*, don't go gadding about at night again. My nerves can't stand it. Where've you been all this time?'

Gradually she took in that Joy looked rather more than all right. She was still dressed in her slinky dance outfit and even despite her pale cheeks, the smudges of mascara and dark circles under her eyes, she appeared somehow all lit up. The war really *was* doing odd things to people.

'We were in a shelter near the markets,' Joy said, sinking down at the kitchen table. 'I mean, first of all we were at the dance – at the Queen's.'

She told her mother a bit about the dance as the kettle heated, whispering on the stove.

'It was nice but then there had to go and be a raid.

167

Norma and I had said we'd go if one started, not just trust to luck.'

'Glad to hear it. And you found a public shelter? What was it like?'

There were all sorts of stories about what went on in public shelters.

'It was all right,' Joy shrugged. 'There was one woman who sounded as if she'd got consumption or something – but it was mostly people like us who'd got caught in town one way or another. People were just worn out – I mean, the man next to me slept through the whole thing. There were bombs coming down really close though. The nearest I've known it compared to here. It was really frightening. When we came out there were fires . . . Anyway, Norm and I got the first tram home.'

'You're going to be tired at work.' Ann got up to make the tea.

'Ah well.' Joy didn't seem bothered.

'What it is to be young.'

'I met this bloke – from Southampton.'

Ann's head shot round.

'Southampton?'

'Yes. Southampton.' Joy looked oddly at her. 'What's wrong with Southampton? We don't know anyone there, do we? He's come from the Spitfire factory – it was bombed, he said. Badly. So they'll be doing more up here, at Castle Bromwich, and he was sent to help.'

She had an odd, dreamy expression on her face.

'His train was delayed, so he got stuck in town.'

Ann brought the teapot to the table. She was too tired to make any sense of this. It must be her nerves and lack of sleep, the way the very word 'Southampton' had set her off. His place. Tom Somers's city. Still feeling the imprint of what had happened with Len this morning she pulled

168

her cardigan up close round her neck, hoping he had not left any marks. It felt as if all her old confusions and uncertainties, all the shame she carried which had been the slow ruination of her marriage, had come back up to the surface again and were shimmering there all the time.

Twenty-One

December 1925

'Go on, bab – have an afternoon to yourself,' Margaret said. 'You go and do your Christmas shopping – you can leave the girls with me.'

Nanna Margaret spent as much time as she could with her granddaughters: Sheila, five now and a stolid, serious little girl, and Joy who was two and showing signs of being much more of a handful. With the in-laws living so close by they were in and out of each other's houses. But Ann realized her mother-in-law might have sensed something, noticed she was feeling a bit low and at the end of her tether. She loved her girls with a tiger's passion – but she did just feel worn out.

'You have a break – I can have them all afternoon, eh?' Margaret offered. 'I expect they'll have a little nap, won't they?'

I wouldn't be so sure of that! Ann thought. Especially Joy, who, young as she was, reckoned to keep her eyes open at all times if she possibly could. She was a monkey to get to sleep of a night, which was another thing dragging her down, Ann realized. She felt tired through and through and a break even for an afternoon would be a wonderful change.

The tram swept along the Bristol Road, passing the elegant tower of the university as they slid along through

Edgbaston. But although Ann sat looking out, she hardly took in any of it. She was far too caught up in her thoughts.

She wondered whether Margaret had noticed anything about her and Len. It wasn't anything in particular that was wrong – not something of this month or last month. They had been married for six years now and had two little ones – that all took its toll. Len coming home from France had been a miracle in itself, a huge celebration. Ann had wept with joy, not just for herself but for Margaret and Cyril who had already lost Ron, Len's older brother.

Len seemed older, exhausted, changed – any man would who had survived all the war threw at them. But being Len, he never said much. Everyone knew men who were more than changed. Men who were wild as horses, or others not fit to be allowed out, maimed in body and spirit. She knew she and Len were the lucky ones.

But by then, she had not seen him for almost three years. Len had been quiet before. Now he was more so. He smiled less, had more of a temper on him. He was still Len but he was like a cake that has had its icing taken off, Ann thought. Or an Ascot without a pilot light. It was much harder to make him laugh, to get him excited about anything.

She told herself things would get better. She kept her promise to him, married him, tried to love him. She *did* love him, the very best she could. Wasn't loving someone what you did for them as much as what you felt? She was already part of his family by then. She and Len got married and did what you did – set up home, had a couple of kids . . . She was lucky. So lucky.

She missed working at Cadbury's with Hilda and the gang. But Hilda had left too, to marry Roy, who had not gone away to war. They had both been presented with their personally inscribed bible and red carnation by Mrs Elizabeth Cadbury, gifts that everyone received who was leaving the company's employ. The births of their children kept pace with one another. Hilda had John and Norma, she Sheila and Joy. Joy and Norma were only a month apart in age. Sometimes, she thought, what really kept her going was the other people in her life. Having Hilda nearby and dear old gingernut Roy, a big, bluff, solid man, was always welcoming. And Margaret and Cyril were the best in-laws you could hope for.

They were the ones she relied on when things felt so flat with Len, as if he was just going through the motions of life rather than being alive. She never felt she could say anything. He was a good man, a reliable man, doing his job at Cadbury's. They had a roof over their heads, food on the table, nothing to complain about. And yet – at times even when Len was in the house, she felt as if she lived alone, bringing up the children. He was like someone there but not there – a kind of absence.

But that was marriage, wasn't it? she told herself over the years. It wasn't all hearts and flowers – it was the day-to-day grind, taking the rough with the smooth. But she knew, deep down, that Hilda and Roy had something she and Len didn't – and so did Margaret and Cyril. There was a light between them, of shared laughter and exchanged looks – passion, even – that still glowed bright through the days of drudgery and repetition. And she envied them because she knew it was possible – and that passion was something she had known, just not with Len. And, when she allowed herself to think about it, she still longed for it with an ache that never left her.

Come on, she chivvied herself as the tram drew to a halt in town. Don't be a misery guts. You've got a nice afternoon out – on your own! How odd it felt to go out without two little ones. She mustn't go and spoil it.

Stepping down in Navigation Street felt strange, exciting. She hadn't been into Birmingham for ages. Getting about with two children in tow was all such a business and she did most of her shopping locally. Pushing her sad, longing thoughts away, she set off towards New Street and the Bull Ring.

With Christmas coming up, Birmingham was thronging with shoppers. Delicious smells filled the air as she drew nearer to the markets. She hadn't come to buy food, but she couldn't resist going into the Bull Ring, to be part of the much-loved bustle of the place, drinking in the atmosphere.

As well as the fruit and veg stalls there were people selling toys and crocks and almost anything you could think of, voices raised, their breath misting the cold air as they shouted in competition with each other. Barrows with knife-sharpeners and key-cutters sent arcing orange sparks into the winter gloom . . . The air was filled with a mix of mouth-watering scents: chestnuts roasting on braziers, barrows selling hot potatoes and whiffs of oranges and pipe smoke and roasted meats.

For old times' sake she bobbed along on the tide of people milling in and out of the grand Market Hall building, with its rows of stalls as far as the eye could see, the big clock hanging over everyone in the middle, marking the hours above the sprays of flowers and stalls bright with fruit and vegetables, the light slanting in through the arched windows.

Ann ambled along, remembering coming here with Mom and her sisters, so excited as kids. For old times' sake, she bought a little bag of troach drops from one of the stalls groaning under jars of bright-coloured sweets.

She popped one in her mouth, the pungent aniseed flavour springing her right back to when she was six years old and first tasted one. She'd have to take a few home for Margaret and Cyril – and for Sheila to try one!

Come on, she thought, after a pleasant twenty minutes of wandering about. This isn't going to get Christmas sorted out. She wanted to go to Lewis's. Sheila was mad for a doll and she could get a little something for Joy as well . . .

Avoiding the wiles of the flower sellers who were very keen for her to take 'flowers home to Mom!' she managed to move against the tide, out of the Market Hall, and made her way up to Corporation Street and Lewis's. If she was going to get a doll, she thought, she wanted a good one, not one of those where the eyes dropped out after a week.

She turned into the gracious sweep of Corporation Street, busy with trams and buses, horse-drawn carts, people, people and more people, thinking about the presents she needed to buy. Sheila was easy, but what about Joy – and as for Len . . .

She drew in a breath of the smoky air, looking round at all the bustle of the street. And found herself face to face with Tom Somers.

That was how she remembered it, for ever. Like a dream. She felt she was dreaming right from the start. There he was, as if conjured from her memory, her longing.

They must have been in everyone's way, coming to a dead stop like that in the crowd. But all that stayed with her was his face, the joy in it when he saw who was in front of him, which took him a moment longer than her because all these years had passed and she was wearing a blue hat instead of a veil, her winter coat instead of her nurse's uniform.

And he – suddenly so beautifully familiar, the sleeve of his brown wool jacket pinned up, the dearly remembered shape of him, his face, under a brown trilby. They had written to each other a few times after he left the hospital. But it died out. She found it unbearable and understood that he did too.

His smile grew wider and wider.

'Nurse Williams? Ann!'

'Tom!'

Nine years, more than, since she had seen him. Eight, probably, since she had heard anything from him. He was a little fuller in the face, and the scars were barely visible on his cheeks. But he was the same – he was Tom.

The 'Nurse Williams' business was instantly done away with and they flung their arms round each other, there in the street.

'What on *earth* are you doing here?' she said, pulling back to drink in the sight of his face, that dear, right, face. They did not completely let go of each other, each clinging to the top of each other's arms as if they were a mirage who might vanish at any second.

'I'm here to go to Joseph Lucas's to talk about a new contract for our supplies. That's tomorrow though. I've just come up today so as not to do it all in one. And for old times' sake, in a way.' He laughed. 'I owe a great deal to Birmingham. I'm staying at the Midland, just for a night.'

The shyness only began then. They both said, 'You look well' and 'How are you?' and it all became very awkward, until Tom said, 'Look – why don't you come and have some tea? Then we can have a proper conversation.'

And the dream began – like a time out of time. An afternoon that was like a capsule sealed off from her life but every bit as real and true.

They went to the Midland Hotel, drank tea, spoke of their lives. Tom told her he was still unmarried, still working at the chandler's. Even after half an hour she knew, with the inevitability of someone washed over a waterfall, what was going to happen. Her knees almost gave way as they walked hand in hand up the shadowy staircase.

An hour later, they were still in bed in Tom's room, clothes strewn on the floor, lying pressed close after loving each other, sobbing with desire and pleasure, with pain for the lost time during which these two longing, seeking bodies had been held apart from each other.

Twenty-Two

24 October 1940

There was a lull in the raid, the guns quiet, just for a time, so they could hear each other. Ann and Joy had gone down to Margaret and Cyril's shelter. Miss Prince of the loose dentures was also there – she would have been on her own every night otherwise.

Cyril had done a lovely job of making the shelter as comfortable as any such place could be, with a little table and cushions along the benches that they brought in every day to stop them getting damp.

'I'd bring the wireless in only it's such a kerfuffle,' he said. 'Home from home!'

This was Martin's first night out during a raid with the Scouts, running messages on his bike between ARP posts.

'Don't fret, bab.' Ann jumped as her mother-in-law's hand suddenly came to rest on hers, comfortingly warm from the hot-water bottle she was nursing in her lap. 'He's a good lad – he can take care of himself. Like a cat with nine lives, that one.'

Ann smiled, her face hollowed by the glowing light of the Tilley lamp.

'That's what he said about you, the night you got caught out,' she said to Joy.

'Well, he was right, wasn't he?' Joy grinned. 'I came home and here I am.'

'Here . . .' Margaret lifted a big Thermos from beside her on the floor. 'Time for a cuppa, I'd say.' She poured tots of sweet tea into cups and they all sipped. 'You all right, Grace?' she asked Miss Prince.

'I'm all right,' Miss Prince said in her gentle way. 'The only thing is . . .' She leaned in close to Margaret. 'I could really do with spending a penny.'

'Oh, bab – just pop into the house while it's quiet,' Margaret said kindly. 'Or give the garden a little water – whichever you think best!'

Miss Prince gave an embarrassed chuckle, pushed the door of the shelter open and disappeared. Margaret and Cyril exchanged a wry smile.

'Bless her,' Margaret said. 'I hope she doesn't trip over anything.'

They could not see or hear much outside at that moment. It was not clear exactly which of the options Miss Prince had chosen in terms of relieving herself, but she was back just as the guns started banging again.

'Oooh!' she squealed, reappearing a lot faster than she had gone out. 'I thought I was done for!'

'Here we go,' Cyril said grimly.

Silence fell in the shelter. They could hear the low, growling rumble of the planes. Ann sat back, shoulder to shoulder with Margaret who was beside Miss Prince. Joy was facing them, next to her grandfather. Ann smiled, seeing Joy and Cyril holding hands. Joy had always been the apple of Cyril's eye. When she was little, he would sit for hours, watching her dance about and perform, the perfect, devoted audience for her.

Ann closed her eyes. Shame washed through her. She had not only been thinking about Martin – or about Len, as Margaret supposed – though God knew, she *was* worried.

Instead, today she could not seem to stop thinking about that afternoon with Tom Somers, so long ago now – nearly fifteen years, though when she called it to mind it could have been the day before. The memory of that afternoon felt separate from all the rest of her life. It stood out, diamond sharp.

Closing her eyes as the planes passed over, moving towards the centre of the city as the first bombs began to fall, she prayed that Tom was safe in Southampton. It was a relief to take her mind elsewhere: she was back in that hotel room with him, in the silence that came over both of them when they had drained their teacups, climbed the stairs and stood in the room's shrouded grey light, facing each other. Never, other than in those moments, had her eyes gazed so frankly into those of another or found the same gaze, in Tom's one eye, that grey, lovely eye, communicating back to her. Love spoke, longing spoke, across the years.

It was she who reached out first, laid her hand gently on Tom's shoulder, felt its broken shape, which she knew and remembered, from where his arm had been amputated. In that moment they exchanged another look. He knew that she knew his body. Ann never asked whether anyone else had known it since.

Under the blackness of her lids, she lived those moments, the drawing together, the feel of holding his body, their fast, desperate kisses, the air on her skin as they pulled at each other's clothes and fell, shivering and laughing, into the bed, to love each other. All judgement had gone from her, all caution, all the things 'nice girls' and 'married women' do not do. His pale, familiar, lovely face close to hers, his hand hungrily exploring her. There was just him and her; nothing else. It was life, now, and it was love.

And afterwards – just days – the last letter he had ever

written to her, promising that, although he loved her, he would leave her alone. Inside, on another sheet of paper, was the poem. She had every word of it, of Elizabeth Barrett Browning's love poem, carved on her heart.

> *How do I love thee? Let me count the ways.*
> *I love thee to the depth and breadth and height*
> *My soul can reach . . .*

There were more explosions, the faint shudder reaching them from not too far off.

'Oh, dear God,' Margaret murmured. 'Hark at that. Dear, oh dear.'

Ann's mind crashed back to the present, calculating feverishly. Martin was in Selly Oak, wasn't he? Where had that noise come from? Her heart raced. Not Bournville, anyway, Len would be all right . . . An image came to her of her husband's enraged face close over hers, pinning her to the bed, like a cold hand squeezing her heart. After all this time, it was as if Len had cracked under the pressure. Is that what she had done to him? She hated herself in those moments. She must get rid of those letters, all that blasted hankering for the past – she had betrayed her husband and she must stop all this nonsense about something that could never be.

There were more muffled explosions as the planes moved further north over Birmingham and the ack-ack guns stopped. It felt almost eerily quiet suddenly.

'Anyone fancy a biscuit?' Margaret said. 'Rich Tea?'

Ann shook her head gently, tied up in her own emotions. She kept her head tilted back against the tin wall as if she were asleep, or as near to asleep as you ever got in a shelter. She heard the crackle of the packet as Margaret offered biscuits round.

'There's a drop more tea – might as well have it before it goes cold. Grace? Cyril?'

And now she was upstairs in the back bedroom, *29 September 1926*, her body tensing and straining, the voice of the midwife, Miss Carew, coming to her from somewhere miles away, it seemed, between her splayed legs as the child's tunnelling force broke her open.

'That's it now – keep it going!' the voice cried.

Miss Carew was a young woman who had never given birth in her life. She sounded much too cheerful, Ann thought savagely, as if she was cheering in a horse race instead of assisting in the effort of trying to bring forth something so impossibly enormous from inside one's body. She may even have come out with something to that effect to the woman, though she could not exactly remember and did not like to think what it might have been.

She groaned under the cudgel of the next bout of contractions. 'Oh God – let it be over . . .'

It was not as if it was her first. Sheila's birth had been a long and agonizing business and she had torn badly at the end. The midwife then was not a nice woman and Ann had taken a long time to recover. Her memories of the whole experience were tainted by a feeling of doom and pain. When Joy arrived though, it had been an easier experience. To her surprise, she had not torn at all though she had thought it would be inevitable after the first time.

'Your third?' Miss Carew said when she first arrived with her little bag and angel smile. 'You know what you're doing then – we'll have him out in no time!'

I have girls so far, Ann wanted to say. It's probably another. But by the time this labour went on and on and seemed to stall so that at one point she was weeping with frustration, she decided it would be a boy. Just like a flaming man to keep you waiting.

And it was. And from the moment Martin arrived she recognized him. She could see his father so clearly in him that she was afraid of anyone else seeing him at first. And she loved him the way she loved both her girls, with a deep passion. But with Martin her love carried an extra little flame that no one else could ever know about because even as a tiny baby, he was so beautifully, so much, like *him*.

As soon as the pains had passed, she could quite like and appreciate Miss Carew again, with her blonde hair tucked under a veil, her light freckles and wholesomely smiling face. And she cared for Ann well. Before long she was sitting up in bed, drinking a cup of tea, eating toast and suckling the latest addition to the Gilby family, who lay angelic in her arms. It was four o'clock in the afternoon and Margaret was downstairs with the girls.

'Well,' Miss Carew beamed at her. 'You're looking very well – and you have a lovely baby! Have you got a name for him?'

'We thought Martin,' Ann said, smiling back at her. 'Martin, and then Tom – after my father,' she added hastily. It was half true at least – that had been her father's name.

'Lovely.' Miss Carew leaned over her and brushed Martin's cheek with her finger. 'Well, get some rest when you can. I'll pop in and see you tomorrow. I'm sure there are some little girls downstairs who will be very keen to come and see their new brother – for a few minutes anyway.'

She went to the door.

'And your husband will be home soon, I expect – and you can introduce this one to his father.'

She closed the door softly behind her, not seeing the blush tinting Ann's cheeks. A blush which spoke the truth that she was never going to be able to tell.

*

'Oh, thank heavens,' Miss Prince said, as the All Clear sirens moaned out across the city. 'We should all be able to get a few hours in our own beds now.'

They got stiffly to their feet, carrying blankets and flasks and cushions.

'Margaret?' Ann said, once Miss Prince had gone and they were wending their way back along the garden. 'That lady from the WVS – she asked if I could help out on the mobile canteens.'

Margaret turned to her in the gloom. 'Are they short then?'

'Sometimes – well, quite often, I think. It depends on the night.'

Ann thought for a moment that her mother-in-law was disapproving, would try to stop her volunteering.

But, into the smoky air of the garden she said, 'Perhaps I could lend a hand as well.'

'You? Oh no! I didn't mean to make you feel you had to – I just thought, with Martin out sometimes – and Joy could come over to you. I mean, some of the women have got younger children at home but really, mine are old enough to look after themselves.'

They stopped close to the back of the house before Ann and Joy went back to their own.

'Look – you do what you think best, Annie,' Margaret said. 'If they are short any time, let me know? I may be getting on a bit, but I'm still up to pouring tea. Cyril's talking about going into the Cadbury's Home Guard with Len now – seems age is no bar these days!'

'Is he? Gracious – that's good of him.' Ann smiled, suddenly relieved. She could not stand too many more nights sitting trapped in one shelter or another. 'Come on, Joy . . .'

'Night, Nanna, Grandad,' Joy called.

'Night, bab,' Cyril called from the kitchen door. 'Mind how you go. And send the lad round to see us tomorrow, all right?'

They all called their 'Goodnight's – or should it be mornings? – and 'Get some sleep's and walked the few houses along the street to find Martin just dismounting from his bicycle outside, looking exhausted but grinning from ear to ear.

'Oh,' Ann said, her body relaxing. 'Thank heavens.'

Later that morning, when she had the house to herself, Ann carried Tom's letters down the garden. There was an old tin bath they used for lugging soil and weeds. In the weak winter light she kissed each letter and laid them in a fan shape inside on its mucky base. Taking a box of matches from her apron pocket, she lit one, bending over the bath, so that the flame caught the corner of one of them. She gripped her hands, fighting the impulse to save them, to pull one out at least . . . And she could not bear it. Thrusting her hand in, she grasped the blue one – the last one, already singed at the corner, and blew on it before pressing it to her chest. Sobs rose in her, and she swallowed them down, tears coursing down her cheeks. The fire hastily licked its way across the rest of the well-worn paper, all Tom's other words reduced to soft grey ash. But she couldn't do it – not that last, loving, kind, longing letter . . . Aching with regret, she waited for the flames to die, then raked the ash around with a stick. Slipping the letter into her skirt pocket, she shovelled the cooling ash on to the vegetable patch and stirred it with a hoe until it was mixed in.

She walked slowly back to the house with the one precious thing she had kept: that last letter, containing the poem. *How do I love thee . . .?* With her hand in her pocket, she pressed it, caressingly, against her thigh.

Twenty-Three

5 November 1940

'Letters for you,' Audrey said, as Sheila carried Elaine down into the kitchen.

Elaine caught sight of Audrey and beamed, bouncing in Sheila's arms. A smile broke across Audrey's pale, strained face.

'What a little lamb she is!' She came up and took Elaine's plump, waggling hand and kissed it and Elaine gurgled with laughter. 'She's a tonic – she really is.'

Sheila waited to come down in the mornings until Audrey had seen the boys off to school. It was all a bit of a bustle, Edward being stubborn about putting his shoes on, Charlie forgetting something and them having to rush back inside. Fortunately, both boys seemed to enjoy school.

'Your family are faithful correspondents,' Audrey remarked.

Sheila sat Elaine in the high-chair, cut up some pieces of apple for her, and quickly looked through the letters. One from Kenneth! Her heartbeat picked up – relief! And Mom . . .

'Yes, they are.' She looked up, suddenly realizing she knew nothing about Audrey's parents. 'Does your mother . . .? I mean, where is she?'

'Mother? Oh, in Cheltenham. And my father. Yes, she writes from time to time.' Audrey slipped the lid on to the delicate china teapot. 'Life goes on much the same where they are. She's doing her bit – they have some evacuees, not in their house, but she helps out with keeping them entertained. I expect you'll meet her one day – she does come to see us occasionally. And we go there . . . Well, I do.' She hesitated, then turned away with a rueful smile. 'Not Maurice's idea of a relaxing weekend, listening to my father. But Daddy still gets called out quite a bit, of course. He's a doctor.'

'Oh,' Sheila said. 'That's nice.' She was itching to read her letters but it would be rude to open them while Audrey was talking. She picked up the bits of apple Elaine had dropped on the floor and cut her some slices of toast.

Audrey came and sat at the table. She slumped, seeming suddenly exhausted.

'I suppose we could switch the wireless on – but I'm not sure I can face it.'

'Yes,' Sheila said. 'Let's not.' She was reassured by having a letter from her mother in her pocket – although there had been a night between her writing and now, and what might have happened in Birmingham then? She tried to tell herself not to be silly. Bournville did not seem to be high on the list of bombers' targets. And here, in this place of trees and birdsong and quiet, it was hard to imagine . . .

'Are you feeling all right?' she asked Audrey timidly. 'I mean, the bombing in London sounds bad . . .?' Underneath all that valiant cheer she must be worried to death about her husband.

'I . . .' For a moment it looked as if Audrey's mask of cheer was about to slip, but she tried to recover herself. 'Maurice could get back here for the night, if he so chose . . .' She seemed close to tears. 'He just . . . Well, he prefers not. There doesn't seem to be anything I can say.'

Sheila had no idea what to say either. It all seemed very

odd to her that Maurice Vellacott would stay in London when he could catch a train and see his wife and sons, not to mention avoiding having bombs raining down around him almost every night. She couldn't help but think about what she had overheard, the strange, angry man on the landing in the half-darkness and Audrey's heartbroken sobbing. She had no idea whether Audrey had heard him talking to her on the landing – she thought not.

'It would be a bit tiring – and not very convenient for him,' she said tactfully. 'I can see that.'

Audrey looked into her eyes with a cool, guarded look, almost as if she was weighing up whether she might say something. Then the smile was back. More and more Sheila could see the mask Audrey kept on almost all the time, the effort it must take – but she did not understand really what was going on behind it.

'Yes, I'm sure you're right,' Audrey said. 'The journey would be very tiring. Only of course, I can't help but *worry*.' She leaned over to Elaine. 'Is that nice, darling? You're a good girl, aren't you? So nice to have a daughter,' she said wistfully. 'She's a little poppet.'

She sat up straighter, changing the subject. 'Oh yes – look, it's Guy Fawkes night tonight. Normally, of course, the village has a lovely show with a fire and fireworks but we're not allowed to this year . . . But I thought we could give the children a nice surprise indoors!'

As soon as she could get away, Sheila went up to her room with Elaine. She was desperate to read her letters. And Audrey did seem in an odd mood – peculiar and on edge, as if she might explode any moment even though she had an almost permanent smile fixed on her face. It was all beginning to wear Sheila down.

She liked Audrey, but there was something very tiring

about having all these contradictory currents of feeling coming at her when she could not really work out what they all meant.

Longing to feel the straightforward love of her mother and husband, before setting to wash and dress Elaine, she settled her on the floor with a couple of little toys and opened both the envelopes, sitting on the side of the bed. Mom's letter was short and sweet as usual.

We've had rather a lot of it in the last two weeks – Jerry paying Birmingham a bit too much attention. But we're all safe here in Bournville. I've sat with Nanna and Grandad quite a few nights and they send their love. Your Dad's all right too. Hilda came round yesterday and she and the family are getting along all right.

They've talked me into doing some work with the WVS – seems as if every other woman at home is helping out like that one way or another. We're all going along well – you mustn't worry. I hope you and Elaine are safe and well down there. I'm glad you're out of it. Joy's all right as well – she's gone over to war work – at Cadbury's but doing work for Lucas or Austin – one or the other, making parts for planes, I think. Maybe you already know that. Can't think straight at the moment – must be the lack of sleep.

I hope you can get home for a visit soon – we are all missing you and Elaine. Give her a kiss from her Nanna.
With love
Mom

Kenneth's letter was not long either. They were not allowed to discuss what they were doing so he would comment on the weather or say everyone was all right and talk about Frank and one of his other pals who she met while she was there and their pub high jinks when off duty. None of it was all that interesting and she skipped down to the best bit at the end where Kenneth signed off.

> *I wish you could be here with me, Sheila – but I know it'd be hard for you. Glad you're with a nice lady and other kids for Elaine and that you're safe – but I miss my wife truth to tell – miss you being here. I love you so much and every night before I go to sleep I lie here thinking about you and wishing I could put my arms round you and our little Lainy. Give her lots of kisses from her Dad won't you? I hope I'll get some leave sometime but things are busy and no hope of it at the moment. Just know that I love you and I always will.*
> *Kenneth xx*

Tears rose and rolled down her cheeks.

'Oh Kenneth . . .' She keeled over sideways on the bed and took the pillow in her arms, wanting to lie and weep and weep. This horrible, cruel, stupid war meaning that she and her beloved Kenneth were parted and he could not see his little girl who seemed to be growing up so fast. But she also knew she would have gone mad if she had had to stay much longer in the freezing winds of Grimsby.

Elaine crawled over and was tugging at her leg, so Sheila sat up and took the little girl in her arms.

'That was a letter from your daddy, Lainy,' she said, kissing her. Her warm skin and wriggling body were comforting, at least. 'He loves you and he sends all his love, babby.' There was no time to lie there crying and feeling sorry for herself – she had to look after her little girl.

*

'Now,' Audrey said, once the children's tea was over, the air full of the delicious smell of fried sausage and mash which Audrey and Sheila had also eaten with them. 'I've got a little surprise. D'you know what day it is today?'

'Guy Fawkes!' Edward shouted.

'Not so loud, darling,' Audrey said. 'But yes.'

'We did some firework pictures at school,' Charlie said. 'Whoosh! Bang!' He thrust his arms in the air.

Sheila watched the boys. They looked relaxed, happy little lads – which they did far more of the time when their father was not around. He seemed to expect them to behave like adults, as if he had forgotten what it was like to be a child himself.

'Well, we can't go out to the field for fireworks this year, or have a big bonfire. Do you know why?'

''Cause of stinking old Hitler!' Edward said.

'I don't *like* stinking old Hitler,' Charlie joined in, banging his fist on the table.

Audrey and Sheila exchanged amused glances.

'Well, that's true – and we can't go outside for fireworks. But –' she leaned over and produced a box from under her chair – 'look what I've got. Fireworks we can have indoors!'

Elaine clapped her hands, watching the boys' excitement.

'What on earth are they?' Sheila said.

'I don't think we're going to set the house on fire,' Audrey said, laughing. 'That would rather defeat the object, wouldn't it? Here – let me see.'

She opened the box and laid little paper shapes on a plate.

'They're not fireworks,' Edward said, but Sheila could see he was intrigued. She watched the children's faces as Audrey put a match to them. The coloured papers took life, wiggling about all over the plate as they burned.

'Oh! Snakes!' Charlie cried.

'Burning snakes!' Edward laughed. Sheila had hardly ever seen him look so young and excited. Elaine started chortling when she saw the boys laugh and that made them giggle even more.

'Now, what have we here?' Audrey said, once the squiggles of paper were reduced to black ash. She lit the rest of the little shapes on another plate. They caught light and suddenly launched, seemingly weightless, towards the ceiling. They all gasped, Sheila included.

'Oh – look how pretty, Lainy!'

'Whooo!' Edward and Charlie both laughed with delight as well, watching as the flames died out and drifted into nothing but a few ashy flakes.

There were a few more of each kind left and Audrey lit them again, the children growing even more excited.

'Bonfire night, indoors!' Charlie yelled, delighted. Sheila felt tears come into her eyes. It was rare to see these little boys look so happy, so carefree and enchanted, as if someone had cast a spell over them.

She looked towards Audrey, smiling, wanting to share the moment. But she saw that Audrey's eyes were fixed on her two sons, on their joy and relaxed sense of fun. And a moment later she convulsed, her face creasing as if in torment, and ran from the room.

Twenty-Four

Joy was coming downstairs on her way out to work as the letters plopped in through the letterbox, and Mom came flying along from the kitchen in her apron.

'Oh good – one from Sheila!' Her voice lightened as she straightened up, pushing her hair back. 'Joy?' She turned, holding another white envelope and frowning in puzzlement. 'This one's for you?'

'Oh – is it?' Joy managed to sound casual.

The handwriting was unfamiliar – who did she ever get letters from anyway? But she had given Lawrence Dayton her address, not really imagining he would actually get in touch. Or so she had told herself. Deep down, as she remembered the look in his eyes when they parted that morning, her own feeling of . . . of what? Of excitement, of being with someone who was like no one she had ever met before . . .

'Who's that from then?'

She took the letter while Mom was watching her beadily. Martin was in the doorway of the kitchen, chewing toast and peering at them.

'Oh, I'm not sure,' she said. 'It might be someone I met – the other night.'

'Oooh,' Martin said – annoyingly. '*Migh*t be. Joy's got secrets!'

'No, I haven't,' she said crossly, slipping it into her bag. 'I've got to go – the bull's going to go off any minute.'

*

192

The letter was burning a hole in her bag as she hurried up Linden Road towards Cadbury's. They had gradually got used to the strange look of the factory: a scattering of sheep fenced in on the grass of Bournville Green, the works all swathed in green camouflage netting, the spotters up there with their binoculars, looking out for enemy planes. It was all becoming normal.

But even if she had not been used to it, Joy was oblivious to everything that morning. The letter . . . His letter? It was all she could think about. Could it be that he was in love with her, this exciting man, the way his eyes seemed to say he was?

She hurried in among all the other workers heading for the morning shift. She had to remind herself not to go to the filling room where her feet would automatically have taken her, but to the chocolate-moulding department to where she and Norma had been reassigned for war work.

It was all change at Cadbury's – quite a few employees being moved out to work at other sites and some, like herself, being reassigned within the Bournville works to 'Bournville Utilities Ltd' for the duration – and it was not chocolate they were making.

Time was short – she really needed to start working her shift – but she could not bear to go in without opening her letter. Standing to one side up against a wall, she pulled it from her bag, fumbling to get the envelope open. It was from an address in Erdington.

Dear Joy,

What an enjoyable time it was meeting you and talking and dancing! I should so like to see you again. Time off is going to be in short supply here the way things are but as it happens, it will be possible this Saturday. I could perhaps wend my way into

Birmingham? I gather there is to be a dance at the Grand Hotel. How would you like that?

Might you be able to drop a line here? I do hope we can meet!

Yours with regard and in high hopes,
Lawrence Dayton

The handwriting was neat and precise. His face came to her mind's eye: so lively and interesting, the little moustache, those strongly marked eyebrows . . . The fact that he was older made him even more exciting. Alan suddenly seemed like a child in comparison.

Heart pounding, Joy slipped the letter back into her bag. He did like her! She was flattered that this man seemed to find her as attractive as she found him. And the Grand Hotel! She nearly jumped up and down with excitement. Well, that was going to be fancy!

'Hey, what're you doing standing around here? Come on!' Norma almost jumped on her.

The bull sounded, blaring over the factory site as they scuttled inside. Instead of working in their white overalls packing up boxes of Milk Tray, they were now in dull grey ones, having had re-training to make parts for – Joy was told – aeroplanes.

'What are these things?' she asked the man supervising them.

'It's a bit of a plane,' he said with a slightly sarcastic air of patience.

'Well, I know *that*.' They had at least been told the basics. 'I'd like to know what it is that's messing up my hands, that's all.'

'You don't really need to know, love. Just do it.'

'But—'

'That little bit you're making's just part of the thing the

gun goes on, all right?' he said with a sigh. 'Look – just get on with it. There's bits of these made all over. You're just a *very* small part of a very big picture, all right?'

That, she realized, would have to do. The bloke hardly knew himself, she realized. She pulled the belt of her overall tighter, accentuating her curvy figure, gave him a wink and set to work.

'The dance at the Grand Hotel sounds very nice, thank you,' was the understatement with which she had written back to Lawrence. *'Shall we meet just outside? The hotel's right by the Cathedral so you shouldn't have any trouble finding it.'*

This time, she did not tell Norma she was going out, let alone mention who with, although she felt bad about it. She and Norma did not usually keep secrets from each other. She didn't know why she wanted to keep it all to herself but she did – and anyway, Norma had Danny and she didn't want to keep hanging about with Joy all the time, did she?

After Alan, she felt so humiliated and unwanted. How had she been so sure that Alan was in love with her when, looking back, he had not given her any sign except his smiles, his dancing with her . . . And the occasional kiss. Her angry thoughts came whirling through again. Surely if you kiss someone that means something? Honestly, Alan didn't know what the hell he was doing!

This now, with Lawrence, was exciting. She needed to feel that someone was attracted to her. She badly wanted love. But something also made her want a chance to get to know this exciting man – and without an audience.

It seemed an age until Saturday. The day dawned bright and in preparation she carefully rinsed through her favourite dance dress. Each time she caught sight of it, rippling gently on the washing line in the weak sunshine, a thrill of excitement ran through her. *Tonight! The Grand Hotel!* By evening it was just about dry and carefully pressed, the iron not too hot. She made herself up – just a touch, nothing too flashy – and polished her dance shoes, wrapping them carefully and nestling them into her bag.

In the privacy of her room, she put a touch of cologne behind each ear. Leaning towards the mirror she took a last look: her big, shining eyes, the lashes accentuated with a touch of mascara, the dark waves of her hair which she was growing, brushed and pinned away from her face and falling down her back. She gave herself a smile and the dimple appeared in her left cheek. She was ready!

'I know you're young and you want some life, Joy,' Mom said when she went downstairs. 'But I do wish you wouldn't go out. Not into Birmingham anyway.'

She looked anxious and, Joy realized, tired. She felt a pang of guilt, but nothing was going to stop her meeting Lawrence at the Grand!

'They've been over once,' she said, slipping her coat on. There had been a daylight raid on Cotteridge earlier – they had all run into the shelter. No one had told them of much damage. 'Surely that'll keep them quiet for one day?'

Her mother folded her arms, realizing she was not going to win. 'Got your torch – and your gas mask?'

'Oh yes.' She went to pick it up, hanging the box casually from her shoulder by its string. Blasted thing, having to carry that around all the time! 'Don't worry, Mom. We'll be all right. If there's any trouble we'll get to a shelter – promise.'

'You meeting Norma?' Ann asked, as Joy went to the front door.

'See you later!' She pretended not to hear and blew a

kiss as she stepped out into the smoky night. She felt bad as she walked carefully along, her eyes adjusting to the darkness. It wasn't as if she had anything terrible to hide, it was just that whatever she did, the whole family seemed determined to put their fourpence ha'penny in and she wanted a chance to get to know Lawrence in private, just for once, before the running commentary began.

It was cold and as she walked across, past the Cathedral, from Navigation Street she hoped Lawrence would not be late. But only a moment after she reached the grand frontage of the hotel, hearing the faint strain of dance music from inside, she heard footsteps and saw someone walking briskly towards her. Even in the murk she could tell it was Lawrence.

'Joy?'

'Yes.' She smiled, stepping forwards. 'That was good timing!'

Lawrence raised his hat and took her arm.

'Shall we go in? It's pretty cold out here. This is on me, of course.'

He paid the entrance fee and soon they were stepping into the grand ballroom of the hotel, with its white arches along the walls and pale, ornate ceiling. The windows were of course blacked out and shrouded with heavy curtains and it felt warm and cosy and already rather stuffy. The floor was more than half full of couples, a rhythmic mass of movement, all dancing the cha-cha-cha as she and Lawrence walked in.

'Shall we wait for the next?' he smiled at her as they stood at the side of the room and Joy found herself beaming back. 'I assume you are expert in every dance?'

'Yes!' she grinned. 'I am!'

She had never seen him in any sort of light and his face

was leaner and a little more weary-looking than she remembered. But there was that liveliness, and she liked the way his face moved as he talked. Excitement welled in her. Here was the atmosphere she loved best, of dance dresses and the infectious beat of the music – and she was with him! Her feet were already tapping, ready to go.

'How've you been?' he asked.

'Oh, I'm all right, thanks!'

She didn't feel she could go into detail because they had to lean close to hear each other over the music and the chatter in the room. This felt nice, as if they were already close and a couple, or at least that everyone else might think so. Close up, she could see the little ripple of the hairs of his moustache as he spoke. She enjoyed the way his eyes fastened on her, with twinkling humour, with liking. He was a cheerful person, she realized and she, also of a happy disposition, felt cheerful in return. There was liking on both sides and they laughed easily together – she remembered that from the last time they met.

The dance ended in clapping and laughter and a reshuffling of partners.

'Now, you are mine for the night – agreed?' Lawrence asked. It was said with humour, nothing more. 'I might as well make sure I bag the best dancer in the room for myself!'

'Oh, I don't know about that,' Joy laughed. But she knew that if it was not true, it could be true and she was on her mettle to dance her very best.

'I don't imagine we'll be jitterbugging in here,' he said, looking round at the rather respectable-looking crowd. 'I'm not sure I'm up to that. Can you do it?'

She nodded, laughing. 'Oh yes – it's fun! I can do them all!'

Lawrence looked rather worried. 'Even the tango?'

She dimpled at him. 'Has been known.' She and Alan had learned the dance together. Was that passionate dance what had misled her about him? It was all the theatre of that dance and nothing real?

'Goodness,' Lawrence said, pulling a nervous expression which made her laugh. The band started up and he made a different, relieved face. 'Ah, foxtrot – now that's one I can manage! It's been quite a while since I was let loose on a dance floor!'

But Lawrence was a good dancer. She had felt that, even dancing with no music, out under the smoke-hazy moon. He had a lithe figure, moved lightly on his feet and held her as if she was something delicate but precious, as a good dancing partner should. Joy blossomed into the familiar steps.

They moved through dance after dance, stopping every now and then for a rest and a drink – 'Just lemonade for me, thank you,' she said. 'I get thirsty when I'm dancing!' Each of them knew the steps well and did not have to think. For much of the time, she felt Lawrence's dark, amused eyes fastened on her face and before long, she was looking straight back. They made a fine couple, she knew, could sense the gaze of others lingering on them as they moved past in the dances.

Coming to the end of a waltz, they stood together clapping and smiling at the sheer joy of it.

'Wonderful.' Lawrence looked deeply at her again. It was as if he was fascinated by her, could not stop looking at her face, and she felt herself blossoming, full of excitement and energy. This was more like it – how life was supposed to be – back in the swing of things, with a handsome man gazing at her! Nothing seemed to matter except this moment, with this person about whom she knew next to nothing, and yet she could sense how much attraction was growing between them.

And then the air-raid siren went off.

They could not hear it at first but a man who worked for the hotel went over to the band and the music stopped abruptly. The sound came whining through then and a groan went round the room. The man took the microphone.

'Ladies and gentlemen, could you please make your way down to the basement . . .'

The raid did not last too long, nor, that night, was it centred on the middle of Birmingham. Joy sat on a bench beside Lawrence Dayton with the others who had taken refuge in the hotel basement – which seemed to be most people. It was warm, stuffy and crowded. She and Lawrence were crushed in, shoulder to shoulder, and the closeness was something Joy became more aware of as every moment passed. Lawrence reached out, took her hand and held it, caressing her fingers with his warm ones and she leaned into him so that they were sitting warm and close. After a time, she rested her head on his shoulder.

Twenty-Five

16 November 1940

'Here you go.' Ann laid a scrap of bacon on Martin's breakfast plate. When he leaned down, pretending to examine it through a magnifying glass, she cuffed his head fondly. 'Be grateful you're getting any! The rest's for your father – he's been up all night.'

They could hear the creak of the floor as Len moved about upstairs, getting ready for work. He had come home, pale and worn out. Joy ran downstairs, put her coat on in the hall and called through, 'Ta-ra! See you later!' The front door opened and closed.

'Can I have that bit of toast?' Martin eyed a blackened piece of bread lying slightly curled on a plate. 'I like charcoal.'

Ann made a face at him and sank down at the table, sipping tea and yawning. The sirens had gone off both of the last two nights. The target though, it seemed, had been elsewhere. The only subject on everyone's lips was the bombing of Coventry the night before last.

'We could see it, plain as day,' Len said yesterday morning, when he came in from Home Guard duty. 'The sky was all lit up. They're saying it's really bad.'

When Ann took her ration books along to the shops, everyone was talking about it. Water and gas mains hit, no water for the firemen. Fire and horror and destruction on that clear, moonlit night in an attack so ferocious it felt as if it might never end. The bulletins on the wireless described wave after wave of bombing by five hundred enemy aircraft. There was talk of reprisal for the British raid on Munich. Of mass destruction. Would they come back the next night, of the fifteenth? But no – they did not.

Len hurried out to get to Cadbury's and soon Martin set off for school. Ann sat on in the sudden quiet, hearing the clock tick. I must clear up, she thought, but could not seem to find the energy. She could go and have a little nap? But it felt all wrong when everyone else was having to be up and doing.

She drained her tea and was stacking the plates to wash up, when she heard an urgent rapping on the front door.

Outside was a tall woman not much older than herself, with dark eyes and hair, in the green uniform and dark red beret of the WVS – the letters proclaimed from the badge on the left side of her chest.

'Mrs Gilby?' There was a clipped urgency to her tone.

'Yes?' Ann's head was clearing fast.

'We need you, please.' She squinted at a piece of paper in her left hand. 'I take it you don't have young children at home?' She was well-spoken, her accent smooth and refined rather than cut-glass.

'Well, no, but . . .'

'Good. I know you put down for clothes sorting and that sort of thing, but this is an emergency and we're short. Can you come now? Well, almost now?'

'Well, I suppose I could, but . . .' Her mind was offering objections. I haven't done the washing-up and I've a wash to do and food to buy and . . .

'Splendid. They'll be here to pick you up in ten minutes. Big green sort of lorry. Wait at the end of the road, will you? I'll see you there. And wrap up warm. We're needed in Coventry. Oh – I'm Mrs Starling, by the way.'

'Ann Gilby.'

'Yes, I have you down here!'

Waving the sheet of paper, she strode back along the road.

After almost ten minutes of frantic dashing about – dressing in warm bloomers and an extra jumper under her coat, making sure she went to the lavatory because goodness knows what they were going to be doing, piling the plates in the sink and scrawling a note to leave on the table, *'WVS. GONE TO COVENTRY'*, she was as ready as she was ever going to be. And she dashed out and along to the end of the road.

A couple of moments later the vehicle lumbered into view – murky green motor cab with a square-ish, box-like extension on the back and a WVS sign at the front. As it came bowling along, Ann realized at the last moment that she was waiting on the wrong side and dashed over to the opposite pavement. The driver, a round-faced, surprisingly cheerful-looking (in the circumstances) woman, braked with an alarmed expression and swerved to a halt at the kerb. Beside her sat Mrs Starling who had called earlier. The passenger door swung open.

'Nearly bally well ran you down there! Hop in!'

'Sorry . . .' Ann had scarcely got her backside on to the seat than they drove off again, while she was pulling the door shut.

'Well done,' the driver said. 'Good for you – rather short notice.' She was a buxom person of an age Ann found hard to guess, with collar-length, curly hair of a colour somewhere between blonde and brown, spilling out around the beetroot-coloured beret. Both the other women were in full WVS uniform.

'This is Ann Gilby,' Mrs Starling said.

'Ah, well done!' the woman said, as if Ann having a name was a significant personal achievement. 'Good for you. WVS – Women of Various Sizes, as they say! There are more in the back!'

She chortled and Ann could only join in. Got a right one here, she thought, but couldn't help warming to her.

'My name's Rowbotham,' she announced, bowling the van along at slightly alarming speed. 'Mildred Rowbotham. Bit of a mouthful. I always rather fancied being called "Ann" myself. You can just stick to Mildred if you like. Or Milly if you must.'

'All right,' Ann smiled, uncertain with these two women who seemed much more confident and forceful than she was.

'Call me Edwina,' Mrs Starling said. 'I can't be doing with all this Mrs So-and-So . . .' She gave a gentle jerk of her head. Although I can't speak for the rest of them in the back.'

'What exactly do we have to do?' Ann asked.

'Well, we're extras it seems – called us up rather late. Some of the others set off before dawn,' Mrs Starling said. Ann saw that she was rather beautiful, in a dark-eyed, tired-looking way. 'They wouldn't let any of us in yesterday – we ended up in Leamington. That was a very early start, I can tell you – they telephoned me at half past two in the morning! The raid on Coventry had only just finished when we got there. And they just kept coming – all morning while we were there. Cars – everything on the roof, mattresses and so forth, prams tied on the mud-guards . . . Poor souls.'

She shook her head.

'There was bomb damage in Leamington but nothing compared with Coventry, evidently. They even bombed the Cathedral – you can hardly recognize the place. It's going to take – well, who knows how long? Water's still off and the gas. We've got some extra water on board – some of the girls have been up early making soup. We've got buns, tea, sandwiches and extra bread. We can make up more sandwiches as we go along . . . We've not used this canteen before – it's just been donated. By a bakery, evidently.'

Edwina was silent for a moment, her long face fixed looking forward with a grim expression.

'I'm really not sure quite what we're going to find. The place is overwhelmed.' She reached down for her bag.

'Here, these are for you.'

She held out a badge and armband with the WVS letters and insignia on. Ann took them and silently fixed them on to her coat.

As Mildred Rowbotham roared her way along the Coventry Road in the grey, overcast morning, they saw numerous other vehicles leaving Birmingham in the same direction: police vehicles, fire engines and a variety of other types of mobile canteens. They sat silent for most of the journey. The solemn faces of the other women made Ann's innards twist with nerves.

They smelt Coventry before they could see it. The windows of the vehicle were open a crack and a rank, burned smell started to seep in. As they grew closer, a mucky pall hung over the city and acrid, smoke-filled air rasped into their nostrils, the stink growing stronger all the time.

And coming the other way, there were people walking at the side of the road. Many who did not own cars or other means of transport were only now getting out. Some were individuals, others family groups, draped in blankets or whatever they had been able to salvage, some pushing perambulators or wheelbarrows piled with objects. They were grey with dust and all looked shocked and haunted. They stared longingly at the canteen, a few calling out to them, raising an arm to try and get them to stop.

'Should we park up here?' Mildred Rowbotham asked. Her pink face now wore a stern, shocked expression. 'These poor souls look as if they could do with a cuppa.'

'Well . . .' Edwina Starling hesitated. 'We were told to go into the centre – it's not far now. I think we'd better press on.'

As they travelled further in, there were more people streaming out along the road, more signs of damage and window glass blown out all along the streets. The pall of dust and smoke thickened as they drew nearer to the centre of Coventry. The further they drove, the more rubble there was in the road and Mildred Rowbotham was swerving round bricks and lumps of masonry.

Ann narrowed her eyes, coughing in the stench of it, hardly able to make sense of what she was seeing ahead of her. It did not seem to be a city at all – more a tangle of ruins and masonry. They all quietly took in the shocking sights around them, the enormity of the chaos and destruction. Buildings left with charred, skeletal timbers pointing at the grey morning sky, and piles of rubble. Rescue workers were still toiling around the buildings; here and there, tucked in as discreetly as possible, lay a body covered by some salvaged covering. There seemed to be nothing to say – it was too much to take in, how the shape of what would be considered a normal city, the streets and buildings, shops and lights and factories, were now smashed into something close to unrecognizable.

People were searching among the rubble, distraught or aimless, moving in a strange daze, as if they must move, must do something, but could not think what.

'The poor dears,' Edwina Starling murmured. 'Poor, poor dears.'

And as they inched their way slowly round a corner, people in the street staring, dazed, at them, Mildred Rowbotham gasped, a hand going to her mouth, her eyes wide, unbelieving.

'Oh – the *utter* barbaric *bastards*!'

They were faced by the gutted remains of Coventry Cathedral.

Twenty-Six

Mildred parked up within sight of the department store Owen Owen, which at first Ann thought had got away unscathed as she could see the shop sign against the sky. Later, taking it in more closely, she could see that its roof was gone. Even though by now the fires had all been put out, a thin trail of smoke was still seeping out through the blackened windows.

When Edwina opened up the back, Ann saw the two other members of their team who had been perching on stools and clinging on during the journey and both looked relieved to be let out. One was a quiet, plump woman whose name Ann did not catch; the other a tiny insect of a person in steel spectacles, called Dorrie Rudge.

There was no time for small talk and they immediately got busy, handing out soup – some very thin vegetable concoction, kept warm in an urn with rugs wrapped round it – and buns and sandwiches and tea. Ann, who was put in charge of the urn, handed out cup after cup of tea – the thing people seemed to want most – and Dorrie was kept busy rinsing out cups in a tin bowl for re-use.

They worked like mad. As well as the lack of water, there was no gas supply in the city, and many people had lost their homes. The queues never ended, of dust-covered, distraught people. Ann was glad she did not have too much time to stop and absorb the terrible reality of sights and sounds around her – the bodies she knew must be being recovered, the hysterical weeping she could hear from somewhere in the distance. But the thing that she could not shut out, that none of them could, was the stench. The mixture of charred things, the whiffs of gas and hints of something much worse mixed in with it – a foul, animal smell like burning meat – was something her mind did not want to linger on even for a second, but she could not escape it either.

She felt almost overwhelmed by the number of people – they seemed to keep coming and coming, all of them shocked, either into a sort of stunned silence, or chattering endlessly from nerves.

A lady approached the van, a stout, matronly person with black, oily hair pinned back with a grip on one side. She wore rough, patched clothes and what looked like an army trench coat from the last war draped over her shoulders and almost reaching the ground. She was carrying a child in her arms, between one and two years of age, Ann gauged, and a gaggle of others – six more – all following, like a mother goose with her brood.

'Ooh – a cuppa'd see me right, that it would!' she said, with surprising cheerfulness, revealing few remaining teeth.

Oh Lor', Ann thought. They had just run out. She felt terrible.

'Here, children,' Mildred said from beside her. 'There are a few buns left – you share these out between you. There's a drop of milk for the little ones as well.'

The eldest girl, a skinny thing who looked about thirteen, took the buns and solemnly broke them into pieces for the rest.

'I'm ever so sorry,' Ann was saying, when they heard the rumble of an engine and a miraculous sight met her eyes behind the woman who was looking up at her.

'Water!' the bloke shouted from the cab. 'D'yer want some?'

'Do we just!' Mildred boomed at him. 'You're a lifesaver!'

'You'll 'ave to get it out the cut if you want any more,' a middle-aged ARP warden called out in passing. His face was so filthy with brick dust and soot it was not possible to see what he really looked like.

'I'm afraid you'll have to wait while it heats up,' Ann said to the woman as Edwina and Dorrie filled the urns.

'Oh, that's all right, bab,' the woman said.

'Have you lost your house?' Ann asked carefully.

'Well – summat's come through the roof at the back and we ain't got water – or gas. It's just over there.' She jerked her thumb vaguely. 'We're doing the best we can, but . . . What with this lot . . .' She cast an eye over her gaggle of children. 'Me ole man was on fire watch at Herbert's while it was going on but 'e come 'ome again, thank the Lord. So we're all right, but not as all right as we'd be if we could 'ave a cuppa, and any road I saw you girls and I thought, I'll see to all this when I've 'ad a cuppa. I'll just sit down over there and give this one a bit of a go.'

She wandered over to a remaining lump of wall, sat down, tucked the smallest child on her lap and reached into her blouse to latch the suckling child on. The other children stood round, chewing on bits of bun.

'Well, she's got her work cut out,' Edwina said. 'Right, come on, ladies – let's knock up the last of the sandwiches while we're waiting for the water. At least there's a bit of meat paste left.'

It had not taken long for them to be on first-name terms even though Ann was having a bit of trouble getting her mouth around 'Edwina'. But she was grateful. Two of them at a time would take food or drinks through the hatch from outside and help hand them round. Inside, the other three who stood crammed into the small space of the canteen with its paraffin stove and urns and fast-emptying trays of sandwiches and buns had to work carefully so as not to trip over each other. It was all very close and intimate and soon they were working well as a team, familiar with each other in a way which Ann realized would have taken many weeks in different circumstances.

She spooned tea for the urn and was starting on the sugar when Ann found her arm grabbed by her tall companion.

'Ah no, don't put the sugar straight in the top!' Edwina instructed. 'You'll never get it mixed in. Look – we make a syrup.'

She picked up a jug, tipped sugar in and mixed it with a measure of hot water from the urn.

'There you are.' Edwina handed the jug to her and they exchanged smiles. Ann liked Edwina – she had no airs about her and was rather beautiful in her bony way. 'You can pour it in now.'

'Thanks.' Ann poured the syrup into the urn, then went to the serving hatch. Mildred Rowbotham was handing sandwiches to another little woman who looked a poor thing, with several children.

'Take some tea over to her, will you?' she said to Mildred, nodding towards the stout madonna seated on the wall. She watched, smiling, as the woman raised her hands to take the tea as if it was a sacred gift and gave a toothless grin.

A pale young woman was at the head of the tea queue with a toddler perched on her hip. She looked exhausted.

'Tea?' Ann said. 'What about a drop of milk for the little one?'

'Yes, please.' The woman was quite young, rather

211

pretty, with ginger hair. As Ann was pouring she started talking, but not as if she was addressing her words to anyone in particular.

'It was ringing out all night . . . The bells – every hour. And the hymns it plays . . . Just like normal, you see, so I thought . . . I heard it last night as well, I'm sure I did – I mean, it can't have gone, can it – not if it was going on all night?'

Ann saw Edwina Starling's face as the woman talked – full of sadness and pity. A lot of people were saying it. Not the Cathedral. How could they have hit our Cathedral? Because in this city they had all known, all the narrow streets and pubs, shops and alleys, of all the familiar landmarks, that was the one that had stood tallest and longest, which could be seen for miles around, ringing out the hours and pointing proudly to the heavens.

'We've run out of everything now,' Edwina Starling said. In the shadow of the van her long face looked stretched further by exhaustion. 'I think we'd better wend our way back – there are others coming with new supplies.'

Gradually as the day wore on, more and more vehicles had been arriving bringing relief to the city in the form of hot tea and food. It was almost dark when they drove slowly into Birmingham. The journey back felt very different to Ann from the one going, this morning, which now felt like several lifetimes ago.

'Let's see if we can get home before those Kraut buggers start on us all over again!' Mildred Rowbotham said. 'After what I've seen here today, I'd string up the whole bloody lot if I could lay hands on them!'

Both Ann and Edwina Starling had, by the end of the day, got used to Mildred Rowbotham's colourful outbursts. In the circumstances they felt much the same and a bit of swearing didn't seem like the worst thing in the world.

The journey home, despite them all being tired out, was far more talkative than when they set off. Ann sat pressed up against the passenger door and shoulder to shoulder with Edwina Starling, seeing the darkening Warwickshire fields slide by outside and full of a strange feeling she had not felt for a long time. She clasped her dusty hands in her lap, trying to remember when she had felt like this before. This sense of excitement, of being fully, truly alive. Realization flooded her – and guilt. It was when she had met Tom Somers. That had given her this same feeling of being wide awake – of being in love with life and of it having truly *started*.

She drew in a deep breath, trying to push Tom from her mind. He was like a ragged end in her life, a door never quite closed. She had never written and told him about all that had happened after that afternoon in the Midland Hotel. About Martin, who arose out of that beautiful, enshrined memory of a time out of time, of love, with the man she truly loved . . .

I can't, she said to him, that afternoon as they lay, so close and warm in those timeless few hours, both of them wanting it just to go on and on. *I'm sorry, I just can't do it – to Len, to the girls . . .*

'Are you all right?' she heard Edwina say, in her smooth voice.

'Oh yes – thank you,' Ann said. 'Not as tired as I'd've thought I'd be.'

'You'll come down with a crash later, I expect – it tends to take you like that, when you've been all strung up and on the go all day.'

'And half the night.' She laughed.

How strange it was that they were all so comfortable

213

together, Ann thought. They had had the most terrible day, in one respect – but why did it feel like one of the best days of her life? As if she had just woken up?

'You've children, I suppose?' Mildred called across to her.

'Yes, three,' Ann said. 'My son, the youngest, is fourteen.'

'And what are they all up to?' Mildred enquired heartily.

'We've all worked at Cadbury's,' Ann said. 'All of us – except Martin, so far.'

'Ah, Cadbury's,' Edwina said. 'I believe they're very good employers?'

'Oh yes – they are,' Ann agreed. Normally she would never have asked questions of women like this but now it didn't seem to matter. 'What about yourselves?'

'Children – me?' Mildred laughed heartily. 'No, no, sooner have a horse, any time! I work for Dowd and Hutchinson, the solicitors. Mr Dowd's personal secretary, no less, or I was before the war – still am, some of the time. The poor darling would forget his own name if I didn't remind him.'

She had to bellow a bit to be heard over the sound of the engine.

'When all this lot started, I thought well, I'm not going to just moulder away in these blasted offices for the rest of my life – there are *things to be done*. So I told him, "Look, Mr Dowd, I'm going to do my bit for the war effort. I'll stay on here part of the time and work three days – that'll keep things in order." There's another old girl in the offices, been there since the Ark, so between them they'll have to keep things under control.'

'How did he take that?' Edwina Starling asked, sounding amused.

'Like a lamb, in fact. Do him good to be reminded what it is I do all the time. I'll be back when this shooting match is over – he knows that. In fact, he said, "Good for you, young lady." He thinks anyone is young if they're under fifty, which has its flattering side, of course.'

'You learned to drive though?' Edwina said.

'Horseboxes – and the odd tractor,' Mildred replied, as if this needed no further explanation. She turned to Edwina Starling. 'What about you?'

'Oh – I haven't worked for years. Brought up our two sons. My husband is at the university. I mean, I rather wanted something like that myself – academic life, teaching and so on, but . . .' She shrugged in a self-mocking way. 'That was not to be. I married, the boys came along rather quickly and . . . Well, that was that. The boys are both in the RAF now.'

Ann listened to the wistful tone in her voice – something she would never have guessed of, this past and these feelings, had they not just spent the day working together at full tilt. She felt a swell of great liking for both of them.

'Right, Ann,' Mildred said as they chugged their way into Bournville. 'I can drop you off almost where I picked you up! We seem to have got you back before the blasted siren goes off anyway!'

Once again she pulled up so abruptly that they were all thrown about and Ann slithered down to the pavement.

'Ann –' Edwina leaned out as Mildred revved up once more – 'can I put you down for relief work again?'

'Yes!' Her eagerness surprised even herself. 'Course you can!'

'Toodle-pip then!' Mildred called through the window. 'See you soon!'

Smiling, Ann watched the squat shape of the vehicle

disappearing into the blacked-out gloom. How blessed she felt to be back here, walking along the familiar street to her own house. She would have to rustle up something to eat, quickly. And perhaps she would soak her feet in a bowl of hot water. It was a blissful thought.

But the reality of the day, the horrors and fears and griefs of Coventry began to fall in on her now she was alone. She went to open the front door, feeling for the lock in the darkness, and found she could barely get the key into it, her hand was shaking so much.

Hardly had she shut the front door behind her when Joy came rushing out from the kitchen.

'Mom – what on earth's going on? Where've you *been?*'

Martin followed her and Len, who was smiling mysteriously.

'Look who's here!' he said.

Sheila came into the hall, carrying Elaine.

'*Sheila?*' Ann could not make sense of anything. 'What on earth're *you* doing here?'

Twenty-Seven

'Well, you've come out of the frying pan into the fire coming back here, all right!' Ann said.

'I came on the spur of the moment – to get out of the way,' Sheila said.

'Oh Lainy – look at you, darlin'! Come and give Nanna a love!'

But Ann realized Sheila was looking strangely at her and Elaine, instead of tipping herself happily into her arms as she would have done before, clung fearfully to Sheila.

'You haven't forgotten your nanna, have you, babby?' Ann hardly realized that she was trembling all over, nor that there were suddenly tears trickling down her grimy cheeks. She felt drifty, detached from herself.

'Mom!' Sheila said, with mounting concern. 'Are you all right? I don't think Lainy quite knows who you are. Your face is absolutely filthy – and you're . . . What's happened?'

Ann looked round and saw that her whole family were standing crushed into the hall, staring at her in bewilderment. All she could think was, we're here, all together – my family. Suddenly, she felt as if her legs would not hold her any longer.

'I need to sit down,' she said faintly. She groped her way into the front room and fell into a chair. Curling forward, she then burst fully into tears.

*

'Ann? Annie?'

Len was kneeling by the chair looking up into her face, his eyes wide and frightened. He took her hands which were clenched in her lap and held them between his own. They felt warm and comforting and started to bring her back to herself.

The children were standing round, watching, all really worried. They had never seen her break down before, not Mom – she wasn't much of a crier in the general run of things. Joy had run to get her a hanky.

'Here, Mom –' She handed over the soft, cotton square and Ann buried her nose in it, saw the filth that had appeared on it when she laid it in her lap. She looked round, dazed.

'I wasn't expecting that,' she said.

'What's happened?' Len said.

Her eyes met his. 'Coventry.'

'We got your note,' Joy said. 'But . . .' She shrugged. 'Anyway, Mart and me got the tea on – just baked spud, but . . .'

Ann realized suddenly that the delicious smell wafting through the house was baking-hot potatoes and she smiled, full of love for them and the way they had all rallied round.

'Good kids,' she said.

She went upstairs to wash and saw what they meant – a swarthy-faced stranger stared at her from the mirror, coated with filth, the way the inside of her mouth had felt full of dust all day, and now her cheeks were also smeared by her tears – what a sight!

Elaine was prepared to go to her for a cuddle when she came down after a wash and found everyone sorting out the tea – Len laying the table, Joy and Martin bustling about in the kitchen. It was a quite new feeling – a lovely feeling.

'I could get used to this,' she joked, beginning to feel more like herself.

They had the potatoes with a scraping of leftover stew and some cabbage, all well sprinkled with pepper.

'This tastes like the best meal I've ever had!' she said as they sat round the table.

'Ha flaming ha,' Joy said.

'No, I'm not joking,' Ann beamed at her.

'It's because you didn't have to cook it yourself,' Sheila said.

'And I cooked the cabbage with hardly any water,' Joy said. 'Nanna told me it's s'posed to be better.'

'It is,' Len agreed, eating hungrily. 'More flavour.'

'I made blancmange,' Martin said. He pronounced it 'blank-mange'. 'It's chocolate.'

'Oh, that won't've set yet,' Joy said. 'You only did it after school.'

Ann smiled round at them, alight with the sense of being alive, safe in her own house, with her family. When they asked about Coventry, she hardly knew where to begin.

'I've never seen anything like it . . .' Tears rose in her eyes again. 'Complete . . . devastation. No one knows where they are – I mean, the middle of the city's all smashed up. So much destroyed, burned. And all these poor people wandering about like lost souls. All we could do was offer them a cup of tea and a bun . . .'

'Oh, that cup of tea'll mean a lot,' Len said.

Ann looked round the table, seized inside by a cold, terrible fear. If that was what they had done to Coventry, where there were a lot of factories, surely

Birmingham must be next? But she did not want to say this, not now.

'Anyway, Sheila, let's hear about you.' She turned to her. 'How long're you staying?'

It was lovely to have Sheila and Elaine home and they spent a relaxed Sunday – until the siren went off in the evening.

'Oh, blast it!' Len said, shooting off upstairs to get into his Home Guard uniform.

'Have you got to go?' Ann asked Martin.

'No, not tonight.'

'Thank heavens for that.' The thought of Martin having to head off into a raid after what she had seen in Coventry would have been almost too much. So far though, Martin had done some bits of message-carrying on his bike around Bournville and Selly Oak and nothing worse than a puncture had happened to him. But now Joy had said she was soon switching to the night shift at Cadbury's so that would be someone else to worry about. At least tonight most of them were together.

'Put the kettle on, Joy!' she called, running to get the rugs for the shelter. The siren jarred her exhausted nerves into action again. 'Martin, run down to Nanna and Grandad's and see if they want to come and sit with us, as Sheila and Elaine are here? Tell them I'm making tea.'

Martin soon came back with his grandparents, already in their coats and hats and carrying blankets. They all trooped along to the shelter. The criss-cross of searchlights always made the darkness below seem even deeper and the air was cold and dank.

'Mind that loose bit of paving,' Ann reminded them all as they stumbled along, single file.

'I've brought some biscuits – and a bit of leftover cake,' Ann heard Margaret say into the dark garden.

'You don't have to feed us,' Ann said, smiling to herself. Margaret always went about like a one-woman mobile canteen.

'Oh, it's too much for Cyril and me – isn't it, Cyril?'

'Oh yes,' his jovial tones came out of the gloom. 'You know me – I never eat cake.' Cyril, who had a good tummy on him, was especially fond of cake – and chips. If there was one thing he could cook, it was chips.

'Anyway, it's got a bit of desiccated coconut in – I found it at the back of the cupboard.'

'Ooh – thanks, Nanna,' Martin's voice came from behind them.

'Bucket-guts,' Joy said, half-shouting over all the racket.

'I'm a growing boy if you don't mind.'

It was far too early and noisy to think of sleep. They all got settled, squeezed on to the little benches. Sheila settled a sleepy Elaine down in the far corner all cuddled up in blankets and sat by her. Margaret sat next to Sheila who had Joy on the other side of her by the door. Ann sat between Cyril and Martin on the other side.

'So this is how it is most nights now, is it?' Sheila said. But she sounded pleased to be home all the same.

'Quite a few, bab, yes,' Cyril said. 'You ain't missing much.'

'Except my family,' Sheila said.

Joy ran inside when there was a lull after a while and made tea for everyone.

Ann felt rather like a princess, sitting there in the shelter with everyone waiting on her all of a sudden. The Tilley lamp was on the stool in the middle. Martin was reading a book by torchlight.

'You'll strain your eyes doing that,' Ann said fondly, leaning to look round at him. How lovely he was, she thought, seeing his long, thin face – so much his father's shape of face – accentuated by the torchlight.

'Better feed me more carrots then,' Martin said, going on with his reading. 'I've got to do it – it's homework. *Macbeth.*'

Ann and Margaret made faces at each other, as if to say, *Oooh, Macbeth!* Martin was the only one who had shown any sign of wanting to go to the grammar school and had passed with flying colours. Sheila was always middling and unambitious and Joy had always been far more interested in dancing and games lessons than anything else.

'How's the little 'un, Sheila?' Cyril said. 'She asleep?'

'She's fine thanks, Grandad,' Sheila said. 'She'll sleep through anything!'

There had already been some muffled thumps and bangs from a distance when Joy's voice came from outside.

'Open the door, quick!'

Ann let her in. 'What the hell've you gone and brought that for?' She started laughing at the sight of Joy trying to balance the tray of cups and saucers and the teapot in its cosy. 'This isn't a garden party, you know!'

'All right, all right!' Joy said crossly. 'I just don't know where the Thermos is. If you get that lamp off the stool I can put it down. It's tea, all right? Let's just drink it and not complain!'

'Here. Offer these round . . .' Margaret leaned and handed over her food parcel.

'Thanks, Mom,' Ann said. It was very comforting having Margaret and Cyril there.

As Joy poured the tea, the noises from outside started to build. They all sat quiet, huddled up, waiting until it passed. Soon she was going to be hearing this in the factory, she thought.

'I wonder where they're going,' Sheila said on an outrush of breath as the planes moved further north.

'Why did you come home?' Ann said. 'Not that I'm not pleased to see you – and little 'un, of course. But you mustn't stay, Sheila . . .' Her mind flashed terrible images of Coventry. 'It's only going to get worse.'

'I know. I just wanted to see everyone,' Sheila said, holding her cup and saucer up close to her face. Ann could see Joy's eyes shining in the lamplight as she leaned forward, sipping tea, watching Sheila. She looked so beautiful. Sheila looked lovely too. Everyone looked especially extraordinary tonight, she realized.

'You getting on all right down there, bab?' Cyril asked. 'It's kind of them to have you.'

'Yes – the lady's very nice and I know it's much safer down there. But I don't like being there at weekends.'

'Why not?' Martin said, looking up from his book.

'It's *him*,' Sheila said. 'He's only there at the weekend – he stays in London all week.'

'But London's having raids all the time, isn't it?' Joy said.

'I know.' Sheila shrugged. 'It's all a bit peculiar. But it's none of my business, is it? It makes me wonder about him – I mean, who in their right mind would stay where there are air raids like they're having if they can go home?'

'Well, you, for a start,' Martin said.

Sheila reached over to slap his knee playfully and Martin dodged, laughing. Ann smiled – it was like when they were kids again.

'He's not being funny with you, is 'e, love?' Cyril said.

'Cyril!' Margaret said, horrified.

'Well, we don't want our Sheila living with some nasty bloke, do we?' Cyril protested.

'Funny?' Sheila said, as it slowly dawned on her what he meant. 'Oh Lord, no. Not like that.'

'D'you think he's got a "mistress"?' Joy said, in dramatic tones.

Sheila looked shocked. 'Surely not! He wouldn't! He's a barrister – very respectable. He's just – I don't know.' She hesitated, as if about to say something, but stopped herself. 'He's *odd*. I can't work him out. Very charming – but just . . .'

'What?' Ann said, draining her teacup.

'I'm just not comfortable with him. Obviously he doesn't want me there, except to keep her company in the week. Sometimes he's just not very nice.'

'But *she*'s all right?' Ann said.

'Yes, she's nice. And when it's just her and me and the children it can be quite good. But as soon as he comes home I feel I'm in the way and she's not at all relaxed.'

'Is there another drop in that pot, love?' Ann held her cup out to Joy who filled it. 'Thanks. I'm parched. Maggie, Cyril – there's a bit more?' They shook their heads.

'I hear you went dancing?' Margaret said to Joy, once they had sat in silence as another rumble of planes passed overhead. 'I know you want a bit of life, but is that a good idea?'

'They had a shelter,' Joy said. 'We were at the Grand Hotel.'

'The Grand Hotel!' Ann exclaimed. 'You never said!'

'Who with?' Sheila said. 'I thought Alan had joined up.'

'He did, damn him,' Joy said. 'Never even told me he was going.'

'It is a bit peculiar, isn't it?' Margaret said. 'I wonder why?'

'I don't know.' Joy frowned. 'Anyway – I shan't be able to go for a bit now. Working night's'll put paid to that.'

'I asked you a question,' Sheila persisted.

Joy was still leaning forward, resting her elbows on her knees. Her eyes shone round at them all with a look of mischief. But it was more than that, Ann saw suddenly. She looked really lit up.

'You went with Norma didn't you?' Ann said.

'Well, I mean, we did go dancing but I wasn't dancing with her . . .' She was relieved they couldn't see her flaming cheeks in the dark of the shelter. She didn't like telling fibs – wasn't used to it. She was trying to protect them really, from worrying at her going out on her own – but it didn't feel very nice.

Ann watched her. What was going on? Joy was looking coy – but happy. She was definitely hiding something.

'Well, that's nice, bab!' Cyril said. 'I'm sure there's many a lad'd be over the moon to dance with you.'

'I did meet one lad.' Lad didn't seem quite the right word for Lawrence. 'He was the best dancer but he's not from Birmingham. He's been sent up from Southampton to work at the Spitfire factory.'

'Cor!' She had Martin's attention now. 'I wish I could go and work there!'

'Well – one day, lad,' Cyril said. 'Bright boy like you.'

'Yes, but going out in raids,' Margaret said, passing round a packet of custard creams. 'It's bad enough with Len but then he's doing his duty . . .'

'It's not that bad,' Joy said. 'There are shelters near.'

'But . . .' Ann started, but could not think what she wanted to say. A sense of panic was rising in her that she couldn't really explain – a feeling that Joy was not telling them everything. The very word 'Southampton' pulsed in her mind, colliding with her own private memories. Weren't there enough other lads Joy might have met at Cadbury's? 'Is he the one wrote you that letter?'

'It was just to arrange to go dancing again, Mom!'

'But,' Ann protested, 'he could be anyone!'

'Well, he is anyone!' Joy laughed – just a little bit too much, Ann thought. 'Or someone, anyway! He's just a good dancer – someone to go with when he can get away from Castle Bromwich, which isn't that often. Honestly – that's all. Most lads are proper clodhoppers and it's nice to find one who isn't. And like I say – I can't really go any more now, so I'm glad I had a go when I could.'

'Well, that's nice, bab,' Cyril said, putting his arm round her and giving her a squeeze. 'But you just be careful, eh?'

They all fell silent, their faces very sober as another collection of explosions took place somewhere in the distance.

'Where d'you think that was?' Margaret said, once it had passed over.

'West of here, somewhere,' Cyril said. 'I wonder what they're after this time.'

'I hope Len's all right,' Margaret said. 'It makes you feel so useless, just sitting here like this.'

Twenty-Eight

Lawrence was waiting for her at Selly Oak station. Joy dashed along the Bristol Road that Sunday afternoon, afraid she was late and getting all hot and bothered in her coat. She wanted to spend every possible moment with him . . .

This time she had really told Mom a big fib, saying she was meeting Norma and some of the other Cadbury girls for tea and a natter. She had recently started working the night shift and, after sleeping it off in the mornings, the afternoon was a precious time for catching up with things and seeing anyone she could. But the knowledge that she was not being truthful sat heavily inside her, like something bad she had eaten. Why did she feel she needed to hide the way she felt about Lawrence? Some instinct she hardly understood told her to keep their meetings secret. It was his age, she decided, as she rushed along Linden Road. Mom wouldn't like that. And was it because of Alan – the way things with him were somehow not finished? She pushed those thoughts from her mind.

The last time she and Lawrence had met was at the dance cut short by the raid. Afterwards he had walked her back to the tram stop. They did not hurry, walking arm in arm, talking lightly, laughing. Wrapped in that intimate cloak of darkness, Joy felt her desire and excitement at being with him grow. She was intensely aware of the feel of his arm pressed against hers.

At the same time she could hardly believe it was

happening, that she was really there . . . Almost as if she was someone else watching herself from the outside. They stopped to look up at the grand edifice of the Cathedral, a darker solidity in the night's blackness.

'I must come and see it in the daytime,' Lawrence said, leaning his head back. 'It looks very fine, though it's hard to make much of it out like this.'

His face was a pale smudge in the gloom. Joy turned to him and suddenly Lawrence pulled her fiercely into his arms. She felt the prickle of his moustache as their lips found each other's . . . It had been a while until they actually got to her tram stop and the feel of him, those kisses, his urgent, slender body in her arms . . .

And now, seeing him as she drew near the railway station, leaning on the iron rail and looking down into the cut, her whole being leapt with excitement. The shape of Lawrence's shoulders, the way he was standing, already felt so familiar and the sight thrilled her. Yet at the same time, as she went towards him, he also seemed like a stranger – and a man much older than herself. (How old was he exactly?) So that as he turned to greet her, dark eyes twinkling at her from under the brim of his hat which shaded his eyes from the wintry sun – she felt suddenly so nervous that she could hardly manage to say hello.

'Spot on time!' he said, leaning to kiss her cheek.

'Am I?' she panted. Then she admitted, 'I ran half the way here!'

'Well, it's given you roses on your cheeks at least – I don't suppose working the night shift does much for anyone's complexion.'

'I've not been doing it long enough to look like a grub!' she laughed.

She had had a hurriedly scrawled letter from him on

Friday, saying that he would most likely be able to get away for Sunday afternoon and how did she fancy a trip out of town – the train to Lichfield perhaps? She had written back explaining that she had to be back in time for the night shift, so they decided to stay nearer home and save the treat of a trip out for another time. The Lickeys, she had suggested. They could manage that.

'Well,' he said, 'now you lead the way! To the mysterious "Lickeys"!'

He took her arm and they walked, comfortably, to the tram stop, Joy explaining about the Lickey Hills, a tram ride south to the edge of the city. Lawrence, smiling down at her, looked happy and energetic as he always seemed to, as if he had a little brazier of energy burning away inside him at all times. It was one of the things she liked about him – he was someone who seemed to pull you onwards, who did not move through life with the brake on as so many people seemed to.

'I like your hat,' he said. 'Suits you.'

The hat was of dark green felt to match her green coat, with a shapely brim, her hair curling prettily from under it. She had thought carefully about shoes – her sturdy work lace-ups weren't flattering but they would have to do for walking in the country.

'Thanks,' she said pertly and gave him a smile, knowing that it would light up her face with dimples. She could see that she enchanted him – he could not seem to stop looking at her. 'I suppose we've never seen each other in daylight before, have we?'

'No!' he laughed. 'I suppose not!'

The tram appeared, trundling up the hill under the bridge, and they climbed aboard. Lawrence took her hand and held it as they sat side by side.

Joy felt sadly how different this was from being with

Alan. He had only ever touched her when they were dancing. I was kidding myself all that time, she thought, thinking he liked me. But she felt a pang of misery. Alan really had seemed keen on her – so what had happened? Had he just met that girl he was dancing with and turned his back on her? This thought really hurt. Well, she said to herself defiantly, at least with Lawrence – older, much more interesting and attractive – it was obvious that he did like her and she was basking in it!

She felt very conscious of being with him – this man, turned slightly away from her to allow him to cross one slim leg over the other, his foot in a sturdy black shoe, the weave of his black coat . . . She was filled with a feeling of strangeness. What did she really know about Lawrence? She had never even seen him in daylight before, never mind knowing anything about him or his life! He could be married with a gaggle of kids for all she knew!

But, she told herself, Lawrence seemed honest and straightforward. He would have said, surely? Or she could just ask and clear the air? But she realized she didn't want to. Now was now. She did not want to talk much about herself or hear about his life outside of these times they spent together. Who knew what was going to happen? They could all be dead tomorrow anyway.

'Here –' she fished in her bag and brought out a little bag of chocolates – 'd'you fancy one of these?'

'Not stolen goods, I presume?' Lawrence teased, peering into the bag.

'No, misshapes. Anyone who works for Cadbury's can go to the shop and get things cheap.'

Lawrence dipped in the bag and held up a chocolate.

'Hmm – this one has definitely had a mishap. What's in it?'

'Not sure.' She laughed. 'Normally I'd be able to tell

you because I know all the moulds – but the state of that one, you'll just have to suck it and see!'

Lawrence put the chocolate whole into his mouth and chewed, clowning around, pulling faces, one eyebrow raised, as if trying very hard to guess what he was eating.

'A trace of nuts, perhaps . . .'

Joy giggled. 'So – not orange cream then?'

'I think it's safe to say not orange cream.' He swallowed. 'I went into Woolworths in town – and I was on the point of buying chocolate biscuits for you until I realized that might be what you're standing looking at all day . . .'

'No – and not any more. I'm on munitions.'

'Of course you are.'

'Anyway, I went out and bought some apples instead. But I thought we might find a tea room? After a walk, of course.'

'That'd be lovely,' she smiled. She glanced out of the murky window. 'At least it's not raining.'

The Lickey Hills, at the end of the Rednal tram route, were busy with weekend people escaping from Birmingham to breathe in some fresh air and get away from air-raid shelters and sandbags and the smoke and grime in general. But there was plenty of space to spread out and wander the wooded hill paths. They stood, arm in arm, looking at the view back over Birmingham, the barrage balloons strung high over the city.

'They look like giant whales swimming in a tank, don't they?' Lawrence said, and she laughed.

'What will you do, when it's over?' Joy asked a bit later. 'Go back to Southampton?'

He looked down at her. 'It's where I live.'

231

'Do you visit much?' She felt as if she was fishing for information, which at the same time she did not want.

'Hardly get the chance.' He sighed. 'I have a nasty feeling that it being "over" is not going to happen for a long time. Look at Europe. What if they succeed – invade? Whatever Mr Churchill says, they have a lot of power on their side.'

A chill went through her, so much so that she actually shivered. 'I try not to think about it.'

'I think we all do. You could go mad. It's better just to get on with what needs doing on the day, isn't it? Look – we're here to get away from it. Let's think about something happier – anything but bombs and making aeroplanes and work in general. You tell me all about your dance-school plans!'

They walked in the cold breeze, between the bright sun and thin shade of winter trees. Joy chatted away about her dreams – premises with huge spaces, rooms with long mirrors and barres for ballet, employing a team of other teachers, halls full of couples whirling round in a floating sea of crêpe and satin . . .

Lawrence laughed and said he would be along for more lessons and soon.

'My mother taught me to dance,' he said. 'I think she just wanted someone to dance with because my father was never keen. She's still at it – tea dances and so on, even if she's partnered with another woman a lot of the time! But it was a way of entertaining my brother and me. She'd put a record on the gramophone and teach us all the steps. When I was starting off she would get me to stand with my feet on hers and teach me the steps like that!'

'Well, she must have been good,' Joy said. 'You dance very well.'

'You too. In fact, I've never enjoyed dancing with anyone as much – after my mother, of course.'

They had reached a part of the path where the ground was a carpet of sodden leaves, light straining between the mainly leafless trees. It felt private and Lawrence looked down into her eyes, suddenly intense.

'You are so lovely.' He stroked her cheek with his finger, then leaned and gently kissed her nose. 'Real peaches and cream.'

It was almost as if he hypnotized her, a cool hand placed on each of her cheeks, his lips moving towards her like someone about to taste something delicious. Any other lads she had kissed now seemed like children. She felt as if her body had woken to something powerful and grown up, a wanting which left no room for questions or shame or of any other time than the present. She wanted to pour out her feelings – I love you! She was full up with feeling, but perhaps he'd think she was just a silly thing, coming out with that?

Lawrence kissed her again, then he drew back and looked down at her.

'There's something I need to say,' he said.

'You're married, I suppose?' The words just dropped out of her mouth, though as if half-joking.

His head jerked back in surprise, almost as if she had hit him. He looked straight into her eyes.

'Yes,' he said.

She was dumbstruck for a moment, then rage lit in her and she pushed him away, hard, recoiling back from him. 'Yes? What do you mean, yes?'

Lawrence shrugged. 'I mean, *yes*. I am married. I have been married for two years to a woman called—'

'No! Don't tell me – I don't want to know!' She could feel tears brimming in her, the rage turning to a sad, limp feeling of hurt and more hurt. Of course – how could she have been so silly? She turned away, facing the thin trunk of tree, the curled, mustard-coloured fringes of lichen on the bark. 'So what the hell are you doing here with me?'

'I'm . . .' He stumbled, his voice soft, emotional. 'I'm . . . in love with you. You're so beautiful I can't stop thinking about you.'

'Oh, can't you?' She swung round, so upset she could hardly speak. 'What am I then – your little factory girl, your bit on the side?'

Lawrence held his hand up to stop her. He looked truly upset.

'Look, I can understand how you feel. It's not . . . I'm not usually someone who . . . Only, these days . . . I saw what happened – at the factory in Southampton. The Supermarine. It was – a horror. So many dead – just like that . . .' As he spoke, his voice roughened with emotion.

'Jen, my wife, is a nurse at the General. I don't know – she doesn't know – if any of us are going to make it through the night every night. I don't know when I can go back there again . . .' He stopped, turning his face up to the sky. 'Call me a wicked person. A fool. But I'm just trying to have a little bit of life while I still have one. And quite honestly, I sort of hope she's doing exactly the same – even if I don't necessarily want to know about it.'

'But you are married? You *want* to be married – to her?'

'Yes, I do. In normal times I would not be here. None of this would be happening. But nothing is normal. We are living in a . . . a sliver of time . . . Something so frail, like a candle flame that might be blown out at any moment. And when things go back to normal – if they do – it will blow out this flame, as if it had never been.

But for now, that's where we are living. And in that flame I can only see you.'

Joy stared at him, moved. She had never heard logic spoken of quite like this before. Take every moment – you might be dead soon. All the things she had been brought up to take for granted, that faithfulness and vows and marriage – everything considered sacrosanct and respectable – were suddenly set against the fact that death was falling from the sky every night. It was as if her head was spinning. She could see Lawrence today – and never more after this. He might never see his wife again. None of them might reach the next dawn . . . Something shifted in her.

Today is today. It's all we might ever have. And she stepped into his arms. They stood embracing and kissing for a long time.

'Do you get frightened?' she asked him later as they wandered down to the tea room on Bilberry Hill. 'During the raids, I mean?'

'Yes. Of course.' He paused. 'Sometimes we're working – and we just carry on. It's vital we get production up. If you have something to fix your mind on it's not quite so bad, in a way. If you go to the shelters – well, you're just stuck there, like a sitting duck . . .'

'We play cards – at home, I mean. Or Ludo. My brother – he's really brainy – he reads. And my nan and grandad come and sit with us sometimes. We try to talk and keep our minds occupied – but you know it's getting worse when everyone goes quiet.'

Over the teacups in the old tea room, she said, 'This was built by the Cadburys as well, you know – Barrow Cadbury. He gave this land round here to the city, as a park.'

'Goodness,' Lawrence said, pouring milk into the cups. 'Is there anything in this city not donated by the Cadbury family?'

'A few things.' She laughed. She watched his hands. Even the sight of him handling his teacup filled her with desire. This was just the passing flame he had talked about, she told herself – exciting, burning, but destined to die.

She knew then that the words she might have said, if everything were different – *Lawrence, will you come and meet my family?* – were never going to come out of her mouth. Because they could not know, and she could not have him, not for the rest of their lives. She could only live here and now and burn within this consuming flame – of this time out of time of war, of the strength of her feelings – or walk away from him, for ever.

Twenty-Nine

'Don't be silly,' Audrey had said, before Sheila left for Birmingham for the weekend. 'Of course I'll come and collect you when you get back! The boys'll be at school and you can't walk all the way up here carrying Lainy and all your things.'

They had agreed on the train Sheila would catch and sure enough, Audrey was sitting waiting in the car when she carried Elaine and her little case out from the station. Sheila was touched – both because Audrey had kept her promise and even more, by the smile and wave she gave when she saw them both, leaping out of the car into the greyness and drizzle. Although she knew that Audrey always tried desperately hard to be 'nice' she did seem genuinely pleased to see them.

'Hello, Sheila! Hello, Lainy, darling! That's it – pop your bag in the back and do get in. What a miserable day!'

Sheila settled Elaine on her lap and Audrey revved away down the road through the village.

'I'd like to learn to drive,' Sheila said. She had never given it a thought before but now it seemed very nice to be able to get in a car and take off on your own wherever you wanted.

'I could teach you.' Audrey glanced at her with a mischievous grin. 'No, I could – really! Maurice taught me as a matter of fact. I prefer to do the driving – he drives like a madman.' She swallowed. 'It scares the boys, but he just doesn't seem to see it.'

'All right – maybe,' Sheila said, though she was still not sure Audrey meant it – or whether she really did either.

There was a silence and then Audrey said, 'So how did you find things?'

'Well, there was a raid last night – we were in the shelter for hours. Apart from that it wasn't too bad. But our Mom's joined the WVS. They were sent to Coventry on Saturday so I didn't see her until she got back.'

'My God,' Audrey said as they waited to turn on to the main road. 'Were they handing out cups of tea and suchlike?'

'Yes, mobile canteen. She didn't say all that much . . .' Sheila found she had tears in her eyes and wiped them away quickly. The sight of Mom breaking down like that had really affected her. 'But she was upset – she just said that it was very bad.'

Audrey nodded, her face grave. 'It sounds terrible.'

'Did you have a nice weekend?' Sheila asked, out of politeness.

'Oh yes, thank you very much!'

Sheila, having the advantage of being the passenger, watched Audrey's face. More and more she could see how tense Audrey was under the bright exterior. She flashed a quick smile.

'It's very nice to have you both back though.'

Sheila could tell she meant it and it gave her a warm feeling, of welcome.

On the table, when they got in, was a letter from Kenneth.

'Oh!' Sheila practically fell on it.

'I knew you'd be pleased,' Audrey said. 'Why don't you leave her down here with me and take your bag up and read your nice letter? I'll make us a cup of tea.'

Upstairs, Sheila sank on to the bed and stared at Kenneth's looped handwriting. His letters were never exciting as such, but – and this was no exception when she opened it – always full of his steady love. And it was enough to know he was there and still all right, because all she could do was wait and worry. The tears ran down her cheeks as she read it. Going back home had brought the realities of the war much closer again.

'*I'm missing you, my lovely wife,*' he said at the end. '*Sending you all my love.*'

She had a proper little cry at that. She could still feel the love of her family wrapped round her – Nanna and Grandad as well as her own parents and Joy and Martin. They had their squabbles, of course – especially she and Joy – but they were her family.

When she went downstairs, Elaine was in her highchair eating a finger of toast. Audrey was standing with her back to the sink, just staring, seeming to be lost in her thoughts, and she did not notice Sheila straight away, padding in quietly in her slippers.

Audrey was wearing a soft brown skirt with a coffee-coloured twinset and looking neat and smart. The country Englishwoman. But her face was so tense and sad that Sheila almost found courage to ask her what was wrong. She knew it was something to do with Maurice Vellacott but she could not make sense of any of it – this charming man who could be so vile and unkind but who Audrey seemed almost to worship.

As soon as she noticed Sheila, Audrey's face lit up with her social smile.

'Ah, here we are! Let's have a cup of tea. Mrs B isn't due for half an hour, so you can tell me all about it.'

*

'Oh, *she*'s back again,' Edward said when he walked in after school that day. Charlie just put his things down and went upstairs, but Edward stared rudely at Sheila, his eyes narrowed. 'I thought she had gone for ever.'

'Don't be so rude, Edward.' Audrey bent over him, looking horrified. 'You must apologize to Mrs Carson at once!'

Sheila was about to open her mouth and say that it was all right, there was no need, but she stopped herself. Let the rude little sod apologize, she thought.

He stared at her contemptuously and said, 'Sorry,' with rude insincerity as he barged past. Audrey looked at Sheila, stricken.

'I do apologize for my son.' Dropping her voice almost to a whisper, she mouthed, *Difficult weekend.* And looked away again quickly, as if not wanting Sheila to ask anything. Which she still did not feel she could.

III

November – December 1940

Thirty

19 November, 1940

'Ah, well done!' Edwina Starling, tall and elegant in her WVS uniform, greeted Ann warmly as she came into the Methodist church hall on the Bristol Road. 'It's a nuisance not everyone having a telephone, but we seem to have all got here nevertheless!'

Ann, being one of the households with no telephone for sudden emergencies, had agreed to come on duty three nights a week.

The hall was abuzz with activity. Lines of trestle tables were arranged across it, piled with mounds of bread, bent over by busy rows of women wielding round-ended knives. The air was full of the smells of fish paste and sulphurous whiffs of hard-boiled egg.

'There's a space over there with Mrs Parrott,' Edwina Starling instructed. Seeing Ann's amused face, she laughed. 'I know, Starling, Parrott – all we need now is for Mother Goose to walk in!'

Ann saw Mildred Rowbotham across the room and they waved at each other. Mildred, pink-faced and rather harassed-looking, was wearing slacks and a tightly belted black coat.

'Are you Mrs Parrott?' Ann asked the big bruiser of a woman who had been pointed out to her, with all her hair scraped back under the WVS beret. An apron was tied over her sizeable, uniform-clad girth, and she wore black ankle boots which zipped up the front. Her face was pink and fleshy as a pork joint and she gave off an air of energy and force. Not pausing for a moment in her work of spreading, she merely turned her head.

'I am. Gladys Parrott. Who're you then?'

'Ann Gilby. I was told to come over here.'

'Grab a knife,' she instructed, nodding towards a ramshackle collection of blunt knives. Clearly she wasn't one to waste any breath but Ann liked the down-to-earth look of her. 'There's the bread.'

Ann moved in next to her and got cracking. The other women round the table smiled and said hello. They were all working so fast they scarcely had the space to talk. Ann had been working for about half an hour, spreading slices of bread with margarine at top speed on the production line of sandwiches when they heard the air-raid siren.

'Oh!' She jumped. The sound always made her feel a bit sick. 'What do we do now?'

'We keep going,' Gladys Parrott said, without even looking up.

Every so often, Mildred Rowbotham went outside and brought back a bulletin. *They're dropping flares! And incendiaries – all over the place!* Several ripe swear words accompanied what she actually said which seemed to shock some of the women, but no one commented except for a few head shakes: *Is that really necessary?* But for Mildred, it seemed that it was. And then the first bombs began to fall across the city.

Ann tried not to think about anything: of Martin, out on his bike between ARP posts; of Len and the others staring up at the skies around the Cadbury factory with

Joy working the night shift on her stamping machine; of Margaret and Cyril crouched in their shelter. It could send you mad, dwelling on things. She was glad just to pick up each stiff slice of bread and smear it with margarine, again and again.

Everyone worked like mad, piling up trays of sandwiches and buns, while others heated up urns of water for making tea. Every last crumb of bread used, they cleared the tables and hastily tidied up, while others packed everything into the vans outside, all struggling not to think about the racket going on out there.

But as Ann was wiping down the table, Gladys Parrott leaned her perspiring face close to her and said, 'Sounds bad, don't it? Got anyone out in it?'

'Everyone.' Ann straightened up, jolted into what she had been trying so hard not to think about. Explaining to this woman brought her close to tears. Gladys's ham joint face looked into hers, her stony coloured eyes seeming to see Ann for the first time. Ann saw a look of sympathy spread across her features.

'Oh, bab –' She folded her brawny arms beneath her shelf of a chest. 'Well, it's a worry, if yer let it be.'

'What about you – your family?' Ann said.

'I've three sons in the forces – Army,' she rattled off. 'And four in factories and one in a home.'

'Eight sons?!'

Gladys gave her a serious nod. 'We worked out what was causing it – eventually.'

Ann stared at her and Gladys suddenly burst out laughing, her large bust heaving.

'Look at yower face, bab! We'd've liked a girl somewhere along the line, my old man and me, but it weren't to be. All lads – and there it is. I lost another along the way – and the one went blind when he was three.'

Ann nodded, trying to take all this in. Gladys Parrott spoke about everything with a matter-of-fact flatness of tone. She was trying to think what to say when a hoarse shout interrupted them.

'Right!' Edwina Starling had her hands cupped round her mouth. She was not a woman used to shouting. 'Things are hotting up out there and we need to get going. In the first vehicle . . .' She reeled off five names. 'And in the second will be Miss Rowbotham driving, Mrs Parrott, Mrs Gilby, Miss Rudge and myself.'

'I thought this was for after the All Clear?' Ann said, looking aghast at Gladys Parrott. 'We're not going out in this, are we?'

Edwina Starling was walking past as she said it and she turned.

'We'll take cover if it gets really bad,' she said crisply. 'But there are all sorts of people out there braving their lives – ARP workers, the ambulances, rescue people – not to mention any of the poor souls bombed out of their houses. The least we can offer them is a cup of tea.'

Mildred Rowbotham's face was round and determined under her beret as she looked out through the wind-screen. Beside her were Gladys Parrott and the tiny twiglike lady with round, steel spectacles, Dorrie Rudge. Ann had scarcely yet heard Dorrie say a word, even after working all day with her before, though she was given to muttering to herself under her breath. Ann and Edwina Starling went round and climbed into the back, Edwina slamming the door closed.

They perched precariously on cork-topped stools as Mildred Rowbotham roared out along the Bristol Road. Ann tried to peer through the only window – a small rectangle in the back door.

'Yes, you can't see very much in here,' Edwina said.

'Well, that's probably for the best.'

Edwina gave a snort of laughter. 'I'm glad you have a good sense of humour.'

Do I? Ann thought. She could just see Edwina's tall outline, holding on to the stool with both hands for dear life: this woman who had been a stranger to her a week ago and yet now they were caught up in this adventure together. Because in one respect, heading out, away from the humdrum life of every day, into the unknown, felt like an adventure. And, despite being completely churned up with fear inside, Ann was also loving every minute of it.

She did not know then, though, what kind of night it was going to be.

Facing out of the back of the canteen, they could see nothing of what was ahead. But as they reached further into Birmingham they could hear the fury of explosions from outside and see the sky lit orange with flames. They slowed, crawling, swerving, and once stopped and turned round. Smoke seeped into the back, making them cough, and Ann's eyes started to smart.

'What time is it?' Ann asked, almost having to shout. They had stopped again. Edwina had a fob watch pinned to her jacket.

'Half past ten.'

They sat, uneasy, not wanting to show they were frightened, but the air was filled with the whistle of bombs and both of them would instinctively bend in half, arms over their heads. Ann felt the rough wool of her coat against her forehead as she crouched praying. *Not here, not us . . . Please . . .* A few minutes more and they crawled onwards. Peering out of the back, Ann saw a tram abandoned on the tracks in the middle of the road, and whichever way she looked there were fires burning.

'My God,' she murmured. The city was like a strange planet, like nowhere she recognized. It felt as if they had been driving for hours, twisting and turning. At last they stopped and the engine went off with a shudder.

'Right . . .' Almost instantly Mildred appeared, opening the doors. 'There's been an incident here.'

Edwina immediately went to check the paraffin urn that was heating water; they already had urns of hot tea ready, wrapped in rugs. Ann stepped down out of the back. For a moment she could see only a blackness above her. Mildred had parked in the lee of the great blue-brick span of the viaduct. She was outside, a plump, determined figure silhouetted against the flames, and with her the unmistakeable outlines of Gladys Parrott and Dorrie Rudge. Ann went to join them.

'Where are we?' she asked.

'Deritend,' Mildred said. 'One of the wardens directed me over here. It's a right mess out there.'

Behind her, Dorrie Rudge's eyes were stretched wide behind her specs. The first words Ann ever heard her say, thick with adenoids, were, 'It looks like Armageddon!'

'That's as maybe,' Mildred Rowbotham said. 'A big one's come down behind the pub over there – there are people trapped and injured. We've got work to do.'

Bewildered, shocked people started to line up outside the serving hatch. Some were draped in shawls or blankets, some were silent, others wept hysterically. Everyone was coughing in the dust and smoke.

Ann and the rest of the WVS women were kept busy, managing to move round each other in the cramped conditions of the van, trying to avoid trampling on each other's toes. Or they stood outside handing out drinks. Rescue teams were busy digging amid the rubble and dust. Dazed neighbours stood watching as the fire brigade pointed their hoses towards the inferno. There was a sense of loud chaos, the air full of smoke and dust and the stink of bombs – and still the raid was going on.

Ann took a turn outside the van, handing out tea and sandwiches. A middle-aged woman stood near her, a sheet or something half-draped round her and her hair all a tangle. She kept saying, 'I don't know where I put them. I knew on Friday but now I just can't think . . .'

An elderly couple mutely held hands, staring at the ruins of their house, and a young woman stood with two small children both clinging to her legs. She came up to the hatch and said, 'Can Tommy have a bit of milk, please?'

'Yes, of course he can.' Edwina was pouring some milk into a cup when the woman said, 'I don't know where Ada is . . .' and wandered off.

The bombardment was not easing up – in fact it was getting worse. People stood under the high arch of the railway viaduct for cover as stretchers were carried to ambulances which drove away fast, the sound of their bells fading into the general din. Ann saw some stretchers covered completely by a sheet and felt her insides twist. She was not familiar with the sight of the dead. People were still trapped under the buildings.

'Come along now . . .' An ARP warden came into view in a white steel helmet, shouting against all the noise. 'Under cover, those of you who can. It's not over yet! Get yourselves into a shelter – now!'

Just as he spoke the whistle of heavy bombs falling started again and everyone ducked, some people screaming. Ann felt like screaming herself. She just managed to hold on to herself. How much longer would this terrible night go on for? How could they keep going?

'Right,' Mildred said. 'I think we've done what we can here – we'll move on. Back in, everyone!'

Thirty-One

Ann thought her bladder might give way with fear as they drove further in under the bombs. *Don't you think we ought to go and get in a shelter somewhere?* she kept wanting to say, but it seemed she was the only one with these cowardly thoughts.

Mildred Rowbotham drove with what Ann could only admire as astonishing aplomb and courage. This time, she was in the back with Dorrie Rudge – it was silently concluded that the stools in the back might not be equal to Gladys Parrott. Dorrie, Ann decided, was a religious fanatic. The odd glint in her eyes was not just a reaction to this hellish night. All the way she kept up an intense muttering to herself of what sounded like prayers and bits of psalms. It was rather a lonely business being in the back with her because her attention was so fully fixed on the Almighty that it was like being there by yourself. Ann almost wished she was more religious herself.

They made their way to another central neighbourhood. The air was filled with dust and smoke. As they arrived, another wave of planes passed over.

'Oh, Lord Our Saviour!' Dorrie breathed.

Both of them crouched, by instinct, right down on the floor in the back of the canteen. Ann pulled herself in as small as she could, arms clasped round her legs, pressing her head on to her knees and her eyes squeezed shut while the whistle and crash, the hammering from the

251

ack-ack emplacements and the exploding and destruction, seemed to go on for an eternity outside.

'Please . . .' All she knew was the smoky smell of her skirt, the words pouring from her lips almost as if someone else had taken them over. 'Please, please . . .'

And it passed. She felt someone patting her shoulder and she reached up and grasped the hand that was reaching out to her. She had not even noticed the doors opening and Edwina coming to crouch beside her. For a moment she stayed there, each of them clutching the other's hand.

'Oh.' Ann surfaced. 'Edwina! Where's Dorrie?'

'Out there,' Edwina said. 'I came to see if you were all right.'

'Thanks, yes. I'm fine.' She felt foolish. Everyone else had got out and she had just stayed crouched in there!

Shaken, she got to her feet and for a moment they looked out. Ann gasped. Without the sheltering obstruction of the viaduct, and from a higher vantage point, they could see more. The night was full of smoke and dust and noise – sirens and bells, shouts and guns banging. Across the city the sky was red, beams of searchlights dancing across it, flames leaping from buildings not far away. And the place where they were standing – once a street, it seemed – was a wasteland, any familiar lines of the city or streets smashed into a queer, disorientating strangeness. It felt like Coventry and it filled her with a sense of dread and desolation. Would they do this to the whole country? Where would any of this end?

She saw the rounded steel hats of two ARP wardens in the glowing distance. There was a fire engine, jets of water vanishing in arcs. The water never looked enough to have any effect on such a blaze. A few people were wandering, stunned, among the rubble.

Rage suddenly filled her. An utter outrage, stronger than

fear, that this should be done to their city, their home and country. She wanted to scream and curse at the sky. And then she heard the very words she wanted to hurl at the heavens being yelled out. She turned to see Mildred Rowbotham, fist raised to the sky, bawling with all her might.

'You bastards! You evil, filthy Kraut bastards!'

The All Clear sounded at four-thirty in the morning. They stayed in the same street in the middle of Birmingham until dawn, by which time every last drop of water from their supplies had been converted into the comfort of cups of tea, passed over into trembling hands.

Ann had rinsed out cups, and made fresh urns of tea, which outlasted the food. As well as people from the houses around, shocked, shivering, but knowing they were lucky to be alive, they sustained firemen and rescue workers who stood round the canteen as if it were a candle in the darkness.

'Ta, love,' one fireman said to Ann as she handed him the one pathetic offering of help she could – sweet tea. For a moment he took his spectacles off to clean them and his eyes were round white patches. He gave her a fleeting smile and his teeth looked film-star white as well. 'Makes all the difference. Washes all the dust down.'

Eventually they packed up and began the long, difficult crawl home.

'You go up front,' Gladys said to Ann and Edwina, to Ann's surprise. The stools would have to do their best to survive. Gladys jerked her head at Dorrie who scuttled in after her.

Ann sat between Edwina and Mildred as they drove slowly through the grey, mizzling dawn, too tired to talk much. Ann felt exhausted, yet full of a jumpy kind of energy, as if she would never be able to sleep again. They had to wind their way, turning back once or twice in roads blocked by debris, hoses snaking across the rubble. All the time, there was the foul, acrid stench of burning.

Ann could still hardly believe all of it. There were people trying to rescue possessions from the rubble, others at the side of the road, whole families, walking with whatever they could carry. She saw a woman, face red with brick dust and a blanket draped over her head, pushing a pram with one arm and a child balanced on the other hip. The pram was piled with objects – pans, bits of clothing, what looked like the legs of a stool sticking out. She was a poor, thin-looking thing.

Houses and businesses were now pitiful mounds of wreckage. In one street, half blocked by rubble, they passed another canteen, a fan-shaped huddle of people standing close to it as if it were a rock in a shipwreck, some sipping from cups held between both their hands. On the side of the canteen Ann read the sign: 'Cadbury's YMCA Cocoa Van'.

'Aha,' Edwina said. 'One of yours.'

'They call them Misery Vans at work,' she said.

Edwina leaned round to look as they passed. 'When you're doing it – handing out tea and those stale buns – it seems like nothing, doesn't it. But look at them. Just the fact that someone has come to help, give something – it really does make a difference.'

'Life always looks better with a cup of tea,' Ann said. 'Although I think they hand out cocoa.'

'Same difference,' Mildred said. 'Hot and comforting. And the fact that someone's bothering. I know I'd be pleased to see us if it was me.'

Once they reached the main road it became easier to get along. The tram still stood stationary. A car had been blown right across the road on its side. As they moved further out, the chaos and damage lessened.

Ann looked down at Edwina's hands, clasped in her lap, then at Mildred, her face coated with dust and muck – they must all look like that, Ann realized. Mildred's plump face was set in a tight, serious expression. She hardly knew these women, in one way. But she found, after all they had done and lived through, that she felt a warm love for them.

'You'll be glad to get home and get some sleep?' she said to Mildred.

'No, I need to get into the office today. I promised Mr Dowd.'

'Goodness,' Ann said. 'You've got a long day ahead then. Bit of a tartar, is he?'

'Mr Dowd? Oh no!' Ann could hear something in Mildred's tone – an odd mixture of harsh and reverential – that made her look round. Even though Mildred was coated in dust, Ann thought she could see a flush of feeling spreading through her face.

'He's a very clever man,' Mildred added heartily. 'He just needs someone to organize him.'

'Sounds like my husband,' Edwina said with a chuckle.

It was as if now, away from the heart of the destruction of last night, they desperately needed to think about something else.

'What's your husband like, Ann?' Edwina asked kindly. 'He's at Cadbury's as well, you said?'

'Oh, he's . . .' What on earth do you say about your husband? 'He's quite organized really,' she said, hoping this was what was wanted. 'You know – quite practical.'

'How marvellous,' Edwina said. 'All I can say is thank heavens we have a cellar because I wouldn't have wanted to see Richard having to put up an Anderson shelter. It really doesn't bear thinking about.'

'Oh, I helped Mr Dowd with his,' Mildred said. 'He has a house in Moseley with a garden – but he's hopeless.'

'*Did* you?' Edwina said. She and Ann exchanged glances. This did seem odd. 'Does Mr Dowd have a family?'

'Oh no . . .' Mildred said briskly. 'A confirmed bachelor – and he's rattling around in that great big house . . .'

'It sounds as if he's in need of a good woman,' Edwina said. Ann could see that she was half-joking, but Mildred Rowbotham suddenly made her face a blank and looked away, though not before a look of pain – of longing – had crossed her face.

Oh dear, Ann thought. She found herself suddenly close to tears. After this night, emotions were raw. But she recognized that longing, knew it of old, like a familiar pain.

Mildred turned the van in at the side of the church. It felt like years since they were last here.

'Well,' Edwina said, in the quiet as the engine died. 'Who's on tonight?'

'Me, as ever,' Mildred said. Drivers were in short supply.

'And me,' Ann said.

Edwina drew in a deep breath and released it slowly. Her dark eyes smiled affectionately at each of them, before they climbed stiffly out to release Gladys and Dorrie.

'Make sure you get some sleep if you can, both of you,' she said.

Gladys emerged, rubbing her backside. 'That cowing stool's like perching on a pinhead . . .'

Ann and Edwina exchanged little smiles.

Dorrie stood, staring as if some sort of vision was going on before her eyes.

'Thank you, ladies,' Edwina said. 'And well done – that was a good job, in the circumstances. See you tonight, those of you who are on duty.'

Ann stood looking along the main road. It had started to rain gently. Everything felt so quiet after the endless, terrifying racket of the night. There was very little traffic. A tram rumbled past, then it fell quiet again. She could hear pigeons crooning on the rooftops. She was not sure of the time, but people were beginning to emerge from the side streets, hurrying to their places of work.

She was about to set off along the Bristol Road when, out of curiosity, she decided to walk round along the nearest street, past the copper works which backed on to the cut and along one of the little back streets of terraced houses. How had the raid affected this part of town, she wondered? It had been so heavy; the worst yet by far.

The little street seemed unharmed. A few people were emerging from their houses, some calling greetings to each other: 'Morning, Ivy. That was a bad 'un!' 'All right, Harry?' Others keeping their heads down, breath steaming in the cold and damp. Well, this didn't look too bad. Compared to the havoc and destruction of the night she had just seen in the middle of town, it looked peaceful here, like a normal morning.

At the corner she turned along towards the main road again and was getting near the end when someone came out of a house on the left a few yards in front of her. He stepped out, coat on, a scarf knotted tightly at his neck, and turned to say something to whoever was standing in the doorway. Another sound came from inside – the brief wail of a child or a cat, it was hard to tell. The man raised his hand, said, 'Soon as I can,' and turned left out of the gate and down the road.

The rain was falling more heavily but she did not even notice. It took seconds for her exhausted mind to latch on to the fact that the man she was walking only ten or so yards behind was closely familiar: that jacket, the scarf, the shoulders, his particular gait. Intimately familiar. But it was so strange, so impossible to explain, that as she stopped to let him progress further away from her up the road, it still took her a moment to take in.

Her mind clicked between each new realization and the next: that the man ahead of her was her husband, Len Gilby; that he was not wearing ARP uniform, despite his saying that he was on duty last night. And that she had no idea what he was doing in this little street where neither of them, so far as she was aware, had ever known anybody.

Thirty-Two

20 November 1940

Joy hurried into work amid the crowd of people, many holding umbrellas, as they poured into Cadbury's for the night shift. The smell of burning from last night's raid was still drifting from the middle of Birmingham but it had all been dampened by the rain, bucketing down most of the day.

They streamed into the factory, coats shaken out and hung up, overalls on. The odd joke was cracked, a burst of laughter, but the atmosphere was serious, subdued, and literally dampened. The city had just come through the worst night of bombing so far.

When Mom got home that morning and saw that she and Martin had both arrived back safely, she burst into tears and flung her arms round them. They were just as relieved to see her because when they heard where she'd been all night it was far worse than anything they had seen.

'Your dad's all right,' Mom said. 'I saw him on my way back, on his way to work.'

Mom's face was covered in muck and she looked exhausted but she was so wound up she couldn't stop chattering. She made tea and they all sat at the kitchen table full of everything they had seen and done last night.

'Pop in and see Nanna on your way to school, Martin,' Mom said. 'She'll've been worried to death.'

But that had not even been necessary because a few minutes later Margaret arrived, limping in on her bunioned feet, took one look at them and said, 'Oh, thank the Lord.' And Mom told her Dad was all right.

Mom really hadn't been her usual self, Joy thought, settling at her machine to work through the night. She looked strained and very serious and older, somehow, unless it was just the morning light making her face seem bonier, the shadows deeper under her eyes.

'I've said to the WVS I'll go and help out today,' Nanna said. 'Wherever I'm needed. Have you heard about the BSA?'

The Birmingham Small Arms factory in Small Heath was pouring out guns and motorcycles for the war. One of the blocks had taken a direct hit and there were people trapped underneath who had gone to shelter in the basement. No one knew too much detail but it played on everyone's mind. Joy could not stop thinking about it, a chill going through her imagining those poor people under there and what they must be enduring.

Everyone was talking about it at the factory. Most days now there seemed to be a number of pieces of terrible news of the destruction of something dear, of lost lives. Have you heard about . . . The Art Gallery? The Carlton Cinema? That shelter in . . .? It was random, terrifying – you could not make sense out of any of it. And now it was night once more and the whole terror might begin all over again.

In the clatter and din of the night shift, Joy really did feel like a cog in a machine. Voices were raised above the racket of the machines in singing or jokes or, as the night wore on, fell into exhausted silence as everyone worked endlessly, repetitively, with their hands. Birmingham's industries were turning, more each week, into one huge machine powering the war. Tyres for motor vehicles at Fort Dunlop, aircraft parts at Lucas's, tank parts and radar vehicles at Metropolitan Cammell, tools for Spitfires and Lancasters at Turner Brothers, shells, grenades, bomb cases and jerrycans at Parkinson Cowan, vehicle parts at Morris Commercial, Wolseley and BSA . . . The list went on and on.

All the city's skills of motor manufacture, of toolmaking and every variety of engineering was now directed to one thing day and night: winning the war against Hitler. They would fight – the way Mr Churchill said they would fight – with everything they had. And as Joy stood there, stamping holes in the flat, rounded little piece of metal that she hardly knew the use of, she did feel that she was part of it all.

The work was hypnotic. She sang with the others, 'Roll Out the Barrel!' and 'Run, Adolf, Run, Adolf, Run, Run, Run!' And then it went quiet for a while and her mind began to churn along its own paths.

Lawrence Dayton . . . He was in her thoughts day and night. She could not seem to control her feelings for him. Repeating the same actions on her machine again and again, pulling the handle down to stamp the little piece of metal, the night shift often passed in a dream world, in which she and Lawrence were together in some secret spot. His face was close to hers . . .

I love you, Joy. You're like no one else I have ever met . . .

And her dreams had progressed until she was imagining far more than just their passionate kisses. She would visualize Lawrence's body, naked and lean . . . At least, she would imagine it down as far as the waist and after that things got rather difficult and she would be blushing over her machine because she wasn't entirely sure exactly how things would look any further down, not on a grown-up man who was . . . And she both wanted and did not want to find out.

She just could not stop picturing herself lying naked beside Lawrence. He would be gazing at her and making love to her. *My love, my beautiful darling . . .* But other than that, she only had a rather hazy idea about what that actually meant – except that it filled her body with a hot, melting longing.

Since she last saw Lawrence she had spent an awful lot of time in this fantasy world. It felt safe to be there because it was not real. Lawrence was a married man. She could dream and imagine, but that was not the same as doing anything in reality – was it?

'You all right, Joy?' Norma called over to her. She worked on a machine just behind Joy. 'You're a proper little Dolly Daydream these days!'

'Yeah, I'm all right!' Joy nodded, pausing to tuck her hair back under her white snood. Their eyes met for a moment and then Joy looked away, blushing. There were things now she could not even tell Norma.

But this morning there had been something else that had, for the moment, knocked her dreams sideways.

'There's another letter for you,' Mom said. Both of them were about to head up and catch a few hours' sleep. 'It's on the side in the kitchen.'

Joy's heart started pounding like a piston. A letter – was it from Lawrence? Did he want to meet, or was it a letter telling her they must never see each other again? She was already feeling queasy from lack of sleep. She was in quite a state before she had even got to the kitchen.

But the handwriting on the cheap blue envelope was none she recognized. She breathed out hard, sinking down at the table. Opening the letter, her eyes raced to the signature at the bottom and her pulse began racing all over again: '*Alan*'.

His handwriting was neat but childish, sloping down the page.

> *Dear Joy,*
>
> *Sorry not to have been in touch. I'm no good at writing letters. Sorry I didn't tell you I was joining up. I know it was a shock and you must have found it hard. I did it all on the spur of the moment and then couldn't face telling you. I hope you're OK and still dancing. I miss our dances a lot.*
>
> *The army's all right if you keep your head down. I'll be posted soon – don't know where yet. Please don't think badly of me Joy – you're a great girl. I hope to see you when I get leave – we should be due some again before we go.*
>
> *Yours sincerely,*
> *Alan*

Joy stared, dazed, at the letter, her tiredness making it even harder to sort out her feelings. She found herself crying, very suddenly, without even knowing she was going to. Luckily Mom was upstairs because she really sobbed and cried, as quietly as she could for a few minutes, bent over the kitchen table.

Wiping her eyes, she sat up straight and read the little letter again, anger rising in her. It was Alan all over – say something and nothing so that she never knew where she was with him! All her hurt and sadness over Alan surfaced again and her relationship with Lawrence was forgotten.

She got up, about to go up to bed, then stopped in the hall. Tired as she was, her confusion would not let her rest. She had no real idea who Alan was – he was as slippery as an eel. So, she murmured to herself, putting her coat on again, since he's never invited me to his house, I'll go and have a look for myself!

She decided to catch the tram into Birmingham and walk from there. It was the first time she had been into town for a long time and she was shocked by the damage she saw. Looking along side streets, she could see a mess of broken buildings and rubble which had had to be pushed to the side of the street for people to make their way through.

Everyone seemed to be carrying on with their lives but you could see the shock in their faces. And the smells were the worst – a demoralizing, burned, mouldy cocktail of wet plaster and dust and charred masonry. Walking across town in the direction of where Alan lived, she felt an ache of terrible sadness in her chest. It felt as if the world was falling apart around her.

The only reason she had any idea of Alan's address was because she had glimpsed it on his ration book. When she caught sight of it sticking out of his pocket she had tweaked it out and looked at the address.

'Stour Street! Ah, so that's where you live, is it?' She held the book up teasingly before handing it back.

Alan laughed, tucking it right down in his pocket. 'Bit of a way off,' he said. 'Edgbaston.' He cycled to Cadbury's for work every day – said it helped his dancing muscles.

'You keep everything so secret I'm starting to think you're a spy or something.'

'Yeah, that's me.' He clowned around. 'Spying for the government.' But still, he had not told her anything more.

It was a bit of a walk to get there, but she kept going, asking people along the way.

'Stour Street?' The policeman, a skinny man in his thirties, blushed when she spoke to him. Joy knew she had that effect on men because she was pretty. 'Right, well, that's off Monument Road and Cope Street.'

'So if I just keep walking this way, I'm on the right road to Edgbaston?'

'Well, that's if you want to go to Edgbaston,' he said, twinkling at her. 'But if you want Stour Street you're going to Ladywood.'

'Oh.' Joy had a sinking feeling. 'Not Edgbaston then?'

She had never had any reason to go to Ladywood but she knew it was one of the old wards, close to the middle of town. It was somewhere you thought of as poorer, with old back-to-back houses – certainly far more scruffy and tightly packed than Bournville, where she had grown up. Was that why Alan had stretched the truth about his address? It seemed a sad reason.

'It's quite near the rezza. Not a good place to live at the moment – Mr Hitler's lot're using that for target practice.'

She stared at him, not understanding.

'The reservoir. You get the moon shining right in it at night – like a beacon for 'em.'

'Oh, I see,' she said. 'Well – thanks.'

She walked and walked, wondering if this was just a foolish idea after all. She had to be back on the line tonight. But she was past tiredness now.

There were signs of destruction all the way – smashed

sections of streets, houses with their private innards ruptured and turned outward on to the road and the same musty, charred stink that the city had taken on. And the closer she got, the more the neighbourhood felt cramped and drab compared with Bournville's green streets. The railway was close by and she could hear a train whooping up steam and no doubt pouring smuts all over the neighbourhood to add to the soot from all the factory chimneys.

As soon as she turned into Stour Street she realized how ridiculous she was being, because she did not know the house number. She had thought that just by coming to the street she would somehow know which house was Alan's and of course, staring along the straight road of terraced houses, she had no idea.

A few people passed her, one or two giving her a curious look, and she felt shy and out of place in her neat coat and hat. What a stupid idea this had been coming here! Did Alan really live here? And if he did, what did she think she was going to do about it? The Alan she thought she knew seemed further and further away.

She was just thinking about going into a corner shop to ask when she saw a coal merchant's cart further along the street. It was piled with sacks, the skewbald horse standing patiently, swishing its tail. She saw the man come back to the cart having tipped the latest delivery down into a cellar.

''Scuse me,' she said, hurrying up to him. 'Sorry to bother you.'

A soot-smeared face grinned cheerfully at her. 'I never mind being bothered by pretty ladies,' he said, as if he was constantly assailed by a swarm of them. ''Ow can I 'elp yer?'

'I've forgotten the house number,' she said, struggling

to think what to say. 'I'm looking for a . . . a Mr Bishop . . .'

He gave her a look. 'Well, you won't find Alf Bishop in, will yer? He's inside still.'

Her mind tried to follow this. If he was inside why would she not find him?

'In the Green,' he explained patiently. 'The nick. The prison – in Winson Green.'

Joy stared, simply unable to take this in. 'Mr Bishop?' She forced the words out. 'Is that the right Mr Bishop? He has a son called Alan.'

'Ar, that's the one. Number fifty-two. A front house – just there, look. Nice lad, Alan . . . The womenfolk'll likely be in, although . . .' His eye wandered. 'Renie's the one you want to speak to – you won't 'ave much luck if 'er ain't in.'

Joy nodded, as if she had any idea what he was on about.

'All right,' she said, now feeling very nervous and still wondering, despite what he said, whether she was in completely the wrong street. 'Fifty-two, you say?'

'Good luck to yer, bab,' he called after her, with a sincerity which was no help to her nerves either.

She was quite close to number fifty-two. An entry ran between the houses two doors down and she realized that they led to the yards of houses behind. The door was black, the paint chipped, but otherwise clean as if recently washed. Not knowing really why she felt so ill at ease, she rapped on the door.

It flew open so smartly that Joy took a step back. The young woman on the step was upstanding, with hair Joy recognized as being the same strong brown as Alan's, caught up into a ponytail, out of her way. She had an apron on over her skirt and blouse and her strong features and direct blue-eyed gaze looked Joy up and down, making no bones about sizing her up. Alan had mentioned he had an older sister – Irene – and this must surely be her.

'Yeah?' she said, with impatience as if she had things to get on with. 'What d'*you* want?'

'Er – are you Irene Bishop?' Joy said, now cursing herself for having knocked at all. She felt like taking off along the road at a run. But curiosity had brought her this far and would not let her just dash off home.

The woman folded her arms. 'I am, yeah.'

Joy was about to introduce herself when a strange sound came from inside, behind her. It was a distressed sound, a little sobbing noise, and suddenly there was a long wail, so strange and heart-rending that it brought her up in goose pimples.

'Hang on, I'll be in in a moment!' Irene called over her shoulder.

She stepped outside and almost closed the door.

'Sorry,' Joy said. 'Only I'm a friend of Alan's – your brother?' Still, she could hardly believe she was in the right place.

'Yes, I know who Alan is,' Irene said as if she was a halfwit.

'Only we work together . . .'

'You'd be Joy?' She smiled suddenly and Joy saw what a handsome woman she was, full-mouthed, strong-looking. 'He's talked a lot about you – the dancing and that.'

Relief flooded through Joy. This was beginning to feel like a more normal sort of conversation. And Alan had talked about her! This pleased her more than she could say.

'Has he?' She smiled. 'Only . . . I don't know why I

came really. I had a little note from him – when I hadn't heard anything in ages. And I remembered the street he lives in but I didn't know the number and I just wanted to say hello because he—'

'Oh, he's half-soaked at times, that one . . .' she said to Joy's surprise. 'Look, it'd be better if . . .'

She did not get to the end of the sentence then because the door slowly opened behind her. Joy saw a person staring at her whose appearance made her shrink inside with dread and sorrow. A terribly thin, ill-looking woman standing behind Renie, hugging herself with pin-thin arms; lank, colourless hair hanging all straggly round her face and watery, deranged-looking eyes. In a high, whining voice, she said, 'Who's that?'

Thirty-Three

When Ann came down again that morning, after a wash and change, Martin was heading off to school.

'Joy gone to bed?' she said.

'No,' Martin said, checking the books in his satchel. 'She went out.'

'*Out?*' Ann took her tea and a couple of Shredded Wheat and sank down at the table. 'Why on earth? Oh well, she can sleep later, I s'pose.'

She looked up at Martin. Seeing his face now, her slender, active boy with his lively personality, there seemed something different about him but she couldn't put her finger on it exactly. He looked serious, as if his mind was weighed down, but she put that down to tiredness as well. He had been up most of the night, the poor lamb. T war was changing all of them. She stroked his arm as he went past. 'I don't know how you keep going.'

'I'll be all right.' Martin's pale face lifted into a smile. 'See you later.'

'Martin?' she called, her heart full, as he went to the hall. He turned in the doorway. 'Proud of you – eh?'

He smiled then, properly. 'Aww – thanks, Mom.'

The house quietened: she could hear the soft tick of the clock from the front room. Ann sat at the table in her old dressing gown, having washed her feet in warm water – at last! – and cosy in her slippers. She cradled her teacup in her hands, waves of exhaustion passing over her. But she was not sleepy in the least.

Usually after a night on duty, all the sights and sounds of the raid would hammer through her mind, making it difficult to sleep. This morning, even these were pushed aside . . . She had only gone down Elliott Road and along the back this morning on a whim, for a change. But it felt like fate. Len, appearing out of that house, that woman, the child . . .

How was she ever meant to sleep after that?

Half an hour later she was dressed again, hat and coat on, her WVS armband fastened on her sleeve and the badge pinned to her chest. She rummaged under the stairs for a basket, blew the dust off it and went out into the grey morning with it hanging over her arm. Both her mind and body felt nervy and overwrought. As she stepped out of the house she ran straight into her mother-in-law and nearly jumped out of her skin.

'Oh God, you startled me!' She laid a hand over her pounding heart. She must be in even more of a state than she realized.

'Sorry, Annie – dain't you see me coming?' Margaret said kindly. She had her WVS band and badge on as well. 'You only just got in, have you? I'm just popping up to give a hand with whatever they need.' She peered at Ann more closely. 'Are you all right, bab? You're white as a sheet.'

'I'm all right, Maggie.' She did not want to be held up, not now. 'It was a terrible night. I'll come down this afternoon when I've had a rest, all right? Just got a couple of errands to run.'

'Well, you get some sleep afterwards,' Margaret said. 'And then come and have a cuppa with us later?'

All the way she kept rehearsing the name of the street in her mind as if it was an evil spell. Katie Road, Katie

271

Road . . . But none of this felt real as she turned in to the little street again. There was no one much about – a couple of women heading to the shops.

Standing outside the house's green door, she knocked, then stepped back. Her heart was thudding, but she knew she could hide behind the WVS uniform and no one would question it. Putting on a welcoming smile, she waited as the door opened.

The details only settled into Ann's mind afterwards: that the woman standing in the doorway was in her early thirties, that she was attractive in a country-girl sort of way, a few freckles across her nose, blonde hair loose and swept back from her face as if she had just lowered her head and swung it back out of the way. She wore a plain navy dress with a white V-neck collar and some worn-out pink slippers. Her expression was not hostile but it was not friendly either and she looked harassed, sad even, Ann thought. She also seemed vaguely – very vaguely – familiar.

'Yes?' she said irritably.

'I'm sorry to disturb you, dear,' Ann said. She found it quite easy just to act the part. 'I'm collecting for the WVS – any spare clothes you might have for those who've been bombed out? A lot of the poor things have only got what they're standing up in . . . Whole families sometimes.'

'Oh – well, I don't know . . .' the woman said distractedly. She kept looking back into the room and Ann heard a faint sound, the cooing of a child. 'Hang on a minute . . .'

She disappeared and came back with the little one on her hip. Ann stared and her blood started to beat so hard round her body that she had to stop herself exclaiming out loud.

'Hello. Who's this then?' She forced herself to sound pleasant.

The woman softened slightly. 'This is George – he's ten months, nearly.'

'Aren't you lovely?' The little boy was gazing curiously at her. 'And is his daddy around?'

'Oh yes! Well – no, I mean not at the moment,' she said hurriedly. 'He's . . . he's away. In the Army.'

'Oh, what a shame,' Ann said. 'That must be very hard for you, being left on your own. Is he your first?'

'Yes, just this one.' She was blushing and Ann could see she did not like being asked questions. 'Anyway – I haven't got any clothes to spare, sorry . . .' She stepped back, ready to close the door. Ann had an impulse to ask her name, but she knew this would be too peculiar.

'Well, thank you anyway – and good luck to you,' she said, in such a hearty tone she realized she was beginning to sound like Mildred Rowbotham. That was what being in the WVS did for you.

Ann saw the young woman standing in the window, looking out with the child on her hip, so she stepped up to the house next door and knocked. The door opened, letting out stale air smelling of cabbage and musty clothes. The elderly woman inside handed her a pair of threadbare men's trousers. ''E won't be needing them no more,' she remarked, without further explanation.

'Oh dear – sorry to hear that,' Ann said, eyeing the window next door. The young woman was no longer looking out. 'Thanks, bab – that'll be a help to someone.'

Back home, she lay on her bed, still dressed, trying to make sense of what she had seen. Her mind felt like a room where all the furniture was being rearranged at such speed that it seemed like a place she did not know at all.

The evidence of her eyes was all there. She had seen her husband coming out of a house, saying goodbye to a woman . . .

But was she wrong? She tried to make this not be true, to give Len the benefit of the doubt. Could this young woman be a cousin, some other friend or relative that she had never met? But she knew in her heart. She had known Len for so long – each of them knew more or less everyone that the other knew. And not once had he ever mentioned this person or anyone else living in Katie Road.

Jumping off the bed, she went downstairs to fetch their family photograph album. She sat back on the bed, turning to the earliest few pictures they had had taken of Sheila as a baby. Sheila, who everyone always said was the image of her father . . . Ten months old . . . She turned over a page and there was Sheila at about that age, sitting up on a white fluffy blanket, her round face looking out, bright-eyed and eager. They had gone to a studio to have it done and it was a beautiful portrait. Ann stared and stared for an age before lying back on the bed again, heart thudding dully. Apart from the girlish frills on her little romper, this could be a portrait of George, the child she had just seen.

Len had been odd lately. She tried to think back to when that had begun, but it was hard to say. What with the war and the Home Guard and everyone being so tired and with so much on their minds . . . But there had been something else – what happened the last time they had had intimate relations together, because that in itself was rare enough these days.

Hurt and fury blazed through her. All this time, her husband must have been falling in – love? Or something? Attraction anyway, and temptation. With this young, pretty woman, Because she *was* pretty and fresh-faced.

And all this time, he had been thinking of *her* – going to see her? God knew how he'd managed it, with everything else that was going on. What with the Home Guard and ARP . . . Her mind buckled. Unless . . . Where was Len really going? She felt suddenly sick and winded, as if someone had physically punched her in the belly. Lies and more lies – was that what was going on?

But mixed with all this hurt, there was a tiny thread of relief. That day, three years ago, when Len stood there, just in front of where she was lying now, with that stiff piece of paper in his hand. The day that she knew had changed everything for ever. His face – she would never forget that as long as she lived . . .

As Miss Carew the midwife was leaving after Martin's birth in 1926, she had turned, smiling, in the bedroom door.

'Now, don't forget to register his birth, will you? In the next week or two – no rush, but it has to be done!'

Ann made sure she went by herself while Len was at work, carrying Martin in her arms. In the offices where she had to register the birth, the middle-aged woman in horn-rimmed glasses looked up at her forbiddingly, or so it seemed to Ann, who became so flustered she could hardly speak.

'It's all right, dear.' The woman softened a fraction, seeing how nervous she looked. 'Is this your first baby?'

Ann shook her head, her chest aching with the sobs of guilt that wanted to burst from her. At that moment she longed to pour out the whole story of her terrible sinfulness and deceit to this stranger. The woman looked at her with an air of having seen everything many times before.

'Well then – you know it only takes a few moments. And it doesn't hurt anything like as much as having the baby, does it?'

She arranged her papers in front of her.

'Now, father's name?'

Ann couldn't help it – the tears started to roll down her cheeks. There were people waiting behind her and she felt utterly mortified.

'Look, dear,' the lady said, leaning close to her. 'I don't know anyone involved in your situation. My job is simply to register the birth and the child's identity. It's just the basics he needs to know about himself when he's older. And it's the law, of course. Now – a little boy, is it?'

Ann nodded, still crying. She felt so ashamed, even though the lady was not the judgemental harridan that she might have been.

She had only a second to think.

Just the basics he needs to know about himself . . .

That December afternoon in Tom's arms. That time out of time – impossible that it could continue in any way. *We can't keep doing this*, she had said, clinging to him. *I'm sorry . . .* Although she could not – would not want to, ever – undo that afternoon and even everything that flowed from it. And his words – distraught but kind, trying to do the best for her. *I will leave you alone, Ann – I promise . . .* But she did not want to wipe him out of her life, out of Martin, his little son . . . *How do I love thee . . .?* She did not want Martin's life based on a lie right from the start.

'His name's Thomas John Somers,' she said. 'He's a marine chandler and he lives in Southampton.'

'Thank you.' The woman wrote the details without further comment.

Ann had put the birth certificate away once she was home, tucked underneath Sheila's and Joy's, going hot and cold every time she thought about that moment in the hospital when she could not bear to deny the truth.

Tom. Martin was Tom's – her beloved Tom's. But it was not something you ever looked at, was it, that bit of paper? It would just lie there, in a bundle with the others, for years ...

Until, eleven years later, Len went looking for some insurance certificate or other, and stumbled on the children's birth certificates. That moment, when he stood holding Martin's – looking at her.

'What's this?' he said quietly.

In those moments, she knew, something shattered that could never be put back together, not quite ever be the same. She had had to tell him. *He was someone I knew in the war. I never thought I'd see him again – and I was promised to you. It was something that happened, that never should have happened.*

'I'm sorry, Len,' she sobbed. 'So, so sorry.'

Never would she tell him how much love there was between her and Tom, how much she had longed for it. There was only so much truth she could inflict on him. Both of them went on from then, these last three years, day after day, in a marriage that would persist because it had to and was held together by the love of so many people. Len loved Martin, sunny, easy Martin, had loved him to bits as his own son for eleven years. She watched for any trace of difference in the way Len treated him now, but nothing had seemed to change. And their marriage was sustained by the love of Margaret and Cyril, Len's Mom and Dad – and that never changed either. But privately, in so many little details of their life together, between herself and Len, a gulf had opened and things had never been the same.

Lying there, jarred, guilty, every cell of her body pounding with today's discovery, she thought about the woman in Katie Road. Pretty, young. And she knew it was her betrayal of Len that had driven him into this woman's arms. Did she love Len, or was it all a big mistake from her point of view? Did she feel about Len the way she, Ann, had felt about Tom?

And as she brought the young woman's face to mind she knew in a flash where she had seen her before. The Rowheath Pavilion. She had had some job – selling tea or some such – at Rowheath, the Cadbury sports grounds where Len had played football since long before the war.

Thirty-Four

'Ah, there you are – come in, bab!' Cyril opened the door that afternoon. 'No Joy with you?'

'She only came in a while ago.' Ann wiped her feet thoroughly. 'I've left her to sleep.'

'Not been at work all this time, has 'er?' Cyril asked, closing the front door. They stood in the linoleum gloom of the hall.

'No, she went off somewhere . . . All right, Margaret!' she called to the back.

She was about to go through but Cyril said softly, very urgently, 'Ann!' He took her arm, his face wearing a solemn expression. ''Er's only just got in 'erself – had a bit of a shock, like.'

He released her, clearly not about to explain any more. Ann nodded, feeling a clench of dread. Oh dear – what now?

She expected to find Margaret prostrate in a chair, but she was by the table, putting the cosy on the teapot and looking much as usual, until Ann got closer and saw that her mother-in-law's face was blotchy from recent tears.

'No Joy or Martin?' Margaret asked, obviously trying to sound normal – but she didn't because her nose was all stuffed up.

Ann explained again. 'I 'spect Martin'll be along in a bit to eat you out of house and home.'

'Well, we hope so!' Cyril said. 'I can make the lad some chips if 'e'd like – we've still got potatoes left.'

'When has Martin ever said no to your chips?' Ann couldn't help smiling. There was something so comforting about Cyril, in his baggy old jumper and predictable ways. Almost his whole garden that summer had been turned into a potato patch.

'I hope you got some sleep, bab.' Margaret pointed at one of the chairs. 'Come on, you must have had a night of it. Sit down and I'll pour us a cup of tea.'

There was a plate of broken biscuits – Martin's favourite because he always said you could eat more biscuits than with the whole ones and get away with it. Ann glanced at Cyril as they sat down. He still looked very serious.

'You might as well tell her what's happened, Maggie,' he said.

Margaret sank back in her chair, clasping her hands, with their swollen knuckles, on the brown, woolly material of her lap. Ann saw that the flesh round her wedding ring was puffed up – she'd never get her ring off without cutting it now. Margaret looked almost as if she didn't want to say anything, to begin on it, and she gave a tired sigh.

'I must admit, I've had a bit of a shock,' she said.

'Maggie's found out summat she never expected—' Cyril began for her. Margaret waved at him to be quiet.

'Let me tell her, Cyril.' She picked up her tea and took a sip, but Ann saw that her hands were shaking and she had to help her put the cup and saucer back on the table.

'When I saw you this morning, I was going to help with the WVS, as I told yer . . . I'd said I'd help – not at nights, that's too much. But after the night we had there's plenty to do. Any road, a few of us went – were

280

driven – to one of the rest centres, in a church on the Moseley Road. St Paul's, that one on the corner . . .'

Ann listened in astonishment to the story her mother-in-law told her.

The church was in Balsall Heath, which had been heavily bombed, and there was damage in most of the streets around, a lot of people without their homes. The gloomy, cavernous space inside the church was crowded and as Margaret and the other WVS ladies went in, they were hit by the stink of unwashed humanity, many of whom had also been doused in plaster and brick dust or water or both. It felt like barely organized chaos, some people crying, babies bawling and everyone in shock.

Margaret was full of misgivings about how she was going to cope. But she told herself to *come on, buck up – what if it was you, bombed out of your house? Just set to and do what needs to be done.*

In the morning light there was a feeling of such bewilderment and desolation that it brought tears to her eyes. All around were people and family groups. An old lady all in black, in a hat with a veil, sat bolt upright on a pew, staring ahead of her, seemingly quite alone as children sat about her feet and mothers tried to gather their little ones, change dirty nappies or get a drink for them from the WVS ladies who were already there.

In the aisle, on his own, stood a thin, sagging man. He was barefoot and dressed only in a pair of ragged striped pyjamas. He stood with tears rolling down his face but without making a sound.

Margaret and the other three WVS women exchanged looks.

'You go and help with the tea,' one of them said to her. 'I'll go and speak to him, poor soul.'

Margaret was soon busy with the others, getting fresh urns of hot tea on to a table with cups and buns and sandwiches to hand out. She was just getting ready to start serving when a young woman ran into the church, screaming, distraught.

'Denny? Joe? Are you here? Oh God, they must be here!' She ran along the aisle, pushing past the crying man, and her voice echoed round the whole building. 'My boys! Has anyone seen my little lads? Six and three! My boys! Denny! Joe! Come to Mom – I'm 'ere!'

Someone helped her search. The noise died down. Margaret never heard what had happened in that case and she and the others busied themselves as people came up and queued for the tea and whatever they could get to eat and she had to set to and wash up cups in a bowl of hot water at top speed, for someone else to use as soon as they were finished with.

All this kept her busy for a good while as more people arrived and needed comfort and tea and somewhere to sit, and in some cases first aid. At last, the number of newcomers died down. The place was packed. Margaret had a moment to look round, her heart buckling with sorrow for them all. Where on earth were they going to go?

And then a middle-aged lady came up to her and said, 'There's an old girl sitting along there and I asked her if she wanted a cup of tea but she seems a bit – I dunno what. Wouldn't answer me. She don't 'alf pen-and-ink as well. I'm just helping that other woman out over there – but I thought p'raps the old girl'd be more herself if she had a cup of tea?'

'Don't worry, love,' Margaret said, glad to help. 'We're just waiting for the water to heat again but I'll bring one along as soon as it's ready.'

'She's just behind that pillar,' the woman said, pointing.

Margaret carried the cup of sweet tea along the aisle. Eyes turned to look at her. On a pew behind the pillar she found an elderly lady sitting on her own. Everyone was giving her a wide berth because the smell coming off her was pungent. She wore an old black coat of slubbed wool, broken-down little boots with zips up the front and a crushed-looking felt hat pushed down over long, straggly grey hair. She was sitting quietly, staring straight ahead as if unaware of anyone else around her.

'Here's a cup of tea for you, bab,' Margaret said. The old girl must be well into her eighties, she thought, by the wizened look of her.

She held out the cup and the woman looked up at her with big, grey eyes.

'Oh,' she said. Her voice was high, rather childlike. 'That's nice. That for me?'

'Yes – and there's a couple of biscuits too.'

She was about to walk away but the old girl seemed such a lonely figure that Margaret thought she really ought to try and ignore the unwashed, urine-laced miasma that hung about her and see if she was all right or if she needed further help. She sat down on the pew beside her and the old lady turned to her with an air of astonishment.

'You gunna sit there, with me?'

'Well, yes – for a minute or two, if you like,' Margaret said, touched by this. It seemed pitiful, how surprised and grateful she was that anyone would spend time with her.

The old lady took several surprisingly genteel sips of her tea and said, 'Aah. That's nice.'

'What's your name, bab?' Margaret said, half-wondering whether she'd even remember.

'Lizzie One,' came back the prompt reply.

'Lizzie One?' Surely this could not be right?

'There's three Lizzies,' she said conversationally. 'And I got there first, so I'm Lizzie One. Always have been, while I was Lizzie.'

'I see,' Margaret said, even though this was far from true. She sat on, not liking to get up and leave but unsure what to say.

'Was your house hit, Lizzie?' she asked. 'Where do you live?'

'Oh – *there*,' she said. 'You know.'

Out of her depth, Margaret said, 'I hope your house has not been damaged. Have you always lived – *there*?'

'Oh no! Course not!' Lizzie laughed as if this was a ridiculous question. 'No one ever starts off *there*, do they?'

She turned to Margaret then, still smiling as if enjoying this as a joke of some kind. And then it was not just those eyes, large and grey. It was everything: the tone of voice, even though higher now, and odder. And it was the shape of her face; just something essentially familiar about it. And then for a second Margaret thought that she *was* in a dream or going off her head.

'Ida?' The word shot out of her mouth like an impulse that preceded thought.

The grey eyes narrowed for a second and Margaret felt for an instant that she was being regarded by something hostile and not quite human, like a lizard. But as soon as she opened her eyes wider again, she seemed gentle once more.

'But I'm Lizzie now.'

Margaret forgot to breathe for a long moment and then gasped, panting the air in.

'You want to be careful,' the old girl observed.

'Ida,' Margaret repeated. Her mind was reeling. 'But . . . You can't be . . . But you *are*, I can see . . .'

And then came the moment that completely floored her.

'You're Margaret, aren't you?' Lizzie-who-was-Ida said, matter-of-factly. 'Can tell by your eyes. We always had the same eyes, dain't we? Never thought I'd see any of you again. Not after all this time.'

There was a stunned silence round the table. As Margaret was speaking, all Ann's own preoccupations and worries vanished and she was caught up in this strange story. Sinbad, seeming to sense all the emotion in the room, jumped up and sat on Margaret's lap, and she stroked him as he settled himself down.

Tears started to pour down Margaret's cheeks.

'They told me she was dead. First of all, she was in hospital – that's what they said. That she was very ill. And she never came back – she was so ill, she died. And . . .' She looked taken aback all over again, realizing another of the lies that had been told to her.

'I never went to her funeral because they said I was too young. She was supposed to have been buried at Lodge Hill – I mean, I've been, of course, because that's where . . .' She looked at Cyril, distraught. 'Ron's grave is there.' Her son's war grave, which she visited regularly and faithfully. 'I never knew where Ida's was. I never even asked . . .'

She sobbed for a few moments in grief and remorse. Cyril leaned over and laid his hand over hers, on the cat's warm back.

'If you'd asked at the cemetery and she weren't there you'd've still been none the wiser though, love, would you?' he said.

Ann was still completely in the dark about this. 'So as well as your brother, you had a sister?'

Margaret nodded. 'She was – is – ten years older than me. Eight years older than my brother. So when she died . . . or . . . Anyway, I was seven. I still don't know what happened. She said – Ida, I mean – there was a "naughty man" – that's whose fault it was. So what went on exactly, I don't know . . .'

She sat silently for a moment and then her face darkened. 'I knew my mother and father were strict, but to do that . . . To put her away!'

Her shoulders began to shake with sobs again and she lowered her head. Ann heard the back door opening and Martin appeared. He could sense the strangeness of the atmosphere immediately and his eyes met Ann's.

'Eh, love . . .' Cyril got up and stood by his wife, gently laying a hand on her shoulder. Martin, not even knowing what had happened, stepped forward and caressed his grandmother's other shoulder.

'Go and see your mother,' Ann called to Len from the kitchen, as soon as he walked through the door a couple of hours later.

He appeared in front of her, his face clouded with irritation.

'What, now? I've got to get out again – ARP.'

'Have you?' Ann came up close to him. ARP – or did that mean a house in Katie Road? *That woman*. Rage rose in her so that she almost choked on it. All the guilt she had kept inside her all these years. And he had been lying to her, deceiving her all this time! But no – not now. This wasn't the moment. She wanted more time to think and take in what this meant.

'Something's happened,' she said, more gently. 'Your mom's ever so upset. It won't take long – just pop along and see her, eh?'

He came back almost an hour later, during which time she had cooked some liver with the smallest amount of onion and potatoes.

'I can't stay – I ate something at Mom's,' Len said.

'They don't seem to have given you an ARP uniform?' Ann said. Had he eaten at his mother's, or would he get a meal with *her*?

'Yeah, they still haven't got enough for everyone – and I'm not on often.' He paused, then looked into her face, softening. If there was one thing they had always been in accord about it was their love of Margaret and Cyril, who had always been the kindest in-laws she could have wished for. 'Strange do, that, eh – with Mom? Terrible really.' He went to go and get his coat. Ann stared at his back, the clipped hair, strong neck, his shoulders, this stranger who was her husband. Putting his head back round the door he said, 'Are you on tonight?'

'If there's a raid. Martin's not – he can go to your mom and dad.'

Len hesitated for a moment, then walked over and pecked her on the cheek. She did not kiss him back.

'Let's hope it's quiet,' he said, turning away.

The front door closed behind him. Ann followed his steps in her mind. Was he really going to the ARP post, or . . . Her mind went with him all along the road, up to Selly Oak, to that house and *her* – was that where he was really going?

She was on edge, waiting all evening – but for once, it was quiet. Only she and Martin were in the house.

'Fancy a game of cards?' she asked him, desperate to take her mind off her thoughts of Len, of what he might be doing. And because here she was with her boy and she loved spending time with him. 'Finished your homework?'

'Yes.' He was sprawled across a chair, one leg over the arm, already in his pyjamas. 'OK – one quick game,' he said, yawning. 'But I'm all in. Need to catch up with some sleep.'

'I'll make some cocoa if you like,' she said. From the kitchen she called, 'It's that Red Label stuff – I've run out of the other.' Another wartime economy at Cadbury's – the difficulty of getting enough milk and sugar into the factory meant the cocoa was an economy version – more saccharin than sugar.

'It doesn't taste too bad,' she heard Martin call. 'And I've found the cards.'

Ann carried the cups in and over to the wobbly folding table with its green felt top that Martin had put up close to the gas fire.

'This is cosy,' she said.

He looked up from shuffling the pack. There was a veiled manner to him somehow these days, as if he had things on his mind that he did not want her to see. But tonight he looked back at her directly and smiled. She felt herself lurch inwardly. At times, and more as he got older, he was so like Tom. Most of all when he smiled. Love surged in her – of him, of both of them. Followed by bitter guilt and sorrow. If anyone had caused the pain and deceit in this marriage it was her. She was angry with Len, hurt, furious – but she could not condemn him completely. Had her heart not been turned away, and for a long time, no matter how much she tried to twist it towards him? She deserved it, because he had been true up until recently – she was sure of it.

And in the meantime, she had these moments of quiet with her boy – the child of the man she had loved so much. All they had for certain were moments, because from day to day you never knew what fate might fall from the sky.

'You deal, love,' she said softly. And as she spoke, the siren went off again.

Martin made a face. 'Looks as if I'll have to deal in the shelter.'

Thirty-Five

22 November 1940

'Oh goodness,' Sheila said, rushing to look at the letters on the table. 'It's from my sister! I wonder what I've done to deserve this!'

'Joy, is it?' Audrey said, stirring a pan of porridge.

'Yes, Joy. She's not much of a letter writer usually . . .'

But as she took it upstairs to read, leaving Elaine downstairs with Audrey, Sheila felt a tingle of pleasure and excitement. It was always nice to get a letter. She had not seen a lot of Joy last week and they had been so different growing up. Joy: always the pretty one, the one who seemed to have all the outward energy and confidence that Sheila lacked. She had often envied Joy because she was so lively and dimply and popular. This had been the case up until she met Kenneth and realized that he was really in love with her, that she loved him and they were just right together. When she introduced him to Joy the first time, she was almost afraid he would prefer her young sister with her dancing eyes and feet. But Kenneth showed no sign of that.

'She's a nice kid,' Kenneth said, in his solid, earnest way. 'And she is a looker, I grant you – but not my type. Not like you are, Sheila. You're more of a homebird and that suits me just right!'

Once she was settled with Kenneth and had Elaine, she

felt no envy at all of Joy. This lad Alan seemed to mess her about no end and she knew Joy was hiding just how much that had hurt. She had sometimes wondered in any case whether the prettiest girls always had the best time because it often did not seem to turn out that way. All in all, now she was away from home and everything felt so fragile, it would be so nice if she and Joy could be closer.

Sitting on the bed she slit the envelope open with her nail scissors. Joy's handwriting was large and uneven; she was too impatient to shape her letters carefully.

Dear Sheila,

Thought I'd drop you a line because we didn't have much time last weekend. Sorry about that. I'd had an invitation I couldn't refuse and I must say it turned out to be quite a day.

What's happened is that since Alan left – with hardly a word to me so I give up, he obviously doesn't like me the way I thought he did – I've met someone else. He's quite a character, working on the Spitfires at Castle Brom, of all things, we met in an air raid shelter and we danced out in the moonlight after the raid was over! I haven't told Mom anything because he's a bit older than me and you know what she's like. But the best thing is, he's ever so interesting and talks to me and he's a really good dancer. We went to a dance at the Grand Hotel a few weeks ago!

The letter rambled on, all about how she was working nights and was hardly ever free to go out but what a romantic time they had had on the Lickeys, going to a tea shop.

Sheila folded the letter back into the envelope, feeling disappointed and fed up with Joy. She was obviously having a very good time and Sheila knew she ought to be happy for her. Joy did just about manage to ask at the end how she was getting along and about Elaine. But there was nothing about anyone else – Mom and Dad, their grandparents, Martin.

All me, me, me, Sheila thought, getting up and dropping the letter into a drawer. Well, that was Joy for you – what had she been expecting? The war didn't change people *that* much, evidently.

She wondered though why Joy, who she hardly ever heard from, had written at all – and why now?

Later, Sheila sat feeding Elaine her dinner of mashed carrot and swede and gravy while Audrey moved about in the kitchen, heating soup – another version of the carrot and swede – for the two of them.

'There you are – at least we managed to get some of it into your mouth.' Sheila wiped Elaine's plump cheeks. The little girl shook her head emphatically. 'Just keep still, will you, you wiggly worm!'

She heard Audrey laugh at this and a moment later she appeared with some slices of bread on a plate and a small lump of cheese.

'She's a very good girl though, aren't you, Lainy?' She ruffled Elaine's hair as she went past. 'She doesn't get in half the mess the boys used to. Shall I bring the soup in now?'

'Yes – lovely, thanks,' Sheila said. 'I'll give her a bit of apple – that should keep her quiet while we have ours.'

They settled companionably to their simple meal. As the weeks went by the two of them had become more relaxed together. Able to talk about the things they had in common – children and families and the day-to-day irritations and sadnesses of the war. Sheila sometimes told her a few stories about Kenneth – happy memories. Audrey missed her sister Evelyn and talked about her. The one thing they never discussed, a no-go area in the conversation, it seemed, was Audrey's husband.

The weeks passed harmoniously – two women, plus Mrs Blisset coming in three mornings a week, and three children. The boys were easier when their father was not there. Sheila and Audrey passed the time companionably, mostly keeping their attention on practical things, and both of them good-natured and cooperative.

But now it was Friday and the dreaded weekend loomed. Although she had only come back on Monday, Sheila wished she could just scuttle straight back to Birmingham again to get out of the way.

'I'll wash up,' she said as she and Audrey cleared the table together afterwards. 'You put your feet up.'

'Tell you what,' Audrey said, folding the tablecloth. 'Let's take the children down to the river after school, shall we? Give them all a good blow-around. We can feed the ducks—'

She was interrupted by the telephone ringing.

'Oh *bother* – I hope this isn't the WVS after me for something . . .'

Sheila dragged the high-chair into the kitchen so that Elaine could be with her as she worked. She turned on the tap, hearing the faint 'whoomp!' of the Ascot water heater. Audrey's voice spoke faintly in the background.

She was putting the glasses into the warm, soapy water when she heard something else. A strange sound which she could not decipher – a shriek, a sob? It went quiet. Sheila tiptoed to the door to listen and heard Audrey, in the next room, making strange sounds – gulping, panting, almost as if she was choking.

Audrey was on the floor of the wide hall, beside the

telephone table. The receiver had been neatly returned to its place and Audrey was on her knees, curled into a ball beside the table, her head on the tiled floor.

Sheila dashed to her, stepping round to kneel in front of her.

'Audrey? What is it? What's happened?'

Almost frightened, she dared to touch Audrey's shoulder. Audrey shot upright suddenly, arms flailing with a crazed movement, her face stretched and wild with some emotion that Sheila could not fathom at all. Audrey let out a shriek, a howl, from the bottom of her lungs, so loud that Sheila recoiled. Audrey drew in a deep, shuddering breath, then put her head back again.

'Oh, thank God!' she roared. 'Thank God, thank God!'

She seemed to come to herself then, almost as if she had been possessed. Her arms lowered to her sides, her face sobered and she looked at Sheila, dazed, as if reality was catching up with her.

'That was one of Maurice's colleagues in chambers,' she said. 'He's been killed.'

Sheila, now in shock herself, helped Audrey get up, led her to a chair in the sitting room, made sweet tea and brought Elaine in to play on the rug. Cautiously, she sat down beside Audrey.

'Can you tell me what's happened?' she said softly.

'His flat.' Audrey was sitting hunched forward on the edge of the chair, her fists clenched in her lap. 'It was quite early in the evening. He was there – in the flat – not in the shelter in the basement.' She paused for a long moment, her eyes seeming huge, dark rings underneath them. 'Probably working . . . on something. He was taken to hospital but he died soon after . . .'

Sheila was so shocked, she started to wonder if she had

dreamt Audrey's outburst a few minutes earlier. All she could do was gently look after Audrey and reserve any kind of thought or judgement. She sat carefully on the chair opposite her.

'He said – this man who telephoned, I mean, I don't know him, I never knew Maurice's life, not really – that he did not think he would have suffered. He wouldn't have known anything about it.' Suddenly she straightened her back and looked directly at Sheila, her expression naked, more honest than Sheila had ever seen it.

'You must think I'm wicked.'

'No.' Sheila leaned over to touch her hand for a moment. 'Of course not.' Though she had no real idea what to think.

When the boys came back from school, and after a slice of bread and jam, they wrapped all the children up warm, put Elaine into the pushchair and walked down the road, over the two bridges into the village and down to the river. The day was grey with a heavy, lowering sky and cold breeze, but there was no rain.

'I won't say anything to the boys just yet,' Audrey said, before Edward and Charlie came home from school. 'Let's just go out and give them a run around. I can't get my own head straight yet.'

Later, at home, both pink-cheeked and eating their tea, Edward asked if his father was coming home. Audrey told him that he had been delayed and the boys accepted this without protest. They passed a normal evening, playing and bathing and getting ready for bed. Sheila started to wonder during those hours if she was the one going mad. She felt a constant sense of curled-up dread and horror inside while Audrey behaved in a bright way as if nothing had happened at all, even after the children were in bed.

Later though, after she had turned in herself, she heard a knock on the door. Sheila had been just falling asleep, but she leapt up, her heart hammering.

'May I come in?' Audrey asked, from the doorway.

'Yes. Course.' Sheila switched on the bedside light, expecting Audrey to curl up on the chair. But she came and pulled the covers back and slipped into the other side of the bed.

'Sorry,' she said. 'Do put the light out again. We mustn't wake Lainy . . . It's too cold to stay out of bed. I just wanted to explain—'

She broke off. Sheila could feel that Audrey was still sitting upright. After a moment of silence, she started to cry. Sheila had just switched the light off and wondered if she ought to put it on again, but as she was reaching for the switch, Audrey grabbed at her arm.

'No, leave it off. It makes it easier to talk. You must think I'm—' she began again.

'I don't,' Sheila interrupted. 'I don't, honestly . . . I mean, I'm just here staying in your house, I don't really know anything about . . . well, anything.'

'Oh, you do,' Audrey said. Words suddenly poured out of her. 'I've seen it in your face. And that's partly why I wanted you – wanted someone here. Another woman. To protect us – but to *see* as well. Maurice was such a catch – a barrister, no less! Even Evie, my sister, can never see how he is – was. Not really. I don't see much of her anyway – Cheltenham is hardly on the doorstep and what with all the petrol shortages now . . . We're like chalk and cheese in any case. And she's got no idea! She's happy with her chap – and you, you've got a nice husband too.' Her voice rose, quickly close to hysterical.

'You don't know what it's like being trapped in a marriage to a . . . a cold, mean *bully* like Maurice! Having to put on a show all the time, be the perfect wife, in front of the children, in front of everyone. Having a part-time marriage in any case because he's hardly here – off living his bachelor life with me here, giving him everything he needs on a plate. I don't mind that – not really. Lots of men do that. If he had only been . . . But he's only half-human, I swear it! He's an arrogant bully – a torturing, soulless . . . *animal*. I *hate* him. I never knew I could hate anyone until I was married to him.' She seemed to sober down then, abruptly. 'Hated. Hated. And he's gone. I can't believe it . . . I am honourably . . .' With an outrush of breath, she finished, 'Free.'

Sheila was in shock, really shaken by these torrents of pent-up emotion. The horror of it all seemed to swamp her. She had seen glimpses, but had never been sure how to make sense of it.

'He only hit me occasionally,' Audrey said. Her tone was even more disturbing now – light and sarcastic. 'He wasn't able to control it all properly – Maurice had to control everything, you see. And a few times he left bruises where people could see them and that wasn't on, of course. So instead, he used to—' Her voice broke. 'Hitting someone isn't the only way you can—' She broke off again. 'You do believe me, don't you?'

'Yes!' Sheila said. 'Of course I do!' She didn't doubt anything Audrey was saying – she was still trying to understand. She had seen how he could be in the daytime – disagreeable, bad-tempered. But just that one night, shivering on the landing, had opened a door into the dark depths of Audrey's marriage.

'I shan't be able to say this to anyone else – ever. I put on a show in the village, of course, do my best. I didn't expect to be able to talk to you – I didn't know who would be coming, I just hoped . . . You must believe me!'

Sheila pushed herself up in bed to sit beside her.

'I do, Audrey,' she said, moved. The room was completely dark, but she could feel Audrey's shoulder up against her own, smell the scent she wore, still flower fresh. After a moment she reached out and put her arm around her. Audrey sagged against her.

'I'm sorry,' Sheila said. 'For all you've had to put up with.'

'Thank you. You're very kind. A kind, kind person,' Audrey said. She gave a long sigh. 'I'm going to have to break it to the boys.'

They sat for a moment and gradually something arose in the silence; a rise-and-fall throb from outside.

'Hark at that,' Sheila whispered. It was a rare sound here, but she knew it well from Birmingham – the disjointed rumble of engines, German ones. 'Jerry planes.'

Without a word they both leapt out of bed and pulled back the curtain and the blackout.

'I'll just open the window a crack,' Audrey whispered, speaking even more quietly as if the plane might be able to hear them. She pushed the casement open and the sound grew more distinct before fading away and dying into silence.

'I hope they're not heading for Birmingham,' Sheila said.

Thirty-Six

'What's up with *her*?' Gladys Parrott said.

Gladys was resplendent in full WVS uniform, this time with a coiled plait of her steel-grey hair visible just behind each ear beneath the beret. Ann and some of the others who were part-timers still only wore their own coat with a badge, band and beret to go with it. Gladys liked her uniform and wore it with great pride.

They were all piling up sandwiches again like mad when Mildred Rowbotham strode across the church hall, her usually bouncing curls straight and flat about her cheeks and looking like the wrath of God.

Ann looked up and shrugged. Gladys winked at her suddenly and they exchanged little smiles. Edwina and Mildred were nice people, but of a different class from them.

'She must be worn out,' Ann said. Mildred, as a driver, was in constant demand. 'It's been quite a week.'

Gladys acknowledged this. She kept smearing margarine on to the bread at lightning speed. 'You all right? Family?'

Ann nodded. 'They're all right. So far. All tired out, of course.'

'You just have to keep going,' Gladys said. 'Best not to dwell on it.'

Ann knew Gladys was right but as she bent over the table to start work on the sandwich production line, she felt a wave of exhaustion and a queasiness in her belly. It didn't do anyone any good, all this worry, being up odd hours. Not to mention all that was going round and round in her mind. She did her usual mental scan of the family – what were they doing? Were they safe? Joy was on the night shift at Cadbury's. Martin would be with Margaret and Cyril tonight, thank the Lord. And Len too, one of the rare nights when he would be home.

Women's voices were calling orders and chatting. There were occasional outbursts of singing and the constant toing and froing of feet starting to load trays heaped with sandwiches into the vans. Ann found the repetitive task left her mind free to wander, however much she tried not to think about Len – and *her*?

Whenever the steps of her mind found their way to Katie Road and *her*, she felt overwhelmed by hurt and rage, by his betrayal. At the same time, it still felt unreal. All these years *she* had been the betrayer and Len forever the injured party, the always virtuous husband. Didn't it just serve her right . . . And yet how *could* he? she raged in her mind. How *could* he?

But had she got it wrong? Was she going mad? Had Len called on *that woman* as part of some ARP duty? Was it true that her husband was really in the Army and away – and of course the baby was his, not Len's . . .

But Len had not been wearing the ARP uniform that morning. She could call to memory his back moving away from her as clear as day, in his everyday coat. And the way he had said goodbye, looking back through the door, raised his hand in a wave . . . It was familiar. It was the look and wave of a lover, a father . . . Her throat ached violently and suddenly she was on the point of weeping. When had either she or Len last looked at each other the way she saw him look back at *her*? And that child – the baby who could almost, very nearly, be Sheila at the same age?

Her insides bucked and she flung the knife down and dashed to the dank lavatory at the back of the church, only just managing to get inside before she was heaving violently over the pan. She knelt on the hard floor, sweat cooling under her arms and down her back until she was shivering.

'Oh God . . .' she groaned to herself. All she most dearly wanted was to lie down there on the shabby linoleum and go to sleep. The night loomed ahead, like an eternity she had to live through.

After a few moments she began to recover.

'Better out than in,' she murmured, getting exhaustedly to her feet. A bit of a waste of a dinner but that couldn't be helped. She hadn't realized quite what a state she was in, but a lot of people were complaining about their indigestion, about feeling queasy. Everyone was living on their nerves. Leaning over the basin she drank down handfuls of water, then straightened, patting her hair, and went back to the bread and marge.

Afterwards, she remembered that night as a series of shattered fragments. The siren went off at seven. Wave after wave of incendiaries were dropped, then the heavy bombs. As the night wore on it seemed that half the city was on fire.

The usual team was aboard – Mildred driving, and Edwina, Gladys and Dorrie, who Ann sat with in the back and who was crouched over on the stool, wringing her hands and frantically muttering prayers.

'Well, the Lord's having his ear bent tonight all right,' Ann murmured to Gladys, once they had parked up near the middle of town and they were all standing out at the back.

'Now, now,' Gladys said, mock reproachful, but giving her a wink.

They handed out tea to the firemen who they could see silhouetted against the flames, all working frantically. Ann sat for some time on the edge of the kerb in Gooch Street with an ARP warden who had had an incendiary blow up in his face. They waited for an ambulance while the inferno roared around them. The man's face was in a terrible state but he was admirably calm. He leaned forward, moaning every so often, and she felt terrible that she could do no more for him. The pavement was hard and freezing cold under her backside and all her nerves were on red alert for the next lot of bombers overhead. She thought of all those people from the tightly packed houses around her with no cellars or gardens. Were they all safe in their public shelters behind? Soon, mercifully, she heard the ambulance bell.

They moved carefully about the southern inner ring of the city, trying not to think about the danger and handing out tea and sandwiches to the grateful wardens and rescue teams. Ann thankfully drank a cup of the hot sweet tea herself, knowing that if she didn't she was not going to be able to keep going.

'It's getting very bad again,' Edwina said anxiously. It was almost three in the morning and there had been a brief lull, but once again, the bombers were back. And it was bad – bomb after bomb falling with terrifying frequency.

Mildred, who had been crawling the van along, braked abruptly. The engine went off and a moment later the back door opened.

'Come on, all of you.' It never occurred to anyone

to disobey. 'We can't stay out in this – it's getting ridiculous.'

They were parked close to the entrance to Snow Hill. Mildred slammed the doors of the vehicle shut behind them and they all fled into the railway station.

An ARP warden emerged from the shadows in his steel helmet.

'Go on, ladies – you want to go down that way!'

He pointed them in the direction of steps to the underground part of the station, where they joined the edge of the crowd huddled down there. It was dark, except for the pencil light of a few torches or occasional flash of a lit match, and the air was fuggy with cigarette smoke and staleness. Ann could hear children crying, people murmuring.

'They've already bombed here once,' Ann heard someone saying close to her. 'Smashed all the glass ceiling in the booking hall.'

Ann's stomach was growling, a mixture of hunger and queasiness, she could not tell which. She was standing next to Mildred who had Dorrie on the other side of her. Dorrie was still muttering away to herself. Mildred turned to her suddenly.

'Oh, for goodness' *sake*,' she hissed. 'Can't you just put a sock in it for once?'

This, delivered with Mildred's plummy vowels and the shock on poor Dorrie's face, made Ann suddenly want to giggle hysterically. She could feel the pressure building in her chest as she fought to control the laughter that threatened to erupt out of her.

As they stood in the darkness though, she realized, choking back her own feeling of hysteria, that others were not succeeding so well. They had come down here to shelter but they felt like sitting ducks all crushed in together. A woman started crying loudly and other people told her to pack it in. The voices were rising, harsh in their panic and fear.

Cutting through this came a man's booming voice. Even over the racket and confusion, his voice was so clear and authoritative that Ann heard every word.

'Come along now! Let us gather ourselves. *"Ar Hyd y Nos".*'

A low sound began in the cramped, echoing space, building from just one male voice as more and more joined in, softly, then gathering power.

'*Holl amrantau'r sêr ddywedant, Ar hyd y nos.*'

Soon she heard Mildred and Edwina joining in very softly, in English, '*All through the night.*'

The beauty of the men's voices gathered, as if emitting from a powerful, yet gentle instrument, swelling until it beat against the walls as the screaming of bombs went on above them outside and the ground shook under their feet. The singing continued until they could feel it moving right through them, so that by the end of the beautiful hymn, all of them had tears streaming down their faces.

What a whole Welsh male-voice choir was doing in the bowels of a Birmingham railway station at three in the morning was not something they asked about until afterwards. (The answer being obvious: waiting to travel back to Wales.) It was like a miracle and Ann's chest felt as if it might tear open with emotion.

All her life seemed to come before her – and above all, Len's face. The husband with whom she had lived all these years. Whatever she felt for Tom Somers, whatever mistakes she had made, it was Len who had been her husband, there in all the ordinary days, through the children being born, the days of happiness, of disappointments, of day-to-day grind. Steady Len. And, she had thought, faithful old Len – not like her. Better than her. She wondered again if she was mistaken about that woman. Was she seeing Sheila's face in that little boy on her hip when it was not really like that? Maybe all the time she was imagining things – that there had been some innocent reason why Len was in the street that morning.

As the last bars of the song were sung, low, reverberating round the cave-like space, she felt ashamed and contrite. I must make everything better, she thought. We might die – at any moment, either of us, and I won't have done anything to mend things . . . Suddenly she was full of a new sense of calm. That was what she must do. Go back to Len – be more loving. Show him that he is the one I have married and cared for. Be a better wife. Make everything right.

And burn Tom's letter. That last one she had been unable to bear parting with. She must put all that behind her – it was a dream world of the past, and she must attend now to everything and everyone who was dear to her.

The choir kept singing, filling the space with this loveliness, and they all listened entranced. Now that her own storm of emotion had blown through her, Ann wiped her eyes and listened, humming softly when she knew a tune, aware of her surroundings again.

And during a lull when the choir were taking a rest, she realized with a shock that Mildred, beside her, had her hands over her face and was sobbing and snorting uncontrollably. Ann hesitated, shy of saying anything to her. Surely Mildred would stop crying soon – they were all emotional. But her usually curt and stalwart driver seemed overcome by her feelings.

'Are you all right?' Ann took courage and leaned towards her. There was so little light in the place that she could only see the outline of Mildred's head and shoulders. Mildred was shaking her head.

'No, I'm *not* all right! It's . . . it's Mr Dowd . . .' Ann had to think quickly to realize that Mildred meant her boss in the solicitor's firm where she worked. 'He was killed – the night before last.'

'Oh my goodness.' Ann dared to lay a hand on Mildred's plump shoulder. 'How terrible . . .'

'He was at home – alone . . .' She was crying again. Ann was at a loss what to say except for 'Oh dear' and 'What a terrible thing.'

'I'm a silly fool,' Mildred said, tugging a hanky from her pocket and fiercely blowing her nose. 'I know Ernest never felt the same for me as I did for him. He was twenty years older than me anyway. But he was a bachelor and I always rather hoped that he might . . . You know, notice me.'

Ann was even more dumbstruck at this point and to her relief the choir leader announced gently, 'Now then, "*Rhyfelgyrch Gwŷr Harlech*".'

The haunting sound of their voices rose in the gloom singing 'Men of Harlech'. Ann's eyes filled with tears again. She imagined Mildred in her flat shoes, her brisk and competent manner, working her socks off for this Mr Dowd who quite honestly sounded rather a dry old stick – hoping he would say a fond word to her and him never taking the slightest notice.

I have been loved, at least, she thought amid all the confusion of now. I know how it feels. And her tears flowed again. Laying a hand on Mildred's arm as the hymn drew to a close, she said, 'There'll be someone for you – I'm sure there will.'

Mildred sniffed and Ann saw her give a little nod. 'Thanks. Nice of you. Not much sign so far is all I can say.'

Thirty-Seven

The All Clear did not sound until nearly six in the morning and by the time they had crawled back towards Selly Oak before dawn, the destruction was enormous. Ann sat in the front with Gladys, Mildred driving grim-faced through the battered, smoky city, lit by the glow of scattered, still-burning fires. In one rubble-strewn street, members of a rescue team headed hopefully towards them. Mildred lowered the window.

'Sorry, chaps, we've been out all night. We're cleaned out – and there's no water.'

'Yeah, you're telling us!' someone quipped. 'No cowing water anywhere – not even for a cuppa!'

'Someone else'll be along soon,' Mildred tried to reassure them.

'Ah, here's the trouble,' she said when they reached the Bristol Road where suddenly they were driving along a stream bed, a whole section of the road awash with water. High-explosive bombs had hit the mains and they had seen the firemen desperately struggling to find water to put out the fires. 'My God, there's no water anywhere. If they come back tonight, we'll be done for.'

Ann sat with her arms folded, cold and utterly spent. Her hands were icy and her stomach felt acid and horrible. Even with all the horror and destruction all around them, the only thing she could think of was getting home and sinking into bed for a long sleep . . .

'Well, we can't just knock off,' Gladys said, as if her

thoughts had been going along the same track. 'There's people all over with nothing. We'll have to go and stock up . . .'

Ann glanced at her. Was she serious? The way she felt at the moment she could hardly put one foot in front of the other. She almost groaned out loud.

'I'll have a conflab with Edwina,' Mildred said. The two of them were always the seniors of the group. 'We – or someone – can set up a field kitchen in town if we can get the right supplies in time – get some food into people. But let's hope to God there will be enough volunteers to take over from us.'

She swung the van in along the side of the chapel where they had started out.

'Ann, you go home and get some rest. The rest of us will manage.'

'Are you sure?' Ann said. She found she was almost in tears at the thought of having to go on and do anything else. 'I must say I don't feel too good.'

'You don't look it either,' Mildred said cheerfully, hoicking the handbrake into place. 'In fact, you look quite green round the gills. Go on – off you go.' She touched Ann's arm for a second. 'Sorry, by the way, about earlier. Silly old fool.'

'No,' Ann said. For a moment she touched Mildred's arm. 'Not silly at all.'

Hurrying back along the Bristol Road, Ann was praying that everyone was all right at home, that Martin and the others had been safe all night, that Joy would come home and then Len . . . And from this very day she was going somehow to make it up to him . . .

She was coughing again even before she turned down Oak Tree Lane . . . Along the street were smashed rooftops and mess and rubble all over the ground. So that was why the air was thick with dust! As she drew nearer, the damage became clearer, charred beams at jagged angles like jackstraws, windows blown out – the destruction of a section of Katie Road.

Her tired brain made sense of this in jerking steps. In the centre of Birmingham, she had seen so many neighbourhoods destroyed, people losing everything in one stroke including their lives. But now this was a street she knew well, close to home and where she had been recently because although she did not know anyone there – not really – she had been to that house . . .

And, turning into the wrecked mess of Katie Road, she could see that the very spot where she had stood on the step was blocked with the remains of a half-destroyed house . . .

'Oh my God.' Her feet stopped moving and she stood staring, hardly able to take all this in.

'You all right, missus?' A man in fireman's uniform came over to her, his face black with filth. It was only the voice that made her realize he was her friend Hilda's husband, Roy, his usually ginger looks disguised by the helmet and the grime. 'Oh sorry, Annie, it's you! Bad do, this – a bit close for comfort.'

Ann nodded. 'Many injured . . .? Is anyone stuck inside?'

'Not sure yet,' Roy said, his kindly face smiling at her. It was a comfort to see him – she had known him most of her life.

'I'll let you get on, Roy,' she said, after a few moments. 'See you soon.'

'Yeah, you get off home, bab.' Roy narrowed his eyes suddenly, nodding in the direction of the bombed houses. 'Hey, hang on – isn't that Len over there?'

Ann's heart started thudding, as if some instinct in her told her what she was going to see before she even turned round. As she did so, two figures immediately came to her notice, further along the pavement. A half-familiar woman with a brown blanket round her shoulders and her blonde hair, loose and dishevelled, stood holding a child and talking to someone. The someone, standing beside her, also came into focus. The wavy hair, the shape of his face and body . . . Everything completely familiar because, once again, she was standing looking at her husband.

'Oh!' she cried shrilly. 'So it is! Maybe we can walk home together! See you, Roy.'

She waited a few seconds, trying to look as if everything was normal until Roy turned away, before going over to them. Len was talking to the woman, seeming to be trying to comfort her. He was not dressed in ARP uniform, or a tin hat; he was just himself, here, with that woman, who she could see he knew very well.

She did not feel tired now, or sick, or anything but clear and purposeful. She picked her way across to where the two of them were standing. The woman was the first to notice her. Her face was a mess of tears and grit and the baby's face was also grimy and had slug trails of tears down it. Len went stiff with astonishment. He had had one hand on the woman's shoulder but he let it drop as if she was suddenly red hot.

'Oh my goodness,' Ann said. 'What a night – and what a terrible mess! Are you all right, bab?'

She saw the bewildered woman take a moment to recognize her, but as she was dressed almost exactly as she had been when she had called previously, this was not too difficult.

'We're all right,' the young woman said, though her

voice broke and she was struggling not to break down again. 'We were under the stairs, the two of us. But the house . . .' She trailed off.

Seeing into what confusion she had thrown everything, Ann turned to Len with a dazzling smile. 'I called on this lady the other day, for the WVS, met her little boy – isn't he lovely?' She beamed at the child who was staring woefully at her. She had not been imagining it – he really was the spitting image of Sheila. 'You know each other, do you?'

There was the strangest of awkward silences. She could sense the young woman longing for her to go away so that she could carry on pouring out her woes to Len. Which was probably nothing compared to how much Len was longing for her to leave as well.

'Oh,' she added, to the young woman, 'sorry – this is my husband.' She paused for a moment. Len was ashen, looking as if he was desperately trying to think of something to say.

'Well, I'll let you get on,' Ann said. 'I've been up all night – in town. Terrible there. Really bad. I 'spect you've got all sorts to do, reporting back to your ARP post and everything,' she said to Len. To the young woman she said, 'Good luck to you, dear.'

And she took off along the road. Once she had turned into Oak Tree Lane, she realized she was shaking and she had to stop and lean against a wall and breathe. The scene kept crashing through her mind. All her hopes and resolve to make things right with Len seemed so ridiculous now. They had turned to dust and ashes. She saw his face, the shock and confusion. Anger burned in her, like a pilot light just waiting to be sparked into something much more destructive.

Outside the hospital, her insides rebelled, and she

found herself bending over, retching into the gutter. There was nothing but bile in her stomach and luckily no one was around. She bent over, panting for a moment before walking on.

'Mom! Wait!' she heard, when she had just got past the Cadbury works. Joy came dashing down the road to catch her up and Ann stopped, her spirits lifting at seeing her daughter and that she was all right. Joy came and flung her arms round her and they held each other for a moment – something they would normally not have done but after a night like that, it seemed anything was possible.

'Oh Mom, you're all right!' Joy said tearfully. 'They said it was terrible in town and I thought you might be there – I was worried sick.'

'It *was* bad,' she said, linking arms with Joy. My children, she thought. They're my family now. She felt a surge of love for each of them. 'But we survived. I don't know if there's any water – I could murder a cup of tea.'

'There is,' Joy said. 'Nanna told Martin to fill all the pans just in case.'

Ann smiled. 'She did, didn't she? Bless her.'

Martin had even half-filled the bath with water.

'Oh, thank God,' Ann said. 'I can soak my feet as well! They're like blocks of ice!'

They had boiled a kettle and Ann was sitting in the kitchen, sipping tea, her feet in a tin bowl of soothingly warm water, when Len came in. He didn't look at her.

'All right, Dad?' Joy asked. If anyone could get a rise out of him it would be Joy and he glanced at her and nodded. 'There's a drop of tea in the pot.'

Len nodded again and Joy poured him a cup, then got to her feet, yawning.

'I'm all in. I need to get to bed,' she said. 'I'll see you later.'

Len sipped his tea, standing up against the sink. Ann kept her head down to begin with, but angry, bursting emotions rose in her and she looked up, directly at him.

'You were never even in the ARP, Len, were you?'

Thirty-Eight

Ann slid into bed, her nerves so jangled that she knew it would be a miracle if she slept. Her whole body was shaky with rage and frustration. Because the moment she had opened her mouth to say anything Len had stormed off outside into the garden as if she was the one at fault, avoiding all of it. But she also felt so hurt and frightened. Her husband had suddenly become a complete stranger who seemed to have no regard for her or her feelings at all.

She was lying on her back, taking deep breaths to try and calm herself, when she heard Len come upstairs. Of course – he was not working today. He was coming to bed. She turned quickly on to her side, away from him.

Len tiptoed into the room in his socks. Lying turned away from him, eyes closed, as he started to undress, she could picture each move he made – unbuttoning his shirt, sliding his braces down over his shoulders, letting his trousers fall to the floor where he would often leave them, forgetting to pick them up. A moment later the bed shook as he sat on the side to take off his socks.

Still in underpants and vest, he slid in beside her, tossing about before he settled. Every second he was in the room she felt wound up. Now that he was lying here beside her, she kept having to remind herself to breathe. Was he going to speak to her – tell her honestly what was going on?

'I'm not asleep,' she said eventually, into the stillness.

The silence went on, but she could hear from his

breathing that he was not asleep either. Ann turned over to face him. She had closed the curtains but not put up the blackout frames, so there was a murky light in the room. Len was lying on his back, his familiar profile so close to her.

A part of her wanted to curl up, to put her arms round him, Len, her husband of twenty-one years. She wanted to make things better, pretend that nothing had ever happened in their marriage except faithful sweetness – because that had also been there – and their children and her loving in-laws and so many good things . . . And at the same time her body was throbbing with a tense longing to rear up and scream at Len – even to hit him – for betraying her, and to at least make him speak.

The silence went on. *Say something!* her mind was roaring inside. Why do I have to start every conversation that needs to be had? Just open your mouth and damn well *speak to me*! She had reached a point where she felt she might explode and her voice came out harsh and forced.

'Well. Are you ever going to *say* anything?'

Len immediately pulled away and turned huffily on to his side.

'Don't you just turn your back on me!' She thumped the bed with her hand. 'I wasn't born yesterday – I can see what's going on! That baby – he's the image of Sheila, and as for *her*, pretending her husband's away . . .'

'Her name's Marianne,' Len said, without moving. His voice was so hostile she hardly recognized it. 'Not *her*.'

Even though she knew already, she had wanted him to deny it – at least to try to. His words were like a blow. She stayed, raised up on one elbow, staring down at him. All she could see was the side of Len's face, the tip of his ear. The silence went on and on until eventually he turned over again on to his back.

'She loves me.'

It was like being punched. Len saying these words – the Len she had believed would always love her because he couldn't help it. Len, faithful and true. However much she had let him down, he would love her, solidly and eternally. She could hear the unspoken accusation: *You don't love me – you never have.* Not that this was completely true. But there was justice in it, she knew. She was the one who had betrayed him – terribly badly. But she felt stunned, as if this very conversation was unreal.

'Does she really have a husband?' she asked, trying to keep her voice calm.

'No.'

A hundred other questions flocked noisily into her mind like geese. How long, when, how, do you love her, are you going to leave me . . .? Tell me . . .

'And that little boy. He's yours?'

He was silent, as if he could not quite bear to admit it. He was looking away from her, straight up at the ceiling. Eventually, very quietly, he said, 'It was . . . I never meant that to happen.'

'No,' she said, keeping her voice even. She felt triumphant, almost – so I'm not the only one, the only terrible wicked sinner! – and angry, and above all, sad. So very sad. 'I don't s'pose you did.'

She never did sleep and was affronted that Len dropped off quite quickly. Could he just fall asleep through *anything*? Of course, they could not sort all this out straight away, but even so! Ann gave up trying to get to sleep herself with him snoring beside her and got furiously out of bed and dressed again.

316

To her surprise, Joy was still downstairs, dark rings under her eyes and yawning her head off.

'Thought you'd gone to bed,' Ann said.

'I couldn't sleep.'

'I'll make some more tea.'

Ann turned on the gas, keeping her face turned away from Joy because she was afraid she'd start blarting. She felt so exhausted and sick and wrung out. 'What a night.'

'It sounded really bad,' Joy said, yawning again, and Ann did turn round then.

'Go on – you ought to have another go at getting some sleep.' She nearly added, *Don't wake your father*, but then somehow didn't feel like being that considerate. 'You coming to Nanna and Grandad's this afternoon?' she called softly up the stairs behind Joy.

'Yeah. Wake me if I'm not down, all right?'

'All right.' Trying to sound more normal, she added, 'Hope the bugs don't bite.'

'Ooh – ham sandwiches! What are we celebrating?' Martin said, casting the professional eye of an ever-hungry lad over the spread on the table as they all trooped into Margaret and Cyril's back room.

'I thought it was time to open that tin I've been hanging on to,' Margaret said.

She had also made a cake with the faintest dusting of icing sugar on the top. Ann had brought along a plate of paste sandwiches and some plain scones and there were Cadbury's Teatime biscuits and some misshapes from the factory shop.

'So – are you celebrating, Nanna?' Joy asked. The sight of her made Ann smile. Here was she feeling utterly exhausted and Joy, after only a few hours' sleep, looked bright, rosy-cheeked and full of beans. What it was to be young, she thought.

'I suppose I am.' Margaret carried the teapot to the table and Cyril, well-trained, immediately slipped the brown-and-white knitted cosy over the top. Margaret looked round at them all. 'I was saving that tin for Christmas but I thought . . . You know, every day counts, doesn't it? Especially at the moment. And – thing is, I went to see Ida . . .'

They all looked at each other and Margaret held up a hand.

'No, nothing to get upset about.' But there was a catch in her voice and Cyril leaned and touched her arm. 'I'm all right, love. Look – you pour for me, will you? Everyone needs their tea. Come on. Martin, you pass the plates round for me, bab.' She sank on to a chair as if suddenly exhausted. 'It's all just been a bit of a shock.'

Ann sat on the edge of one of the armchairs near the gas fire, which was blasting out heat. It was a wonder Margaret hadn't got bacon burns on her legs, the way she nursed the fire, she thought, looking at her mother-in-law opposite her, as usual huddled as close to it as she could get. Margaret always felt the cold. Ann didn't look at Len. They were there for his mom and dad – acting normal, whatever else was going on between them. And Joy and Martin sat by the table with Cyril.

Margaret held the little flowered plate on her lap with a sandwich on it.

'When I saw her in the church she just kept talking about this place where she'd been. "There", she called it. I didn't ask straight away but in the end some of us tried to find out what had happened – other WVS people, I mean. Where did she live? She didn't seem to know. She said "in the home" and things like that but she had no idea what the address was. It was in town somewhere – she said a few things about that. I honestly don't know still how she managed to get all the way down there where we were – she must have got out and been wandering around.

'Anyway, someone found out – I don't know how – that she was talking about the Agatha Stacey Home on Bath Row. A woman went to enquire and they said someone called Lizzie Patch lived there and had gone missing. Evidently she had started wandering off but this time, because of the raid, she'd gone for much longer and they didn't know where to start looking. She was still there in the church when I left and I felt bad enough not bringing her back here. I did suggest it – I asked her if she wanted to come.' Margaret sounded anxious that they should not think badly of her. 'I said, "Ida" – she was Elizabeth Ida, you see, but she was always Ida at home. "Ida – would you like to come home with me?"'

Margaret paused, shaking her head gently.

'I feel bad saying this but I didn't really want her to. I mean, I barely know who she is – but she's my flesh and blood and it seemed sinful not to offer . . .'

Ann was startled by 'sinful'. It was not the sort of word Margaret used as a rule.

'But she sort of gave me a look – not with any emotion really. It was just as if I'd offered her a cup of tea – something every day. And she said, "Oh no, ta very much. No." And she just kept saying, 'No, no, no . . ." Not sort of angrily or anything like that – it was more as if it was just something she couldn't even imagine.

'So I said, "Well, it's going to be time for me to get off home soon." And she just nodded and said, "Oh ar – all right. Well, you'd best get off, bab."'

Margaret wiped her eyes. Again, Cyril reached over and stroked her arm.

'You did your best, Margaret.'

'You did, Mom,' Len said.

'I know. And I was relieved, to tell you the truth.'

'She's used to what she's used to, isn't she, Nanna?' Martin said, on completion of a scone.

'She must've been there years,' Cyril said. ''Er wouldn't know anything else.'

'You can go and see her, can't you?' Joy said. 'I expect she'd like that.'

'You can get to know each other again,' Ann said.

'Yes, I know.' Margaret picked up her sandwich and then put it down again. 'I just keep thinking – all these years. I mean, she was put away – like putting something at the back of a cupboard and forgetting about it. It seems terrible. Wicked. Whatever she was supposed to have done I don't s'pose it was all her fault.'

They all reassured her that it was not her fault either and there was nothing that she could have done. They all made the tea a celebration – of their life together, of these moments.

But, Ann thought, staring into the glow of the gas fire, it was awful and cruel, the way people – women above all, she noticed – were punished for their mistakes while the men got off scot-free. And even in her anger with Len she could see that overall she might have got off lightly.

As soon as they stepped out into the dark street, the warmth of the family tea faded and immediately there was only one thought.

'Quick,' Joy said. 'Let's get inside. Oh, please don't let us have to spend the night out there . . .'

If they come tonight, I'll have to go on duty, Ann thought. She was so tired now, she felt almost dizzy. And

320

the gas and water were off in town – how on earth were the fire brigade going to manage if there was a raid?

Although their house was barely a couple of minutes away, getting home before the siren seemed like an achievement. Len got the door open and stood back for the family to run inside. And the minutes ticked by, all of them with ears pricked, waiting. But it didn't come and didn't come . . .

And Ann and Len, once alone, didn't have the heart to talk about anything more. They were both so tired and it was as if the tea with Margaret and Cyril, what had happened over Ida and just the sense of home, of things being as they always had, made everything else fade into the background.

Tomorrow, Ann thought as she slipped into sleep beside Len. We'll have to face things. But not now. And she slept and slept.

Thirty-Nine

It was early afternoon, two days later, and Joy had been sleeping off the night shift. She came down fresh from a good kip to find her mother chopping vegetables, throwing them into a pan as if they were, if not quite enemies, at least things against which she held a strong personal grudge.

'What've those parsnips ever done?' Joy joked, but Mom took no notice.

'Here –' She nodded towards the table. 'Letter for you.'

Joy glanced at her as she picked up the envelope with Lawrence's handwriting on it, waiting for the questions to start. But Mom didn't seem bothered or curious – in fact, lately she seemed to be off with the fairies most of the time. And Dad was just as bad. It was the war, Joy thought. People their age couldn't cope with missing a bit of sleep.

She slipped the letter into her pocket and ran upstairs again, her limbs feeling weak and watery. All she had been able to think of for the last days, since she went to Ladywood, was Alan. Alan who she had thought she knew. Alan who was soon due home on leave before they sent him off to goodness knew where. And now this, Lawrence, bursting back into her life, into her feelings again. Breathless, she sat on the edge of the bed.

Dearest Lovely Girl,

I can be free on Tuesday afternoon. Any good? Sorry it's short notice. We could meet in town – how about at New Street, say 2.30 p.m.? I'll go anyway and hope you can make it. Just longing to see you.

Lawrence x

Joy sat on her bed, still in her nightclothes, and stared at the letter. Lawrence's note filled her with colliding emotions: excitement at the desire she could read through the words, longing – of course she would go and meet him! But with these feelings a growing anger and resentment walked hand in hand. This was a married man who was being unfaithful to his wife, who had no intention of making any kind of future with her. Lawrence was using her, wasn't he? Why did she not just tear up the letter and have nothing more to do with him?

She looked out of the window, facing over the back, at the bare trees. It had been a bleak month in a bleak time. What Lawrence had said to her, about the Supermarine in Southampton – about how they could all be dead soon . . . When he spoke, everything he said had made sense. She did not think he was a chancer – not really. He had been honest. He had spoken of this as a time unconnected to their other lives which – if they were spared – would go on, afterwards. Life in brackets, she thought. A time when we seize all the life we can get. Separate from normal. Of course she would meet him.

On the way, she told herself to hold back. She could just have a bit of fun, but nothing serious. But as soon as she set eyes on Lawrence, she felt anything but detached. The very sight of him, in his overcoat, leaning up against a wall outside the station – something about the very shape of him – made her want him all over again.

'Hello!' He pushed off against the wall with his usual energy and came to kiss her. His eyes, dark and expressive, seemed to glow at the sight of her, along with a twinkle of humour, as if he found her amusing.

He took her hand and they started to walk, slowly, glancing at each other amid the crowds along New Street, smiling in happiness at seeing each other.

Forget everything, she said to herself. Just be here.

'Fancy some tea?' Lawrence said.

'I've not long had dinner,' she laughed.

'Ah, but you've got a healthy appetite,' he said. 'And I didn't mean straight away necessarily.' He stopped and pulled her to one side of the pavement. Serious now, he looked down at her. 'Thing is – I've got a room. In the Midland. I just thought, it's very hard to find any time – or a place where we can just relax and be together . . .'

Joy listened, her breath becoming shallow. A hotel room . . . Did this mean . . .? What did this mean – and what did Lawrence expect of her? She was suddenly aware, as she was not normally, of the difference in their ages. Lawrence was ten years older, experienced, while she . . . Suddenly she felt under pressure to do things she was not ready for – was she? She felt young and foolish and her cheeks burned.

'I . . .' she began, but did not know how to go on.

'It's all right,' he said gently. 'We can order some tea later if you like. It would just be nice to be able to sit down somewhere in peace and in the warm, wouldn't it? Instead of having to move on all the time.'

Put like that, it would. She replaced her hand in his and they walked into the main entrance of the hotel.

*

Upstairs, in the rather gloomy room facing out from the back of the hotel, she tried not to dwell on what anyone had been thinking of her when they booked in as Mr and Mrs Dayton. She kept her gloves on, thinking they might look for a ring on her hand, but the receptionist did not even glance at her. If he had, she thought her blushes would have given her away. She stood there feeling like a fish out of water and trying to look relaxed and as Mrs Dayton-ish as she could manage. It was as if she was in a dream suddenly, hardly able to believe where she was or what she was doing.

'Here – you have the chair,' Lawrence said, helping her off with her coat. Was it that the room was not very warm – was that why she was shivering? She folded her arms and huddled into herself. He peeled his own coat off and hung them both up before sitting on the edge of the bed.

'It *is* chilly in here,' he said. 'Sure you won't change your mind about the tea?'

'All right.' She smiled, relieved. Tea would be something to do and they could talk and not feel so awkward. Lawrence popped out to order a tray and she sat looking round her at the drab, neutral-coloured decor in the room, the fawn bedspread, pale walls, soft green curtains.

They chatted for a time – he on the bed, she on the chair. The tea arrived and they drank it. Its warmth made her relax. Joy told him about the night shift, about the ENSA troop who had come in to sing last night.

'They were ever so good,' she said. 'You know, lots of songs and some good playing – the man on the piano was fantastic. Usually it's just one of our lot and they're not bad – they play while we're eating in the dining room. It keeps everyone cheerful.'

'Yes, it's good,' Lawrence said. 'Nothing like a sing-song

to cheer you up – and a dance, of course.' He put his cup down. 'Come on. I know there's no music but we could make our own! Fancy a bit of a dance?'

She stood, laughing at the idea, and soon they had cleared the chair and little table out of the way and were cha-cha-cha-ing up and down the room, both singing along, beaming at each other. They did a few numbers and gradually as they danced, their eyes met and they hummed more softly and stopped laughing and their feet were moving automatically, expertly, as they slid around the floor, each fastened in the other's gaze.

When they stopped, she hardly noticed, because Lawrence was holding her more tightly, looking deep into her eyes. All she could see, all she wanted to see, was his face. Soon they were kissing, deeply, urgently, in a way she never had with anyone before.

It all became quickly very passionate. Lawrence's hands moved over the silky softness of her dress, over her breasts. A small, alarmed corner of her mind signalled to her to make him stop. But a much larger part of it desperately wanted those hands to go on and on exploring – her body lit up, curious and full of need. This is really life, her own voice said in her mind. You're a real woman now.

'Will you come and lie with me?' Lawrence said. She could see all the longing, a hypnotized look in his eyes, and wondered if she looked the same because all she felt was the desire to go on and on, however this went, to follow it until the end.

He led her gently to the bed and they lay clothed, holding and kissing, their hands exploring each other fiercely. Every so often Lawrence stopped and just lay looking at her. He reached to stroke her face.

'You really are so lovely,' he said wistfully. And after a time, he sat up and said, 'Look, I don't know if you want to give yourself to me – fully. I would understand if you didn't.' He was facing away from her. Now that he had sat up she could feel the cold air descending on her and she wanted him to come back and warm her again.

'You know how things are. I can't pretend they are any different. All I'd say is – if you would . . .' He reached over into the pocket of his jacket, which he had taken off and flung on the chair, and brought out a little packet which he held up. 'I'd protect you, of course. I don't want you getting into any trouble on account of me.'

Joy lay, vulnerable, caught in the moment, staring back at him as he turned to her.

'You know I can't promise anything – only that it would make me very, very happy to . . .' She realized then that he was also embarrassed, having to put any of this into words. 'To be with you – like that.' He lay down and laid his palm on her cheek again. 'You are the loveliest girl.' Very gently he kissed her lips.

She should say no, she knew. All correct behaviour pointed that way, every sensible piece of advice that she might be given. This married man, using her. This man, who had left her lying there, weak, almost boneless with desire.

'I haven't done it before,' she said, her voice small.

'I know.' Lawrence had his eyes fixed on hers. He must have seen her answer in them – her trembling, fearful answer, because he said, 'I know, my sweet. We must be very gentle.'

He got up and helped her to her feet, then pulled back the sheet and blankets and the cover. Bending down, he took the hem of her dress and carefully lifted it over her head.

*

On the tram, riding back along the Bristol Road – for she had to get to work that night – it felt like another day, another age, compared with her journey earlier. As she had got on at Navigation Street, she was able to get a seat and keep her face turned towards the window. It felt as if everyone was looking at her – that girl who had just . . . Well, almost just . . .

There was a throbbing between her legs – not because they had gone the whole way, in the end. More because they had not. It was as if the cold on her skin when he pulled her slip over her head had brought her back to herself. Lawrence was reaching round to unfasten her bra, while she was becoming more aware of how aroused he was and suddenly her whole being withdrew. What was she doing here, with this man? She loved Alan – Alan who had hurt her so badly, but yet she still felt there must be a reason because he was a good man – she *knew* he was, at heart.

'No!' She put her hand on his chest and began to push him away. 'I'm sorry, I can't. Not like this.' And she burst into tears, feeling foolish and frightened and disappointed but she knew this was not right. Not where she was meant to be.

For a moment he looked stunned, seeming to come back to himself. Then he put his arms round her.

'It's all right. It's OK. Look, come – we'll just lie here . . .'

He had even put her slip over her head again as if she were a little child and Joy felt almost worse saying no to him because he was being so kind and nice to her. They got under the bedclothes and held each other, getting warm again.

Tides of feeling clashed in her now. Dreamily she recalled Lawrence's face, his taut look of need before she

328

pushed him away. Tears rose in her eyes – disappointment for him and for herself as well. He was a nice man, a good man – she knew she loved him, or would, if she was allowed to. But in the end he was not for her, and he had not hidden that from her, or not for long. She knew she had done the right thing – hadn't she? But why was she full of such cold, sad feelings?

She dabbed her eyes with the edge of her coat sleeve. Perhaps she would never have another chance to become a woman in that way. There might never be another man who wanted her like that . . .

If only Sheila was at home, she found herself thinking. If only they could sit together and she could tell her everything that was happening with Lawrence, with Alan – just pour her heart out. But that fantasy – of a sister who she could sit with, tell all her secrets to, who would listen and understand – soon vanished, like a soap bubble. It was partly her fault that she and Sheila had never been close. Joy was so often impatient with Sheila's stolid, rather fearful ways. Sheila was married to the only boyfriend she had ever had. How could she tell her that, at the age of only eighteen and *out of wedlock* as Sheila would have said, she had come so close to losing her virginity to a married man? Sheila would have a fit! She almost giggled thinking about it. And she couldn't talk to Norma either – not about Lawrence, this stranger ten years older than them. It just didn't feel right.

Joy drew in a long breath and sighed. She had been living in a dream bubble, full of her romance with Lawrence, and she was bewitched by desire and curiosity. But now it had been pricked and vanished into nothing and life felt grey and cold. Lawrence was a nice man – a good companion, gentle. He had looked after her. But all she and he could have was a love affair to help them get through the war. She had not given herself to him today, but if she kept seeing him, she knew it would happen sooner or later because she couldn't keep saying no to him. And in the end, he had a wife, who he loved.

And there was Alan. Her body fluttered with nerves at the thought. Foreboding filled her. The day after tomorrow Alan would be in Birmingham. Alan who she had last seen dancing with that girl. Alan the stranger who she had thought she loved. The sight of Alan's mother, looking so sick and deranged, chilled her through again. And what the coalman said about his father – no wonder Alan had secrets to hide. How could she trust to loving him after all that? And yet she wanted to with all her heart.

Leaning her forehead against the window she looked out through the grimy glass, feeling suddenly exhausted by all of it.

Forty

'Hello, Alan!' Joy heard her mother's voice float upstairs from the hall. 'Look at you – don't you look well! Come on in out of the wet.'

Joy was perched on the side of the bed, her stomach churning and her hands clenched in her lap.

'All right, Mrs Gilby.' Even from up here she could tell Alan sounded nervous. 'Yeah, they keep us fit, that's for sure – a lot of square-bashing.'

'I can see that,' Mom said. 'Now, you'll be wanting Joy. Staying for a cup of tea?'

'I dunno,' Alan said with a little laugh. 'Have to ask the boss, won't we?'

'Joy?' Mom shouted upstairs. 'Alan's here!'

It was funny how people thought you couldn't hear a word just because you were upstairs, Joy thought. Getting to her feet she found her legs were shaky. She had put on her favourite skirt, in a green-and-fawn check and a matching green blouse. Taking a second to look at her hair, longer now and pinned back at each side so that it hung in waves over her shoulders, she went to the stairs. She made herself go down slowly, casually, as if she did not have butterflies fluttering in her belly and hands moist from nerves.

'All right, Joy?'

Alan had come in his uniform. The shoulders were dark with rain and he looked very spruce and handsome with the cap settled on his cropped hair, eyes smiling up at her.

'Hello, Al.'

'Cup of tea?' Mom said.

'Yes, all right.' It would be nice to talk with Mom for a while, Joy thought, smooth things over. But she'd have to get him out of here to have a proper conversation.

Mom disappeared into the kitchen and Joy was conscious of Alan following her into the back room, could almost feel his eyes tracing her outline from behind. Her breathing was shallow with nerves, but she was damned if she was going to show it.

'Have a seat,' she said, cool and detached.

Alan took off his cap, shook the wet off it and sat forward, arms resting on his thighs, the cap between his hands.

'Want me to hang that up?'

'Oh no, yer all right.' He put it on the floor near the fire. 'Soon dry out.'

'So, how's the army?' She was sitting on the edge of her chair, feet together.

'It's all right.'

'All right? Is that all you've got to say?' She could feel she was being pert, aggressive in a way. The hurt she had been carrying inside her all these weeks was hard to keep at bay. Luckily Mom came in with a tray of tea then and chatted with Alan, asking him questions.

Joy watched him, that handsome face she had known – loved, she thought – for two years now, lit up with the attention Mom was giving him. Joy thought for a moment of Alan's mother and she was suddenly flooded with bafflement and pity. When had that woman ever sat him down with tea and asked him about himself? What on earth had things been like for him at home?

They drank tea and Mom offered some biscuits –
Cadbury misshapes, of course.

'Aha!' Alan said. 'Now this feels like home, all right!
I've missed it. How are things?' He looked at Joy.

'Oh, it's much the same – except it isn't, what with all
the war work.'

'Joy's working nights now,' Ann said proudly. Joy had
told Alan this already in her letters, but never mind, she
thought. 'You're on some sort of stamping machine,
aren't you, love?'

'Yeah.' Joy grinned. 'Bit different.'

Her eyes met Alan's, seeing the warmth in his, but a
second later his eyes clouded over into uncertainty. This
hurt, and Joy looked away, feeling as if she might cry, and
she fought against the tightness growing in her chest. It
was so lovely to see him, have him here again like old
times – but now she realized she hardly knew Alan,
really.

When they had made polite conversation with Mom
and drunk their tea, all of which seemed to take an eternity, Alan looked across at her.

'Fancy a little walk, Joy? I wouldn't mind a look at the
old place.'

'You don't want to go out in this, do you?' Mom said.
Rain was falling steadily outside again.

'I've got an umbrella,' Joy said.

The rain was easing up when they went out, the sun
straining to appear in a watery sky. They headed up
Linden Road, Joy under the umbrella. The atmosphere
changed immediately. She could not keep up her pretence
of normality any longer. Her heart was thudding, her
breath shallow and for some time neither of them spoke.
She watched the ground, the rivulets of water running

along the kerb. Alan didn't speak either and eventually Joy felt that if she didn't speak, she would explode.

'So.' She heard herself, the harsh upset in her voice. 'You going to explain any of this?'

Out of the corner of her eye she saw him look at her, then away. 'This?'

She stopped and turned furiously to face him. 'Well, for a start, I was at that dance at the Y when you came home on leave the first time and never even bothered to tell me you were there. You didn't see me, did you? But I saw you, all right, with *that girl*, whoever she was. And that's just the start of all the things you've never got around to telling me.'

She looked up then and Alan was staring at her in complete bewilderment.

'I dunno what the hell you're going on about,' he said. 'What Y – where? And when?'

'When you came home after training – I *suppose*, since you never even got in touch.' She couldn't help her hurt spilling out. 'You've been hopeless about writing. That's why I stopped writing to you!' That and Lawrence, she thought guiltily. But Lawrence was in the past now. She wasn't going to go into all that.

Alan looked wretched. 'I know. I didn't get in touch then. My mom was – she's not well and she was really bad then and I didn't want to . . .' He trailed off miserably. 'Honest to God, Joy, I don't know anything about any dance because there was no chance to go out anywhere. That wasn't me.'

'But . . .' She thought back: that lad with his cropped hair, the shape of his face, arm round the girl's shoulders . . . 'It *was* you!'

'No,' Alan said quietly. 'It wasn't.'

Joy had the wind taken right out of her sails. She had

been so sure – so quick to leap to accusing him because of her wounded feelings. That other lad had looked so like Alan, but she could tell by his tone that he was telling the truth and she felt very stupid. She was cold suddenly, and miserable, all her stored-up feelings coming to the surface, and as they walked on, she could not hold back her tears.

'I just . . . I don't feel you've been telling me the truth, Al – about all sorts of things. At least, not telling lies exactly, just not telling me anything. I went to your house.'

She expected an eruption, rage from him, but all he did was frown.

'You what?'

'I went to Stour Street. Al, I'm so sick of all this – of never knowing what you feel about me, or anything about you. It hurts – can't you see that? I thought we were . . . Anyway, I went. I met Irene, your sister – and your mom.'

There was a silence and they walked on, slowly, Joy wiping her eyes. Then he said quietly, 'You went all the way over there?' He glanced at her, shamefaced. 'Can you blame me, then? You saw our mom. And my father . . .'

'I know where he is,' Joy said, more gently now. 'What did he do?'

'Oh, went down for burglary.' His voice was hard, contemptuous. 'Not for the first time. He can't seem to help himself. Anything rather than make the effort and hold down a job. He's a waster – and a boozer.' He looked at her fearfully. 'Not a lot to be proud of, is it? Our mom's always suffered with her nerves and it just got worse and worse 'cause of him. He's not a nice man. Takes it out on anyone but himself.'

'Irene – she's very nice.'

She looked up at Alan and he smiled sadly. 'Everything I've had, I owe to Irene . . . She's been like a mom to me as well as a sister. Our older brother, Phil – he's married with kids now. He's all right. But it was Renie held everything together. Things were – well, they weren't good a lot of the time. She and Phil went out and earned the money. She did well, Irene did. She got me my first dance lessons before I was working and could pay for it myself. She was the one said I should apply to work at Cadbury's. She always looked out, looked bigger than anyone else. She's the best.'

Joy listened, moved. 'I wish you'd told me before,' she said.

'You saw it – not much to be proud of. I just wanted to get out. Dancing's always been my way of getting away. I always danced, just natural like, from when I was small and . . . Well, Renie saved me. She did. But I didn't want any of that near Cadbury's – or near you.'

They had turned down Bournville Lane and were walking towards the lodges at the entrance to Cadbury's. They stopped at the steps leading down to Birdcage Walk and looked across the grand, brick frontage of Cadbury's, flanked by beautiful, sweeping playing fields and a cricket pavilion, the perimeter edged with trees.

'This place's meant everything to me,' he said. 'I was over the moon when I got in.' He laughed. 'Not like in your family where it's practically a birthright!'

Joy pulled him aside as someone else wanted to get past down the steps.

'I just wish you'd said.' Even though it had been a sho͏ͨ seeing Alan's home, and all of it made her uneasy, ͏ such a relief. This was about his family, not any- ͏ had done, nothing to do with her. The way he ͏ g, it was that he didn't feel good enough for her, and she was moved by him and all he must have had to suffer. Alan put his hands in his pockets, his blue eyes looking across the sports pitches, the buildings swathed in camouflage. His face was so handsome, so lovely, she just wanted to put her arms round him, but he seemed far away in himself and she held back.

'I s'pose all this'll be over eventually.'

'When've you got to go back?' Joy asked.

'Monday.' He looked round at her. 'Then we're going – I don't even know where. More training of some sort I think. Come on, let's walk through.' Alan set off down the steps and she followed. He looked fondly around him as they passed through the factory.

'I've missed this place.'

'Well, did anyone ask you to join up?' she said tartly.

'No, but they would've sooner or later. And I wanted—'

He stopped abruptly and turned to her as they reached the other side of the factory. He looked very tense.

'Thing is, Joy . . .' He seemed to dry up, looked upset and wretched.

'Come on, Al, just say what you've got to say.' She was immediately sorry and put her hand on his arm. 'I mean, look. I'm not being nasty, but I never know where I am with you. And it's . . . It's upsetting . . .' Her voice went high and her throat had gone all tight again. Alan was looking down at her now, seeming afraid, almost. But he could hear how she sounded and saw the tears in her eyes.

'The thing is . . .' He stalled, then started again. 'I just need to get away. Sort myself out. I'm frightened to be with you – or with any woman. The way I feel sometimes . . .'

His face was strained. 'I just get so angry at times . . . I'm scared what I might do.'

Joy looked back at him, tears trickling down her cheeks. She did not really know what he meant but she was full of tenderness for him because she could see what it was costing him to tell her this.

'That night – remember? When I got sort of steamed up with you? In town?'

She nodded. Not something she would ever forget. It had been strange and frightening at the time, but it was not the Alan she usually saw.

'Sometimes, the way I feel . . . And the way my dad is, when he's . . . I don't let it out, hardly ever. I try to be better than I feel. Better than *him*. But I know that one day . . . It's like this rage I can't control. And that night I came that close to . . .' He looked into her face. 'It's not your fault. I've got this animal inside me when it comes to women. I'm frightened even to kiss you because then we might be, you know, we might end up getting wed and you'd be mine and then, if you was to do one thing out of line . . .' He half-turned away from her. 'I can't explain it. It's just there, in me. I thought, if I went into the Army maybe it'd sort me out – cure me, sort of thing.'

'Oh, Alan!' She wept now. 'I'm sure it's not that bad – you don't need curing! Look, if we just keep being honest with each other . . . I love you, Al – I've loved you for ages and I just want to be with you, help you! Oh, come here.' She held her arms out and after a moment's hesitation, Alan stepped forward. Joy held him tight, feeling his arms round her, and she wept, just so happy and relieved that he was here and they were talking.

'I really love you,' she sobbed.

'I love you, too,' she heard him say gruffly. 'I just don't think I'm good enough for you.'

'Don't talk daft.' She held him even closer. 'You're lovely, Al. And – you're the best dancer ever.'

'Dancing *is* the best,' he said, his lips close to her ear. 'You and me – the way we dance together . . . But you don't want me, Joy. Not for anything else.'

'But I do – course I do!' She stepped back to look up at him. His face wore such a sad, defeated expression, it made her ache. 'I know you got angry that once. But all the rest of the time . . .' She looked into his eyes, showing him her tears, her hurt. 'I've been in love with you for ages, Al, and I know you love me. And if we're together we can get over anything!'

He looked at her, seemingly in wonder. 'Have you really – been in love with me all this time?'

'You must know I have,' she said.

He looked away for a moment, as if struggling with himself, then turned suddenly and put his arms tight around her again, his lips finding hers, kissing her as if he had a well of passion inside him he had been holding back. And she wrapped her arms tightly round him, feeling the khaki drill under her fingers that meant soon he would have to go away, when they were only just truly finding one another now . . . Tears ran down her cheeks.

'That's it, lad, you go for it!' a man said as he walked past and they both pulled back, embarrassed – laughing, crying.

Alan held her by the shoulders, looking at her as if drinking her in.

'I've always loved you too, Joy,' he said. 'But the thing is – I've felt I was living in two different lives. There's home – with our dad. And then Mom – she was . . .' He trailed off, a look of deep shame coming over him. But he forced himself to go on. 'There was a time she was in the asylum for a bit – at Winston Green. How could I say that, at work? Any of it? Or to you. It was another world for me, over here, and the dancing and that. The thought

339

of you coming to our house . . .' He stopped, shaking his head.

'Well, now I know,' Joy said. She couldn't lie and say she had not found the sight of Mrs Bishop disturbing, frightening even. Just the memory of that prematurely aged, deranged-looking face made her want to recoil. But it sounded as if the poor woman had been driven to it and now at least Alan was talking to her, telling her the truth. It made sense of all of it – and it meant everything. This was the Alan she loved and wanted to be with. 'I suppose she can't help it, Al – if she's poorly.'

He nodded, a painful expression on his face. He took her arm and they started walking slowly back along Birdcage Walk.

'Look, we've not got long. Let's not spend it talking about that.'

She leaned her head on his shoulder for a moment, so happy now. Her Alan – he did love her and she loved him! It made all the difference to everything. And Lawrence – that had just been her being hurt and angry and looking for something to make herself feel better. Her and Alan – that was what was true.

'Thing is,' he said. 'Maybe going off – the Army and that – will make a better man of me. I want to come back better, for you. If I do come back.'

Joy went cold. She clung to his arm. 'Don't say that! You've got to come back! Of course you will!'

'Yeah, course I will.' He pulled her into his arms again. 'You're my girl, Joy – that's what I want, if you know all there is to know about me and you'll still have me.'

'Oh, Al – of course I'll have you. I love you, love you, love you . . .' She stood on tiptoes and kissed his face all over.

'And I love you, girl!' He was laughing.

She wrapped her arms round him again and they stood under the umbrella, caught up in each other and their happiness, not caring about the grey and the wet, not caring about anything else at that moment, together, joyful as the rain fell, swishing down all around them.

Forty-One

Arrangements for Maurice Vellacott's funeral, to be held at the little village church in Goring, were under way. A London undertaker was to drive his remains back home and a service was to be held. Audrey had been to see the vicar and discuss everything.

'I played the dutiful mourning wife,' she said when she returned late one afternoon, from making arrangements in London. Sheila could read the strain of it all in her face. 'I don't want anyone in the village knowing the truth of things.'

'But you are mourning – in a way,' Sheila pointed out. She could see the shock and sadness in every line of Audrey. 'He was still your sons' father and you had part of your life with him.'

'He wasn't all bad,' Audrey admitted, sinking on to a kitchen chair exhaustedly, still in her coat and hat. 'We got along all right for brief intervals, I suppose. It's just that when someone has treated you a certain way it's hard to behave as if nothing has happened afterwards.' She sighed. 'Is there any tea left in the pot, Sheila?'

As Sheila poured, she said thoughtfully, 'I blame Maurice's father. He was in the Army. A complete bastard.'

Sheila almost poured tea all over the tablecloth.

'He *was* though.' Audrey looked up. Suddenly she laughed, seeing Sheila's face. 'Sorry to shock you – again. But there's no other word for it. Thanks, Sheila. The vicar has fixed the funeral for next Monday. His brother and family will be coming, of course . . .'

'I'll help however I can,' Sheila said.

'I know you will. And you won't give away my sorry little secrets, will you?'

'Of course I won't.' It was not hard to promise – why ever would she go gossiping about Audrey?

Audrey smiled at her. 'You're a gem, Sheila.'

Sheila did everything she could to be a help and comfort to Audrey and the boys during those awful, shocking days. She was surprised by her own strength, that she could take charge of things when she needed to. Audrey's initial reaction when she heard about Maurice's death sank into something sadder and more regretful.

'I just wish,' she said as they sat together by the fire a couple of evenings after the news, 'that Maurice had been the person I thought I was marrying.'

She was hunched forward on her armchair, looking into the hearth. The room was cosy, smelling of coal dust and woodsmoke, the curtains closed over the blackout blinds. Audrey was wearing a dark brown frock – she had no black clothes except a cocktail dress, she said – and it made her face look even more pale and pinched. Sheila sat with her knitting in her lap – a little yellow jersey for Elaine – but she did not manage a stitch because it felt insensitive to be busy when Audrey was talking.

'We met at my cousin's wedding in London, would you believe.' She looked across at Sheila with a faint smile. 'Quite a society do – I felt a very frumpy country mouse set against that side of the family. Maurice was a friend of the groom and we . . . Well, we clicked. He was very entertaining, nice-looking . . . He could be very charming.' Her voice lowered into bitterness. 'And of course I thought I had fallen in love, silly little thing. I had, in a way, but I had fallen for a mirage.

'He was all an act, Maurice was. I've never seen him in court but my golly I can imagine – the charm, the charisma. The mighty barrister. Anyway . . .' She brushed something off her dress, her face twisting as if she had a nasty taste in her mouth. 'He kept up the charm until after the wedding, of course. And then I found out what he was really like. Mean. A bully. A joyless . . .' She tailed off as if ashamed to be saying such things. 'And when I was pregnant – oh my Lord. He sulked through both pregnancies because I was sick and then tired and not just there on tap all the time.'

Sheila watched her, feeling embarrassed, in a way, to be let in on all this, but also bewildered and sad for Audrey.

'I mean, I've heard other women say their husband changed after marriage. You know, they make little jokes – "Oh yes, he was all over me until the knot was tied," or "Of course you never really know a man until you've lived with him." And I've thought, do they mean their husbands are like mine? Do they virtually rape them every time they demand marital relations?'

Her voice had become high and shrill, her eyes stretched and full of rage.

'I'd always be listening out for some sort of sign, that someone lived the way I did. But no, I don't think they *did* mean that! They were talking about . . . I don't know, their husbands leaving their clothes on the floor like spoilt children or belching loudly or some other such charm. But small things . . . And all the time I was thinking, You have no idea – your husband is a tame sheep compared with mine who's a vile wild animal! And my boys . . . I've so often wished we'd had girls so that they would not think they had to be like him . . .'

344

She started sobbing then, her shoulders shaking. Sheila got up and went to kneel beside her, feeling helpless.

'I'm ever so sorry,' she said. 'It sounds terrible – having to put up with all that.'

'*I hated him so much!*' Audrey half-screamed, gripping Sheila's hand. 'Sometimes I thought I'd go mad – when I was supposed to love him, was *trying* to be a loving wife. And I wanted someone else to see – that's partly why I offered to have someone to stay. Maurice agreed which surprised me, but then he's hardly here and I think he just thought you'd vanish in a puff of smoke for his convenience at the weekend. God, the strain he must have been under trying to be reasonably civil when you were here!'

She laughed, wildly, then suddenly looked down at Sheila.

'Your husband – did he change when you got married?'

'No.' Sheila shook her head, feeling almost guilty at having a husband who was loving and kind. 'It wasn't easy when we first had Elaine – we were in his lodgings in Grimsby and we hardly saw each other. I was worried about him going out to sea – he's in the RAF but the air-sea rescue people work off boats. But I hated it there in the end and I went home. It wasn't his fault, it was just all new to us both. Kenneth's never moody or anything – he's just as he is. And very grown up really.'

'Well, Maurice had another side to him, all right.' Audrey's voice was hard. 'And he kept it well hidden from me, innocent little fool that I was.' She stared into the fire. 'I would have so loved a nice marriage. I'm very loyal and biddable really – good wife material.'

'Course you are.' Sheila squeezed her hand, before getting up and going back to her chair. 'The boys seem to be doing quite well?' she said carefully.

Audrey had broken the news to the two of them the day before. Sheila had been waiting for them to act up and be difficult – Edward especially. So far though, they had been subdued, in fact sweet-natured. She wondered what they were feeling and realized they had probably not taken any of this in yet.

Audrey nodded. 'Poor darlings. I suppose the funeral will bring it all home.'

Some of the time it was hard to take in that Maurice Vellacott was dead because the days seemed so much as they had been before. Children's routines, little walks in the village, shopping and cooking, managing the rations and the news, always the news; sitting by the wireless on those dark winter evenings hearing the smooth voices of Stuart Hibberd, Alvar Lidell and the other newsreaders recounting more terrible developments of the war, more nights of bombing.

It came home to them more on that first Saturday, when he did not come home and nothing changed. It was another dull, mizzling day – the sort of day of which there had been too many.

'I'll take the boys out in the garden for a while,' Audrey said, wearily putting her mac on. 'They can kick a ball around for a bit. I can't face another walk in this.'

So when the doorbell rang soon afterwards, it was Sheila who hurried to open up before the person rang again and woke Elaine who she had just put down for a nap. She guessed it might be someone from the church come to talk to Audrey about flowers or arrangements. When she pulled the heavy front door open, she saw an unknown woman in a smart, emerald-green coat and hat. She was tall, slender and well made-up, with coppery brown hair under the hat. Standing just behind her were two little girls. Was it a flag day or something? Sheila thought, wondering if she had any small change.

'Er – hello,' she said. Then trying to sound a bit more respectable she added, 'Good afternoon.'

The woman jutted her chin out in a defiant-looking way that Sheila could not make sense of.

'Mrs Vellacott?'

'No . . . I'm, er . . . That's not me. I can fetch her for you,' Sheila said. She was about to hurry away before adding, 'What is it concerning?'

'Oh . . . Look . . .' the woman snapped back, seeming suddenly flummoxed. 'It's too difficult to explain. Just fetch her for me, would you?'

Sheila, realizing she had been cast as the maid, went out to fetch Audrey.

'You carry on, boys!' Audrey said. 'Back in a minute!'

Sheila, no longer needed, went into the back sitting room and settled for a few minutes' rest now Elaine was asleep. She picked up a magazine. Voices came from the front and she expected the door to close and Audrey to come through and go back into the garden. Instead of which she realized the woman and children were being invited into the house. The front door thudded closed and a moment later, Audrey led them into the room.

Her eyes were glittering strangely, her mouth fixed in something that was trying to be a smile but did not quite come off.

'Right.' She turned to the strange woman who also looked as if her nerves were being shredded one by one. 'If we are to have this conversation, I should like it to be here – in front of my friend. This is Sheila Carson. And this –' she indicated the stranger – 'is . . .?'

'Monica Gordon,' the woman said.

The hostility in her voice was thinning and she now

347

sounded close to tears. The girls, pretty little things with a ribbon tied in their coppery curls, and who Sheila realized must be twins of about three years old, stood round-eyed and mute.

'Monica Gordon,' Audrey said, digesting this. 'Well, Sheila – according to Miss Gordon, or is it Mrs?'

'How could it be?' she snapped.

'Well, yes, indeed,' Audrey said. 'Monica is Maurice's other wife, apparently. Well, not wife, of course – even he was legal man enough not to act as a bigamist. And these are Maurice's daughters.'

Sheila actually felt her mouth drop open. Even in that moment her next letter to Kenneth was forming. *I thought when I came down here I'd learn how the other half live but I certainly wasn't expecting any of this . . .*

And then as she focused again, Audrey was saying, to her disbelief, 'I imagine, if you've come all this way to find out about the funeral, you might like a cup of tea?'

'I'll make it!' Sheila said, jumping up at once.

As she came back in with the tray of tea, the boys erupted into the house.

Audrey jumped up as if to stop them coming in before realizing she couldn't.

'I hope you've taken your shoes off?' she shouted.

Edward and Charlie appeared at the door and stared.

'Who're they?' Edward said warily. 'Have they got to live with us as well?'

'No!' Audrey said. 'They have just come for a visit.'

Sheila watched, fascinated, as both women fell into behaving well in front of the children. All, as they must both have been realizing, Maurice's children and therefore each other's half-brothers and -sisters.

'This is . . .' Audrey looked at Monica who seemed to

be relaxing more by the moment. Sheila wondered what she had expected.

'This is Barbara,' Monica said. 'And Ella.'

'They're twins,' Audrey said brightly. 'Have you ever seen any twins before?'

'No,' Edward said, sounding as if he definitely didn't want to either.

'Charlie . . .' Sheila straightened up from pouring tea and spoke softly to him. 'Why don't you take the girls into the other room and find something for them to play with?'

'But they're girls,' Edward objected.

'I was speaking to Charlie,' Sheila said, giving Edward a forbidding look. 'You can get some of the toys out, can't you, Charlie?'

'And be nice,' Audrey warned.

There was a long moment of silence after they had gone. Sheila wished she could follow them, anything to escape the tension in this room.

'You knew he was married, I suppose,' Audrey said. Sheila could only feel admiration for her – for her dignity in not scratching the other woman's eyes out. Maurice was not exactly the love of her life as it turned out, but even so, she had been terribly deceived.

'Not at first,' Monica said. She spoke fast, seeming to need to pour out her story. 'I worked in the Inns of Court – PA to someone else, who Maurice worked with from time to time. I had to leave my job, of course,' she added bitterly. 'I found myself expecting a baby – two as it turned out. I was sick as a dog right at the beginning but in the long run I'd've had to go. Maurice helped me – financially, anyway. But . . .'

'I suppose that's why you're here.' Audrey's voice was harsh suddenly. 'After all, you won't be in the will.'

Monica's eyes filled with tears suddenly and she lowered her head.

'I never meant for this to happen,' she said. 'It's utterly humiliating. And you must think I'm the most terrible person – but he was so charming, so persuasive . . .'

'Oh, I know,' Audrey said, brittle, breezy. 'Could charm a bird off a branch.'

'But then . . .' She shook her head as if not knowing how to go on, then looked across at Audrey. 'I did really come to find out about the funeral – and because I wanted to meet you, come clean. I can't pretend I'm not worried sick about the future. I'll go back to work somehow eventually but I have to pay our rent, find a nanny . . . I've no one much, you see.'

'The funeral's on Monday – day after tomorrow – two o'clock sharp,' Audrey said. 'Down in the village here, only a few minutes' walk from the station. I suppose you can say you were his secretary?' She got up and went into the other room, to Maurice's office, returning with an envelope. 'Here – have this for the train fare. But I want you to go back today. You can't stay here.'

'No! I never thought, or expected . . .' All blushes of embarrassment, Monica took the envelope, not meeting Audrey's eyes. 'Thank you. Thank you so much. I thought you'd be – different. I was expecting . . . I mean, I didn't know whether to come.'

Audrey sat and there was another long, awkward pause. Sheila felt twisted up inside watching this whole situation. Audrey, her face tense, leaned forward.

'Did you love him?'

Did he love you? That was what she was really asking, Sheila thought, watching Audrey's face.

'I don't . . . know.' Monica was blushing, deeply uncomfortable. 'I suppose at first he was very exciting and entertaining and then of course . . . But once you're in the situation I was in – mortifying, desperate . . . To tell you the truth you don't think about the lovey-dovey part any more. I was trying to survive. And he did help. But he was so nasty sometimes. I realized he was a bully. Jekyll and Hyde – two sides to him.' She looked across at Audrey. 'Before, I had been jealous of you. Then I started to feel sorry for you, even though you had the house and the security and all that. Even in spite of everything I was glad not to have married him and been trapped by that. I'm sorry to say it but I found him a nasty piece of work in some ways.'

Audrey sat up and Sheila saw something in her release, like a knot being untied.

'I need time to take all this in,' she said. Her voice was cool, but not unkind. 'Come to the funeral and then we'll have to work out what's best to be done.'

Forty-Two

2 December 1940

I can't go on like this, Ann thought, overwrought, fit to explode with the pressure of all her thoughts and feelings. She had queued for her bits of shopping, done a whole load of washing even though the air was so damp that hanging it out felt chancy. All morning she had kept frenziedly busy while Joy slept off her night shift.

She had had a letter from Sheila saying that today was the funeral of the husband of her hostess down south. Poor soul, Ann thought. London was really getting a basinful. And she sounded such a kindly lady.

But none of this could stop her thoughts whirring round and round. Len and that woman. Marianne. The little boy – George. What were they going to do? Len seemed paralysed. Ann was frantic. Was he going to leave them and set up with her in Selly Oak – or what?

'Len . . .' She kept trying to get him to talk about it, whenever there was a chance – which was not that often. They were so busy, so exhausted. 'Len, I need to know what you're going to do . . .'

He did not know, she could see. It was as if he was paralysed and could not even think straight.

'Don't tell our mom, will you?' he'd said last night when she'd managed to force a few words out of him, like trying to shake farthings out of a piggy bank. 'I can't stand for Mom to know.'

'Well, you might've thought of that,' Ann said furiously. 'I'm not going to be the one who tells her – that's your flaming job!'

'She doesn't need to know,' he said desperately.

'So what does that mean?' Ann flared at him. 'Are you just going to go on as if nothing's happened?'

Again, she could get no sense out of him.

Round and round it all went in Ann's head and by the time she had had a cup of tea and a couple of slices of toast at dinnertime, and before Joy could come down, she pulled her coat on and slammed out of the house into the wind.

That'll get the washing dry anyway, she thought, hurrying along to her mother-in-law's. She was pretty sure Margaret was not out doing WVS work today.

Standing on the step of the solid brick house with its ornate, tapering arches over the window and front door, she felt suddenly like weeping. Coming here was like coming home. Margaret and Cyril had lived there since soon after they were married and they had made Ann so welcome there from the beginning, always offering kindness and comfort and a sense of home. It had always felt as if they and this sense of family would go on for ever, stable and unchanging.

And both of them – first she and now Len – had broken that precious thing and now she doubted it could ever be repaired.

Pulling herself together she wiped her nose and knocked on the door.

'Hello, Ann!' You all right?' Margaret said. She had on a comfortable old winter dress in rusty shades, and her slippers, her hair taken back and fastened up exactly as it always was. This made Ann want to cry even more.

'Cyril's just having forty winks,' she said, speaking quietly as she let Ann into the hall. 'I could fancy a breath of fresh air – want to come with me?'

'All right,' Ann said. 'I'll keep my coat on.'

They went to Rowheath, the leisure area and pavilion provided by Cadbury's, walking in the blustery air which buffeted their faces but held back its rain.

'Nice memories,' Margaret sighed, as they stood looking back at the gracious pavilion building. 'All the times we've had here.'

The days of the football matches and picnics and socials over the years came back to both of them. Winter snowball fights on the grass or cosy dances inside; summer days of games and swimming in the lido pool, of paddling and ice cream, the evenings with the sun low in the sky, children playing, not wanting to go home, gnats hovering near the water and everything peaceful.

It feels like a lost world, Ann thought. But she knew it was not just the war that made everything feel lost.

Now there was a barrage balloon stationed to one side of the park. The football pitches were a brown acreage of sodden ground planted with winter cabbages.

'It'll all be back one day, Annie,' Margaret said, threading her arm through Ann's. 'It'll all be over – just like the last one was.'

'I know,' she said huskily, stepping round a puddle. She felt even more like crying and struggled to keep herself together. As she had said to Len, it was not up to her to break any news to her mother-in-law. But how she longed to pour out all that was on her mind to someone. She must try and get her thoughts off the subject.

But she was immediately thwarted by Margaret saying, 'Is Len all right? He seems a bit preoccupied these days.'

'Oh – I think so,' Ann said, keeping her voice light. 'No one's getting enough sleep and he's doing a lot, what with the Home Guard and everything . . .'

'But there's nothing else on his mind?' Margaret probed.

'Like what?' Ann almost hoped she knew something.

'Oh, I don't know. He just seems a bit – just not quite himself.'

Ann knew she had to change the subject before she burst into tears and poured out everything about Len and Marianne and a baby called George.

'What're you going to do about Ida?' she asked.

Margaret's face clouded. 'I don't know, bab. There doesn't seem to be a lot I can do. I'll go and visit her now and again, but she's been there – or similar – most of her life now.' She stopped talking and Ann could feel that she was close to tears now as well.

'There's nothing else you can do, is there?' Ann reassured her.

'No,' Margaret said, with sudden force. 'But my God, it makes me see our parents in a new light and it's not one I'm proud of.'

Later Ann hurried home, took in all the still-damp washing, hung some of it on the clothes horse inside and gave Joy and Martin their tea before Joy had to go to work. Martin went up to do homework and once more Ann was left alone.

She thought about turning the wireless on but knew she wouldn't take anything in. She sank down at the table, exhausted from the turmoil of her mind. All the time she was waiting for Len to make some announcement, wondering what he was going to do. Her feelings boiled up suddenly.

Why am I waiting for him to make up his mind, keeping me stringing along? She could see that Len could not face up to it all – had no idea what to do.

Well, damn him, she thought. He could do what he flaming well wanted. He had never once even said he was sorry. Not like the way she was over Martin. She had said sorry so many times she had almost worn out the word. Len had not shown any sign of fellow feeling with her. She could wait for ever for him to make up his mind whether he was going to break up his whole family – or what? Stay with a kept mistress along the road? And what kind of secrets would that involve her keeping for years to come?

What did she, Ann Gilby, want for herself? What was *she* going to do?

Full of rage she wanted to go stamping up the stairs, slam doors, shriek and yell. Instead she tiptoed up to their bedroom and closed the door. Going to her chest of drawers, she saw in the mirror the reflection of her own hand going to slide open the top drawer, burrowing to the back, under the undies and the knitting patterns, to that dear, well-worn brown envelope.

It was so many years since she had seen or heard from Tom Somers. They were all in their forties now. Tom must be married with a growing family, surely?

Opening that one precious letter she had not been able to bear throwing into the flames, she read as tears blurred her eyes. '*My dearest Ann . . .*'

She could even hear his voice in those loving words, speaking to her across the years. Her heart buckled. And the last thing he had sent – that poem, *How do I love thee . . .?*

She sat holding those precious, fragile sheets of paper and lifted them gently, pressing them close against her heart.

Forty-Three

11 December 1940

'Martin?' Ann called up the stairs.

There was a pause, then his door opened. 'Yeah?'

'You're out tonight?'

'Yep. A bit later.'

She ran up the stairs, superstitious suddenly. He stood on the landing, still in his school uniform, but seeming suddenly taller. He looked questioningly at her.

'Just . . . be careful, love.' Since last week, it had all come closer to them. A bomb landed on the canal bridge in Bournville Lane, flooding the streets around, and Cadbury's were having to clear water out of some departments. It made Ann even more nervous to think of Martin, out in a raid.

'I will.' He gave her his easy smile.

On an impulse she flung her arms round him, pulling him tight. 'You're a good lad.'

'Aww – thanks, Mom.' He returned her embrace lightly, embarrassed but touched as well. 'And you.'

'Joy?' She stood outside her daughter's door. 'I've got to go in a minute. You all right?'

Joy emerged from her room. She looked different suddenly, Ann realized. Lately she had been so quiet and moody and Ann had suspected something was wrong.

But since she had seen Alan, Joy looked quite different, all lit up.

'Nice to see you looking so chirpy,' Ann said. She gave Joy's cheek an affectionate stroke. 'I know you'll miss him but I'm glad you made it up, the pair of you.'

'I know.' Joy dimpled at her. 'I'd almost decided to give up on men – they never seem to know what they want! But then . . .' She grinned. 'We had a good chat. And Alan's special – I've always known that.'

'Well, I'm glad for you, bab,' Ann said. 'Look, I'm running late. Have a good night. We'll have a sit-down when we're back in tomorrow, eh?' She started off down the stairs. 'Hope the night doesn't seem too long. I'll see you in the morning – oh, and tell your dad his tea's in the oven, will you?'

Hurrying along to the church hall, she felt a bit guilty about not having asked Joy anything much about Alan sooner. Her head was so full of her own thoughts and worries these days that she hardly had space for anyone else's.

Even when there was a quiet night she could not sleep. If Len was there, she lay beside him, enraged that he was asleep when she was lying staring into the darkness, full of an unpleasant, jarring energy, even though in the daytime she was often reeling with exhaustion.

If Len was not there, she could not stop herself picturing the same thing over and over again: him going to that house, being with *her* . . . Even though she told herself this could not be. The house had been so badly damaged that the woman (Ann could not use her name) must surely have gone somewhere else? Maybe Len was with her wherever she was? Her mind could not rest.

And worst of all, something that had been needling her now for a couple of weeks was beginning to come home to her. She could hardly bear to think about it. She had put all her queasy feelings, her utter exhaustion, down to the odd hours she was working, the lost sleep, but now she could tell from how she had felt before, that it wasn't just that. The only time she and Len had been intimate lately was that terrible night when he put his hands round her throat, had been like a terrible angry stranger. But once with no precautions was enough, even at her age. Especially at her age.

Oh God, she whispered, anguished, as she hurried towards the Bristol Road. *What the hell am I going to do?*

She stepped into the now familiar surroundings of the church hall, its blacked-out windows, the dim overhead lights and the tables surrounded by WVS women, some talking and laughing and all working very fast.

'Evening, Ann!' Mildred greeted her, giving a brief smile as she strode past.

Ann felt better immediately, having something practical to do. Mildred seemed to be almost permanently on duty and she could see Gladys's ample form bent over a table laden with tottering piles of cut bread. She went over to join in and saw Dorrie Rudge, looking as bonkers as ever and spreading margarine in a frenzy.

'Evening!' she said, sounding as cheerful as she was able. There was space on the table for her to work and she had just picked up a knife when the siren went off.

Dorrie Rudge stood bolt upright, held her arms out and declared in a loud, reedy voice, 'Cast forth thy lightning and tear them: shoot out thin arrows and consume them!'

'Oh, do just get *on* with it, Dorrie,' Mildred said, advancing on them. 'Are you ladies nearly ready to load up?'

*

Even in all the busyness, Ann could not stop her thoughts. Len and that woman. And now herself, expecting his child as well – she was as certain as she could be. What a flaming awful mess they were all in.

She helped load the canteen with sandwiches, made sure the urns were already hot and that the big churns of extra water were full. As Mildred was leaning down, pulling on them to check their weight in the confined, dark space, she suddenly blurted out, 'I had to clear out Mr Dowd's flat today.'

Ann, stowing sandwiches into the wagon, dragged herself out of her own obsessions to remember who Mr Dowd was.

'Oh . . . dear! That must have been difficult for you.'

'I'd never been in there before,' Mildred added hurriedly, standing upright again. 'Only there seemed to be no one else. So, as his secretary, I felt it was . . . Hello, what's . . .? That's the All Clear!'

They looked at each other. This was very odd. But soon after they had trooped back inside, the air-raid warning sounded again.

'Oh, for goodness' sake,' Mildred said.

Ann sat in the front, squeezed between Mildred and Gladys Parrott's capacious hips. Dorrie was in the back with another woman who had come to replace Edwina Starling, who was unwell.

The raid was already under way and none of them spoke. Ann stared out through the windscreen at the flickering lights above.

And she knew what she was going to do. Suddenly, there in the darkness, in the night-time flashes and thundering bangs of the raid, she thought, I'm going to write to Tom. She felt her heart swell, as if it had been an empty shell, waiting all these years to be filled, the way Tom had filled it. The thought gave her a strange sense of relief even though it offered no clear answer to anything.

For all these days she had felt like a tripwire of tension and exhaustion – waiting to know what Len would do, what he would choose. He could not seem to confront the situation at all, wouldn't speak to her about it. The only sign of emotion he had shown was when he heard that a bomb had fallen on his beloved St Andrew's, the ground of Birmingham City Football Club. He actually cried. Ann had, for the first time in their long marriage, felt like hitting him.

Wife or mistress? she thought, bitterly. That sounded so bad – such loose morals. She must remember to say it to him. Are you going to face up to that? And are you going to cry about that too?

The thought of Tom – her Tom, her love – was like a refuge. I can write to him, she thought. Even if he's married and happy and has forgotten all about me. Whatever Len does, I don't have to wait for him to make up his blasted mind – I can do this because I *want to*. I just want to hear from him, to know he's there. It made her feel stronger.

They were getting to the middle of town and the raid was fully under way, the ragged glow of flames lighting up the sky ahead of them.

'Dear Lord – look!' Dorrie squeaked, stepping out of the back of the wagon when they pulled up in a new spot later in the night. In all the racket she sounded like a little bird. 'Oh, how evil – just evil!'

All of them had grubby faces and judging by what they had already seen, the destruction being unleashed everywhere, all the fires and the hard-pressed firemen fighting to contain them, this was going to be another long and terrible night.

And now, parked in Bath Row, they were confronted by the smashed ruins of one of the city's gracious old churches, St Thomas's, shattered and mysterious-looking amid the smoke.

'Oh no.' Gladys's voice was husky. 'Look at that . . .'

They all seemed unable to leave. There was so much rubble it was hard to get near, but stepping round the edges of the destruction, they were all silenced by the strange horror of seeing something so solid, so beloved and seemingly unchangeable humbled into a chaotic mess.

In the eerie glow they saw charred beams lying criss-cross, some of which had been hurled across the graveyard. Tombstones, blown out of the ground, lay jumbled and smashed. And the main body of the church itself was broken open, leaving the bell tower standing like a forlorn sentry. Inside, they could make out the scattered shapes of organ pipes, contorted and pale like entrails.

'Hark!' Mildred, eyeing the sky, held up a hand. Ann heard the drone of another wave of planes and her heart rate picked up again.

'We must get on,' Mildred ordered. 'I'm sure those firemen along there could do with a cuppa. I'll drive a bit further along. No need to get in – just follow me.'

She jumped into the cab. Gladys, Dorrie and the other woman trailed after her. Ann hesitated a moment, looking up at the church. *O come, all ye faithful* . . . The words rang round her mind. Faithful. What did that mean? She had no idea any more. Everything seemed smashed and broken. She had tried to be faithful to Len and she had failed. Was it all her fault – had she been the one to drive him away, slowly, year by year? But Tom – she knew that somehow, deep within her, her feelings at least had been true to him . . . *How do I love thee? Let me count the ways . . .*

'Ann!' She heard Mildred's voice calling her along the street, then something that she sensed, rather than heard: a rushing, a terror which seemed to make every hair stand up on her body. The black sky came down on her and – nothing more.

Forty-Four

Joy was walking wearily home the next morning when she saw Martin cycling towards her. Her eyes anxiously scanned his face – he was all in one piece. Full of relief, she waited at the front door.

'All right?' she called. Normally she greeted him with some sarky big-sister remark but today she was surprised to find she had tears in her eyes at the sight of him. Her little pest of a brother in his coat and scarf and knitted hat, pale from being up all night. Here he was and here she was – both alive and safe for another day.

'Yep.' He swung his leg over, dismounting, and went to the side gate. 'Be in in a minute – get the kettle on, will you? I'm blinking freezing.'

Martin came in the back door and they huddled in the kitchen, waiting for the kettle to heat.

'That was a *long* night,' Martin said, white with exhaustion. He kept his coat and gloves on, blowing hot breath into his hands. The All Clear had finally gone at seven. 'Longest yet.'

Joy looked at him. With only the two of them there she noticed him more completely. Her little brother was no longer little, she realized with a pang, looking at the young man sitting hunched at the table. He had grown and his face looked different – his cheekbones more pronounced. And though cheerful by nature, he seemed weighed down. But then who wouldn't be after a night like last night?

'Mom and Dad should be back soon.' She had just sunk

on to a chair with her tea when someone knocked at the front door. Joy shot up again. 'Why's she knocking?'

She found a stranger on the front step: a wide-hipped, pink-faced woman in WVS uniform. Joy stared blankly at her until she took in the expression on the woman's face. They both went to speak at once.

'Is it . . .?' Joy felt her voice go very small and high. 'Are you . . .? Mom – where's Mom?'

'My dear.' The woman sounded so distraught she could hardly speak. 'I'm Mildred Rowbotham – I work with your mother in the WVS. I'm afraid I come bearing bad news . . .'

'You'd better come in,' Joy said, hardly knowing why she was saying it, except she wanted to cut the woman off before she said anything else.

Later, when they had time to take in what had happened, Joy thought back with admiration on Mildred Rowbotham, coming like that, straight to their house when she was obviously in such a state of shock herself. At the time it was all so strange and unreal, as if everything was moving very slowly and her mind could not take anything in.

'Would you like a cup of tea?' she said. And, 'This is my brother Martin. What's happened? Please tell us. It's Mom, isn't it? Is she . . . is she . . . in hospital or something?'

'Yes, my dears, she is . . .' But then Mildred Rowbotham seemed to take in the sight of the two of them. She sank down at the table as if her legs had given way and burst into sobs. Martin sat like a statue. Mildred recovered herself very quickly.

'You sweet young things! Please try not to worry. Your mother is alive but she is injured – quite seriously, I think.

She and two of our other ladies were caught out last night. A bomb came down nearby. One lady was killed but your mother and the other, Mrs Parrott, are both in the General. We must hope and pray that she pulls through.'

Joy and Martin sat, numb, staring at her. Joy saw a movement outside then – their father bringing his bike along the side of the house. Oh God, she thought . . . Dad had just a few moments left of not knowing, and then he was going to walk in here through the back door . . .

'That's our father.' Joy nodded towards the window.

'Oh dear,' Mildred said wretchedly. But, not flinching away from the difficulty of it, she stayed sitting with them. The back door opened and Len appeared in his Home Guard uniform and cycle clips, immediately startled to see this stranger at his table. He stopped in the doorway.

'What's going on?'

There was a moment of silence, before Mildred Rowbotham managed to say, 'Mr Gilby . . .'

And Joy said, 'It's Mom. She got caught by a bomb.'

It was Sheila who, through the window, saw the telegraph boy trundle his bicycle up the steep drive later that day when she was at the table, feeding Elaine.

It took her mind an instant to connect this with any meaning before she leapt to her feet, her body pulsating in alarm. 'No . . . Oh no, no . . .!'

A few seconds and her legs went from under her. The carpet came up to greet her and she sprawled groggily across the floor.

'Sheila? Whatever's wrong?' Audrey was hurrying to her when the doorbell rang. 'Oh heavens . . .'

She came back holding the telegram away from her

like something red hot. Sheila sat up, hugging her knees, shaking her head from side to side.

'No, don't open it. I don't want to know . . . Oh Kenneth, my Kenneth, my lovely husband . . .' She burst into sobs, burying her head in her knees. 'No, take it away, make it disappear . . . I don't want to know!'

Audrey stood helplessly, almost in tears herself.

'Shall I open it?' she ventured after a while.

'No!' Sheila cried. Then, more quietly, 'Yes. You open it.'

Audrey slid a knife along the envelope and with shaking fingers pulled out the slip of paper. Sheila watched Audrey's face as her expression altered from dread to confusion and finally to a wary kind of sorrow as she raised her eyes to look at her.

'Sheila . . .' She lowered herself on to a chair beside Sheila. 'It's not Kenneth, dear. This is from your sister. It's about your mother . . .'

'Oh, Sheila – this is just too awful. But thank heaven she's at least still alive.'

Audrey walked round the car as they got out at Goring railway station the next morning. She flung her arms round Sheila and Elaine. It was a watery-bright December morning. Both of them were tearful. A weight of worry and sadness hung over everything.

'We shall miss both of you so much!' Audrey wept. 'Shall you be back, do you think?'

'I don't know,' Sheila said helplessly. 'I just have no idea.' She was in a fog, could not think about anything except getting on the train, heading back to Birmingham and seeing Mom, getting there as soon as possible, just in case . . .

'Of course you don't – silly, selfish me,' Audrey said.

'Your poor head's in a spin. Only . . .' She stepped back, gently stroking Elaine's cheek with her finger. 'Do keep in touch, won't you? Please let me know – I shall be so worried for you all and . . . Well, things won't be the same without you and Lainy here.'

The pair of them were such a picture of woe that a few people on their way into the little station gave them a wide berth, with looks of dread as if sadness might be catching.

'I'll keep in touch – course I will,' Sheila said distractedly.

Audrey helped her with her luggage and waited on the platform until the train came puffing into view.

'Thank you, Audrey,' Sheila said, tears filling her eyes. 'For everything. And say goodbye to the boys for me, will you? I hope we'll see you again soon.'

She stood inside, suitcase at her feet and holding Elaine, not wanting to find a seat until she had parted with Audrey, who now felt like a real friend.

'Goodbye!' she called, as the train gave a jolt, ducking her face level with the half-open window.

Audrey, attempting a watery smile, waved bravely as they eased away.

'Not goodbye – *au revoir*!' she called. And her neat, slender little figure was soon wrapped in smoke from the train and faded out of sight.

Sheila did something she had never done in her life before. She took a taxi home from Birmingham New Street, staring around her in horror as they drove away from the station. Even though Mom had told her in her letters, she had not really been able to take in the destruction in her home city: seeing it was another matter.

Mom. A sick feeling, as if she had been punched in the

belly. But she could not believe that either. There was not enough news – how was Mom really? Was she even still with them? She was desperate to get back to Bournville, longed to hear that the situation was not as bad as they all feared.

Everyone was in when she got to the house – Joy, Martin, Dad and Nanny Margaret and Grandad Cyril. As soon as she climbed out of the taxi Joy came rushing out, flinging her arms round both of them and sobbing her heart out.

'Sheila! And Lainy – come here to Auntie! Oh, she's grown so much! Come and give Auntie a love, darlin'.'

Dad came and greeted her, seeming so strange: far off and stunned. It was as if he could not take any of this in – none of them could. They all went inside and Martin came and silently hugged her, his face white and strained. Her grandparents, their faces tight with sorrow, embraced her gently and made a fuss of Elaine. Joy made tea and they sat round and told her what they knew which was not much.

'They say we need to wait a while, because . . .' Joy could not go on.

'It came down somewhere near here,' Dad said hoarsely. Margaret laid her hand over his, her face full of distress. 'We don't know what the full damage is.'

'Have you seen her?' Sheila asked. Now that she was home it was hitting her hard. Her whole body felt heavy with sorrow.

'No,' her father said. 'I went in but they said she couldn't see anyone. They were having to . . . I dunno. Sort her out. It's pretty bad, I think . . .' He stumbled over his words, hoarse, stunned. 'They said I'd be able to go in tomorrow and p'raps see her then. Best if I just go on my own, I think, to start with.'

No one seemed to know what to do or say, how to pass the time. They were all numb and shocked. Little Elaine was a godsend that afternoon as everyone made a big fuss of her, cuddling and playing with her. They went through the motions of making a meal and trying to eat it. None of them could take in that Mom wasn't there, in the kitchen or about to walk in from her WVS duty. It was like a dream that you wanted to wake up from but could not. Joy and Martin were a little bit more used to her being out these days but for Sheila, Mom had always been there, cooking, washing, back and forth along the passage, up and down the stairs – the person at the heart of the house. It was such a relief that Nanny and Grandad were there.

Somehow, they all sleepwalked through the rest of that terrible afternoon. It was after dark, when Elaine was already asleep and they were all huddled in the back room, that there was another knock at the front door. Joy hurriedly got up to answer it, almost as if she might be expecting someone.

'Yes,' Sheila heard her say in a low voice. 'She's back. Come on in.'

A moment later, there in the doorway, seeming taller, wider than before, in a thick white rollneck sweater and RAF jacket, stood the beloved person Sheila yearned with all her soul to see. Her man, her love.

'Kenneth!' Her voice sounded faint even to herself. 'Oh my God – how . . .? Why are you here?'

'I sent him a telegram as well,' Joy said.

Kenneth, with a stricken expression, nodded his hellos to them all: 'Mr Gilby . . .' And a moment later Sheila felt the arms she had longed for for so many weeks wrapped round her and she was sobbing into his chest.

Forty-Five

'You going in soon, Dad?' Sheila asked her father the next afternoon. He was sitting at the table in the back room, a cup of tea fast cooling beside him. He seemed so lost and stunned, his shoulders sagging, staring straight ahead of him with haunted eyes. Was she imagining it or did his hair seem suddenly more than tinged with grey?

'She'll be all right,' she said, touching his shoulder. Wanting it to be true. He nodded. 'Don't forget your tea, Dad.'

'Sheila?' he said as she was about to leave the room. 'I ought to take some things in – for your mother.'

'Oh yes – nightdress, a wash bag? I'll pack them up for her.'

'Yes, course.'

She went into the kitchen. Joy had appeared and was sipping tea.

'Dad says we need to pack Mom a night bag.' It was nice talking like that. It made it sound as if she would soon be up and about, needing a towel, a toothbrush . . .

'All right, I'll give you a hand once I'm dressed,' Joy said.

'Ta. That'd be good.' It wasn't as if she really needed help but it was nice. Their eyes met. Sisters. They wanted each other to rely on, differences forgotten. Wanted to be close.

*

Sheila had spent every waking moment with Kenneth so far, but he had popped out for a while to see his own family and Sheila took the opportunity to unpack properly, emptying her own small overnight case up in the attic. It was an old one of Mom's anyway, a saggy-topped cream thing, the peach-coloured inner lining faded and torn off along one side. She had been using it to store some of Elaine's baby clothes in. It was the best they could do for now. She left the clothes in neat piles on the bed, blew the dust off the lid and took it down to the first-floor landing.

'Joy?' she called. 'I'm ready.'

'Here!' To her surprise Joy was already in Mom and Dad's room. She was sitting on the side of the bed. The top drawer of the chest of drawers was open and there were some things on the bed – underwear, a nightie. It felt a bit funny going through Mom's things, but it had to be done.

'Oh good – you've made a start . . . Elaine might wake soon so we need to get on with it.' Sheila leaned over and looked at what Joy had selected. 'We must find some wash things . . . Oh look – her Cadbury Bible!'

Sheila leafed through the delicate pages for a moment. She had a similar Bible herself, from when she had got married and stopped working at Cadbury's. Everyone was given one when they left the company's employ. She stroked the cover. Inside, pressed down tight, she found the carnation Ann had been given with it, dry now and brown. The good wishes from George and Elizabeth Cadbury were dated 1919.

'Sheila.' Joy was sitting still, various things in her lap. Something in her voice made Sheila take notice.

'What?' Sheila straightened up, pushing her hair out of her eyes.

'I wasn't being nosey. Well, I mean I was, I s'pose . . . But . . .' She was blushing. 'I was getting some of her undies out and I found . . . And I just thought . . . Anyway, look at this.'

Sheila walked round the bed and sat down. An old manila envelope lay in Joy's lap, so worn that it was velvety, with slits along each side. She took the piece of paper Joy was holding out, covered in lines of precise, sloping handwriting.

'Sonnet 43,' she read. 'From the Portuguese. Elizabeth Barrett Browning. *How do I love thee? Let me count the ways . . .*'

Her eyes hurried down the words, and even in the rush of her senses she saw that they were beautiful lines and then she reached the last: '*I shall but love thee better after death.*'

And underneath, in a neat hand, '*With all my love, my darling one.*'

She frowned up at Joy. 'What is this?'

Joy's eyes were wide, strange, as if there was something she already knew that Sheila didn't.

'Where did you get it?' Sheila said stupidly. Her voice came out sharply, as if this was yet another thing being thrown at her by life that she did not want to know about and could not contend with.

'I told you. In her drawer. With her undies. I've never been in the drawer before, honestly. And it was funny because it felt nice, looking through it. Her things – it was like feeling her near . . .'

They both filled up then, sitting on their parents' bed like lost children. *Mom, come back . . .*

Sheila stared at the slip of paper. 'It's not Dad's writing.'

'It's not like Dad at all, is it?' Joy said sadly. 'That was

373

the thing. When I saw this envelope, put away at the back, what I thought was . . . Dad must have written to her when they were engaged, in the last war, and they must have been in love *then*, mustn't they?' She looked at Sheila, eyes full of appeal. 'I mean, I know not everyone's the best at writing letters. Al's not all that good but he does *try* – I had a lovely letter from him yesterday. And I wanted to know what Mom and Dad were like when they were young and in love. They never really seem it, do they? Not now.' Her voice cracked. 'But there's nothing from Dad. Not one letter. There're these pictures of us . . .' She held up a handful of baby pictures. 'And this.' She pointed at the poem, then fished inside the envelope. 'Just one letter.'

My dearest Ann . . .

The letter was brief, but in every line they could read love.

I know I must leave you alone – you have your life, your family and I would not endanger that, or you, for any selfish desire of mine. Just know that whatever our situation now, the responsibilities we have, the roads to walk while we must, I have loved you and will continue to love you – always. I just can't imagine it being any other way.
Goodbye, my dear one.
Yours ever,
Tom

They sat, both tearful and astounded.
'If someone wrote me a letter like that . . .' Joy said longingly. 'But *Mom*? Who is this person? It says

Southampton, the address. I mean, how on earth did she ever meet him?'

Sheila shrugged, leafing through the rest of the envelope's contents. 'She must have known him before the war or something. I don't s'pose we'll ever know anyway. Seems as if Mom was more of a dark horse than you might think . . .'

'No,' Joy argued. 'Look.' On the envelope, she could just read the postmark – Jan '26.

'But . . . I was six then. Nearly. And you must have been . . .'

'Four.'

They shook their heads. How could any of this be?

'I just don't know,' Sheila said helplessly. Her hands got busy again. 'Look – here's Mom and Dad's marriage certificate. Oh, and here's your birth certificate – and mine.' She smiled momentarily. '*Father – Chocolate Maker . . .*'

She unfolded the third one. And stopped, staring.

'Joy . . .'

Wide-eyed again, she handed it over.

'What? Martin Thomas Gilby . . .' Joy looked up at Sheila, then back at the certificate again. '*Father: Thomas John Somers . . . Marine Engineer . . .* What? This *can't* be right? Thomas John . . .? Tom!'

'My God,' Sheila said. She got up suddenly and shut the door, even though Martin was not in, had gone to school. But their father was downstairs still. They kept staring at the birth certificate. 'I always knew there was something different about him,' Sheila whispered. 'He's *clever*, for a start. Not like us.'

They sat, talking in scraps, while this sank in. *What on earth? How?*

'The date on the letter's January 1926,' Sheila said, calculating rapidly. 'Eight months before Martin was born.'

They were silent.

'D'you think Dad knows?' Joy said.

'Let alone Martin!'

It was all so impossible to believe. Mom. Not their mom. How could this be true? It felt like a continuation of a bad dream they were already living in. Sheila slumped, her shoulders rounding, exhausted.

'I just can't take all this in.'

'And who the hell,' Joy said, 'is Tom Somers?'

It was as if a chasm had opened in front of them, the secrets, the events happening somewhere behind a screen in their lives that they had never suspected. If it was true . . . If it was not all a mistake . . .

'We can't mention it to Martin, can we?' Sheila said. 'If he doesn't know, he doesn't need to.'

'But won't he have to have his birth certificate – one day at least?' Joy said. 'He'll have to know some time.'

Another silence.

'Not yet though,' Sheila said. 'Not now. And it's not up to us to tell him, is it?'

Joy picked up the letter again and the poem and stared wistfully at them. 'He really loved her, didn't he?' Her eyes filled with tears. 'It's all so sad. Maybe he still does? And maybe she . . .?'

Sheila looked at her. 'Poor Dad.'

Forty-Six

That afternoon, Joy said she was popping out to run a few errands and buy extra milk. There had already been a good many visitors to the house in Bournville. Hilda and Roy came as soon as they heard, and Norma with them, and as soon as they had been it was a foregone conclusion that there would be others.

'I can't believe it,' Norma kept saying. 'Just can't.'

'I know.' Joy sobbed, enjoying the comfort of her old friend's arms round her. 'Nothing feels right with our mom not here.'

'So your father's gone to the hospital?' Hilda said, as they sat drinking tea. 'Poor Annie – what a terrible thing. Now – anything we can do, girls, you just tell us straight away,' she said to Sheila and Joy, her eyes filling. 'Oh, you poor loves . . . And you, bab . . .' She hugged Martin who was suddenly trying desperately not to cry.

By the time Joy came back after hurrying to the shops on the Green at Bournville, some of the loyal little gang of 'Cadbury girls' who Ann had worked with before leaving to get married had been there for some time and the air in the house felt warm and breathed in. She could hear the low murmur of tactful conversation from the front room. Word had obviously got round at the factory – one word from Hilda and bingo! It was a nice feeling, Mom having all these old pals even if they had had barely a minute to see each other, once they had homes and families to tend to.

'Oh, thank goodness – we're down to the last drop,' Sheila said as she walked in. She took the bottle of milk and poured it into the jug. 'It's not bad having something to keep us busy though,' she whispered. 'I don't think I've ever made so many cups of tea in one day! It's a good thing Dad's not in – he'd never be able to deal with all this lot.' She peered more closely at Joy. 'You all right? You look a bit . . . I don't know what.'

Joy blushed, but before she could even reply, there was another knock at the door and she hurried along to open it, escaping Sheila's interrogation. Two ladies in WVS uniforms were outside: one, the solid, pink-faced lady who had broken the news to them; the other tall, dark-eyed and rather beautiful.

'Oh, Miss Rowbotham . . .' Joy felt pleased to see her. She was a reassuring kind of lady.

'Hello, dear – this is my colleague, Edwina Starling. We thought we'd pay a call to see if you are all managing all right?'

'Would you like to come in?' Joy stood back to let them in.

The Cadbury girls were on their way out, showering everyone with good wishes. Sheila hurried to put the kettle on yet again.

'It's very nice of you to come,' Joy said, showing them into the front room. As they sat, Sheila came in.

'We were so sorry to hear about the other lady,' she said.

'Yes, poor Dorrie,' Mildred said. 'A frail soul. Mrs Parrott, our other volunteer, is in hospital, but I gather it's cuts and bruises mainly. She's making good progress.'

Edwina Starling was nodding sympathetically.

'One feels it might take rather more than a bomb to do much damage to Gladys Parrott,' Miss Rowbotham added. Which Joy found rather shocking and was not sure what to say.

'Your mother gave of herself unstintingly,' Mrs Starling said quickly, as if to compensate. There were tears in her brown eyes. 'And such a sympathetic person. Have you any more news?'

'No,' Sheila said. She was perched on the edge of her chair. 'Our father's at the hospital now.'

'Well, if any of you need anything, call on us in the WVS,' Mildred Rowbotham said. 'Don't hesitate. We're here to help and especially our Ann's family.'

This final comment brought Joy to tears all over again.

'You're so kind – thank you ever so much,' Sheila said, getting up. 'I'll just go and fill the pot.'

'I'm sorry, Mr Gilby. I don't think your wife is well enough to see anyone yet,' the ward sister said. She was a middle-aged, rather statuesque woman with a calm manner. 'She has not fully regained consciousness. She has lost a great deal of blood, I'm afraid. In fact, if you have a moment . . .'

Len, holding his hat in one hand and the little cream overnight bag in the other, followed her nervously. The fact that Ann had briefly been a nurse did not make him feel any less intimidated by this woman. She led him out into the corridor which was, for the moment, quiet.

'When you see her, you will be shocked. There is a lot of superficial wounding which of course looks bad but will heal. She has several broken ribs – very painful but they have to heal themselves. And her ankle was smashed up as well. But when she was brought in we thought things were worse than they in fact are. She seemed to be haemorrhaging badly. We thought there were severe internal injuries. But in fact . . .' She lowered her voice even further. 'I don't know if you were aware that your wife was expecting a child?'

Len recoiled, shocked. 'Er . . . No. No, I wasn't.'

'Well, sadly, that is no longer the case. She was very knocked about. But – do feel encouraged. She needs time, but the signs are good.'

'Right,' he said. 'Thanks. Very much. So. She can't . . .?'

'I don't think she can receive anyone today, no. But it won't be long. Please try not to worry. Are those her things?' She held her hand out for the bag.

'Oh. Yes. Right. Well, I'll come back tomorrow then.'

Forty-Seven

'Ann?'

'I think she was awake earlier.' The nurse was speaking. She knew the woman's voice now. 'You might sit with her for a little while? I expect she'll come round.'

At some time, which could have been the middle of the night, someone had said, 'Your husband came to see you today. I'm sure he'll be back tomorrow – and I expect you'll feel a bit stronger.' Or was that a dream? As she lay under the maroon darkness of her eyelids, the waking world and the room around her came back to her from time to time. She had very little idea how she'd got there, but she knew that the war was going on and she was in a hospital and that, when she surfaced, every inch of her body hurt: the broken ribs, her ankle, her face stinging raw. And in her belly was an endless dull, griping pain . . .

She also knew that Gladys Parrott was in here somewhere but not as badly hurt as she was because yesterday Ann had opened her eyes for a moment to see Gladys's moon face peering down at her, peppered with cuts and bruises.

'You're gunna be all right, our Annie,' Gladys said in her big, kind voice. 'Don't fret, bab. Just get yerself well rested up.'

Ann had tried to speak but by the time she found any words the face had disappeared.

The other thing that she knew was that she had in some way died and come back to life and that this life was different from the one she had before. This was not something she understood in any sort of detail: she just felt that it was the case.

'Ann?' the voice said again.

Slowly, she opened her eyes as much as she could. The left one was swollen and she could only prise the lids apart a crack. Her eyes felt gritty and she tried to blink the feeling away and gave a low moan because moving even her eyelids hurt so much.

Len was sitting down on the chair beside her, gingerly, as if he was not sure he was allowed to. His face was a mask of shock and he seemed almost afraid of her. Ann wondered what she must look like. She managed to turn her head just a fraction and when he realized she was looking at him, he said, 'How are you?'

'Sore,' she managed. Her jaw felt all right, she realized, although her lips were parched, her mouth dusty, and every breath hurt.

'Thank God – they say you're going to be all right.'

'Umm,' she said.

'Everyone's at home. Sheila's come back, with Elaine.'

'Umm?'

'Yeah, she came straight back. They're all – you know, rallying round. Send their love, of course – all of 'em.'

She was glad to hear it. If Sheila had come home, things must have looked serious. She didn't know quite how it had been, no one had said. But it set her mind at rest to think of them all – Sheila, Joy, Martin and no doubt with Margaret and Cyril's help – being old enough to manage things and all pulling together. About Len himself, she felt nothing, that she could identify.

Len didn't touch her, didn't reach for her hand. He looked down between his knees and couldn't seem to think of anything to say. Ann was not in a fit state to fill in the gaps, to do all the work like that. Not now.

'They said . . . there was a baby,' Len said eventually. He looked up then, ashamed, embarrassed. 'But you . . . lost it.'

She answered with her eyes. *Lost it.* As if she had mislaid it somewhere like a shopping bag. The pain in her guts. They had had to wash and wash her, there was so much blood. She felt weak as a half-drowned kitten. Even to move an arm, she had to think about it, work up to it.

'Maybe it's for the best,' Len said.

She felt a tear run down her cheek even though she didn't know she was crying, did not know what she felt. Someone had told her this. But she had hardly got used to the idea that there was a baby and now it was gone and yes, maybe it was for the best, but it still felt like a terrible sorrow.

Silence followed. A silence that had been there a long time, except it had been covered up by the daily round of work and children, by Margaret and Cyril and yes, by her filling it with chatter when it hung too heavy. It was a silence like a lack of life.

Len was staring at the floor again. He said quietly, 'I thought you'd love me always.'

She licked her lips, got her mouth to open.

'I do . . . love you . . . Len.'

He lowered his head into his hands and his shoulders started shaking. He sobbed, as quietly as he could, distraught. Tears ran down her cheeks but she could not do anything for him, could not say all she needed to say. That she loved him for all they had been, for their family, for their past, for all those days together and that even if that was not all the love she might feel, it was something, it was a great deal . . .

Eventually he got himself under control, wiping his face, embarrassed. His watery eyes looked into hers. 'I . . . I love you as well, Annie. Only . . .' He stopped, obviously thinking better of beginning on any of this now.

'Yes.' She drew in a painful breath. She understood what he was trying to say. This is all such a mess. We love each other for all our past, our family. But. We each have someone else, tugging on us. There are children. There are consequences . . .

He leaned forward, whispering desperately, 'What are we going to do, Annie?'

Forty-Eight

'I might as well go back to work,' Joy said, the next evening. They had been to the General to see Mom and were all feeling much better. 'I think I need to be busy – and anyway, they were really expecting me back.'

The three of them went to the hospital together, taking a few copies of *Woman's Own* from Hilda and some cake that Nanny Margaret had sent with messages of love and that she would be in to see her soon. They were only allowed two at the bedside, so Sheila and Martin went in first, then Joy took Martin's place. They had found Ann propped up on pillows and looking better than their father had described.

'Blimey,' Martin said. 'Who've you been in the ring with?' And that brought a smile to her lips.

'I'll be all right,' she said. They could see how pleased she was to see them, a bit tearful, in fact. 'It all looks worse than it is. Thing that hurts most is my ribs – and my ankle's broken.' She pulled back the bedclothes, which were raised from underneath by some kind of frame, to show them her plaster.

'Oh, Mom,' Sheila said. 'D'you remember what happened?'

Ann tried to shake her head, but thought better of it, wincing at the pain in her neck. 'No. Hardly a thing. I was looking at the church – it had been bombed out . . . And then, nothing after that – 'til I woke up here.'

'Maybe it's just as well.' Sheila found herself feeling

really emotional. Nearly losing Mom – did her mother know how close it had been? – and all the things she and Joy had discovered but could not talk about . . . But the main thing was, Mom was still here – and she might even be home for Christmas, which was only just over a week away.

'As long as you all take *very* good care of her!' the young nurse said, twinkling at them.

'Oh, we will!' Martin said earnestly and the nurse gave Ann a *'what a lovely boy!'* look.

They each, very gently, kissed her goodbye and went off feeling lifted, as if life and light were returning. Mom was going to be all right.

Sheila had received a kindly letter from Audrey, wishing them all well and saying that she and the boys were missing them. After they had been to the hospital, Sheila managed to sit down and write a short note back.

> *We're all in a bit of a state here. I hardly know*
> *whether I'm coming or going to be honest with*
> *all there has been to do. But it looks as if my*
> *mother is going to be all right and we are all so*
> *relieved. I'll write a better letter when things*
> *have calmed down a bit. But give the boys*
> *my love, won't you?*

She had developed quite a fondness for those little boys after nearly three months in the Vellacotts' house. The nastiness she had had from them at the beginning was something they had learned from their father and they could be nice lads really. Would she ever see them again? she wondered. Even though Kenneth was home and there was nowhere she would rather be, she found she was missing Audrey and she finished the letter feeling affectionate towards her.

That night, Sheila and Kenneth crept up to the attic, leaving the light off as usual because Elaine was asleep in her cot. Very quietly they undressed. Kenneth was soon in his pyjamas and got into bed first. They were sharing a single bed and he shifted right up by the wall.

'Come on, love . . .' He patted the mattress beside him. 'She's all right – leave her.'

Sheila, in her long winter nightie, got in beside him, shivering.

'Come 'ere. I'll warm you up.' Cuddled up close, she was soon flooded by the heat of his body. His heartbeat was like an echo of her own.

'You're like an oil stove,' she teased.

'Your very own. Warmer now?'

'Umm. I could stay like this for ever.' She was warm and cosy in the bed and she felt safe and loved, trying to shut everything out, just for a while. But the things she and Joy had discovered soon came rushing back into her mind. Her mother, some love who she had never spoken about. Tom. This unknown man, Tom . . .

She had not said anything to Kenneth yet and she was torn between wanting to pour it all out – all these things they had no idea of that Mom had kept to herself – to get it off her chest. But she could not bear to start. It was all too fresh and raw in her mind. And it felt shameful to admit any of it.

Kenneth's hand moved to her breast. Gratefully, she pushed away any other thought but the flow of desire that began with his touch and led from one to another, feeling Kenneth's hot, firm skin under her hands, their breathing, their desire growing until she could lose herself in it completely.

And when he was lying on top of her, both of them spent with pleasure, hot and naked, she burst into tears, releasing some of the fear and worry of the past few days, and all the missing of Kenneth and worrying about him too and he held her, kissing away her tears.

'It's all right,' he murmured. 'It's all right, sweetheart. It's all gunna be OK.'

He lay at her side and they held one another. She rested her hand on him, feeling complete now that he was here. She was about to ask him to tell her about his work and what he had been doing since he was not able to tell her in letters. But suddenly, she did not want to hear it. He was here now. Safe. That was what she needed to know.

'We're so lucky,' she whispered. 'That they let you stay for Christmas. Even when you go back, I know where you are. If I really needed to, I could get on a train and come and see you. Not like some people. Even though I can't bear to think of you going away again – not even to Grimsby!'

Kenneth didn't say anything. He was stroking the upper part of her arm, his lips kissing her hair.

'It's terrible,' Sheila went on. 'All these children growing up without their dads. Not even forces people – poor Audrey, the woman I was living with. Her husband was killed in London. I don't think they wanted any more children, but now she certainly won't be . . . Oh!' She pushed herself up on to her elbow suddenly. 'My God – we didn't take any precautions! D'you think . . .?'

She felt Kenneth shrug. 'I don't know. You caught quite quickly last time. We can be careful from now on if you want, but . . .' He turned on his side, as if to look into her eyes, even though neither of them could see a thing. 'Would it be the worst thing if you did?'

A warm feeling filled her. Life, and more life. 'No. Of course it wouldn't. Oh, Kenneth – shall we try for another baby? While you're here? We don't know when you'll get leave again, do we?'

Forty-Nine

Ann was managing to move slowly about the ward now, even though her ribs were still painful. And they were talking about her going home in a day or two – definitely about being home for Christmas.

Sitting up in bed, she looked around her. Gladys Parrott had already been discharged. Before she went she came and sat with Ann and chatted cheerfully, saying she wondered how on earth all her lads had been faring at home without her, but how she thought 'the Old Man and the little so-and-sos' would likely have done her proud.

'See you back on duty, bab,' she said as she was leaving. Ann was startled. She had somehow felt that what had happened would mean she would not be going back into the WVS. But why should that be? The war was still on and she was like a wounded serviceman – she would be sent back to the front.

'S'pose I will,' she smiled. 'Mind how you go, Gladys.'

Gladys gave her a wink and Ann watched, affectionately, as Gladys made her way regally between the rows of beds to the door of the ward, like a tanker taking leave of a wharf.

'So – I hear they're letting you out tomorrow, bab?'

Ann turned as she hobbled back along the ward from the lavatory, to smile at the elderly lady who was calling to her.

'I think so. That's what they've said, anyway.'

'Good for you – I hope you have a lovely Christmas at home with your family.'

Ann felt wistful as she climbed back into bed. She had thanked the lady and wished her the same, but whatever was wrong with her – she was so thin and fragile – it did not look as if she would be leaving the hospital for some time yet and she was touched by her kindness. Everyone had been very good to her. Because her own reasons for being there were bomb injuries from being in the WVS, she had been treated like some kind of hero.

Just as she had got settled, one of the nurses came to her bed and helped her get comfortable.

'There – that's you sitting pretty,' she said. 'There's one of your visitors here already – even though it's barely time yet. Must be very keen to see you!'

'Oh, is there?' Ann was surprised. She never quite knew who to expect day by day because Len and the children and Margaret and Cyril were all taking turns to come in when they could, depending on who was at work. But even though it was a Saturday, they hardly ever got here this early. It was most likely Martin, she thought. Or perhaps even Hilda – though she'd said she would come and see Ann once she got home.

'Shall I let him in?'

'Well – yes, if that's all right.'

Ann smoothed the sheet in front of her and patted her hair. Yes, she had brushed it and it didn't seem to be sticking out all over the place.

She heard the ward doors open and someone came in. Not for her though, she thought. It wasn't any of the family. Someone else must have a very keen visitor as well. She looked down at her hands, the healing wound on the back of her right hand, still vivid. I'll have that for ever now, she thought. She was hardly coming to terms with her face yet. Each time she went along to the bathroom she stood and had a good look, having to learn this changed map of her reflection. There were scars across her forehead, one gash in her right cheek so deep she had had to have stitches, and other cuts scattered all over. They would all leave scars. Tears rose in her eyes the first few times she had seen the damage, but now she was coming to terms with it. She would never be the same again. But she was alive . . .

'Ann?'

The voice was soft, uncertain-sounding.

She looked up. He took off his hat and held it. That face. A patch over the left eye. The empty sleeve of his coat. The shape of him. The breath seemed to leave her body and she had to gasp air in before she could say hoarsely, 'Tom?'

They were both paralysed for a moment. And then she was weeping. It took her completely by surprise, but she was convulsed by emotion, leaning forward curled in on herself.

'I'm sorry,' she sobbed at last, as he hurriedly came and sat beside her. 'I'm sorry . . . I just . . .' It came back to her then. Just a flash. That the last thing she had been thinking about before the darkness descended was him. This man who she loved, who she had decided to write to, to reach for him, just to know he was there . . .

She leaned in to him and regardless of anyone else around them, they put their arms around each other. Tom's chin rested on the top of her head and he rocked her gently. She sobbed, held in the cocoon of his arms, the place where she most longed to be.

'Tom . . .' She pulled back at last, staying close, talking very quietly, gazing up at his face, trying to take in that it was him, here . . . It was really happening. 'Oh God, I can't believe it.' She touched his face. 'You're really here. But . . . why are you here? How . . .?'

'Your daughter.' He reached in his pocket and brought out a telegram. 'God alone knows how she found out my address – I'm still at my parents' house. I wanted to come earlier but it was just impossible . . . I was worried to death I'd be too late.'

The telegram read: '*Mother hit by bomb – stop – in General Hospital – stop – serious please come – stop. Joy Gilby – stop – Daughter.*'

'*Joy?*' Ann stared at it, utterly bewildered. Later, she would piece together that they must have been in her chest of drawers. Only later did she realize they knew everything – or Joy did, at least. But now all she could do was be afraid someone else would come and break into these few precious moments she had Tom here, really here. They clasped their hands together and kept their eyes fixed on each other, drinking one another in. There was so much to say – could she ever say all she needed? She took his hand and they held each other, gently.

'I know I look a sight,' she said.

'No.' Tom smiled. 'That'll heal. You have both your eyes intact – what more do you need?'

They laughed.

'The tables are turned,' she said. 'Me in the bed this time. I've got off lightly really – cracked ribs, my ankle . . .' And no baby, not any more. But she was not going to say that. There were other things which needed saying.

'We have a son,' she said. 'Our son, Martin – he's yours, you know.'

'No!' Tom stared at her, the horrified realization of what she was saying moving across his face. 'You mean . . . Surely not . . .? Mine?'

393

Before Tom could even begin to take this in, she gabbled on. '*Yes*. He was born the September after we met – that Christmas. He looks ever so like you and Len found out – not straight away, but later. I wanted your name on the birth certificate because I knew . . . I knew he was yours. And I wanted the certificate to be true at least. But . . . it's been . . .' She shook her head, more tears coming.

'I didn't want to . . . to make things difficult for you – or for me,' she stuttered. Shame washed through her. The lies and pretence. 'I let Len think, for a long time . . . Only he found out. He found Martin's birth certificate . . .'

Tom was reeling. 'So, he – Martin – is . . . fourteen?'

'He's lovely. He's like you. Clever – and . . .'

'My God, Ann.' He sat, stunned. 'A son. And I haven't contributed a thing . . . all this time . . .'

'Are you married, Tom? Other children?'

He lowered his head, shaking it slightly. 'I did marry. A while after I saw you. After we . . .' He let out a deep sigh. 'I just thought I needed to get over things, find a life – for your sake and mine.' He looked up at her, seeming ashamed. 'Poor Jean. She was a good woman. It only lasted a year – just over. She told me – and her parents – that I was not a properly functioning man.'

'Oh, Tom.'

'I don't mean . . . Not the bedroom, not exactly. It was more than that. I just couldn't seem to *be* with her properly, in any way. Couldn't open up to her somehow. I just used to stay out – as much as I properly could. Worked all hours. She didn't fall for a child – fortunately, I suppose. We divorced in the end. It was the only thing if she was to have any chance of another shot at it. I did my best to go through the motions, but I just . . .' He shrugged. 'I seem to be one of those people who love one person. I can't seem to switch it on to anyone else. There was always you – looking at me over her shoulder if I had her in my arms. You, speaking to me when I was alone – me speaking to you. It was a long habit, you see. There's always been just you,' he finished simply.

'I know,' she said.

They sat looking deeply, frankly, at each other – as they had always been able to do.

'Oh, my love. I'm so, so happy to see you. I'm going to have to give Joy a roasting when I see her. But . . . I was thinking about you when . . .' It all came pouring out then – why hold anything back? 'You see, things have been difficult at home. Len has had a child by another woman and I was just standing there by that church – the ruins – and I thought, I must write to Tom. But I was frightened that I'd be disturbing your life. That maybe you'd have a family by now and that would have held me back – but every day these days it feels as if life is short and you never know . . . And then there was . . . I had such a strange feeling and after that I don't remember . . .'

'Oh, my Annie,' Tom said tenderly, seeming to understand even through her confused ramblings. He pressed her hand to his lips. 'What a mess. And a son . . . My God, we have a son . . .'

Ann leaned in to him, against his bad shoulder. Glancing up a second later, to her utter horror she saw two people walking along the ward towards them: Len and Margaret.

'Tom.' The change in her voice and her sitting bolt upright were scarcely enough warning. 'You're going to have to go . . .'

Len and Margaret stopped at the end of the bed and for as long as she lived, Ann would never forget the expression on her mother-in-law's face: a solemn, guarded look which said that in those moments, she who had been so close, a much-loved daughter-in-law, had become an alien and a betrayer.

Len knew, she could see that straight away. This man who looked so like his son.

'What's going on here then?' His voice was quiet, but she could hear the tension in it, the explosion waiting to happen. Tom stood up.

'Len –' There seemed nothing else she could say, but the truth. 'This is Tom Somers. Martin's father.'

Margaret's face froze. But Len, who already knew, had known for so long, released his mother's arm and stepped up to Tom. His voice, harsh and menacing, rose as he spoke, his face full of an ugly contempt.

'So, you're the bloke whose child I've been bringing up, sweating my guts out for, all these years?'

Tom held up his one arm to fend Len off.

'Look, I never knew, I promise you. Please – we can't discuss this here,' he tried to say.

Ann could see heads turned towards them all along the ward, everyone agog at this unfolding drama.

'Oh, and why not?' Len was starting to shout now. He drew back his fist. 'Got summat to hide, have you, pal?'

Nurses came dashing along, even the ward sister. Margaret grabbed him by the sleeve.

'Len, stop it! Just come away, son – come outside . . .'

'If you could leave the ward, please. We can't have this kind of behaviour.' Sister was furious. 'I will not have you disturbing my other patients. There are some very ill people in here!'

'Len – outside,' Margaret ordered.

'Tell him to get out an' all.' Len sounded harsh, childish in his rage. Bowing to the pressure from everyone he

396

went out with Margaret, turning to cast furious looks at Ann and Tom before he disappeared.

'I'm sorry.' Tom stayed standing. He looked distraught. 'I should never have come.'

'What she doesn't know,' Ann said bitterly, 'my mother-in-law, that is – is that she has another grandson by some woman called Marianne. And I don't know who's going to tell her that either. Tom – sit down, please.'

He sank on to the chair, pale and shaken.

'He's right though. My God, all these years. I can at least pay you both – I can pay from now on . . .'

'We'll sort something out,' Ann said. She felt utterly drained suddenly and leaned her head on his shoulder. 'It will all have to be gone through. But you know – I am . . . I'm here. Alive. That's . . . Well, it might not have been like that. I don't know what we're all going to do about all this, but I want to be able to see you – or at least for us to write to one another? All I need to know is that you love me and I love you. I always have loved you, Tom. It may have been wrong, all of it, but that's how it is.'

Tom slid his arm round her back and rested his cheek on her head. People were staring but neither of them gave a damn. Tenderly he stroked her hand. 'It is,' he said. 'That is how it is.'

Fifty

The next afternoon, Len ushered Margaret and Cyril into the house.

Ann had been released from hospital that cold Sunday morning and had come home in a taxi. Everyone was home. Sheila was cooking a dinner for them, the house full of the scents of roasting beef and potatoes, and the children all smiles at seeing her hobble into the house. When Elaine saw her, she started to squeal and clap and everyone laughed.

'Oh, Mom, thank goodness you're back!' Joy cried, flinging her arms round her. As they hugged, Ann whispered, 'I need to have words with you, young lady.' But as she drew back she gave her a tearful smile: *Thank you, my love.*

Len stayed in the background and Kenneth was there, so it was no time for any carry-on. They all managed to get through a celebratory dinner with no upsets.

'Home felt really peculiar without you here,' Martin said. 'Just not right.'

'I told you you'll miss me when I'm gone.'

'Don't say that!' Sheila said. 'It was close, Mom. It really was. That other WVS lady . . .'

'Yes, poor Dorrie,' Ann said.

'The others have been round,' Joy said. 'Miss Rowbotham and Mrs . . .?'

'Starling,' Martin said.

'They've been ever so kind,' Sheila said. 'Very nice people they are.'

'Yes.' Ann's eyes suddenly filled with tears. A memory flashed into her mind. That church. She had been standing outside a church, all smashed up, and it was dark, the air thick with smoke. A shudder passed through her and she had great difficulty swallowing her mouthful of potato.

'You all right, Mom?' Joy said.

She nodded, smiling, wiping her eyes. 'Yeah,' she managed eventually. 'Just glad to be home.'

She and Tom had parted lovingly that afternoon, though neither of them had any real idea what should come next. They embraced and kissed – in a reserved way given the public spectacle they had already made – and Tom said he had to catch a train.

'I'll write,' she said. 'I promise.'

As soon as he had left, Margaret came back on to the ward, her face like thunder.

'Where's Len?' Ann asked.

'I sent him home.' She stood by the bed. Ann felt ashamed, heartbroken, but also defiant. I don't suppose your son has told you the half of it yet, she thought.

'Mom, I'm so sorry—'

Margaret waved her words away.

'Don't start. You'll be home tomorrow. We'll have to deal with this then. But all I can say to you, Annie is . . .' She sighed, her whole body seeming to deflate and her face crumpled as she turned away. 'I thought I knew you like my own. Obviously, I was wrong.'

She went without another word. Ann watched Margaret's sagging shoulders as she left the ward, full of sadness. She thought about her family. About all the truths they did not know – would most likely rather never know. And now there was precious little she could do about any of it. Things would have to unfold how they did. She was a terrible woman, that was the truth of it. And she was horrified and appalled and relieved at the same time.

Exhausted, she settled back, but she found she was lying on something – a crumpled handkerchief. Confused, she stared at it for a moment. It must be Tom's. She lifted it to her nostrils. Tom's – yes, the faint, comforting smell of him. She lay back, cradling it against her chest, and closed her eyes.

Ann and Len sat with Margaret and Cyril in the front room. None of the rest of the family seemed especially surprised: they could tell something was afoot and Ann had realized that it was not just Joy who had found things out. Sheila seemed to be avoiding meeting her eye as well.

She could hardly bear to look at her father-in-law. The sight of him made her ache. He had aged suddenly, seemed shrunken into himself. Instead of greeting her with his usual warmth he had given her a brief nod. Grief and disappointment were written all over him. Margaret, however, appeared upright and stronger than before. She wore a look of resolve. As the four of them sat down, each couple on either side of the fireplace, the atmosphere so tense and strained that no one knew what to say, it was Margaret who eventually took charge.

'Right,' she said. 'It's obviously high time something was said about you two. And I'm going to say it. I'm shocked to the core by all of this. I never thought I'd see any of this kind of carry-on under the roof of my own family. But this seems to be how things are. And I've had a bit of time to mull things over.' She looked at Len, then Ann, as she talked. 'Your father and I have talked about it. I don't know what ideas you might have in your head,

Annie – now things have all come out into the open. I'm not sure I've got much idea who you are at all . . .'

This stung, like an arrow piercing her, but Ann said nothing.

'It's obvious now that a lot more has been going on in your lives than your father and I ever realized. And I can't say either of us are happy about it. We're disappointed in you, Ann. You've betrayed us and you've betrayed your husband. We're shocked, Annie. We're wounded.' She stopped, choked up, fighting to control herself. Cyril put his hand on her shoulder for a moment and Ann thought her chest was going to burst with sorrow. Margaret gained control of herself.

'What we've got to think about is not what you want, or he wants –' She nodded towards each of them. 'You've got to think about the family as a whole. Martin's our grandson as much as he ever was. He's our Martin. And there're the others to think about – Joy especially. So, if you've got any ideas about running off with your fancy man whatever his name is, after all this time, you'd better think again, Annie. You need to put your family first. And Len – angry and hurt as you are, son, you've got to do the same.'

Len hung his head. Ann felt her pulse racing faster and faster. Say something, she thought. For God's sake, Len! If all the truths were spilling out, all the secrets and lies and mistakes they had each made, then they had to empty the bucket, right to the bottom. But Len showed no sign of saying anything.

'Mom . . .' she began, keeping her voice low. 'Margaret . . .' She raised her head and looked directly at her mother-in-law. She had her shame. She had had to wear it for a long time and would continue to do so for ever. She was not going to deny it. But neither was she prepared to do it alone.

'I don't disagree with you. That's what I've been trying to do, all this time. And not just because . . . I mean . . .' Her own composure deserted her and she burst into tears. 'It wasn't to save face or cover up – not just. It was for the family – and because of you and . . . and Dad. I love you both. I always have, and you've been so good to me!'

Out of the corner of her eye she saw Cyril wiping his eyes and it made her cry all the more.

'And I'm sorry. I'm so very sorry about all of it. I am. It should never have happened the way it did. Tom never knew, I never told him. Otherwise he would have helped with Martin – and he will now, I know. But while we're sorting everything out, there's something else you need to know. I think Len's got something to tell you.'

All three of them looked at Len. He seemed to shrink right down into himself. Ann could see that his hands were trembling and he clenched them into fists and thrust them under his legs so that he ended up looking like a little boy on a naughty stool. But he just could not seem to speak.

'Well, whatever it is, I expect it'll keep for another time,' Margaret said, dismissing it as of no importance.

'No,' Ann insisted. 'It won't.'

Len turned to her. In a whisper, he said, 'You tell them.'

'Me?'

Len nodded, looking down into his lap. She could see that he really could not speak. And she found she barely could either, because while she was hurt and angry, she knew it was going to be another heavy blow to her father-and mother-in-law. But it had to be done. In the end she found herself speaking almost apologetically for him.

'Len has been having an affair with a young woman called Marianne. She used to work at Rowheath. And they have a little boy called George who's nearly a year old. She used to live in Katie Road in Selly Oak but they were bombed out. I don't know where they are now. But George is also your grandson.' She waited a second. 'He looks just like Sheila.'

There was a long, ominous silence. Ann could see that blaming her for her mistakes had been easier.

'Is this true, son?' Cyril said eventually.

Len nodded, face, ears, everything red with shame.

'Right.' Margaret sat up straighter, speaking in a harsh, clipped way. 'Well – all the more reason. I never thought I could be as disgusted as I am with the pair of you, but there it is. You've both made your beds and now you're going to lie in them. And that goes for those others who're involved. That . . . *him*, Tom Somers, needs to do what he can for his son – and Len, you need to make sure this child of yours is taken care of.' She looked from one to another and her voice grew tight with fury. 'I could knock your heads together, that I could. But your job is to carry on and look after this family. We'll give you all the help we can, as we always have. You're married and that's that. So pull yourselves together and keep your troubles to your-selves because they're no one else's but your own.' She got up. 'And just get on with it. Come on, Cyril.'

They both left the room and Ann and Len sat as the two of them let themselves out and shut the front door.

A long moment passed. They looked at each other at last. There was a second of conspiratorial humour which reached back into the long past they had shared together – like two children who have just survived a pasting by the headmaster, giggling with relief. Then they sobered up.

'She's right,' Len said. 'Isn't she?'

Ann stared back at him for a moment. This was how it had to be. They had enough between them, enough for a long marriage. She nodded.

Fifty-One

By the time Ann went to bed that night, she was so exhausted she could hardly drag herself up the stairs. Sheila and Joy came up to her room after Margaret and Cyril had left, when she had struggled up to unpack her little case.

'Can we come in, Mom?' Sheila said. She and Joy stood side by side and for a moment, Ann thought, they looked as they had when they were little girls, upset about something, needing her to themselves.

'Everything all right downstairs?' she asked.

'Kenneth's playing rummy with Mart.' Sheila said.

'Dad's asleep, I think,' Joy added.

'Shut the door.' She was already sitting, sagging, on the side of the bed, as her ankle would not let her stand for long. They came and sat each side of her. 'So – you went through my drawers.' She was not cross. It was far too late for that.

'Oh, Mom!' Joy burst out. 'We thought you were going to die! They said you were really bad and then we found his poem and it was so romantic and he really loved you and I thought, what if . . .?'

'He came,' Ann said. Her eyes shone with tears. 'Thank you. He did.'

'Mom,' Sheila said solemnly. 'What about Martin? Are you going to tell him?'

She nodded slowly. 'Just give me a chance. When the right time comes. Don't you tell him.'

'We wouldn't,' Sheila said. 'It's not up to us. But—'

Ann stopped her with a gesture. 'I know. He needs to know.'

'Do you love him?' Joy said. 'I mean – Al's started writing me much better letters. Lovely letters. So I know what that feels like now . . .' She beamed tearfully.

'I do,' Ann said carefully. 'I'll tell you all about it – soon. When I'm not so . . . worn out. But I do love your dad, you know, as well. And we aren't going anywhere.'

They both drank this in and she could see they were relieved. Their world was not about to change after all. She reached round, an arm about each of them.

'There's my girls. You're the best, you know that.' She kissed them, one by one. 'It's all going to be all right – one way or another.'

They each lay their head on a shoulder and took one of her hands. They sat for a while, rocking gently back and forth, all finding comfort in each other.

She lay beside Len that night. They didn't cuddle or kiss, but they lay in the darkness talking – not about Tom, or Marianne and how she must be helped somehow, or any of the secrets and challenges facing them. They talked about the past: *d'you remember when? . . .* Knitting themselves back together again. Each doing their best.

After that, they spent the days preparing for Christmas. There were no air raids, they could sleep in their beds and the hens were laying better again without the shocking night assaults. Martin went out and gathered greenery from somewhere or other and Ann and the three children decorated the house, made streamers, listening to Christmas carols on the wireless and making it a house of warmth and celebration. Hilda came to visit – 'Oh my word, Annie, you don't half get into some scrapes you do!' she said, flinging her arms emotionally round her old friend. And when Margaret called in as well, they all got her to join in. With Hilda there and all the family, the stiffness of her manner began to melt back to something more normal. Because things felt normal. Surprisingly normal, Ann thought, all things considered.

'You're to come to us for your dinner,' Margaret said. 'It's no good you trying to cook Christmas dinner standing on that ankle. And Cyril and I want our family all round us.' She gave Ann a gimlet-like look. Ann met her eye calmly. Margaret was right – somehow they all had to go on together.

'That'd be lovely, Mom,' she said. 'And we'll bring everything we can for the feast.'

'Is this Hettie we're eating?' Martin said, peering at the roasted chicken as Cyril carried it triumphantly from the kitchen.

'Martin!' Ann ticked him off.

''Fraid so, son,' Cyril said. 'Would you rather've just had a plate of mashed turnip?'

Martin made a face. 'It just seems a bit brutal.'

'Well, that's food for you,' Margaret said, carrying in a jug of gravy.

Ann sat quietly as they all squeezed round the table in the cosy back room: she between Joy and Martin, Sheila and Len opposite, with Miss Prince from along the road also invited and Elaine in her high-chair. Margaret and Cyril were at each end. Kenneth was coming later but for now, was eating dinner with his parents. It was only fair, Sheila said, but she wanted to stay with her own family today. Ann felt a bit foolish not being able to do much, but she had made sure they contributed all the rations they could spare and between them they had enough to make a mince tart for afters – *with custard*, as Martin insisted. And Sheila and Joy had rallied round, helping with all the vegetable preparation and cooking.

Cyril carved up and soon they all had a plateful – spuds from the veg patches and sprouts and carrots and Margaret's delicious gravy and bread sauce.

'Right!' Cyril raised his glass of ale. Ann watched. Everything seemed so normal. Was normal. Warm and loving – despite . . . She knew things between herself and her in-laws would never be the same again. Not quite. That her secrets had driven a wedge of mistrust that could never be removed. But they were all there being family, making the future out of love for one another. 'Come on, everyone – Merry Christmas! And here's to 1941 being a better year – heaven help us!'

'Cheers, Grandad!' the children toasted. Elaine banged her hands on her little tray, excited at being part of it all.

'Oh, look at her, bless her!' Margaret said, stroking Elaine's cheek. 'Come on – tuck in, everyone, or it'll get cold. Happy Christmas!'

Later, after the long, leisurely meal, it was time for the King's broadcast.

'Accumulator's all topped up,' Cyril said, clicking on the set as they sat round in the front room. 'Here we go. Oh –' He was about to sit down again, but shot back up at the sound of the National Anthem. 'Up you get!'

Once they were all seated again, Elaine drowsy in Sheila's lap, they heard, amid the crackle, the King's hesitant voice:

'In days of peace, the feast of Christmas is a time when we all gather together in our homes, the young and old . . .'

Ann found her thoughts wandering, hearing the speech in snatches, looking round at her family's pink, for once well-fed, faces in the warm light. We are here, she thought, together. Everything felt fragile, blessed. '*Dearest Tom,*' a letter she would write, began in her head. '*I love you so and we will be in each other's lives, knowing that we love each other. But I must do right by my family – I know you know this. This is where I must be . . .*'

'War brings, among other sorrows,' the King was saying, 'the sadness of separation . . .' She looked at Joy, knew that in her pocket she carried her latest letter from Alan.

'He's telling me things now,' she said to Ann when the letter arrived. 'It's as if things are completely different. He's so loving – I can hardly believe it.'

And Sheila looked pink and happy as well after these precious days she was able to spend with her husband back among them, safe and well. And she was a different Sheila from the one that had left home with Elaine only a few months ago, Ann realized. A braver, stronger person.

Martin, her lovely boy, was sitting next to his grandmother, teasing her. One day he would have to know – would have to endure the shock of knowing about Tom. But not yet, not today.

'Many family circles are broken . . .' the King went on.

But not this one, she prayed, looking at Len, pink-faced and muzzy from the ale, and at her in-laws, still struggling to come to terms with all that had emerged, shocking them to the core – but still here. Still being family, not broken – or not completely. She sent up a prayer of gratitude for all of them – all the people she loved, she so imperfect in this imperfect world.

'The future looks hard . . .' King George went on.

'He hasn't stammered once,' Sheila remarked.

'He's doing well,' Margaret agreed. Everyone felt for the King, trying to get through his speeches.

'. . . but our feet are planted on the path of victory and with the help of God, we shall make our way to justice and to peace.'

The National Anthem boomed out again and all of them got to their feet, even Ann, perched on one leg.

'To justice and to peace!' Cyril toasted with his cup of tea. 'And so say all of us!'

'And so say all of us!' they chimed in. And as they looked round, toasting each other with their teacups, everyone burst into happy laughter.

Acknowledgements

All books written about a large cast of people involve many pieces of research great and small: clips of archive film, maps and photographs, histories and novels. It always involves a certain amount of luck and chance. Trying to research anything in a year of pandemic and lockdown has added unexpected frustrations, so there are areas of research I have been completely unable to access. However there is still the internet and other means of communications with people, who are of course the best sources of detail.

My particular thanks to Margaret Nicklin, a chocolate girl who I spent a lovely afternoon with in Bournville and drinking tea at Rowheath before lockdown was even a speck on the horizon. And thank you also to others who spoke to me and provided all sorts of snippets of interest: Pat Hayward, Roy McCreedy, Emma-Louise Tighe and to the Cadbury Friends thread on Facebook, which is full of wonderful photographs and information. I am especially grateful to Deborah Cadbury for her book *Chocolate Wars*, Fiona Joseph for *Beatrice* and as ever to Carl Chinn for *The Cadbury Story: A Short History*, as well as his book, *Brum Undaunted: Birmingham During the Blitz*.

Gratitude also to Woodbrooke College, Selly Oak – once a home of George Cadbury and now the world's main Quaker study centre, for the beautiful and peaceful hospitality provided there. We all hope you will be able to be up and running again soon.